The KING of the TREES

BOOK SIX

KYLEAH'S MIRRORS

William D. Burt (signature)

WILLIAM D. BURT

WINEPRESS **WP** PUBLISHING

Cover and Chapter Illustrations by Terri L. Lahr.
Text Illustrations by Becky Miller.

Rights to all illustrations transferred to the author, William D. Burt, from Terri L. Lahr and Becky Miller, by assignment.

WinePress Publishing (PO Box 428, Enumclaw, WA 98022) functions only as book publisher. As such, the ultimate design, content, editorial accuracy, and views expressed or implied in this work are those of the author.

ISBN 13: 978-1-57921-903-1
ISBN 10: 1-57921-903-9
Library of Congress Catalog Card Number: 2007923043

"For now we see in a mirror dimly, but then face to face; now I know in part, but then I shall know fully just as I also have been fully known."

(1 Corinthians 13:12, NASB)

CONTENTS

PROLOGUE

"A CHOO!" Having blown the dust off the dented metal box, the Finder sneezed. Didn't these brutish Thalmosians ever tidy up their cellars? This one was crammed with all sorts of useless articles, from broken beehives to chunks of rotten wood. The musty space smelled of beeswax, wilted carrots and sprouting potatoes. A pile of those revolting, pasty tubers lay on the table where he had found the box. He shook it. Inside, a few paltry coins clinked. How anyone could have wallowed in such squalor and still sit upon Lucambra's throne was an absolute outrage.

Licking his lips, the Finder leered to himself. While the half-breed and his witless wife were searching for their fickle eldest daughter in some backwoods torsil world, it was time to clean house in the Hallowfast. Climbing a rickety set of shelves, the Finder found some dusty parchments at the top. Replacing them with a suitable souvenir, he clumsily clambered down with the brittle sheets, his heart thundering in the cellar's confines.

For years, he had been poking through the Hallowfast's dark corners, looking for some long-lost weapon or talisman that would tip the balance of power in his favor. Ironically, the key to victory had finally turned up in despised Thalmos, not in Lucambra.

In his oft-repeated tale of finding the seventh soros, Gannon's son had let drop that he had found something more than his grandmother's box lying on the cellar shelves. Armed with that clue, the Finder had returned to Beechtown, where he discovered the priceless relics just where the half-breed had left them. The fool! Those yellowed parchments would yet prove his undoing.

Now the Finder lacked only Elgathel's reforged sword. That revered symbol of royalty was missing from its hook on the back of Lucambra's throne. No king could rightfully rule Lucambra without Elgathel's legendary blade. Realizing the pretender must have taken the weapon with him, the Finder had flown into a destructive frenzy. After his wrath was spent, he vowed he would one day hang his cloak in the throne room, sword or no sword. Only Emmer and his mooning granddaughter stood in his way.

Clutching his trophies, the Finder climbed out of the cellar and dropped the trapdoor back into place. The cabin was silent. Gannon was conveniently visiting his busybody sister down in Beechtown. The Finder detested busybodies. When he became king, he would exile Lucambra's gossips to some bleak world and let them bore one another to death. To prevent his own exile, he had taken the precaution of copying Rolin's torsil maps, which marked the location of nearly every torsil in Western Lucambra.

The cabin's door creaked as he cautiously opened and closed it. No two-legs, tree, bird or beast raised the alarm. Whistling tunelessly, he set off to climb the nearest Lucambra-torsil.

That night, the Finder sat perched on a stool in the cramped hollow of his oak tree. Looking forward to roomier quarters, he peered at the chart etched on the wall opposite him. At the top, the name "Elgathel" was carved in bold letters. At the bottom, his own name appeared. Let others clutter their homes with faded murals of the One Tree. *His* family tree held far greater promise.

By candlelight, he examined the parchments, and the blood roared in his ears. Though some of the staves were smudged or faded, he was sure the riddle spoke of him. Very soon, he would seize the crown, sword and throne of Lucambra, Land of Light.

CHAPTER 1

KYLEAH'S TEARS

Useless! That's all you are and that's all you ever will be!" Kyleah's face burned as she picked herself off the slick sugarhouse floor and hobbled out the beckoning door.

"And take this with you!" Kyleah instinctively ducked as a sap-bucket sailed over her head. Moments earlier, her makeshift wooden crutch had slipped on a film of water and had overturned the pail, spilling fresh, sticky maple sap across the floor. Unable to catch herself in time, she had landed heavily on cold stones.

Outside, Kyleah wept, her tears dimpling the new-fallen snow. No matter how hard she tried, she always seemed to get in the way. This March morning, her stepsister Gyrta was already in a foul temper since Barlomey, Kyleah's brother, had used Gyrta's best comb to smooth the tangles out of the horse's tail. Knocking over the sap-bucket was all the excuse Gyrta needed to vent her wrath on Kyleah. The sugarhouse would be off limits the rest of the day, unless Kyleah wished to be thrashed with her crutch.

She trudged up the snowy slope toward her home. Behind her, fragrant steam billowed through the door and roof vents of the sugarhouse, as if the building were ablaze. Kyleah loved working inside the rambling old shed at this time of year, when gallons of maple sap frothed in the big copper cauldrons suspended over roaring fires. It was hard, hot work feeding the hungry flames, but Kyleah always looked forward to her favorite treat: a bowlful of fresh snow drenched with maple syrup straight out of the spigot.

"Maple snow" had been their father's invention. As the sugarmaster, Branagan son of Carrigan was responsible for boiling down the maple sap to just the right consistency. If overcooked, the precious sap would crystallize, caramelize or even burn and have to be scraped out of the cauldrons; if undercooked, the syrup tasted bland and watery. Branagan's batches always turned out just right. By all accounts, he was the finest sugarmaster Mapleton had ever seen, and Kyleah was proud to be his only daughter.

She wished he hadn't saddled her with such a shrew of a stepmother. Dolora spent more time primping than disciplining her unruly daughters. At seventeen and fifteen, Gyrta and Garta took after their mean-spirited mother. They were taller and stronger than Kyleah, who was twelve. The two delighted in tormenting her behind Branagan's back. Once, she had caught them smearing grease on her crutch. Telling on them only invited swift revenge.

Kyleah dashed away her tears with cold-stiffened fingers. If only her mother Larissa were still alive, life would be different! Maybe the accident might never have happened, and Einwen . . .

Whump! Something cold and crunchy struck Kyleah's right ear, and she went deaf. "Barlomey!" she yelled, knocking the snow out of her ear. "You know you're not supposed to throw—" She ducked as another icy snowball whizzed past the other ear.

Stooping, she scooped up a handful of snow and molded it into a ball. She would teach that boy a lesson! He was just nipping back through the sugarhouse door. Aiming at him, Kyleah let fly.

Unfortunately, Gyrta was right behind Barlomey. *Smack!* The snowball hit her full in the face. She shrieked and staggered back inside the sugarhouse. Losing her balance, Kyleah toppled into a snowdrift. Now she was in for it! Gyrta would never believe the snowball was meant for Barlomey, and she would not rest until Kyleah was black and blue. Kyleah wanted to sink into the drift and never come out again until the last snowflake had melted.

Sitting up, she spotted Gyrta emerging from the sugarhouse brandishing a long-handled stirring paddle. Murder and mayhem were written all over the blond girl's proud, sharp-featured face, leaving no doubt as to what she intended to do with the paddle.

Sugarmen stirred their evaporating maple sap with wooden paddles to keep it from burning on the kettle bottoms. Applied to other bottoms, those paddles left spectacular bruises. Kyleah grabbed her crutch and struggled to free herself from the snowdrift's clinging embrace. Then footsteps munched through the snow, and Barlomey's mop of curly black hair swam into view.

"What are you doing down there?" he said, his brown eyes laughing. "Hurry up; you don't want Gyrta to catch you!" He pulled his sister out of the snow and shoved the crutch under her arm. Then he brushed her off. At nine years, "Barley," as he was known, enjoyed picking on his sisters, especially Kyleah. Still, she loved the rascally boy. He was her flesh and blood, after all.

"I'll never outrun Gyrta!" she cried. "Can't you toss some snow-balls at her to slow her up? I promise I won't tell Father about the maple-sugar bears you stole and hid under your bed."

Barley's eyes narrowed. "What were you doing in my—?" Then he saw Gyrta plowing toward them through the snow. "Come on!" he yelled, and he began dragging Kyleah along, protesting.

Swish. As swiftly and smoothly as swans gliding on a lake, a sledge slid up with the jangle of harness bells. Perched on the driver's seat, Branagan pulled back on the reins. "Whoa, Sally!" he called to the mare. Dark-haired and clean-shaven, the sugarmaster was a solid man with boulders for shoulders and forearms as thick as knotted barge-cables. Kyleah shrank back. Muffled in a thick ermine coat, Garta glared down at her from beside Branagan.

"How nice of you, dear little sister, to take my place collecting sap-buckets in the sugar bush," Garta sneered. She stepped off the sleigh just in time to catch the fat snowball meant for Kyleah.

"Oooh!" Garta screamed at Gyrta. "You horrid little minx, I'll get you for that!" Surging through the snow, she knocked down her sister. Blonde hair and white snow mingled as the two girls tumbled down the hill, kicking, punching and biting each other.

Barley's freckled face broke into a self-satisfied smirk, as if he had orchestrated the brawl all by himself. Branagan clucked his tongue in mock outrage. "Tsk! Tsk! Such a fuss over a snowball!" he said, helping Kyleah into the sledge. She huddled on the seat beside her father, her teeth chattering. Usually, she wore light clothing when working in the hot, steamy sugarhouse. Now she was thankful for the woolen trousers and fur-lined boots she had pulled on that morning to ward off the lingering winter's chill.

In truth, she didn't mind the cold, so long as she could spend time with her father. Beneath his crusty gruffness shone a love as bright and genuine as a newly polished copper syrup cauldron.

"Shouldn't you go down there and separate Gyrta and Garta before they hurt one another?" she asked him. "I'm afraid they're going to blame their fight on Barley and me. It's just not fair."

He winked at her. "I'd rather separate a couple of quarreling polecats. I've learnt to let those two settle their differences by themselves. Remember, I have to live with their mother."

Barley climbed up behind Kyleah and clung to the seat. Then Branagan flicked the reins. The empty buckets in back rattled as the sledge leapt forward, heading higher into the Tartellan hills.

"These will warm you up," Branagan told Kyleah. He wrapped a fur-tipped cape around her shoulders and pulled a wool cap over her head. She thanked him as her shivering gradually subsided.

"Gyrta and Garta are always picking on me," she confessed. "I wish I were strong and sure-footed enough to stand up to them."

Branagan sighed. "Maybe one day you will be."

A few snowflakes drifted down from a slate sky, but spring was already shrugging off its winter's coat. The streams were thawing and running high with snowmelt. Warm breezes were wandering up from the valley of the Foamwater like flocks of wayward geese. Kyleah loved the promise of spring, when all nature awoke from its hibernation and stretched itself, bearlike. First, the fuzzy pussy willows burst like caterpillars from their brownish bud-cocoons. Then the daffodils nodded farewell to winter and turned their golden faces toward spring. The poplars were next, opening their sticky buds to perfume the air with their spicy-sweet balm.

She also loved sledging through the woods with her father. The evergreen air tasted brisk and clean, free of the chimney haze that hung over Mapleton. "Through the snow, higher we go!" rang the sleigh bells. "Through the snow, higher we go!" sang the sleigh's runners as they hissed over the fresh powder. Presently, Branagan stopped the sledge beside a snowy clearing, where the eternal white blanket muffled all sound but the mournful tinkling of hundreds of tiny bells, each one lamenting a lost soul.

Winter was the safest season of the year, when the Prowlers slept in the forests above Mapleton. No one had ever seen a Prowler and lived to tell the tale, but many townsfolk had glimpsed dark shapes hulking through the woods on moonlit nights. As soon as the trees leafed out, prudent people stayed indoors after dusk.

Whoever or whatever the Prowlers were, they could snatch their prey—usually a girl—through a second-story window as neatly as neat, leaving only a few scratchy tracks behind, if any. And they always seemed to know right where their victims slept.

So many boys and girls had gone missing over the years that parents took to hanging small brass bells around their young ones' necks to foil would-be kidnappers. Since each bell's tone was unique, a sharp ear could track down any particular child by the sound of his bell. "Belltown," the village came to be known. Each spring, the hills resounded with the ringing of the children's chimes. By autumn, some of those bells had already fallen silent.

Now they rang again, but not because carefree children were playing tag, throwing snowballs at one another or making snow-men. These bells rang in the fitful wind that prowled the Grieving Ground, as it was called. Branagan often visited this spot before sledging on to the sugar bush. Like so many boat oars standing in river sand, neat rows of stirring paddles lined this patch of snowy earth. Each stirrer represented one of Mapleton's boys or girls, men or women who had vanished. Jingling and jangling, brass bells on leather cords hung from most of the paddle blades.

"Soon, we'll be staying inside after dusk," Branagan said as he helped Kyleah down from the sleigh. "Then you'll have to wear your bell. I wish your mother had been wearing one that night."

Kyleah made a sour face. "I hate wearing that thing! Bells are for sheep, not for people. Besides, the cord rubs my neck raw."

Branagan turned a stern gaze on his daughter. "'Either thou shalt bear the bell, or the paddlewood shall wear it,'" he told her, quoting a time-worn proverb familiar to all Mapleton's residents.

He was right, of course. Anybody spending time out-of-doors without a bell was "asking for a paddle," as the villagers put it.

Kyleah braved the gauntlet of faceless paddles with her father and brother. She and Barley read out the names engraved on the weathered blades. Linnae . . . Timmon . . . Daniella . . . *Larissa.*

Stopping before the Larissa-paddle, the three bowed their heads in silent grief. "Why did you leave us, Mother?" Kyleah murmured. Tears blurred her vision as she recalled happier days.

One April evening when Kyleah had just turned eight, Larissa had stepped outside to pick a few lilacs for the table. When she failed to return, Branagan went looking for her. He found only some scattered, smudged tracks leading toward the dark forest.

Ding! Kyleah tapped the paddle's bell. Some people believed that ringing those bells would bring back the lost. Though many of the Grieving Ground's wind-wakened bells had rung out the months and years till their paddles rotted, not one of the missing had ever returned. Kyleah's eyes burned as she knelt before her mother's paddle and read the messages scratched into the wooden handle. *Please come back! Where are you? We will always love you.*

Branagan gently scraped the snow away from Larissa's paddle and straightened it. Then he moved on, tears streaking his face.

Kyleah wistfully rang the bell again before she went in search of another snow-bound paddle. This one bore the name, "Anna."

After her sister Einwen's death, Kyleah had found another dear friend in Anna daughter of Dyllis. Full of girlish secrets, spirited Anna had helped ease Kyleah's loneliness. Then one hot summer's eve, Anna had left her bedroom window open. The next morning, her bed was as cold and bare as an empty sap-bucket in January.

Kyleah rejoined Barley and Branagan, and the three sledged onward. A sharp wind knocked snow from the fir boughs, stinging Kyleah's cheek where the cruel carriage wheel had struck her.

The fall following her mother's death, a horse-drawn, runaway carriage had mown down Kyleah and her twin sister, Einwen. The wagon's onslaught had scarred Kyleah's cheek and crippled her right leg, leaving Einwen limp and lifeless in the merciless road.

After a mile or so, the stolid firs gave way to pure stands of sugar maples. Branagan drew the sledge up beside one of the trees, which was decorated with a splash of red. Each sugarman in the village marked his trees with a distinctive color of paint. This tree also sported a sap-bucket, which hung from a wooden tube or *spile* protruding from the maple's trunk. A slab of slate lay across the bucket's top to keep rain and debris from falling into the sap.

Barley tromped through the snow to the tree. After taking off the cover, he carried the brimming bucket back to the sledge, where Kyleah exchanged the full pail for an empty one. Seeing her marred face mirrored in the clear liquid, she quickly turned away, reminded of the accident. In her hazel eyes and reddish-brown hair, she also saw her beloved Einwen's reflection.

She dipped a finger into the pail and tasted the sweet sap. The sugaring season's first sap always tasted the best, like fresh dew sipped from a budding rose. Even so, it still took forty gallons to make a gallon of finished maple syrup. Much more sap went into the making of the shaped maple-sugar candies Barley so coveted.

Barley hung the fresh bucket over the spile and replaced the slate cover. He and Kyleah repeated this routine with one maple tree after another. The sledge was jingling to the next tree when Branagan suddenly hauled back on the reins and jumped out. Kyleah clumsily followed. She found her father standing beside a maple, scratching his head. At the tree's base sat a sap-bucket; the spile had been pulled out of the trunk and lay beside the bucket.

"Who would do such a thing?" Branagan grunted in disgust. "No sugarman I know would steal his neighbor's sap. But why would any thief take out the tap, too?" Bending down, he retrieved the hollow spile and empty pail from the trampled snow. With a wooden mallet, he drove the spile back into its taphole. Then he rehung the bucket on the spout. A few drops of sap dribbled out of the tap and plunked satisfyingly into the pail. *Plock! Plock!*

14

Branagan found several more maple trees missing their spiles. Muttering under his breath, he and Kyleah replaced the spouts and rehung the pails. Then they returned to the sledge and Barley, who was sampling some of the sap. Moving deeper into the sugar bush, they resumed replacing full sap-buckets with empty ones.

The back of the sleigh was nearly full of sloshing buckets when Branagan pulled two burlap sacks from under his seat and motioned to Kyleah and Barley. "Time to set more spiles!" he said. "Bring along a few buckets, and we'll tap some new trees."

Barley grabbed two empty pails, while Kyleah took one of the bags from her father. Her crutch crunched through the snow as she followed Branagan and Barley on foot into leafless groves of untapped maples. Here the trees grew so thickly there was no room for a sledge. Kyleah's foggy breath hung lazily in the biting air, like steam billowing through the sugarhouse doors and roof.

Branagan set his sack down next to a maple. "This one looks old enough," he said. Kyleah knew that tapping a tree younger than about forty years could weaken it. Her father always took care of his trees. From the sack, the sugarmaster removed a short bow, a six-inch iron drill bit and a flat stone. He wrapped the taut bowstring around the drill. Then he fitted the bit's blunt end into a shallow hole in the stone. Pressing the sharp end against the tree trunk with the rock, he began to saw the bow back and forth, twirling the drill first this way, then that. Kyleah had often seen a similar arrangement used for starting fires under the cauldrons in the sugarhouse, using a wooden rod instead of a metal one.

Soon, cream-colored wood shavings were curling out of the taphole Branagan was making in the trunk. After he had bored a couple of inches or so into the tree, he pulled out the drill bit.

"Hand me a spile, will you?" he asked Barley.

The boy dutifully opened Kyleah's sack and handed his father one of the taps. Branagan thoughtfully weighed the spout in his palm before handing it back to Barley. "I'll let you drive this one in," he told the boy. Barley's face split in a toothy grin. Hefting the wooden mallet, he smartly pounded the tap into the tree.

"That's deep enough," Branagan said, taking back the mallet.

He examined his son's handiwork. "You've done a fine job, too," he allowed with a slow smile. "Now hang the bucket." Sap was trickling into the swinging pail when Branagan reached into Kyleah's burlap bag and presented her with a second bow-drill.

"While Barley helps me," he told her, "you go up higher and set some spiles yourself. It's about time you learnt to tap the sap."

Kyleah nearly dropped the bow-drill. Mapleton's women could work in the sugarhouse, but they weren't permitted to set spiles in the sugar bush. Why was Branagan violating this unwritten rule?

Scarcely believing her good fortune, Kyleah limped away with her bag and some buckets before her father could change his mind. Farther up, she came upon a grove of untapped maples. Beneath their outstretched limbs, shadows sullenly defied the bright sun.

Laying the bag and buckets next to a promising tree, she set to work boring a taphole in the trunk. However, she could not work the bow-drill properly. Every time she twisted it, the bit came loose and flew into the snow. After a half-hour, she hadn't made a dent in the maple's tough bark. Exasperated, she plopped down on the snow and wept bitterly. How could she return to her father with the news that she had failed to tap even a single maple tree?

Filled with a sudden fury, she grabbed a spile and shoved it into the scored spot she had left on the trunk. The tap slipped into the tree as smoothly as a knife slicing through soft cheese.

Befuddled, she stared at the spile. With trembling fingers, she pulled on it, and it slid out as readily as it had gone in. The short wooden tube appeared undamaged. Kyleah pushed the tap against the trunk in a different place, and it slipped in again. Around the tree she went, thrusting the tap into the trunk in high spots and low spots, where the bark was thin and where it was thick. When she pulled out the spile, it left no trace of a hole behind.

She took another tap from the bag and pressed it against the trunk. This spout popped into the tree as readily as the first. In a frenzy, Kyleah dumped all the taps out of the sack and tried each in turn. The maple obligingly let them all in with equal ease.

The spiles were magical. They had to be. Kyleah had hit upon a secret worth more than all the gold in Beechtown's treasury!

THE BLACK SWORD

Kyleah couldn't wait to tell her father what had happened. No more drilling holes to insert spiles; from now on, Branagan could tap a hundred trees in the time it took to bore a single hole! No more plugging the tapholes, either. At the end of each sugaring season, Branagan and his fellow sugarmen removed all their taps and filled the holes with birchwood plugs. The Plugger would take care of any holes that were missed.

Every spring, the *tap-tap* of the Plugger's hammer echoed among the peaks like a woodpecker's drumming. Most villagers agreed the old hermit was a harmless eccentric who had nothing better to do than roam the woods looking for tapholes to plug, and he was welcome to them. Kyleah was one of the few people in Mapleton who had spoken with the bearded fellow.

One damp fall day, the Plugger had found Kyleah sobbing in a bracken thicket after Garta and Gyrta had hounded her into the woods again. The Plugger dried her tears and listened to her tale of misery. Afterwards, he told her, "Some people live with crippled bodies, and others with crippled souls. You are suffering with both. You will never find healing until you surrender your pain and loss and forgive your stepsisters from the heart."

Kyleah couldn't quite bring herself to forgive Gyrta and Garta. In the meantime, she wondered what the Plugger would do for work if all the sugarmen started using her magic taps. Then again, perhaps it was the tree that was enchanted and not the taps themselves! Slogging over to the nearest maple, she shoved a spile into its trunk. The tube slipped in as easily as it had into the first tree. Evidently, the taps worked equally well on any maple tree.

After rounding up her tools and supplies, Kyleah scuttled from tree to tree, pushing in spiles and hanging buckets. She avoided any maples with black, oozing holes in their trunks; such trees might yield tainted sap that could spoil an entire batch of syrup.

After hanging her last bucket, she collapsed against a rotten log. Who was "useless" now? She had just proven her worth as a master tapper. Maybe she would take her father's place when he retired. "Sugarmistress Kyleah"—she liked the sound of that!

She stretched and sighed. It was time to go; soon she would be missed. Then she noticed another set of tracks leading from tree to tree. They weren't hers, for these prints lacked that neat round hole her crutch punched in the snow. They were also too large.

Curious, she collected her tapping gear and followed the footprints. Sugarmen rarely visited this remote part of the forest, since the trees were too closely spaced for sledges to pass through.

Kyleah hadn't gone far when she spotted a dark, cloaked shape slinking through the woods. Of course—she should have known. It was the Plugger, making his rounds of the sugar maple groves. But why was the hermit going about his business at this time of the year, when the sap was still flowing heavily in the trees?

She hid behind a maple to observe the elusive Plugger at work. There was a grunting noise and a muted clink. Then the figure sidled past one tree to stop at another. Peering around her maple, Kyleah glimpsed a tall, lean man cloaked in green, his pinched features partially concealed inside a deep hood. He was wielding a heavy iron crowbar. Jamming one end of the crowbar against the tree, he yanked back on the other end with both hands.

That's not the Plugger! Kyleah thought. *He must be the thief who's been pulling out our taps. I must warn Father about him!*

Releasing the bar, the man leaned against the tree, gasping with his exertions. He threw back his hood, revealing a shock of sweaty gray hair. To avoid his roving gaze, Kyleah ducked behind her maple. When she risked another peek, the tap-thief was again prying on the crowbar. With a shriek, the bar gave way, and the man sailed backward into the snow. Picking himself up, he pulled something off the crowbar and dropped it into a bag. Then he moved off to Kyleah's right, where he let out a cry of triumph.

Like a wary squirrel, Kyleah scuttled around the tree to stay hidden. As she moved, a rusty iron spike caught on her cape. Breathlessly, she freed the fabric from the spike. Then she looked out again. Using only his hands, the cursing thief was trying in vain to pull something out of another maple. His neck sinews stood out with the strain. *Clang! Clang!* He struck the stubborn object with his crowbar, yet it still refused to budge or break.

"Kyleah? Kyleah! Where are you, girl?" Branagan's gruff voice echoed through the woods. The green-cloaked man's head snapped up. With a furtive look, he slung the bag and crowbar over his shoulder and slouched off, growling like a disgruntled bear.

Kyleah waited until the tap-thief had safely slunk out of sight. Then she crept over to the tree where he had been working. Her cap fell off as she reeled back in shock. The hilt of a black sword was jutting from the maple's trunk about four feet off the ground. She rubbed her eyes, but the sword was as real as the snow itself. It was difficult to judge the blade's length, but the maple was at least six feet thick at that height, and the point did not poke out.

Kyleah nudged the sword with her crutch-tip. The blade felt firmly embedded. Over the years, the trunk must have grown around it. Why did the stranger wish to pull out the sword? Maybe he hoped to sell it for a princely price at the Beechtown market.

But why would anyone drive a sword into a tree trunk in the first place? Perhaps this maple had witnessed a duel to the death, and one of the combatants' desperate thrusts had missed its mark, piercing wood instead of flesh. A daring thought crystallized in Kyleah's mind, like maple syrup hardening in a candy mold. What if the sword responded to her touch as readily as the spiles had?

Kyleah gripped the weapon's hilt. It felt colder than a frozen sledge-runner. She pulled back, and the blade smoothly slid out with a faint groan, as if the tree itself was moaning with relief.

The sword was seamlessly formed of a substance so black her eyes hurt just looking at it. Even after being trapped in the trunk for so many years, the blade was untarnished. Glistening with fresh sap, it steamed and smoked under the weak winter's sun.

Silvery letters ran along the sword's length. Holding it up to the light, Kyleah read the words, *With this blade he will make them, and with this blade he will break them!* Who was "he," and whom was he supposed to "make" and "break" with this black blade?

More words were carved into the maple just above the dark, dripping gash the sword had left in its trunk. The letters were so overgrown with callus that Kyleah could hardly read them.

> This sword was driven for a reason;
> To capture king of leafy treason;
> Remove the sword, and you will see
> Why he's intrisoned in this tree!

Intrisoned? What an odd word! Surely the writer must have meant, "imprisoned." Yet, how could you lock a person up inside a tree? She walked around the trunk but saw no door or latch or keyhole. Someone must have been playing a prank. Thoughtless lovers often carved their initials, cupid hearts and other messages on smooth-barked trees such as birches and beeches. The worst scars never completely healed, permanently disfiguring the tree.

"Squawk! Squawk!" Kyleah glanced up to spot a magpie perched on a black, crusty growth high on the trunk of another tree. She had never seen such a large tree-burl before. Over three feet across, it displayed grotesque, face-like features. Her father sometimes sawed off those lumpy swellings to carve the highly figured wood into beautiful bowls, plates and pitchers that he sold in the Beechtown market. During the off-season, he also crafted oak syrup-barrels and fine furniture. "His casks won't leak and his chairs won't squeak," the townsfolk said of him. It was a fact, for Branagan took pride in whatever task his hands found to do.

"Kyleah! Why won't you answer me?" Branagan's voice broke the snowy stillness. She had to hurry. Strapping the sword to her right thigh inside her trousers, she stiffly limped back the way she had come. For once, being crippled worked in her favor, for no one would give her awkward gait a second glance. She found her father and brother striding through the snowdrifts to meet her.

"Where were you, anyway?" Branagan scolded her. "I've been a-calling and a-calling for you. Did you tap all these trees?" When Kyleah nodded, her father observed, "You made a right clean job of it, and quick-like, too. I couldn't a-bored such neat holes if I'd tried. What did you do with all the shavings from the drill? I don't see a single speck o' sawdust." He pointed to a tapped tree's base, where the trampled snow was clear of wood flakes and chips.

Kyleah had forgotten her novel method of tree-tapping left no telltale wood waste. Sidestepping her father's questions, she said, "I've just been looking for new trees to tap. I found some very nice maples higher up. Would you like me to show them to you?"

Branagan narrowly eyed her. "Were they wearing any mark?"

Sheepishly, Kyleah replied, "I didn't see any paint. I thought if a tree belonged to no one in particular, anyone could tap it."

Sweeping her remark aside, the sugarmaster brusquely said, "I meant, did you see any nails or spikes driven into the trunks?"

Kyleah recalled the rusty spike sticking out of the maple where she had hidden from the tap-thief. "Well, yes, I did notice at least one," she admitted. "How did you know about that?"

"Don't touch them trees," said Branagan. Fear furrowed his face as he trudged through the snow back toward the sleigh.

"Why not?" Kyleah and Barley asked, hurrying to catch up.

After a brooding silence, Branagan said, "I've heard tales about those trees since I was too young to knock a spile into a maple."

"What kind of tales?" Kyleah eagerly asked him. She loved listening to her father spin stories of the old days in Mapleton, when sugarmen boiled down the maple sap in an open-air kitchen using shallow copper pans. Supposedly, Branagan was the tenth in an unbroken succession of sugarmasters. One of those ancestors, Tapwell son of Tharweld, had actually founded Mapleton.

"Tales that don't bear repeating!" Branagan answered. "Now, help me load the sledge with our tapping gear, and you can sit up front again." He added, "If you want to know about them maples, try asking Wynnagar. She goes back a long way in these parts."

Wynnagar. The spry, silver-haired spinster was a legend in herself. Some said when men first settled the green valley of the Foamwater, they found Wynnagar living in the hills above the river. She was even rumored to have introduced the art of maple sugaring to Mapleton, though she had never been a sugarmaster.

Nowadays, most of the villagers regarded Wynnagar as a bit eccentric, if not downright daft. At the mere mention of her name, townsfolk twirled their fingers around their ears and rolled their eyes. Kyleah's mother had never been among those mockers.

On the contrary, Larissa and Wynnagar had been fast friends. On brisk autumn afternoons, when Kyleah loved to scuffle through the musky maple and oak leaves carpeting the forest floor, she would often come across the two women strolling among the trees, speaking in hushed, earnest tones. Without warning, Larissa might then go away for a day or even a week at a time. "I was just visiting some relatives," she would tell Kyleah, but not even Branagan had met his wife's relations or knew where they lived.

"Womenfolk!" he was fond of muttering. "Who knows what they'll do next? They keep their own counsel, and I keep mine."

Larissa's counsel had died with her. Now Kyleah was anxious to speak with Wynnagar. Unfortunately, no one knew exactly where the reclusive old lady lived. From time to time, she would wander into the village, staff in hand and a sack of taps over her shoulder. Wynnagar whittled the finest spiles in all the valley.

Kyleah slung a bagful of those spiles into the back of the sleigh and stiffly climbed onto the seat in front of a grumbling Barley. On the way home, she sat with her right leg outstretched in hopes her father wouldn't notice the black sword. As soon as the sleigh slid to a stop outside the sugarhouse, she clambered down and toiled up the snowy slope to her rambling cottage. Inside her bedroom, she hid the sword under her mattress before returning to the sledge to help her father and brother unload the full sap-pails.

Forming a human chain, Branagan, Barley, Kyleah and her stepsisters carried the pails inside the sugarhouse. Branagan held the last place, dumping the sap into a cauldron. Then they all took a turn at the stirring paddles, singing as they worked:

Pour the sap in quick; boil it up thick;
Whip it up well with a stirring-stick!
Bubble and churn; don't let it burn;
No sipping syrup till you've taken a turn!

That's how we make the syrup from sap;
Once we've taken it straight from the tap;
There's no finer sweet than sugar from trees;
Poured over pancakes, it's certain to please!

Serve it up hot, right from the pot,
Cool it with snow and you'll hit the spot!
Pour into flasks and Branagan's casks;
Selling the syrup is the last of our tasks!

That's how we make the syrup from sap;
Once we've taken it straight from the tap;
There's no finer sweet than sugar from trees;
Poured over pancakes, it's certain to please!

When Kyleah lay back on her bed that night, she was content. Gyrta and Garta had glared at her in the sugarhouse, but Branagan was also working there, so the spiteful pair couldn't vent their venom on her. To top it all off, she now owned a sword of her very own, not to mention the most magnificent bed in Mapleton.

One day after her father had remarried, Kyleah had fled to her bedroom to escape her stepsisters. Intending to weep alone on her crackly corn-husk mattress, she had instead discovered Branagan sitting on a beautiful new bed, looking pleased with himself.

Shortly before the Prowlers had taken her, Larissa had lugged two rough wooden panels into Branagan's cluttered shop behind the house. "A friend gave me these," she had told him. "Aren't they lovely? One is a headboard and the other is a footboard. Kyleah has been sleeping on corn husks long enough. Now that she has been growing taller, it's about time you built her a proper bed."

"I'll get around to it this fall," he had told her. He never did.

After she was gone, Branagan closed up the woodshop and his heart as well. In his grief and loneliness, he forgot all about the boards. Some months and a wedding later, Dolora's incessant nagging drove him back into the shop, where he came across the headboard and footboard standing just where Larissa had left them. Recalling his promise, he had set about making Kyleah's bed. The careful work helped clear his head—and his heart.

He had enjoyed sanding and varnishing the heavy, fine-grained boards, whose reddish-brown wood had all the best qualities of maple, cherry and walnut. He would have paid dearly for more, if only he knew what kind of wood it was or where to find it.

Kyleah's was a bed to dream upon, a bed to grow into. If she rested her head against the headboard and extended her legs as far as they would go, she couldn't quite reach the footboard with her good leg. She stretched her lame leg every night in hopes of lengthening it, but the broken bones had knitted crookedly. It didn't help that her bed was always cold, even in the summer.

The next day, Kyleah sledged up to the sugar bush again with Barley and Branagan to check on the sap-buckets. One of the pails Kyleah had hung contained a dark, oily liquid with a foul odor.

"Iron-spoilt!" Branagan pronounced in disgust. Kyleah had seen sap tainted by iron before, but this tree's trunk bore no nails or other metal objects. As she gazed into the pail, a hideous face glared back at her. She dropped the bucket, spilling the sap.

Branagan threw the bucket away, but for days afterward, Kyleah could not shake the memory of that awful reflection. Whose face had stared at her from the dark sap? She was reminded of the grotesque burl she had seen by the sword-tree. It was a mystery to crown all the other mysteries the sugar bush had sprung on her.

CHAPTER 3

BURGLED AND BURGLING

A few weeks later, the sap flow dried up and Branagan hung his buckets in the attic. The Plugger's tap-tapping echoed through the forest as the snow retreated into the mountain passes. Creeks thawed, frogs croaked—and Kyleah grew.

First, her sleeves came up short on her wrists. Then she began bumping her head on low-hanging tree limbs. One morning, as she emerged from the woodshed with an armload of firewood, she cracked her head on the lintel. She dropped the firewood to rub the sore spot. Wynnagar was impatiently waiting for her outside.

"You!" cried the crone. She jabbed a bony finger at Kyleah. "I've warned you people not to touch those trees, but what do I find? Someone has pulled the spikes, and that someone is you!"

"What spikes?" Kyleah said, forgetting the nail that had caught on her cape as she hid from the tap-thief. Left in, such spikes would taint the maple sap and leave the trees open to disease.

"These spikes!" Wynnagar shouted at her. Tearing open her canvas bag, she removed a rusted nail and shook it in Kyleah's face. "Phah!" she spat and cast the spike aside. Kyleah noticed the object had left an angry red mark on the hag's dried-up, clawlike hand, no doubt where some of the rust had rubbed off.

Wynnagar grated, "Don't try to deny it! I found your crutch-marks all around those spiked trees. What were you doing up there? Do you want more folk to end up like your poor mother?"

Tears sprang to Kyleah's eyes. "I didn't take those spikes!" she cried, and she told Wynnagar about the green-cloaked tap-thief.

Wynnagar's face softened. "You have inherited your mother's honest heart—and perhaps much more," she said. "You tapped those trees without drilling any holes, didn't you? Your spiles are too perfectly seated." As Kyleah drew back in alarm, Wynnagar grunted, "Do not fear. Your secret is safe with me. However, I must know whether your thief took anything else from those trees."

"He tried to pull out a sword," Kyleah reluctantly replied.

Wynnagar's face blanched and she asked in a hoarse whisper, "Did he . . . did he succeed? Tell me; *has he the sword*?"

Kyleah shook her head. "No—I do."

"Ai! Ai! Ai!" Wynnagar's hands flew to her head. "We are all undone! Alas, alack, what evil has been loosed upon the earth, and who can stand against it? May Gaelathane have mercy upon the children of men." With a terrible strength, she grasped Kyleah's shoulders. "Give it to me!" she ordered. "Give me the sword!"

Kyleah wrenched free of Wynnagar's iron grip. "No!" she cried. "You can't have it! That sword belongs to me. I found it, and I am going to keep it. You have no right to take it from me."

Wynnagar's hands fell limply to her sides, and she turned into a different woman. Her skin tightened and flushed pink, erasing the wrinkles in her face, arms and hands; her hair darkened to a raven-black; her bowed back straightened, and tears fell from her pleading eyes as she said in a strong, vibrant voice, "You do not understand. As long as you keep this thing, you are endangering not only yourself but all of Mapleton! Give me the sword, and I will keep it safe. I will not stoop to taking it from you by force."

Wavering, Kyleah still stood her ground. "No! If the sword must be hidden, I will be the one to hide it. I know just where in these hills to conceal that sword so no one will ever find it."

To Kyleah's horror, Wynnagar withered with age again. "They will find it," she croaked. "Be very sure of that. They will find it."

26

Retreating down the hill, Wynnagar called back, "When they come for you, take to your bed! It is your only way of escape."

As the hollow-eyed old woman melted into the woods, Kyleah shook her head. Who were "they" and why did they covet her sword? Why take refuge in a bed? And how had Wynnagar changed her appearance? Sighing, Kyleah gathered up her firewood.

That night, she could not sleep for thinking of Wynnagar's words. Why was the crone so distraught over a sword and a few spikes? She shivered, setting the bell on her neck to ringing.

That sound sent her back to the day she had spied on the tap-thief. *Clink.* Suddenly, Kyleah realized what the green-cloaked stranger had been up to. One by one, he had been prying out the iron spikes and dropping them into his bag. Trailing behind him, Kyleah had found only the black, dripping holes that remained. The man must have been looking for anything embedded in tree trunks. He had started with Branagan's spiles, but he was really after the spikes. But what could anyone possibly want with a few handfuls of rusted nails, or even a sword, for that matter?

Kyleah reached under the mattress and pulled out the black sword by its hilt. In the morning, she would look for a safer hiding spot. In the meantime, she could put the sword to good use. She bound it to her right leg with some rags, painfully forcing the leg to straighten. Maybe if she splinted her leg every night, it would eventually mend itself. She stretched her legs. For the first time, her left toes just touched the footboard. She *had* been growing! If only her crooked leg would grow properly, too. She fell asleep.

In the dead of the night, she dreamt her mattress was bucking beneath her like an unruly horse. She awoke shivering with the cold. Her window wasn't open; she had made sure to close and bolt it before bed. The fire in the parlor stove must have died out. Burrowing under her thick blankets, Kyleah dozed off till dawn.

After a good yawn and head-to-toes stretch, she emerged from her cocoon of blankets. Her breath fogged in the chill morning air. Hanging askew by one hinge, the window sash swung lazily into the curtains. The door jamb was splintered, and long, deep gouges scored the ceiling and walls. Snow whitened the whole room.

Snow? No wonder she had felt so chilled! But how could snow get into her bedroom? Then she realized the white powder that coated her bed and all her belongings was plaster dust. Her torn clothing, hairbrushes, combs and mementos of her mother were rudely strewn about. Worst of all, Kyleah's prized mirror collection lay smashed across the floor, mingled with the shattered remnants of the maple wardrobe Branagan had lovingly made for her.

After untying the sword from her leg, she shoved the black blade back under the mattress and grabbed the crutch that lay beside her. Then she retrieved her shoes from under the bed and slipped them on. Crunching across the broken glass to the wrecked wardrobe, she cried, "Please, oh please, let it still be there!"

Rummaging through the debris, she glimpsed a buttery gleam under a pile of faded, pressed flowers. With a sob of relief, she dug out the broad golden bracelet her mother had once given her.

Kyleah had kept the bracelet locked in a secret drawer in the wardrobe for fear her stepsisters or Barley would see it and try to take it away from her. Double-looping an old leather shoelace around the bracelet, she hung it from her neck inside her frock.

The cottage was eerily silent, as if she alone had survived this calamity. "Father!" she shouted. "Father, come quickly! Someone has broken into my room." No one came or answered her call.

Hearing shouts and wailing outside, she hobbled through the empty house and pushed open the front door. Down the hill, an agitated crowd of villagers had gathered beside the sugarhouse. For time out of mind, the old building had served as a meeting place during dark days of distress as well as joyous celebration.

Kyleah hurried down the hillside as swiftly as her crippled leg would allow. As soon as she came into sight, the confused babble of angry, grieving and frightened voices died into silence.

"Has anyone seen Branagan son of Carrigan?" she called out.

"Kyleah!" bellowed her father. He plowed through the throng toward her, followed by a bawling Barley. The rest of the family dragged behind. Gyrta and Garta seemed dazed and disappointed to see Kyleah again. Forced to share the same room, the sisters had long hoped one of them could move into Kyleah's space.

Wrapping his thick arms around Kyleah, Branagan squeezed the breath out of her. "My dear daughter!" he wept. "I thought you were lost! Where in thundering tarnation did you go?"

"Oof!" she gasped. "Don't hug me so hard, Papa, or I shall pop! Why are you so upset? What is wrong with everybody?"

"What's wrong?" echoed Branagan. He held her at arm's length, looking dumbfounded. "You were gone, and now you're back!"

If her father's expression hadn't been so serious, Kyleah would have laughed aloud. "I didn't go anywhere! When I woke up this morning, I found my room in a shambles. I'm surprised I slept through it all. Somebody must have played a prank on me."

"This was no prank," said Branagan grimly. Taking her hand, he steered her toward home. Some of the villagers followed them. "Whoever or whatever got into your bedroom," he went on, "they raised enough racket to wake everybody in Mapleton. I thought the house was collapsing. By the time we forced our way into your room, it was empty. When we shouted your name outside, you didn't answer. We were sure we would never see you again."

He flung open the front door. Then the company trooped to the back of the cottage, where Kyleah had her bedroom.

"Stand aside, everyone!" Branagan said. He pushed Kyleah's door open and glanced around. "It's all clear!" he announced.

A collective sigh rose from the onlookers. "Worst mess I ever did see!" said a grizzled sugarman. "Cougars done this, I'd say."

"I don't see any cat hairs," said Branagan. "Besides, cougars don't make marks like those." He pointed at the scarred walls and ceiling, which looked as if they had been attacked with rakes.

"Where were you, anyway?" Kyleah's stepmother asked her. Clutching her favorite copper mixing-bowl, Dolora scratched her long, pointed nose as she often did when perplexed or angry.

Confused, Kyleah stared at her. "I was in my bed, of course."

"That's impossible!" Dolora scoffed. "When we came in here, you were nowhere to be seen! How did you manage to escape?"

"I didn't go anywhere," Kyleah insisted. "I stayed right here in this room all night, from the time I went to sleep till the time I woke up. If you don't believe me, look at my tracks in the dust."

Sure enough, only one set of tracks led from Kyleah's bed to the demolished wardrobe, and from the wardrobe out the door.

"It's what happened betwixt the sleeping and the waking that worries me," muttered her father. He stared fixedly at the ceiling.

"Just look at this disaster!" Dolora said. Her eyes darted around the floor. "How anyone could sleep through this is beyond me."

"She didn't sleep through it," Gyrta declared, her hands on her hips. "She wrecked her room to get attention and hid outside to throw us all off the scent. You won't get away with it, Useless."

"That's right!" said Garta. "You made this mess, so you can jolly well clean it up again. We're not going to help you, either."

"That's ridiculous!" Kyleah snapped. "How could I have made all those marks?" She jabbed her crutch at the gouged ceiling.

"You stood on the bed and used your stick!" sneered Gyrta.

"I did no such thing, and you know it!" Kyleah retorted. "If you and Garta won't help me, I'll straighten things up myself."

"Girls, girls," Dolora said soothingly. "Let's not fight, shall we? Many families in our village have lost loved ones during the night. We should be very thankful our family wasn't among them."

"I'd be thankful if Gimpy here weren't such a lazy whiner," Garta muttered, and she haughtily stalked out of the bedroom.

"Someone needs to take a paddle to that girl!" Branagan said.

Dolora changed the subject. "What do you suppose those Prowlers were after?" She seemed more puzzled than frightened.

Branagan's eyebrows rose. "Why blame the Prowlers?"

Dolora looked flustered. "I don't know. I just thought—"

"Prowlers don't steal *things*; they take *people*!" Branagan said. "If it was Prowlers, I'd be carving Kyleah's name on a paddle. And how did you know others in town have gone missing? I thought ours was the only house in Mapleton them thieves broke into."

"I—I heard people at the sugarhouse talking," said Dolora.

Branagan grunted. "Well, I didn't hear 'em."

When everyone had left her bedroom, Kyleah closed the door, threw herself on her bed and wept until she had left a big wet spot on the bedspread. After her tears had dried, she limped about the room, making a pitiful pile of her few salvageable possessions.

The shattered mirrors troubled her the most. For some odd reason, the burglars had singled out Kyleah's precious mirrors for special treatment, stomping them to splinters. Not that Kyleah ever looked into those mirrors anymore; since the accident, she had turned the hanging mirrors against the wall and laid the hand mirrors face down. She didn't want to be reminded of Einwen.

After sweeping up the broken wood and glass, she dumped the heap outside into a badger hole. Let the old badger mend her mirrors if he wished; she had washed her hands of the whole lot.

Exhausted, she flopped down on her bed. Surrounded by the wreckage of her once-tidy room, she couldn't rest. At last, she gave up trying to sleep and set about putting her bed in order. Even if a tornado had struck everything else in her bedroom, at least she could make up her bed to look as neat as she had once kept it.

First, she fluffed up her pillows and straightened her mattress, which had somehow become quite crooked. She was shaking the plaster dust off the bedspread when a couple of leaves flew up and sailed across the room. Leaves! How had they found a way into her bedroom? Then she remembered the damaged window. Pushing the sash back into place, she fitted the loose hinge into its slot and pounded down the nails with a rock she used to prop her door open. Last of all, she retrieved the leaves from the floor.

They were linden leaves, shiny with the first breath of spring. Yet, no lindens grew anywhere near Mapleton. A windstorm must have carried them up from the Foamwater valley. She thrust them into her pocket. Then she slid the sword from under her mattress. After sandwiching the black blade between two broken wardrobe boards, she tied up the bundle with string. If anyone should ask, she was taking out the wardrobe to be burned, piece by piece.

Leaving the house, she headed up the slope to a thick-limbed chestnut tree where she often came to sit and think. In the fall, she and Barley enjoyed trampling on the chestnut burs to release the glossy, reddish-brown nuts. Larissa used to dry the nuts and grind them to make a sweet, nourishing flour, but Dolora didn't want to bother with them. Kyleah and Barley liked to roast or boil the fresh nuts and eat them steaming hot, right out of the shell.

She glanced about to be sure no one was watching. Then she untied the boards and removed the sword. It shone a dull black in the spring sun. Since she had found the blade in a tree, it was only fitting that she should return it to a tree for safekeeping. With a gentle thrust, she shoved the sword into the trunk up to the hilt.

Here was a new dilemma. If she was going to bury the sword completely in the tree, she would have to push her hand into the trunk, too. What if she got splinters in her fingers? That might be difficult to explain away. And suppose she couldn't pull her hand out again? She would be at the mercy of whoever might happen by—and that usually meant Garta and Gyrta. After making sport of her, they would call Branagan, who would cut open the trunk to free her hand. Then the sword would surely be discovered.

Still, left as it was, the black blade would soon be discovered anyway. She had no other choice. Taking a deep breath, she drove the sword into the chestnut's trunk up to her elbow. A sigh of relief escaped her lips. No splinters had jabbed her. Rather, the chestnut wood felt like chilled maple syrup—cool, thick and moist.

As she withdrew her arm, a sharp pain stabbed her hand. She must have cut it on the black blade! Her palm came out bleeding. Bitter bile boiled up into her throat, filling her mouth. Gagging, she spat out a dark fluid. Her eyes blurred and the world faded into shadows. Terrible voices spoke to her from out of the earth.

"What are you doing outside? You're supposed to be cleaning your room, and here I find you playing with trees again!"

Bell jingling, Kyleah guiltily turned to find Garta glaring at her. Belatedly, she hid her bleeding hand behind her back.

"What have you got back there?" Garta growled. "Show me!"

Reluctantly, Kyleah raised her bloody right hand and lamely explained, "I cut myself picking up the pieces of my wardrobe. I came over here to find some lichens to stanch the flow of blood."

Garta snorted. "A likely story! But I suppose since you're hurt, I'd better take you back to Mother. She has just the thing for cuts and scrapes." Just the thing, indeed! Dolora seemed to delight in pouring whiskey into people's wounds. The potent liquor not only smelled terrible, but it also burned white-hot on raw flesh.

Meekly, Kyleah let herself be led away, wincing as her sliced hand pressed against the crutch. At the cottage, Dolora scolded and fussed over her before wrapping her throbbing gash with yards of fresh bandages. Fortunately, the whiskey bottle was empty, having seen much use lately on blisters raised by stirring paddles.

Kyleah's cut slowly mended, leaving a thin black scar on her palm and a lingering bitter taste on the back of her tongue. At night, waking nightmares still disturbed her sleep. In the dark, she would feel the prickly sensation of air passing across her face. Mutterings, rustlings and whisperings surrounded the bed, too. At other times, she heard scratching and tapping at the iron bars Branagan had set over her window. Terrified, she could only lie still, listening to her pounding heart and hoping for the dawn.

Even before her hand had healed, she began exploring trees again. She discovered that they felt perfectly solid when she leaned against a trunk or climbed onto a limb. Only when she set her mind on getting *inside* a tree did its wood yield to her probing fingers. Nails she found by the bushel-basketful, driven there by careless sugarmen who used them to hang their sap-buckets. Once, she found an ax-head. Another time, she pulled out a horseshoe that someone had nailed to a maple for good luck. The horseshoe had brought only bad luck to the maple, scarring its trunk.

One fine June morning, she found a hand. She was waving her arm through the trunk of a beech tree when other fingers touched hers. She shrieked and yanked back her hand. Flinching with fear, she slipped her fingers back into the beech and wiggled them like a fisherman twitching his lure to attract a trout. She felt only wood. She was ready to give up when another hand grasped her own. Trembling, she drew back, pulling out a bony wrist attached to a thin, shrunken arm. The rest of the body gradually followed.

Kyleah gaped. She had found a long-haired boy about Barley's age. Tattered clothing hung on his gaunt frame, and his neck-bell tinkled. He blinked in the sunlight. "Who are you?" he asked.

"I'm Kyleah," she replied. "What is your name?"

The boy's face scrunched up. "Robin, I think. Where are we?"

"In the forest above Mapleton. Where are your parents?"

More scrunching. "In town. Do you have any food?"

Searching her pockets, Kyleah came up with a stale biscuit. She handed it to Robin, who greedily devoured it on the spot.

"Do you remember how you got here?" Kyleah asked him.

Robin shook his head. Then recollection dawned on him. "I think I got lost chasing squirrels. After sunset, the darkness came. The next thing I knew, you were here. How did you find me?"

Kyleah let out her pent-up breath. Her secret was still safe. Robin didn't remember being freed from the tree. When she took him back to the village, she could say she found him wandering in the woods. Answering his question, she said, "I heard your bell ringing in the forest." She hated lying, but it couldn't be helped.

Finding Robin's family proved unexpectedly difficult. No one recalled him or his parents. "You might try down the mountain and across the water," the villagers suggested, referring to Beechtown. However, Beechtown's young people never wore neck-bells.

The setting sun found Kyleah sitting with Robin on a stone behind the sugarhouse. She couldn't leave him outside after dark, but she couldn't take him home with her, either. Her suspicious stepmother would ask too many questions. In particular, Dolora always wanted to know whether Kyleah's girlfriends were "gifted" in any way. Kyleah was never quite sure what she meant by that.

She was about to hide Robin in the sugarhouse for the night when Wynnagar came out of the woods wrapped in a green shawl, her staff swinging like a clock pendulum. Kyleah cringed as the old woman hurried over and waved a bony finger in her face.

"You've been tree-burgling again, haven't you! Some things are better left alone. You are fortunate it's only Robin son of Rimlin you found. Next time, death might be waiting for you inside a tree! Didn't your mother warn you not to pry into others' affairs?"

"I wasn't prying," Kyleah retorted. "How was I to know Robin was hiding inside that tree? And how did you know his name?"

"No one goes missing in Mapleton without my knowledge," said Wynnagar softly. "I thought you knew that. I am beginning to understand. Your mother hadn't the time to tell you everything."

"Tell me what? Understand what?" Kyleah asked her.

"I cannot explain now, but I suspect we shall meet again soon, if Gaelathane wills it. In the meantime, I must keep my promise to Larissa and look after you, despite your headstrong ways. Let not your hand seek the secret places of a tree again, lest you fall into the darkness whence there is no escaping! Now, come along, boy." Wynnagar steered Robin toward the woods' deepening gloom.

"Where are you taking him?" Kyleah protested. "Someone needs to find his parents. They must live in Beechtown, because nobody in Mapleton knows anything about him or his relatives."

Wynnagar stared bleakly at Kyleah. "I will safely hide Robin from our awakened foes. As for his kinfolk: Robin's last living relative died of old age in this very village over fifty years ago."

Chapter 4

A Treacherous Bed

Kyleah tossed and turned on her bed as she mulled over the day's events. Who was this "Gaelathane" Wynnagar kept mentioning? What enemy had captured Robin? If the crone was correct about the boy's family, he could have been sitting inside that tree over one hundred years! Yet, Robin didn't look a day older than ten. And where had Wynnagar taken him?

When she fell asleep, Kyleah dreamt of the wind in the trees and of fragrant flowers. She awoke to weeping and the awful groan of tortured metal. *Something* was crying in the darkness crouching outside her room. Protesting, an iron window rod curled back.

Kyleah sat bolt upright in her bed just as a second iron bar twisted back with a dreadful screech. Someone in pain was trying to break through her window! She bounded out of bed. Whoever the intruders were, they wouldn't catch her without a fight. But how could she defend herself against a foe that could bend bars of metal? She wished she had not hidden her sword so hastily.

Where is the sword? Give us the sword! Dreadful voices rang in Kyleah's head like a blacksmith's hammers clanging on an anvil.

"I don't have it anymore!" she screamed, covering her ears. "Now go away!" Still the voices gnawed at her tortured mind.

Then she heard angry shouts outside, and the clamoring voices faded. The door flew open and Branagan burst in, his face blackened with soot. He held a smoking torch in one hand and a bow and arrows in the other. Kyleah's father was a dead shot, often bringing home deer and other game to fill his family's larder. Alerted by the intruders' break-in attempts, he had mustered the men of Mapleton and had fallen upon the would-be burglars.

"Those ruffians must have been wearing chain mail," he told Kyleah. "Our arrows and spears just bounced off their hides! Old Bob set his dogs on the lot, but the animals wouldn't go near. Turned tail and ran off, they did. I've seen them dogs bring down a bear, too. Something about this bunch would give anyone the willies. They wouldn't leave till we threw some burning torches at them and set a few on fire. That sent them all packing!"

"What did they look like?" Kyleah asked him, shuddering.

"Big fellers, they were," said Branagan. "They wore black cloaks and hoods, so I couldn't get a good look at 'em. I don't know how they bent your window-bars, but if we hadn't a-chased them off, they'd have broken into your room again. That's twice now. I've stationed men outside your window in shifts until morning. In a day or two, you and I had better take a trip down the mountain and across the water to sell some syrup. Maybe while we're gone, things will cool off a bit. It's just not safe here for you now."

Kyleah brightened at the prospect of a visit to town. Now that Wynnagar had put a stop to Kyleah's "tree-burgling" expeditions, life in Mapleton had become dreary indeed. Beechtown's market square wasn't quite as exciting as exploring the mysterious hearts of maples, but at least Kyleah could expect to come away from a syrup-selling jaunt with more than a pocketful of rusty nails!

Since dawn was reddening the sky, Kyleah stayed up to help her father load his wagon with crates of candies and syrup. Next, a mountain of dirty laundry beckoned. When Branagan wasn't watching, Dolora liked to slough off her daughters' chores on Kyleah. Grumbling, she dragged the sacks of soiled clothes down to the sugarhouse and emptied them into a cauldron. In the off-season, the sugarhouse served double-duty as the village laundry.

Limping back and forth to the well, she drew buckets of water to dump into the gleaming kettle of clothes. Then she kindled a fire underneath. As the water slowly warmed, she stirred soap flakes into the laundry stew with a paddle, singing as she worked:

Where will I find a friend to love me?
Why must I face rejection?
When will I see an end to mis'ry?
Where will I find protection?

In my home I'm but a guest,
And I cannot even rest,
For I work at their request,
Like a pauper or a pest!

Where must I go to find acceptance?
Why must I feel so lonely?
Why must I always be a nuisance?
Why must I look so homely?

Careful vigil I must keep,
For the Prowlers never sleep,
As they softly crawl and creep
And underneath my window weep!

Someday I know my dreams will flourish;
Do I dare hope for better?
Just for today, my faith I'll nourish;
To dreamland I'll be a debtor!

"Hey, whatcha doing, 'Leah?" Barley stood smirking at the sugarhouse door, chewing on a sweet birch twig.

"What does it look like I'm doing?" Kyleah wiped sweat from her brow. Washing laundry over a steaming kettle was hot work.

Barley shuffled his feet. "I hear you're going to town tomorrow. I was hoping I could go, too. You know how Gyrta and Garta pick on me while Papa is away. They always make me do all their work. I can't wait till I'm bigger. Then I'm gonna make them pay!"

Kyleah felt a twinge of guilt. Her stepsisters tormented Barley unmercifully. It was high time those two were put in their place!

"Why don't you ask Father if you can join us?" she said.

Barley scowled petulantly. "I already did. He told me to stay here and help Mother. She's not really my mother, and I don't want to help her! Could I hide in the back of the wagon?" His beaming, upturned face reminded Kyleah of the man-in-the-moon.

"No, silly!" she laughed. "The wagon is already packed, and there's no room left for you. Now drain the kettle for me, please. With my bum leg, it's hard climbing up and down this ladder."

Kyleah's brother scurried beneath her stirring platform and turned a stopcock. Soapy water gurgled down a drainpipe and through a grate in the floor. During the sugaring season, the drain carried away waste water after the kettles had been scrubbed out.

"I know why those men were trying to break into your room," Barley said. "They heard you're the prettiest girl in Mapleton!"

"Oh, go on with you!" Kyleah laughed. As Barley darted for the door, bell ringing, she fished a soggy tunic out of the cauldron, rolled it into a dripping ball and hurled it after him. She missed.

"You throw like a girl!" Barley jeered over his shoulder.

"Of course I throw like a girl; I *am* a girl!" Kyleah muttered.

At the dinner table that night, Kyleah was so worn out that she could barely keep her eyes open. After picking at her food, she went to bed fully clothed and fell into a deep, dreamless sleep.

She awoke to a familiar flowery scent. Someone must have opened her bedroom window! As she got up to shut it, her feet sank into soft earth. A full moon peered down through a gauzy white canopy stretched above her bed. Masses of fragrant linden blossoms hung like sea-foam from the surrounding trees. Kyleah was outside! Clinging to a bedpost, she stared about in fear and wonderment. What was this place, and how had she come here?

She had been sleeping in a magic bed all along and hadn't even known it! She tried to recall all the tales her mother had told her of such things. Many were the fabulous stories of magic beans and magic lamps and magic wands and magic boots—but never had she heard of a magic bed. Now she was sure that if she took her hand off the bedpost even for an instant, the bed would disappear, and she would be trapped in this phantom forest forever.

The fickle bed must have brought her here at least once before, which would explain the leaves she had found on her bedspread. But how could she get back to her bedroom? What made the bed work? Kyleah didn't know any enchantments. Perhaps someone else had spoken the magic words over her while she was asleep.

She climbed back on the bed and gently rocked it this way and that. Nothing changed. She bounced up and down, making her bell ring. Still nothing. Now she became really frightened. If the treacherous bed wouldn't yield up its secrets, she would never see her father or Barley again! Maybe if she went back to sleep, the bed would do the rest. Try as she might, though, she could not calm herself enough to fall asleep. The bed had kidnapped her!

Furious, Kyleah crawled out of the bed and kicked one of the legs. "Drat you, bed!" she hissed. "Why did you bring me here?"

All at once, she realized she was no longer touching the bed. She held her breath. Would her only link to home vanish? Still the moonlit frame stood stolidly among the trees, as if to say, "Never fear; I am not going anywhere without you!" Reaching out, Kyleah patted one of her pillows. It still seemed solid and real enough.

Slowly, she backed away. All she knew and loved was wrapped up in that bed. It stayed put. A breeze sprang up, drawing a white curtain across the moon. Fat raindrops spattered on the leaves.

Moving deeper into the forest, Kyleah was telling herself that Mapleton must lie just beyond the next trees when the ground sickeningly slid out from under her feet. With a scream and the jangling of her neck-bell, she pitched forward into empty space. A vast, silvery plain rushed up to meet her. She had to be dreaming, but her lurching stomach told a frighteningly different story.

Then her fall was checked. A hand had seized the back of her shift and was pulling her upright. Her windmilling feet found level ground. Turning, she came face to face with a young woman clad in black. The stranger's eyes and face struck a familiar chord.

"You have come at last," said the woman. "I was beginning to think we would never meet here. Welcome to Mt. Argel!"

Kyleah instantly recognized that husky voice.

It was Wynnagar.

CHAPTER 5

THE GIFTED GIRL

W ynnagar!" Kyleah gasped. "What are you doing here? You look so *young*." Was Wynnagar also a part of her dream? If not, was the old woman's age an illusion?

Wynnagar chuckled. "At seven hundred and fifty-five years, I can't very well parade about Mapleton looking like this, can I? Just because I'm mortal doesn't mean I must look my age! Now let's find your bed. We must send you back before you are missed."

All the air left Kyleah's lungs. *Seven hundred and fifty-five years?* Most people in her village were fortunate if they lived past forty. She hurried to keep up with Wynnagar's long-legged strides.

On reaching the bed, Wynnagar firmly sat Kyleah down beside her. "Tell me now what you have done with the sword," she said. "I must be certain it lies beyond the reach of our enemies."

She is still worried about her precious sword? Sighing, Kyleah described how she had concealed the sword in the chestnut tree.

Wynnagar groaned. "You hid it in a tree? They are sure to find it there! A tree is the first place they will look. If you had given me that sword, I would have buried it where no one would have ever found it. You have placed us all in grave peril. We must recover the sword before it is too late. Now lie down and stretch out."

"Not until you answer my questions first!" Kyleah said. "Where are we? How did my bed and I get here? Who are 'they' that seek my sword? What happened to my mother? *Who are you?*"

Wynnagar scowled. "Very well," she said. "I suppose I owe your mother that much. I suspect it is too late to save the sword now, anyway. *They* have keen noses! Be forewarned: I shan't tell you more than you need to know, lest you fall into the hands of our enemies. They would squeeze you dry like a ripe grape and cast you aside after they learned all that is hidden in your heart."

Wynnagar looked Kyleah full in the eye. "I am a *worldwalker*," she declared. "Your mother was my closest and dearest friend. I have never forgiven myself for what happened to her that night."

Taken aback, Kyleah asked, "Is a worldwalker someone who walks around the sugar bush hanging sap-buckets on spiles?"

"No, a worldwalker is a *memer*—a nymph or dryad—who has become mortal," Wynnagar explained. "As an ageless wood-nymph, I once lived inside a tree. Like other Wood Folk, I could leave my tree—or *moonslip*—between dusk and dawn, after the moon's rising. If the sun catches us outside our trees, we become long-lived mortals. Then we are known as worldwalkers."

Kyleah had long suspected that living trees possessed their own spirits, but she had never dreamed of meeting one. "How did you become a worldwalker?" she asked. "Was it an accident?"

Wynnagar wearily bowed her head. "I made the choice," she said. "Gaelathane asked me to seek the dawn. 'The mortals of this land need a worldwalker's help,' He said. I obeyed. After you were born, I took upon myself the most solemn oath a memer can make: I swore to Larissa upon my tree to look after you, should anything happen to her. Whether you realize it or not, I have kept my promise to her and to you down to this very day and hour."

Gaelathane. Kyleah now recalled hearing her mother speak that name with love and reverence. "But how is it you can appear either as a maiden or as an old woman?" she asked Wynnagar.

"To help worldwalkers pass for human, Gaelathane gave us the power to appear as young or as old as we wish," she replied.

"Who *is* this Gaelathane person?" Kyleah asked.

"Don't you know?" Wynnagar looked shocked. "Gaelathane is the Creator of this world and every other. All things owe their life and existence to Him. Once, He sacrificed Himself to deliver His creation from the darkness and despair that fester in the soul."

"You still haven't answered my other questions," said Kyleah.

Wynnagar sighed. "All right, if you insist! We are standing on Mt. Argel. It is one of the most ancient gathering places of the *memerren*. Few and secret are the ways into this world of wood, stone and water, and we guard them well. Even if our haven were found out, no foe could scale this mountain's tall, steep flanks."

Kyleah sniffed the night-scent of linden flowers. "If Argel can't be climbed, how did your people get up here in the first place?"

"The same way you did," Wynnagar dryly replied.

"You have a magic bed, too?"

Wynnagar laughed. "There is nothing magical about your bed. The headboard and footboard are made of passage-tree wood. If you climb such a tree to the very top and back down again, it will take you into another world. One of those trees brought me here today. I have visited this spot nearly every night for the past two years, in case you should make passage through the bed. I did not wish you to lose your way—or your wits—up here on Mt. Argel.

"Ages before the Rebellion, we memerren sent a bird up to this mountaintop with half of a passage nut. We planted the other half on the plain below. After the halves had grown into separate trees, we could climb the lower tree to reach the summit of Mt. Argel, and the higher one to return to the plain. Since then, we have planted several more passage trees on the top of this mountain."

Kyleah's head swam. "Then—then how does my bed work?"

"Long ago, Gaelathane told us to fashion two boards from a passage tree that once stood on this very spot. One board was made from the tree's base, the other from the crown. They were to serve as the footboard and headboard of a bed for her of the Oracle that Gaelathane gave us. You'll find a clue on the footboard."

Moving the bedclothes aside, Wynnagar showed Kyleah some spidery writing engraved on the footboard's back. *Head and toes, toes and head, that's the way to work this bed!* the lettering ran.

"You should have told me about this before!" Kyleah said.

"Gaelathane asked us not to reveal the bed's secret to you," the worldwalker patiently explained. "You were supposed to find the riddle when you grew enough on the outside—and the inside—to travel here through the bed. Because of its passage-tree headboard and footboard, your bed occupies two places at once—the top of Mt. Argel here and your Mapleton bedroom. For that reason, I hung a canopy over your bed to protect it from rain and debris."

No wonder my bed always feels so cold, Kyleah thought. *Its twin has been sitting up here on a mountaintop!* "But how—why—did I end up with this bed? I am neither a worldwalker nor a memer."

Wynnagar replied, "As the boards' Custodian, I gave them to your mother, since I believe you are the 'Gifted Girl' foretold in Gaelathane's Oracle. She in turn gave them to your father."

"If I'm so gifted," Kyleah grumbled, "why do I need a crutch to get around? Anyway, this bed doesn't work properly anymore."

"Of course it does," said Wynnagar. "Come lie here beside me, and I will show you. Hurry, now. We haven't much time."

Kyleah lay back on the bed, holding her crutch beside her. She longed to rest, but her lame leg was aching with the cold and damp. If only she could wake up from this dreadful dream!

"Now stretch out and touch the footboard and headboard," Wynnagar instructed her. "It's just like climbing a passage tree to the top and down again." Kyleah pressed her head against the headboard and her toes against the footboard. She blinked. The trees and canopy were gone. She was back in her bedroom! Just before her room was burgled, the bed must have transported her to Mt. Argel. When the thieves had searched under her Mapleton mattress, they had disturbed her Mt. Argel mattress as well!

Wynnagar sprang out of the bed, dragging Kyleah after her. Kyleah had just enough presence of mind to grab her crutch.

"Hurry!" cried the worldwalker. "We must find that chestnut tree of yours. Let us pray the sword is still hidden inside."

The old sentry sitting beneath Kyleah's window was snoring blissfully when two shadowy figures slipped out the door and into the starry night. Kyleah hoped nobody inside had heard them.

"This way!" she whispered, leading Wynnagar to the ancient chestnut. The tree's leaves rattled mournfully in a night breeze as Kyleah pushed her right arm up to the shoulder into the trunk. She fished around with her hand. Nothing solid met her fingers. She tried a different spot, but still, no sword. The heat rose in her face as she sidled around the trunk, flailing high and low through the chestnut's heart. She found not even a single rusted nail.

"It was here!" she wailed. "I know I left it here!"

"Are you certain this is the right tree?" Wynnagar asked her.

"Yes!" Kyleah sobbed. No other chestnuts grew nearby.

Wynnagar aged before Kyleah's horrified eyes. Just when she thought the worldwalker's frame could not shrink any smaller, Wynnagar shook herself and spoke with the voice of death.

"*He* has it," she croaked. "There will be no stopping him now. He will not rest until every two-legs is dead or intrisoned."

"Who has it?" Kyleah cried. "Who will not rest? Who?"

Wynnagar gazed at her with bleary eyes. "What difference does it make now? I had such high hopes you were the 'Gifted Girl' with the passage-wood bed! Alas, I must have been mistaken."

"You are right!" Kyleah declared. "I am just a useless, crippled child. Why would you think I was anything more than that?"

"Do not speak so foolishly!" Wynnagar chided her. "Gaelathane did not err in making and choosing you. Perhaps I have misread the Oracle. Yet, no mortal or memer since creation's dawn has ever reached inside a tree the way you can in broad daylight."

"Even so," said Kyleah, "what use is someone who can move things in and out of trees, other than for tapping maples?"

"You may find tree-burgling a very useful knack some day," Wynnagar replied. "Now we must leave this place at once. Not even I am safe here after dark. Flee this forest while you may!"

Kyleah felt a sudden chill. "When will I see you again?"

"Perhaps we will meet again shortly, and perhaps we will not. Heed well my words!" With a moonsigh, Wynnagar vanished.

Now Kyleah was alone in the dark woods, although she was not far from home. Then a twig snapped down the hill. She froze in dry-mouthed fear. The Prowlers were coming after her!

"'Leah?" called a familiar voice. It was Barley!

Quietly, Kyleah picked her way toward her brother. He was wearing his rumpled nightclothes and an anxious expression.

"What are you doing out here?" she hissed at him crossly.

His tears glittered in the moonlight. "Awhile ago, I heard some noises in the house. I was frightened, so I came to your bedroom, but you were gone again! I looked for you outside, but I couldn't find you anywhere. Later, I saw you and Dolora leaving the house. I followed you here. What were you doing to that chestnut tree?"

"That wasn't Dolora," Kyleah said. "It was—" She whirled around as a heavy tread sounded behind her. *Ding! Ding!* Her neck-bell rang, and she shrank into herself. Instead of protecting her, the little brass chime had given away her location! In quiet desperation, she ever-so-gently removed the bell from around her neck and hurled it into the night. Striking a tree, it jingled once and fell silent. The steps faltered and turned toward the sound.

Kyleah felt sick with fright. With her lame leg, she couldn't possibly outrun a Prowler in the woods—and now she had her little brother to worry about as well. If she sent him home in the dark, the Prowler might catch him. Her hand brushed against a maple trunk, and a desperate plan of action formed in her mind. Grabbing Barley by the arm, she backed into the tree and slowly forced her body inside. Then she pulled her brother in after her.

At first, she could hardly breathe inside the trunk's stifling denseness. Then she found that the tree was actually breathing for her. Cool, fresh air was flowing into her lungs as if the trunk were hollow and not made of solid wood. Beside her, Barley struggled for a soundless minute and then went limp. Kyleah was afraid he had suffocated until she realized he was merely sleeping.

She turned her attention outside. As through a thick fog, she saw the other trees standing about her. A shadowy, angular figure was moving among them. It stopped at Kyleah's maple, picked up a crooked stick lying at the tree's base and softly sniffed at it. Kyleah strangled a gathering scream. Now she had done it. She had left her crutch lying outside in plain view! Finally, the tall, menacing shadow dropped her stick and slouched out of sight.

That night was the longest Kyleah had ever endured. As she stood inside the tree, nagging questions whirled in her mind like smoke twirling from Mapleton's chimneys. Who had stolen her sword, and for what purpose? Was her pursuer a Prowler or some other nightmarish creature of the forest? Was Wynnagar safe?

Not until dawn's first rays were lancing through the trees did Kyleah leave her leafy hideout. After wading out of the molasses-thick trunk, she took up her crutch and pulled a sleepy Barley out after her. Then she began dragging him homeward behind her.

She noticed the awakening forest was unusually noisy. As the sun climbed above the breathing earth, a rapturous rustling rushed through the drowsy maples like a flock of wood-pigeons rousted from their treetop roosts. Kyleah's heart soared with a secret joy as the sound swelled into a melodious symphony of worship.

Blinking groggily, Barley asked her, "Did you hear that music? Mother used to sing songs like that. Why are we in the woods?"

"Hush!" Kyleah told him. "You are just having a bad dream."

The two arrived home before anyone else had risen. To keep Barley's hands busy and his tongue from wagging, Kyleah put him to work peeling potatoes with a flint knife, while she beat some eggs in a bowl. Thanks to Branagan's supply of old copper cauldrons, Dolora's kitchen gleamed with bowls, pots and pans of polished copper. With Barley's help, Kyleah managed to whip up a hearty breakfast. Soon, the odors of hash browns, buckwheat pancakes, maple syrup and scrambled eggs lured her family into the kitchen. As Kyleah had hoped, everyone was too busy eating to ask any awkward questions about her earlier whereabouts.

After clearing away the dishes, Kyleah bundled Branagan out the door. Harnessed to the wagon, Sally was patiently waiting for them. The mare whinnied as the two mounted the wagon seat.

"Let's go sell some syrup!" said Branagan in a blubbery voice, although his lips didn't move. He flicked the reins, and Sally set out for Beechtown. Lulled by the wagon's rhythmic swaying and clattering wheels, Kyleah slept soundly on her father's shoulder. Her dreams played out sweetly, undisturbed by night terrors.

AN URGENT MESSAGE

M eghan sat in her sister's favorite linden tree, picking a few early flowers to dry for tea. It was June, and the tree was covered with clusters of pea-sized blossoms. Meghan loved the flowers' sweet fragrance. So did the bees that came from miles around to sip the linden's nectar, which yielded a superb honey prized as a delicacy. Her father, Rolin, always placed a beehive or two under the tree during the peak honey flow.

Except this year. Listlessly, Meghan dropped another cluster of blooms into her bag. Life simply hadn't been the same since most of her family had left in search of Gwynneth. Climbing the linden reminded Meghan of her missing sister, but she also felt an aching loneliness. Why was she always the one to stay behind when her relatives went off on adventures? Not that she liked to visit other torsil worlds; ever since being kidnapped by the Thalmosians and marched to the Golden Wood, she had lost her taste for travel.

Instead, she enjoyed staying near the Hallowfast, tending the gardens and chatting with the trees. Grandfather Emmer often took her for walks in the woods. Also a homebody, Aunt Mycena occasionally joined them on these leisurely jaunts. Otherwise, life in the Tower of the Tree had become humdrum and predictable.

Meghan had another reason for staying close to home: She had lost her lightstaff, and her parents had evidently taken all the rest with them on their journey. Scouring the Tower of the Tree from top to bottom, she had found only an ashen staff of unusual thickness standing in a throne-room closet. Her father had been whittling on that length of ash just before he left to search for Gwynneth. Meghan couldn't imagine what the king needed with another walking stick. He owned scores of ordinary staffs made from various woods, not to mention an assortment of lightstaffs.

A week later, she had found the throne room in a shambles. Chairs and tables lay smashed on the floor. Amidst the heaps of shattered furniture Meghan also discovered a broken starglass. Normally, the instrument sat in an alcove in the wall. A vengeful, wrathful hand had evidently dashed the tube to pieces, but who would have done such a thing—and why—was still a mystery.

Miraculously, one of the starglass's two lenses had survived intact. Meghan pocketed it to remind her of her father. She tried not to think what would happen if her family failed to return. It seemed ages had passed since her loved ones had stepped into that wretched faery ring. In truth, spring had barely swelled into summer since the search party had set out to find Gwynneth.

Meghan removed the lens from her cloak pocket. It glittered like a diamond in the sun. Putting it experimentally to her eye, she stared down at a linden leaf. A fat, greenish-white monster stared back at her. She recoiled. Sheepishly, she realized the "monster" was only a tiny aphid crawling across the leaf! Apparently, the lens somehow made very small objects appear much larger.

She spent the rest of that morning peering through the lens at leaves and flowers, beetles and butterflies, feathers and bark. Viewed through the oval piece of glass, even sprigs of lowly moss appeared outlandishly exotic. Meghan was studying a ladybug when a movement in the forest caught her eye. She looked up just in time to see a green-cloaked form darting through the woods. The figure stopped behind one tree before moving on to another. Was this some strange Lucambrian version of hide-and-seek? If so, Meghan could see no other players lurking in the woods.

As she watched, the cloaked stranger approached Littleleaf, a Thalmos-torsil. Bearded lips snarled beneath the green hood, and a knife flashed. The wicked blade drove in and out of the trunk, leaving an oozing wound in the hapless tree's checkered bark.

Meghan recoiled. No true Lucambrian would so maliciously harm a living tree, much less a torsil! She was about to shout at the tree-stabber when five other Greencloaks appeared beside a faery ring on the Hallowfast's lawn and began capering for joy.

Startled by the new arrivals, the furtive figure fled. Then Meghan shinnied down the linden and raced across the grass for a tearful reunion with Bembor, Rolin, Marlis, Elwyn and Scanlon.

Meghan was overjoyed to learn the search party had rescued Gwynneth. The other news was more sobering. The royal family had brought back only one lightstaff apiece. That meant twenty or thirty others were still missing. To compound the mystery, those six remaining lightstaffs started disappearing one after another, despite every effort to safeguard them. The troubling losses went on until only King Rolin's rod was left. He kept the glowing staff strapped to his thigh at all times, even sleeping with it.

Lucambra's king was not unduly alarmed; Gaelathane would gladly replace the lightstaffs. However, nobody knew when He would next appear. Until then, the kingdom lay defenseless.

Other objects turned up missing as well. The tower armory was as bare as a winter's twig. Sigarth and Skoglund had to shape new bows of yew and arrows of ash before they could hunt game. Replacing the stolen swords and shields would be more difficult. Lacking metalworking skills, Lucambrians were forced to obtain such weapons of warfare from Thalmos or other torsil worlds.

Moreover, Lucambra's chancellor could not find his sole copy of *The Complete Chronicles of Lucambra from its Discovery to the Present*. Bembor keenly felt the book's loss, for it was his life's work. Assembling his notes, he began dictating another version of the volume to Windsong, who was still handy with a quill pen.

Worst of all, a foul odor clung to the Hallowfast, even after the servants had scrubbed down its walls and floors. Meghan closed her windows at night against the stench or she couldn't sleep.

The next week, Timothy and his bride returned from their Beechtown wedding to find Winona's diary missing from a box of Gwynneth's keepsakes, a loss more grievous than Bembor's. Other items in her room had also vanished or were found out of place. Since Meghan's room was undisturbed, she helped her sister tidy up and pack before the newlyweds left for their honeymoon in the Willowah Mountains, courtesy of Windsong and Ironwing.

The morning after Timothy and Gwynneth arrived home again, Rolin held a breakfast meeting. His face was solemn as he gazed around the table at Bembor, Emmer, Marlis, Gwynneth, Timothy, Meghan, Elwyn, Scanlon, Medwyn and Mycena. All were garbed in green tunics and trousers or skirts, except Medwyn, Queen of the Golden Wood, who wore a purple gown trimmed with gold.

Rolin announced, "My father has left a message with Lightleaf requesting our family's presence. He says it is very important."

"That's odd," Marlis remarked, nibbling on an oatcake. "It's not like Gannon to ask for help. He's quite capable of managing on his own. Why, we wouldn't have known he fell out of that bee-tree last year and broke his arm if Aunt Glenna hadn't told us."

"You're right," Rolin replied. "Maybe he's just lonely and wants some company. After all, we haven't seen him since we returned from Feirian. I'm sure he's been worried about Gwynneth and the rest of our family. It wouldn't hurt to pay him a little visit."

Nobody could argue with that, although Meghan would have preferred to start another oatmeal war. She had sneaked a couple of extra-large serving spoons into the dining room for that very purpose. She sighed. The oatmeal war would have to wait.

The next morning, the royal family disguised themselves as Thalmosian hill-dwellers and set off to find Lightleaf. The torsil hailed them warmly, though not without reproach. "Greetings, two-legged friends!" he rumbled. "By root and branch, leaf and limb I have heard of your return to our fair land. Doubtless you have been climbing other trees-of-passage and enjoying all sorts of grand adventures without me. You certainly have taken your time getting around to my plot of earth, I must say. Ah, but all is forgiven. Now, what can I do for my favorite two-legs today?"

"We wish to pass into Thalmos, good tree," Bembor said.

"My father sent for us," Rolin reminded the torsil.

Lightleaf muttered, "Oh, yes. I remember him now. The first two-legs to speak with me in many a month, he was. He seemed anxious for you to visit him. Made me repeat his message back, he did, to be sure I had not forgotten a single hurried word. Imagine that! I may be old, but my heartwood is still as sound as ever."

"Why does he want to see us?" asked Scanlon.

"That I do not know. He was very abrupt, even for a two-legs. Downright rude, he was, I should say. I was having myself a nice long nap when he rapped on my trunk and started talking to me. He could have brought a little water to pour over my roots. Since we haven't had much rain of late, I have been terribly thirsty."

"That doesn't sound like the Gannon I know," Elwyn said.

Rolin scratched his head. "No, it doesn't." He looked up at Lightleaf. "I hope you won't mind all eleven of us climbing into your top. When we return, I'll bring along some water for you."

"Er, thank you!" Lightleaf replied. "I trust all is well with your father. He always seemed a decent sort and treated me kindly, though he rarely visits except for weddings. I wish I could enjoy a wedding or two myself before I rot, but I'm never invited—and I couldn't pluck up my roots to attend anyway." Lightleaf sighed. "Perhaps some day you two-legs will perform one of those quaint rituals beneath my boughs so I can watch. In that event, I do hope Gannon will leave his sister at home. She carries on worse than a hundred yegs and griffins scrapping. Small wonder he keeps her blindfolded like a nervous falcon while she is making passage."

Meghan rolled her eyes. As the self-appointed town gossip, Glenna was notorious for her sharp tongue and blunt opinions. Not even Mayor Bigglesworth could avoid her scathing remarks.

"It's disgraceful what the mayor has done to Beechtown," she would declare. "A man of his stature ought to have a missus. She'd put a stop to those hideous buildings he's been erecting around town. They're nearly as ugly as that horrid statue he set up in the middle of the market square. I say it's about time the old worm came 'round again and knocked down all those monstrosities."

To Gannon's sister, Gorgorunth would always be "the old worm." Never mind that the dragon had been dead for years or that it had practically flattened Beechtown. In Glenna's mind, the fire-breathing beast would return one day to set matters straight, beginning with Mayor Bigglesworth's garish residence and ending with the petrified batwolf spouting water in the town square.

There was nothing garish about Gannon's home. The rustic creek-side cabin had an endearing charm that Meghan had found nowhere else. Few neighbors lived nearby, making for a stillness broken only by the soothing humming of bees and the sighing of the wind in the tops of the firs and pines. Meghan liked to sit beside Cottonwood Creek, dabbling her feet in its clear waters or plaiting baskets from the willows that grew along its banks. At times, she saw happy scenes from her childhood reflected in the placid pool behind the beaver dam. Here, she could be content.

Grandfather Gannon made her circle of serenity complete. As patient as he was understanding, he had spent many a long hour listening to Meghan's girlish hurts and small triumphs with tender attentiveness. Life always seemed much brighter after a tall stack of Gannon's butter-slathered oatcakes smothered with honey.

On this early June morning, the picturesque cabin looked as peaceful as ever. Peering through a window, Meghan and Elwyn saw Gannon in the kitchen. Sporting a woolen shirt as red as his scraggly beard, he was slicing honeycomb into dripping squares that he placed in a wooden pail to drain. His sister Glenna was holding forth as she sat by the stove knitting a blue shawl to match her dress. Her strident voice cut through the window pane as cleanly as one of Gannon's garden spades through a fresh spud.

"There's another thing," she was saying. "What if thieves come calling up in these hills? That cudgel of yours won't fare very well against a robber's dagger or sword. You'd be better off poling a barge down the Foamwater. I hear Beechtown needs more bargemen. There's the life for you! Think of all the fish you could catch. You might even catch a fine wife in one of the river villages."

Gannon muttered, "More likely I'd catch a case of river-fever, though I'd risk it just to find some peace and quiet for a change."

Just then, Rolin pushed open the door with his thick ashen staff. The rest of the family trooped in after him. A surprised smile creased Glenna's shrewd features, and she laid aside her knitting to enfold Rolin in her plump arms. "So you've decided to move back home after all!" she chortled. "I hope you didn't bring along any of those smelly flying lions. The ones I've met could use a good scrubbing. I don't know why you keep them around."

"To eat gossips!" Elwyn whispered to Meghan. She giggled.

"We came without our griffins this time, Aunt Glenna," Rolin replied, disentangling himself from her clutches. "We received an urgent summons from Father. I feared the cabin had burned down or a bear had broken into the beehives. Are you two all right?"

Gannon ran sticky fingers through flaming hair streaked with gray. "Of course we're all right. Never been better. Still, I could use some help molding more beehives. Lately, my bees have been swarming again, and most of my hives are already plumb full."

"Is that all? I mean, why did you send for us?" Rolin asked.

"I didn't, leastways not as I recollect." The beekeeper wiped his honey-coated hands on a rag and embraced Rolin and Marlis. Next, he greeted the other family members. After everyone was seated on chairs and stools around the kitchen table, Gannon set out cups and plates, together with two pitchers of rich goat's milk and heaping platters of black bread, butter and honeycomb.

"You'll never find finer table fare this side of a torsil than in Gannon's home!" Bembor declared. When all heads were bowed, he blessed the humble beekeeper's bounty in Gaelathane's name.

When Bembor had finished praying, Scanlon began shoveling food onto his plate. "This is more like it!" he said. "Hiking down that mountain has whetted my appetite for a second breakfast."

After everyone had eaten his fill, Gannon propped his boots up on the warm wood stove and said, "I'm right glad to see you all. Glenna visits me now and again, but it's mighty lonely in the cabin without any young folk." He winked at Bembor and Emmer. "I'm partial to the company of graybeards, too. What have you all been up to lately? Poor Gwynneth had Glenna and me powerfully worried when she disappeared on her wedding day!"

Rolin recounted the royal family's adventures in the forbidden land of Feirian. When he had finished, his father could only shake his head. "So I wasn't just seeing things after all!" he said. "That little feller sitting on my hive eating honey was really a *glynnie*."

Aunt Glenna frowned and pinched her nose as she often did when annoyed. "I don't believe a word of it," she sniffed. "Faeries and talking trees, indeed. What poppycock! You must think I've become completely addlepated in my old age. I'll show you!"

With that, Aunt Glenna and her knitting flounced out the door, leaving her listeners speechless. Gannon glanced out the window and chuckled. "She's all bluster but no bite," he said. "She'll huff along the road for a mile or two. Then she'll sit on a log and wait for me to pick her up in the wagon. I need to go to Beechtown on business, anyway." He jabbed his thumb at the honey tub. "The spring market has come and gone, but I still have plenty of honey to sell. If you like, you can all help me clear up these dishes and then ride along with me to town. I'd enjoy the company, and you could take turns listening to Glenna. I love my sister, but she can talk the hind leg off a mule when she gets herself wound up!"

Before you could say, "Bears and honey," the table was cleaner than polished river rocks. Gannon then sent Meghan down into the cellar to fetch the money box. She found it on a swaybacked table piled with potatoes and bunches of carrots. Picking up the box, she fondly recalled how her father's boyhood adventures had begun with his search in this cellar for a misplaced money box.

On a whim, she laid the box down and dragged a sturdy bench over to the sagging shelves where the boy Rolin had discovered his grandmother Adelka's wooden box. Clambering onto the bench, she peered over the topmost shelf. To her disappointment, it looked completely bare. Grandfather Gannon must have thrown out the musty old parchments Rolin had found there years ago.

Then Meghan noticed a chip of green flint lying on the top shelf. She pocketed the shiny object and hopped off the bench.

"Did you find the box?" Gannon's voice echoed down to her.

"Yes, I did!" she called back and hurried up the cellar stairs with the metal container of clinking Thalmosian coins.

CHAPTER 7

THE BLACK-CLOAKS

"You certainly took your time!" Aunt Glenna scolded her brother. She stood beside the rutted mountain road, arms akimbo, her thinning red hair blazing in the sun. "I could have been mauled by a bear or carried off by a mountain lion!"

Gannon pulled back on Nan's reins, and the wagon slowed to a stop. "That hair of yours would scare any critters away!" he told Glenna with a good-natured grin as he helped her up. Since Marlis and Rolin were already sitting in front, Glenna reluctantly joined Meghan and the rest of her family in the back of the wagon amid the sacks of honeycomb. Pouting, Glenna fluffed up her hair and kicked away some castoff, wizened potatoes rolling around on the floorboards. Then Gannon flicked the reins, and Nan plodded down the road, braying in mulish misery over the added weight in the back of the wagon and the distance she was having to travel.

Clutching the money box, Meghan swayed in time with the wagon. Opposite her, Aunt Glenna sat furiously knitting, all the while addressing indignant remarks to no one in particular. Under the numbing influence of Glenna's droning voice, Meghan dozed off. When she awoke, she was slumped against Elwyn's side. Her great-aunt was still chattering and knitting with equal rapidity.

"I can't imagine where I'll find more knitting needles," Glenna was lamenting to herself. "Last week, I lost my favorite pair. They must have fallen out of my knitting bag. I've asked at all the local shops, but the merchants don't know when they'll have more of them in stock. I'm tempted to catch a barge down to Bridgewater. The craftsmen there make the best birch knitting needles."

Meghan grinned. She couldn't picture her finicky great-aunt floating down the Foamwater with a bunch of rough bargemen.

"Why is there such a shortage of needles?" Gwynneth asked.

"There's been a shortage of most goods in town lately," Gannon darkly observed, not turning his head. "The shops are running low on everything from hoe handles to halters. I've had to repair Nan's old worn-out halter with leather bootstraps and a prayer."

"Those straps chafe me, I'll have you know!" Nan grumbled.

Feeling sick to her stomach from riding sideways in the back of the wagon, Meghan leaned against the driver's seat between Gannon and Marlis. "If the merchants don't have hoe handles and halters," she asked, "can't you just buy them at the docks?" She knew some of the rivermen carried on a brisk business selling their wares right off their barges, a practice the staid merchants of Beechtown frowned upon but had so far failed to prohibit.

Gannon fixed his eyes on the potholed road. "The river traffic isn't what it used to be," he said softly. "Dozens of empty boats and barges lie tied up at the docks, because few men will work the Foamwater anymore. Those bargemen who do travel downriver rarely come back. Their barges turn up in the Rattlereed Marshes at the Foamwater's lower end, still laden with the original cargo."

"Do you mean the rivermen just disappear?" asked Meghan.

The beekeeper glanced uneasily back at his sister and nodded. "Nan's halter and Glenna's knitting needles have been sitting on some abandoned barge. Nobody will go down to pick them up."

"Greenies!" Marlis hoarsely exclaimed.

"Lower your voice!" Rolin cautioned her. "Do you want *her* to hear?" Marlis looked stricken. It would never do for Glenna to get wind of the Greenies, those whiney, viney highwaymen who had once terrorized the river traffic for miles north of Beechtown.

Meghan had doubted her family's tales of the leafy, swamp-dwelling robbers. Then Rolin had brought her by torsil to meet Glaslyn, Queen of Vineland, the Greenies' world. Overtaken by the green mist, Meghan had nearly sprouted vines herself.

"I thought Bart and his men had reformed," she said.

"They have!" her father replied. "I ran into Bart the other day. There wasn't a leaf on him. He's still working for Baker Wornick. Besides, Greenies wouldn't leave any loot behind. They would strip those barges down to the bare deck. Windsong and I visited the marshes a couple of weeks ago. We were looking for new spots to plant starworts. Instead, we found twenty or thirty deserted barges stuck in the mud. I don't know what to make of it."

Meghan and her parents were still puzzling over this turn of events when Gannon's wagon rattled over the Beechtown bridge. Meghan glanced down at the Foamwater. Ordinarily packed with rafts, barges and longboats, the river was curiously empty. Only a few dinghies and tipsy coracles plied the roiling water's surface.

Despite the lack of river traffic and a vacant market square, business in Beechtown was still booming. Hawkers crowded around the wagon, noisily thrusting their wares at the visitors. "Sweet perch I've got, just freshly caught!" cried one fishmonger, thrusting a slimy string of scaly fish in Meghan's face. Their dead, bulging eyes and ripe odor made her stomach churn further.

"Garlic! Garlic! Nature's own tonic!" shouted another man, waving a bunch of the stinking bulbs at her. Meghan held her nose. She enjoyed eating garlic, but these cloves smelled putrid.

"Bread and buns straight from the oven! I have scones and muffins!" announced a third vendor. Using a long stick, he swung a fragrant basket above the wagon. Here was something worth smelling! Meghan released her nose and took a long, heady sniff.

All at once, a black-cloaked horseman rode up, shoving the bread man aside. The peddler and his baked goods went flying. "Out of my way, peasant!" growled the rider. He glanced keenly at Rolin and Marlis. Then his mocking gaze strayed to Meghan, and she gripped the money box more protectively. She wouldn't give up Gannon's gilders to this boorish fellow without a fight!

"Guard your money well, mongrel!" the man rasped. "You'll need all those gilders and more besides to survive in Thalmos." Without another word, he reined his horse about and rode away.

"Did you hear what that nasty man called me?" Meghan gasped. "A mongrel!" Nobody had ever cast such an insult at her before. She resisted the urge to throw one of Gannon's old, rotten potatoes at the rider, who had disappeared into an alley. Instead, she hopped off the wagon to join Timothy and Elwyn in helping the distressed vendor salvage his bruised breadstuffs. Accepting a bun each as their reward, the three climbed back into the wagon.

Scowling, Rolin bent over and pulled a polished sword from beneath the seat. After that, it was all Gannon and Marlis could do to restrain him from pursuing the insolent horseman on foot.

"Let him go, Son," said Gannon. "You can't catch him now."

Marlis told her husband, "We must not take our own revenge. Gaelathane will avenge us for this fellow's slight, if He sees fit."

"I suppose you are right," Rolin sighed. "Still, I would have enjoyed teaching that scoundrel some manners at sword-point." He handed the weapon to Gannon, who stowed it under the seat.

"What I should like to know," said Bembor, "is how that rascal could tell so much about us. He not only knew that Meghan was holding a money box but also that her ancestry is mixed."

"And 'Thalmos' is a Lucambrian word," Emmer pointed out.

"That fellow's voice sounded familiar," said Marlis. "I just can't recall where I've heard it before." The others agreed with her.

"I'll have a word with the constable about our black-cloaked friend," Gannon grunted. "We can't have bullies roaming the streets of Beechtown upsetting honest folk." He clucked his tongue, and Nan clip-clopped down the street through the town.

As soon as the creaking wagon rolled into the cobbled market square, buyers scurried over. Word spread quickly in the town, and before long, people had lined up to purchase Gannon's honey and honeycomb. By three o' clock, the wagon was nearly empty.

"That's the lot!" Meghan announced as she sold the last jar of honey. She was footsore and cross from standing for hours on the hard cobbles helping her grandfather peddle his delicious wares.

She and Gwynneth were packing up the empty boxes and sacks when a horse-drawn wagon rolled into the square and pulled up beside Gannon's. The burly driver hopped off his seat and helped a young girl with a crutch climb down. Then he lifted out the back-board and unloaded some clinking crates from the wagon.

A few of Gannon's buyers drifted over to the new arrival. Oblig-ingly, the driver popped the lid off one of his crates. The wooden box was crammed with long-necked, bulbous brown jars stoppered at the top with corks. Meghan smelled a sweet aroma.

Glenna's eyes narrowed. "Why, those are liquor bottles!" she told Gannon. "These hill-folk must have a still. Don't they know you're not supposed to sell strong drink in the market square?"

She was about to descend in wrath upon the unsuspecting vendor when a grin of recognition spread across Gannon's face. Restraining his sister by the arm, he shouted, "Branagan the Sugar-man! What brings you down to Beechtown at this time of the year? The sugar bush must have been good to you this spring."

A matching grin wreathed the other man's face as he pushed through the crowd of customers and pumped Gannon's hand. "Well, I never. If it isn't my old friend the beekeeper! I reckon we're here for the same reason. Folks in this town have a sweet tooth as long as my leg." He nodded at Gannon's empty wagon. "You've done well for yourself today. I see you have some help."

Gannon awkwardly introduced Glenna, Rolin, and his other relations, using first names to conceal the Lucambrians' origins. "And who is this you've brought with you?" he asked Branagan.

"Pardon me!" said the sugarman. "This is my daughter, Kyleah." A wispy waif with shoulder-length, russet hair, Kyleah smiled as she turned adoring, almond-shaped eyes on Branagan.

"Father is Mapleton's sugarmaster," she proudly announced. "I hope to become the sugarmistress after I've learned the trade."

"When I last saw Kyleah, she was just a baby," said Gannon.

"Sugar bush? Sugarmaster?" Elwyn broke in.

Gannon explained, "Branagan son of Carrigan and his hardy forebears have been tapping maple trees for syrup above Mapleton since Beechtown was just a sleepy dock on the Foamwater."

Looking ill at ease, the sugarmaster shuffled his feet and cleared his throat. "See here, Gannon, I didn't mean to horn in on your territory. Fair is fair. You arrived here in the square first. Just say the word, and I'll move along. I don't want no hard feelings."

Gannon clapped Branagan on the shoulder. "Move along? Don't even think of leaving. You aren't horning in. I've already sold out my stock of honey. Besides, Mapleton lies a half-day's journey from here, and I won't have you returning home empty-handed. Now then, let's see about selling some syrup, shall we?"

Afternoon heat-sprites were twirling on the cobblestones as Meghan and her family helped Branagan unload his wagon. They could barely keep up with Kyleah, who was selling paper-wrapped maple-sugar treats and flasks of maple syrup to eager customers. The moon was trading places with the sun when Timothy broke open the last crate of maple syrup and began unpacking it.

"You can put them bottles back in the box," Branagan told him. "I'm leaving them with your family for pitching in. You've all done more than I had any right to ask or expect. 'Leah's lame leg won't let her lift much, but she works well with the customers."

"I'm not as useless as everybody thinks!" Kyleah declared.

Branagan patted her head. "I don't think you're useless," he said tenderly. "Sometimes I don't know what I'd do without—"

The clatter of horses' hooves cut him off. Three black-cloaked riders trotted into the square and stopped beside the wagons. Meghan glared at the middle rider, whom she had already met. The other two were much taller than any man she had ever seen.

Rolin edged closer to his father's wagon, but the sword lay out of his reach. "What do you want with us?" he demanded. "We're sold out of honey and maple syrup, so you can be on your way."

Meghan's tormenter sneered, "We are not here to purchase your pathetic wares. We have come to take back the kingdom."

CHAPTER 8

THE TURNCLOAK UNHOODED

R olin edged closer to Gannon's wagon. "Take back *whose* kingdom?" he asked. "You'll find no kings or castles in this square. You might catch the mayor at home, though I have found it difficult to get in to see him without an appointment."

"Do not play me for a fool!" bellowed the rider. He whipped out a sword and urged his balking mount right into the crowd. Grabbing Gwynneth by the hair, he pressed his sword against her throat. She struggled and screamed, but the man's grip held her fast. "Give me the sword of Elgathel, or the girl dies!" the rider roared. "I know you have been hiding it from me, half-breed!"

Kyleah froze. Had the beekeeper's son stolen her sword? If not, maybe Rolin was the green-cloaked tap-thief. Yet, Rolin's hair was chestnut, not gray, and the sword he had pulled from beneath the wagon seat looked nothing like the black sword. And what was all the fuss over a kingdom? Rolin hardly looked the part of a king. These mounted men in the black cloaks must be mistaken.

"What will it be, pretender?" the rider demanded.

"Very well," said Rolin stiffly, his eyes fixed on Gwynneth. He climbed into Gannon's wagon and retrieved the sword. Then he jumped down and presented it to the black-cloaked horseman.

"Thank you, *Sire*," the man sneered with mock courtesy. He had just released Gwynneth when Rolin's hand shot out and yanked the man's hood back. Kyleah gasped. It was the tap-thief!

"Larkin!" Rolin grunted. "I might have known. Surely you don't expect to usurp the throne with a sword and two goons!"

"That is *Lord* Larkin to you!" The rider's face contorted with hatred and cruelty, and he cackled, "I have not one sword now, but two! One is symbolic, but the other is not. With the first I shall ascend the throne, and with the second, I shall possess it. A direct descendant of King Elgathel shall finally rule Lucambra."

"Bold talk indeed, for a turncloak," Bembor wryly observed.

Larkin waved his sword in Bembor's face. "From where I sit, *you* are the turncloaks and traitors! No more shall Lucambrians wear cloaks of green or swear allegiance to a false standard. Henceforth, Lucambra's true colors shall be red flames and death!"

The horseman on Larkin's right raised a tall flagstaff, unfurling a flapping standard emblazoned with an ebony sword burning on a pallid field. Kyleah gasped. The design depicted her sword!

"Your guilt is greater than mine!" Larkin went on. "With your support and approval, Bembor son of Brenthor, this half-breed has defiled Lucambra's glorious throne. Nonetheless, I am willing to let bygones be bygones." He lowered his weapon. "Bembor . . . Emmer . . . Scanlon—as full-blooded Lucambrians, you may hold honored posts in my new kingdom. Marlis, I fear, would rather die with her renegade husband than swear allegiance to me."

"He's right about that," Marlis acidly muttered.

"That goes for me, too," said Mycena defiantly.

"We all would prefer death to following you, royal pedigree or no," growled Emmer. The others murmured their agreement.

Larkin's lip curled. "I expected as much. You shall have your wish soon enough, if ever you find your way back to Lucambra. I would advise you to remain here in exile—where you belong."

Kyleah had never heard of a place called "Lucambra." What was this man talking about, and why did he hate Rolin's family?

"Who are your friends?" Scanlon asked, pointing at the other riders. "They look rather like overgrown scarecrows to me."

"Perhaps you should ask the queen of the Golden Wood," said Larkin mockingly, pointing his sword at Medwyn. "She knows." Cowering beside her husband, Medwyn shook her head.

Larkin snapped his fingers at the black-cloaked and -hooded standard-bearer, who lowered his flag and rode up to Medwyn. Scanlon desperately threw himself in front of his terrified wife. Knocking him aside, the grim rider grabbed Medwyn by the arm.

Suddenly, the horseman released Medwyn and turned on Kyleah. Sniffing and snuffling, he hissed, "I smell Gundul—and gold!" From his cloak, his gloved hand drew forth a naked black sword—Kyleah's sword. Bile rose in her throat, and her insides burned. When the rider pointed the blade at her, hot knives sliced through her body. She fell to the ground, writhing in agony.

Meghan rushed to her side. "What is the matter?" she asked.

Kyleah couldn't breathe, much less answer. Through a haze of pain, she watched her tormenter slip his sword-tip under her crutch and flip the stick into the air. As it spun, he caught the crutch with the other hand and savagely crushed it to splinters.

"So you have felt the bite of the Black Blade, crutch-girl!" the rider rumbled. "You threw me off the track with your clever bell-ruse the other night. You will not have a second chance. Now you belong to us, for you have tasted of *Felgroth*! I also smell memerren upon you. You can thank them for setting me free. Those maggots hid my sword inside a tree! How very futile. I shall relish teaching their failing race not to meddle in the affairs of tree-kings."

Dismounting, the horseman grabbed a fistful of Kyleah's hair and jerked her off the ground. She clawed at his hand as tears of pain streamed down her cheeks. From out of hooded shadows, the rider glowered at her, his face a wooden mask of malice.

This horrible man must think some memer or worldwalker pulled out that sword! Kyleah thought, struggling in the horseman's grip. *He doesn't realize I removed it and hid it in the chestnut tree myself.*

"Let her go, you ruffian!" Branagan bellowed. Barreling up, he grabbed the man by his cloak and tried to drag him away from Kyleah. Sheathing his sword, the rider solidly punched Branagan in the head with his fist. The sugarmaster dropped like a stone.

"Father!" Kyleah screamed, desperately trying to tear herself loose. Instead, the black-cloak tossed her onto the horse's back and seated himself behind her. No one was making a move to help her. Still struggling, she noticed Rolin pulling a shiny object out of a long, narrow pocket in his trousers leg. Had he hidden a sword there, much as Kyleah had hidden hers on that winter's day?

This was no sword. A blinding light burst from the object, and Kyleah's kidnapper shrieked, covering his face with his hood. Seeing her chance, Kyleah threw herself off the horse, landing on cold, lumpy cobbles. Then she crawled from under the rearing horse's prancing hooves. People scattered in all directions as the black-cloaked rider fought to control his panicked mount.

"You told us you had all their staffs!" he screamed at Larkin.

"I must have overlooked one!" Larkin retorted. "Let the half-breeds be. They cannot stop us, now that we have both swords."

The three reined their horses around and galloped madly out of the square, cloaks and hoods flapping. Watching them go, Kyleah rubbed her sore scalp, weeping in shock and relief. Thanks to Rolin's quick thinking, she had narrowly missed being abducted. However, had the black-cloaks left her and Barley orphans?

Gwynneth and Marlis were bending over Branagan's still form. Gwynneth was wiping his bloodied head with her sleeve. "He'll have a nasty lump here on his temple," she told Kyleah softly. "Otherwise, after some rest, he should make a full recovery."

Kyleah couldn't think or feel. She knelt beside Branagan and kissed him on the cheek. "Please wake up, Papa!" she cried. "Don't leave me here alone! I'm sorry I caused you so much trouble."

Branagan opened one eye. "You're no trouble, 'Leah," he said thickly. "If I'd a-known this would happen, I never would have brought you across the Foamwater. I'll make you a new crutch."

"I have one she can borrow," said Rolin with a thoughtful look. Going to Gannon's wagon, he brought back his staff of ash and handed it to Kyleah. The stick felt sturdier and heavier than her old crutch, but it did have two stubby hand-holds at about the right height for her. The staff held up under her weight when she leaned on it. At least now she could properly get around again.

"Thank you!" she told Rolin. "I will return this staff to you when Father has made me another. But what sort of torch or light or mirror did you use to frighten away those awful men?"

Rolin showed her the glowing stick he had taken from his pocket. The rod resembled a tree branch, but it was as clear as maple sap straight out of the tap. The staff's brightness drove back the evening shadows creeping across the cobbled market square.

"What is it? What makes it shine like that?" Kyleah asked.

Helping Branagan to his feet, Rolin said, "This staff was cut from the Tree of Life and shines with Gaelathane's eternal light."

Gaelathane again. And how could any light last eternally?

"You were wise to hide that lightstaff, Father!" Meghan said.

"Those fellows didn't care much for its glow," said Emmer. "I wonder what that turncloak Larkin did with our other staffs."

Glenna folded her arms and stuck out her chin. "Your friend Larkin seemed very sure of himself. He ought to have been more careful with that sword of his. He could have hurt someone."

"He's no friend of ours," muttered Elwyn.

"And he did hurt me!" Gwynneth said, rubbing her neck.

Glenna ignored them. "I've had enough of hooligans for one day," she announced. "I'm going home!" With that, she marched across the square like a parade marshal without a parade.

Bembor said grimly, "We must return to Lucambra forthwith before that scoundrel Larkin can muster an army and fortify the Hallowfast against us. I wish I knew the origin and powers of the black sword we saw; I fear that blade bodes us ill. It is bad enough that Larkin now possesses Elgathel's sword. Our people are sure to rally behind that weapon's owner, be he turncloak or true."

Rolin laughed. "Then we have nothing to fear at home!"

"What do you mean?" the others asked him.

With a wink, Rolin said, "Surely you don't think I would give up the sword of Elgathel without a fight, do you? It's fortunate for us that Larkin has never looked closely at that blade. As it is, I expect he'll be furious when he discovers he has the wrong one."

A grin spread across Scanlon's face and his green eyes lit up mischievously. "Are you saying that sword wasn't Elgathel's?"

Chewing on a piece of beeswax, Gannon said, "That's right! I bought that sword from Lemmy the blacksmith for ten pounds of honey. It came in handy for whacking prickly blackberry vines."

"I suppose now you'll be wanting me to buy you a new one," Rolin grumbled in mock disgust. "Where am I supposed to find a blackberry-sword, anyway?" His companions laughed.

"Then where *is* Elgathel's sword?" Emmer asked.

Rolin shrugged and raised his eyebrows innocently. "That is a sword I no longer possess. Its location must remain a secret. It is so well hidden that Larkin son of Gaflin will never find it."

Marlis raised her arm to her forehead in a theatrical show of despair. "He won't even tell *me* where it is!" she wailed.

Kyleah looked up from dabbing her father's head-wound. "How can you jest at a time like this?" she said indignantly. "Those men might have killed us all! Just look at my poor father. He has never hurt anyone, but now he's got a big bump on his head."

"We don't mean to make light of your father's suffering," said Bembor. "'Even in laughter, the heart may be weeping.' You see, we have learned to rejoice during times of sorrow, for Gaelathane is our only hope. He is always with us and is ready to help us."

"Will He help Father to get well so we can return home?"

"You cannot go home now," Medwyn said dully. "None of us can ever go home again. We are lost. We are all doomed to die."

"Things aren't *that* bleak!" Marlis said. "Still, maybe we should take Kyleah and Branagan to Gannon's for a day or two until they feel well enough to travel back to Mapleton. Otherwise, Larkin and his black-cloaked thugs might ambush them in the dark."

Although Branagan insisted he didn't want to be a bother, Gannon convinced him it would be for the best. The two wagons set off by moonlight for River Road beside the Foamwater.

Kyleah held the reins while Branagan dozed next to her. An hour later, as her wagon followed the beekeeper's up a steep, stony track, she heard an odd, throaty voice grumbling not far ahead.

"*Harroom!* This is not the way home! Why are we taking this—*reharraharrahurra*—roundabout route? My back aches, my stomach is wanting its supper and these rocks hurt my feet."

Who had been speaking? Branagan was softly snoring as Sally patiently plodded along the rutted dirt road. Sitting in the back of Gannon's wagon, Rolin's people were talking earnestly amongst themselves. Kyleah must have heard one of them complaining.

The stars were spilling across the heavens when Branagan woke up. Rubbing the lump on his head, he muttered dire threats against the black-cloak who had struck him. Shortly afterwards, Gannon's wagon pulled up to a sleepy log cabin. Everyone piled out, straggled onto the porch and filed through the front door.

Kyleah and her father joined them. Kyleah found the cozy cabin cluttered with the sorts of tools and furniture that often lay strewn about Branagan's woodshop. Right away, Gannon and some of the younger folk began bustling about the kitchen. Before long, Mycena was frying eggs, bacon and cornmeal fritters on the roaring wood stove. Then supper was ready, and after Scanlon's heartfelt prayer of thanksgiving, the beekeeper's family and his guests were tucking away the steaming bounty. As hungry as she was, Kyleah was sure she had never enjoyed a finer meal.

Afterwards, the conversation turned to the topic of Larkin's treachery. Everyone agreed he had to be stopped, but no one was sure how. "I'm surprised he didn't kill us all," Emmer remarked.

"Mercy is a virtue beyond Larkin's grasp," Rolin agreed. "With his henchmen's help, he could have done away with five or six of us at least. Still, I doubt he had murder in mind. Seizing Elgathel's sword was at the top of his list, and gloating was a close second."

Bembor nodded. "It appears he has long been planning this rebellion right under our very noses. We should have suspected foul play when our lightstaffs and other weapons went missing. I wouldn't be surprised if Larkin has also stolen our spasels."

"How did Larkin know we would all be gathered in the market square today?" said Elwyn. "He seemed to be expecting us."

A sick look came over Scanlon's face. "I'll bet I know how," he said. "Remember Lightleaf's 'urgent message' from Gannon? Most trees—old ones especially—can't always tell one two-legs from another. If Larkin dressed himself to look like our beekeeper here, he could have tricked the torsil into thinking he was Gannon!"

"It's certainly possible," Bembor allowed.

Gannon snorted. "Hmph! That shifty-eyed character doesn't look anything like me. To begin with, his hair is gray, not red!"

"But why would Larkin go to the trouble of impersonating Gannon and deceiving us through Lightleaf?" asked Marlis.

"He knew we wouldn't refuse a summons from my father," Rolin said. "That way, he could exile us all here at one stroke."

"That's ridiculous!" said Scanlon. "To exile us in Thalmos, he'd have to cut down every last Lucambra-torsil in the land, and not even we know where they all grow. We'll soon find a way back."

"I wouldn't be so sure," Rolin said, helping himself to another cornmeal fritter. "Whatever else we may think of him, Larkin is no fool. There is more than one way to exile a Lucambrian."

Kyleah wondered what a "torsil" was, if cutting one down could prevent her friends from returning home. She suspected it might be similar to the "passage tree" Wynnagar had described.

"Larkin may have gotten away with my sword, but he missed taking something more valuable from my wagon," said Gannon.

"What's that?" everyone asked.

"All our 'honey money'!" he quipped, holding up the dented metal money box. It jingled enticingly when he shook it.

"That reminds me," said Meghan. "When I was fetching that box from the cellar this morning, I noticed some parchments were missing from the top shelf. Did you take them, Grandfather?"

Gannon said, "I don't recollect picking up any old papers in the cellar lately. Are you sure Rolin didn't do something with them?"

"I had forgotten they were there," Rolin confessed. "Those moldy parchments were too faded to read, anyway. Mother wrote her recipes on them, I believe. Why were you looking for them?"

Meghan shrugged. "I wasn't. But I did find this rock lying on the shelf." She dug the curved flake of greenish stone out of her pocket and handed it to her father. "What do you make of it?"

Rolin turned the object over in his hands. "It looks familiar, somehow," he said. "I just can't place it. I'd say it's a mineral chip I left on that shelf when I was a boy. I must have found it up in these mountains years ago. I used to love collecting colorful rocks."

Branagan's head was sagging against his chest and he started to snore again. Kyleah shook his shoulder. "Father! Wake up!"

He opened a bleary eye and nodded off again. Together, Rolin and Gannon helped him up a ladder in the back bedroom and into the attic. Kyleah followed. "I don't have much space in the cabin for guests, since I have few visitors," Gannon apologetically told her. "I've laid out bedding in the loft so my grandchildren can spend the night. You and your father should be comfortable up here. The rest of us won't be going to bed until much later."

After she was sure her father was sleeping peacefully, Kyleah climbed down the ladder and rejoined her hosts. She felt awkward listening to their table talk, and after a few minutes, she excused herself to hobble out the cabin door and into the starry night.

Outside, the fresh mountain air reminded her of home. The rising moon lit up rows of conical clay beehives next to the cabin, their winged occupants crowded inside for the night. Bats flitted erratically across the moon's pocked face. Then someone spoke.

"Heh! Have you any grub around here? I'm famished!"

It was the odd voice Kyleah had heard earlier that evening. She peered into the darkness, seeing no one but the animals. As far as she could tell, Gannon's guests had eaten plenty for supper, except for her father, whose head-wound had left him feeling ill.

"Ee-awr!" said another, higher voice. "I've got lots of fodder, and you're welcome to it. My man is a right decent chap, as two-legs go. A scratch here, a scratch there, a little hay—I'm happy."

Someone touched Kyleah's shoulder, and she jumped. "Who's there?" she gasped. Had the black-cloak returned to kidnap her?

"It's just me, Gannon," said a dark figure. He was carrying a bundle of lumpy sticks. Moving about the bee-yard, he thrust the sticks into the earth, making a rough crescent around the cabin.

Kyleah smelled smoke, and one of the long sticks burst into flame, throwing the beehives into sharp relief. Using that stick, Gannon lit the others. A pleasant, honeyed scent filled the air.

"Beeswax torches," Gannon explained. "If those black-cloaks hate the light, we'll make it hot for them tonight. I'll be barring the door and windows, too. We don't want any uninvited visitors."

"Who else is out here besides us?" Kyleah asked him.

Gannon frowned. "Nobody. The others are inside. Why?"

"I don't know. I thought I heard something a minute ago."

Gannon rubbed his jaw. "Sometimes our mountain winds play queer tricks on the mind. Let's go see whether any fritters are left. That Mycena can work wonders with a cast-iron skillet!"

Kyleah wasn't hungry. While Gannon scrounged for leftover fritters, she headed into the back bedroom and painfully hauled herself up the ladder with her arms and one good leg. Branagan still lay on a mattress in the attic, snoring mightily. Kyleah kissed him lightly on the forehead and went to the bedding that was laid out next to his. She had just lain down when snatches of quiet conversation drifted into her ear from the room below.

Turning over, she discovered a knothole beside her mattress. Lantern light shone weakly up through it. She put her eye to the hole and looked down on Gannon's supper guests, who were still discussing the day's adventures in subdued but anxious voices.

"What were those black-cloaked creatures? Gorks?"

". . . too big for gorks."

"You don't think the griffins will go over to Larkin, do you?"

"What about the trees? . . . bad sorts . . . trouble . . ."

Kyleah dozed off with her ear to the knothole. She awoke to the sounds of thumping, crashing and shouting downstairs.

"Begone, in the name of Gaelathane!" someone cried. After that, Kyleah remained wide awake, drenched with fear-sweat. Had the black-cloaks sprung a surprise attack? Should she pull up the ladder to keep them out of the attic? Were her friends still alive? She spent the rest of that night counting rafters, not daring to look through the knothole for dread of what she might see below.

CHAPTER 9

THE RELUCTANT TORSILS

D awn visited early the next day, peering through a dirty window at the attic's far end. Delicious cooking smells were wafting up from below, making Kyleah's stomach growl and her mouth water. She crept past her sleeping father and clambered down the hatchway ladder. At the bottom, she took up Rolin's ashen staff, which she had left leaning against the wall.

Tap-tap. Someone was hammering. Kyleah limped into the kitchen to find Gannon pounding nails into the door frame. Wood splinters lay everywhere. "What are you doing?" she asked him.

"Your black-cloaked friends came back last night," said the beekeeper. "After they stomped my torches into the ground, they tried to break the door down. The rascals didn't have the common decency to knock first. I had braced the door, but when they forced it open, we menfolk slammed it shut on them. Rolin scared them off with his lightstaff before they could break the windows."

Kyleah's heart pounded painfully. Was there no escaping these cruel riders of the night? "Where is everyone else?" she asked.

"They left about an hour ago," Gannon replied. "I reckon they went off to settle scores with that Larkin fellow. Help yourself to breakfast; the oatcakes are cold, but they're good cold or hot."

As Kyleah stumped her way over to the table, her staff slipped on a piece of wood, and she fell heavily to the floor. Instantly. Gannon was at her side, helping her up and apologizing.

"Forgive me!" he said, his face as red as his beard. "I'm terribly sorry. I should have cleaned away this mess before you got up."

"That's all right," Kyleah mumbled. She hated the pain and humiliation of falling. Onlookers would stare at her with pity and disgust. "Poor Useless!" or, "What a useless cripple!" they would say, and she would hobble off weeping, bruised inside and out.

While Gannon fetched a broom, Kyleah scoured the floor for whatever had tripped her up. Beside the table, she found some long, knobbly twigs that might easily have rolled under her crutch. She pointed out the sticks to Gannon, and he swept them up.

"Eh!" he said. "How did those get in here? Maybe Glenna is right, and I need a wife to keep house for me. Hmph. What woman would marry a beekeeper?" He went back to his repairs. "Hello!" he remarked. "Here are more of those sticks on the threshold."

The hairs prickled on the back of Kyleah's neck, though she could see no reason for her uneasiness. After all, Gannon's home was situated in the midst of a forest, so sticks and twigs were bound to find their way into the cabin, even without human help.

To her delight, Kyleah found oatcakes and honey every bit as tasty as pancakes and maple syrup. She had just finished a tall stack of the cakes when Gannon laid aside his hammer and nails.

"That should do for now!" he said. "If you're done eating, how would you like to help me open one of my hives? If I don't remove some of the honeycomb soon, the bees will swarm for lack of space, and I haven't got any place left to house another colony."

How could Kyleah refuse such a gracious request, especially on a pleasant summer's morning? She followed her host outside. Gannon's bees were already awake and at work, flitting in and out of their clay hives. Removing a long knife from a sheath at his belt, the beekeeper went to one of the hives and jammed the knife between the hive and the board it sat upon. Straining mightily, he managed to peel one side of the hive away from the board. "My sword gave me better leverage than this knife," he grumbled.

He pointed out a black, gooey substance coating the board and the hive's exposed rim. "Bee glue," he said. "The bees scrape this stuff off poplar buds and leaves. They seal their hives with it."

Kyleah helped Gannon finish prying up the hive. Meanwhile, bees were swarming all around, making Kyleah very nervous.

"Won't they sting us?" she asked, swatting at the insects.

Gannon winked. "We have an understanding, these bees and I," he said. "They don't sting me when I rob their hives, and in return, I provide plenty of honey to tide them over the winter."

Cutting into the exposed comb at the hive's base, he showed Kyleah the difference between comb cells filled with honey and those with eggs and hatchlings. Avoiding the "brood cells," Gannon deftly cut out chunks of comb dripping with honey.

Kyleah laid the cut comb in a wooden tub Gannon supplied for that purpose. He was carrying the tub into the cabin when Kyleah made up her mind. She wasn't going to be left behind!

Limping to the rushing creek, she washed the honey off her hands. Having no clear idea of direction, she began following a well beaten path that led higher into the forest. She was growing hot and sweaty when she heard Gannon calling her name below.

"Oh, bother!" she muttered to herself. She loved the gentle man with the red beard, but she still had many questions to ask Rolin and his family. Then she heard other voices, deep, breathy voices that drew her onward. *This way! They went this wayyyyy!*

Following the voices' urging, Kyleah came upon her friends. Rolin, Marlis, Mycena, Scanlon, Bembor, Medwyn, Gwynneth and Emmer were all standing around a large tree, anxiously staring up into it. Seeing Kyleah, they started guiltily, like small children who have just been caught stealing cookies from a cookie jar.

"Kyleah!" Marlis gasped. "What brings you up here?"

"You left without saying good-bye!" she reproachfully replied. "I've been searching all over for you. What are you looking at?"

Rolin wrapped his arm around her shoulders. "I am sorry you came all this way just to see us. I'm surprised you found us! You must be a skilled tracker. Now you must return to your father. I'm sure he is worried about you. Does Gannon know you're here?"

"No, he doesn't—and Father is still sleeping," she said, not daring to mention the strange, whispery voices she had heard in the woods. "Are you all going back to that Lucambra place?"

Rolin jerked his arm away from her as if she were a porcupine. "Where did you hear that name?" he sharply asked her.

"Larkin was talking with you about Lucambra yesterday in the Beechtown square," she replied. "Are you really a king?"

Consternation flamed in the faces of her listeners. Then leaves rustled in the branches above, and a familiar voice rang out.

"It's still not working!" bellowed Elwyn from the tree.

"What's not working?" Kyleah asked.

"You must leave now, do you hear me?" Rolin told her. "You don't belong here. Believe me, this matter doesn't concern you."

"Of course it concerns me!" Kyleah shot back. She shook the staff Rolin had given her. "I want to know why those black-cloaked men tried to kidnap me. Who are they? Where do they come from? I am not leaving until you give me some answers."

"I'm afraid we don't have any answers," said Rolin softly.

"What shall we do now?" Timothy called down from the tree.

"Did you climb to the tippy-top?" Gwynneth shouted back.

"Of course I did! You heard the tree. No passage for anyone!"

"This is a passage tree, isn't it?" Kyleah crowed as the truth dawned on her. "You have to climb it to the very top or it won't work. You are trying to get into the world you call 'Lucambra,' and Rolin is the king of it! I'm right, aren't I? You know I'm right!"

Kyleah thought Rolin and company would faint on the spot. "How do you know about passage trees?" Scanlon demanded.

"Wynnagar told me," she said. "She also told me about nymphs and dryads, moonslipping and worldwalkers. I didn't understand everything she explained, especially the part about the 'Oracle.'"

"Wynnagar!" Medwyn exclaimed. "Why would she tell a mor—, I mean, a *hill-child* our secrets? She is not ordinarily so loose-leaved about such matters. I must speak to her about this."

Just then, Gannon came puffing through the trees. "There you are!" he cried, catching sight of Kyleah. He jogged up to her.

"Why did you run off like that?" he demanded with a scowl.

"I'm sorry," said Kyleah, and she meant it. "I never had a chance to say good-bye to your family before they left your home."

Scanlon rolled his eyes. "All right. Good-bye and fare-thee-well. Now, get going. Gannon will escort you back to his cabin."

"I don't need escorting, because I'm staying right here!"

"What's going on down there?" Meghan hissed from the tree.

"You may as well come down now," sighed Rolin. Timothy, Meghan and Elwyn climbed out of the passage tree. After landing on the ground, Elwyn turned around and kicked the trunk.

"Why won't you grant us passage?" he cried in frustration.

"I cannot let anyone through from Thalmos to Lucambra, by the king's order!" said a gruff voice. "Any tree that disobeys the royal command will be girdled. Now do not ask me again."

Rolin was sputtering. "I never decreed any such thing! Why would anyone punish a torsil tree simply for granting passage?"

"Who said 'girdled,' and what does that mean?" asked Kyleah. The strange, gravelly voice didn't belong to any of her friends.

"She's gotten the Gift!" Marlis exclaimed.

Rolin crouched before Kyleah until they were eye-to-eye. "Did you smell any, ah, *sweet scents* while you were hiking up here?"

Kyleah shook her head. Whatever was he talking about?

"You just heard Greatleaf speaking," Meghan said. "You were right; he is a torsil tree, a tree-of-passage—or he was. He's closed his passage gate on this side. It's quite unlike him to refuse us."

"This tree can *talk*?" Kyleah gasped.

"Of course I can talk!" rumbled Greatleaf, his broad leaves quivering. "Didn't you hear what I just said about the penalty for violating the royal edict? Dear me! What do they teach you two-legs in school? It is no wonder most two-legglings are so fond of hacking us with hatchets and carving their names into us with knives. They assume we are just senseless blocks of wood."

Bembor explained, "Girdling a tree—stripping off a ring of its bark—brings on a horrible, lingering starvation. Most trees would prefer a swift death by ax or saw to a slow death by girdling."

"But I've never heard a tree talk before!" Kyleah said.

"You have now," Gwynneth dryly observed.

Mycena added, "You have received the Gift of Understanding, which comes through the blossom-scent of *amenthils*—trees-of-understanding. Breathing that scent opens the ears and mind to comprehend not only tree-speech but animal-speech as well."

Kyleah felt numb. The grumbly voice she had heard on the way up to Gannon's cabin must have been Sally's. Later that night, she had overheard the horse's conversation with Gannon's mule!

Timothy said, "Greatleaf may have denied us passage, but Lightleaf won't. Let's find him before all the torsils shut us out!"

However, Lightleaf was no more inclined to allow the exiles to make passage than Greatleaf had been. Rolin's family looked very alarmed and frightened. Apparently, nothing like this had ever happened before, and the grown-ups didn't know what to do.

"Larkin did say we might not find our way back to Lucambra," Elwyn said. "How did he know the torsils would turn us down?"

Meghan's face blanched. "Now I remember! The same day you all arrived home from Feirian, I noticed a man skulking through the forest outside the Hallowfast. I couldn't see his face, but I'll bet it was Larkin. He seemed to be talking to himself. Then he jabbed a knife into one of the trees. He must have been impersonating Father, warning all the Thalmos-torsils in the king's name not to grant anyone passage into Lucambra. That filthy turncloak!"

Rolin asked Lightleaf, "Tell me, did Larkin threaten you with girdling, too, if you granted a two-legs passage from Thalmos?"

"Not just with girdling!" wheezed the tree. "You—he told me if I let any two-legs through from this side, he would lop off all my limbs. If it's all the same to you, I'd rather keep my branches. I'm rather attached to them, and I would look undignified as a pole."

"Has Larkin threatened *all* the torsils?" Marlis wondered.

"I fear we have underestimated our foe," said Emmer. "What we need is a tree that doesn't frighten easily or is too old and sleepy to notice that someone is climbing it to make passage."

"What if we didn't need to climb the tree?" Rolin mused. "'Roots and shoots!' You taught me that rhyme, Grandfather."

Bembor laughed aloud. "The torsil cave, of course! We might just get away with it. Kyleah, you had better come along, too."

Torsil cave? Kyleah puzzled. Was Bembor referring to a cave with a passage tree growing inside it, or a passage tree with a hole in it? Whatever it was, her new friends were very determined to find it, leaving Kyleah to catch up as best she could. Stumping along through the forest, she grumbled, "You would think they were still trying to leave me behind on purpose." As usual, she was just unwanted baggage slowing down everybody else.

Sighing, she settled on a boulder. Where did she belong—back with her father in Gannon's cabin—or with these odd folk who claimed to be from another world? If it weren't for Wynnagar and the passage bed, Kyleah would have thought the Greencloaks had concocted the whole notion of torsil trees as an elaborate prank.

She had made up her mind to return to the log cabin when Meghan reappeared. "Why are you sitting there?" she said crossly. "Everybody has been waiting for you. Now follow me, please!"

Kyleah meekly obeyed. She couldn't remember the last time anybody other than her father had waited for her. Most people had little patience for a cripple. She felt a sudden rush of fear. What would Branagan think when he awoke in the attic to find himself alone? She hoped his head-wound wouldn't cause him to lose his balance and fall down the ladder. She would never forgive herself if something were to happen to him because of her neglect.

After a short ramble, Kyleah and Meghan caught up to their companions, who were gathered at the base of a hill. A shadowy opening in the hillside peeked out through some hazel bushes.

"There you are!" Rolin said. "We were wondering what had become of you. Next time, please tell us to slow down and wait."

"You just ordered me to go home!" said Kyleah. "Now you want me to join you after all? Why did you change your mind?"

"You know about Lucambra and the torsils," Emmer said. "For that reason, we can't allow you to return home, at least not yet."

"Besides," said Medwyn, "maybe we can help each other."

"I haven't gone this way in years," Bembor said. "Let us hope the torsil has not died." He stooped and disappeared inside the entrance. A moment later, he reemerged. "The cave still works!" he announced. "We had better go while we have the chance."

Rolin's relatives trooped into the cave. Kyleah entered last, ducking her head to avoid some low-hanging brambles. The place felt cold and dank after the balmy breezes of a summer's bright morning. Once her eyes had adjusted to the darkness, Kyleah saw the cave was empty. What had happened to all her friends?

"Walk through the back, and you'll find them," someone said. It was Gannon. He was standing just inside the cave's mouth.

"I can't walk through solid rock!" Kyleah protested. She could move through living wood, but she refrained from saying so.

"On the hill above this cave you'll find a passage tree," Gannon explained. "If you pass under its roots, you'll go into Lucambra."

"What about you?" Kyleah asked. "Aren't you coming, too?"

"Me?" Gannon snorted. "I visit Lucambra only for weddings, coronations and the like. I must see to my bees and to your father as well. I'll tell him you've gone on a picnic with my son's family. Now, you'd better move on before that torsil changes its mind."

Sunlight filtered through the bushes overhanging the cave's entrance, silhouetting Gannon's lean form. Then he was gone. Kyleah limped up to the rock face at the back of the cave. With her crutch, she tapped the stone wall. It felt as solid as a brick.

Shutting her eyes, she hobbled forward. Her head whirled and she found herself in an echoing passage. At the far end, a light shone reassuringly. As she stumbled toward it, water dripped on her head, and cobwebs brushed her face. At last, the tunnel rose, and she came upon Rolin's lightstaff propped against the wall. Just then, Elwyn flew down the tunnel and picked up the staff.

"Here you are at last!" he said, taking her hand. "We left you this lightstaff to show you the way. *Croeso!* Welcome to Lucambra! You are the first Thalmosian since Timothy to visit our land. Please let me help you the rest of the way. It's tricky footing here."

After a steeper slope of thirty or forty yards, the passage ended in a blaze of daylight. Following Elwyn, Kyleah was climbing out when hands roughly grabbed her and threw her to the ground.

CHAPTER 10

MALROTH'S REBELLION

Kyleah was lying face-up inside the burned-out shell of an enormous dead tree. The blackened snag was about thirty feet high and fifteen wide. A rift gaped in one side. The sun shone down into the shell from directly overhead, though it was mid-morning when Kyleah had entered the torsil cave.

Nine sword-wielding Greencloaks were disarming her friends and roping them together by their waists. One of the men helped Kyleah up and linked her to Bembor. "Lord Larkin has no use for cripples!" the man growled. "You had better keep up—or else!"

"Where are we?" Kyleah whispered to Bembor.

The old Lucambrian wearily hung his shaggy head. "This was once my tree-home," he said huskily. "Then the dragon destroyed it while laying waste to this valley we call 'Liriassa.' Fortunately, the serpent spared many of the other trees, including the cave-torsil through which we just made passage—much to my regret."

"Dragon? You have a dragon here?" asked Kyleah. Her father scoffed at the oft-told tales of the serpent that supposedly had burnt Beechtown nearly to the ground. "Worms that can fly and spit fire?" he would snort. "Preposterous! Sparks escaping from Baker Wornick's dilapidated ovens started the Beechtown fire."

"We *had* a dragon," Bembor corrected her. "Thanks to Gaelathane, we have long since rid our world of such creatures."

"Some vermin still remain," said Elwyn pointedly.

"Shut up, you!" growled the tallest of the rebel Greencloaks. He threw back his silver-tipped hood. The man's gray-bearded face wore a look as disdainful, cruel and proud as Larkin's.

"Runnel son of Runion!" Rolin exclaimed. "Don't tell me that you also have thrown in your lot with the turncloak Larkin!"

"*Lord* Larkin, soon to be *King* Larkin, potato-eater!" the man snarled with barely concealed contempt. "You and your mongrel family should have listened to him and remained in Thalmos, where you belong. We knew you might try to return this way, and we set guards all around this tree. Now you and your followers are under arrest for committing high treason against Lucambra!"

"In what way has Rolin son of Gannon betrayed Lucambra?" Emmer roared. "Through him and my son Scanlon, Gaelathane delivered this land from the sorcerer and his legions, as you know full well! Should you and your traitorous chief have aught against the king, bring your complaint before the Lucambrian council."

"The king?" Runnel mocked Emmer. "Are you referring to this misbegotten son of a Thalmosian bee-breeder? His reign is ended! Nay, the rightful king shall be a pure-blooded Lucambrian, brave and true-hearted. Such a noble ruler has no need of a weak-kneed council of doddering longbeards like Bembor son of Brenthor."

Bembor bristled. "Insult me if you will, but do not presume to slander the king! Have you forgotten my father once dug yours out of the snow after an avalanche in the Brynnmor Mountains? But for that act of kindness, you never would have been born!"

"I had heard it was my father who rescued yours!" Runnel retorted. "No matter. That was then, and this is now. You are in no position to argue. I will bring you all before Lord Larkin, and he will pass judgment upon you. As king, he will make Lucambra great again. First of all, we will avenge ourselves upon the potato-eaters for invading our land. Thalmos and all other torsil worlds will pay tribute to us, just as they once paid tribute to Felgor. Even the trees of the forest will serve Lucambra's lord!"

"Would they not rather serve Gaelathane?" asked Rolin.

Runnel chuckled dryly. "His power is waning in this world, for a new force has arisen that not even He can readily resist."

"You are as mad as your master!" Bembor declared.

"We will see who is mad when Lord Larkin feeds you to his pet!" hissed Runnel. Grabbing Bembor's long beard, he sliced off a handful of white hair with his sword. Then he threw down the hair and viciously ground it into the dirt. Kyleah's friends gasped.

"May your sythan-ar rot, and your beard with it!" Runnel growled. "Now march!" At his command, his men prodded their reluctant prisoners out of the snag. Then Runnel drove them through the burned valley at a brutal pace, stinging stragglers with fresh willow and nettle switches he snatched up along the way.

From the very start, Kyleah was unable to keep up. Time and again, she tripped and fell, dragging Bembor down with her. At last, Runnel stationed two of his men at the back of the line to goad her onward with jabs, jeers and curses. Pushed from behind and pulled from ahead, she stumbled through the trees.

"What's the matter, gimp-girl? Can't you go any faster?" the soldiers taunted her. They kicked the crutch out from under her arm, and she thudded to the ground. The entire procession stopped until she could regain her feet—but not her dignity.

In this faltering fashion, Kyleah was half driven, half dragged through an endless nightmare of pain and terror. She and her friends were force-marched over fallen logs, through bogs and across rivers with never the slightest pause to catch their breath.

Darkness filled Kyleah's mind until the ragged line finally halted before an immense stone tower. Going on ahead, Runnel unlocked a heavy door in the tower's side. Then he and his men herded Kyleah and her companions through the door. Inside, a set of worn stairs spiraled upward into the tower's echoing heart. Runnel climbed to the fourth step and twisted the tread out of its place, revealing another stairway leading the opposite direction—into dark, unseen depths. "Down you go!" he said with a wicked grin. After their ropes were removed, the captives were forced one at a time through the narrow hole into the waiting blackness.

When Kyleah's turn came, she drew back. She hated climbing stairs. Going up was not nearly so difficult as going down, when she risked slipping on a tread and tumbling head-over-heels. Then Runnel shoved her through the hole and slid down after her. With her crutch's help, she stiffly descended one step at a time.

As soon as the darkness closed over her head, she smelled a horrible stench. Something was rotting in the cavernous space beneath her. Then Rolin brought out his lightstaff, and its cheery rays guided her safely down and into Meghan's steadying hands.

The minute he reached level ground, Runnel took Rolin's staff and snuffed out its light under his cloak. Then he and his men marched back up the stairs and squeezed through the open step.

"Wait!" cried Timothy. "Don't leave us down here!"

Runnel laughed, his voice echoing unpleasantly in the airless chamber. "A worse fate than this awaits you! Do not try to follow us. Death guards these stairs, both at the top and at the bottom."

The step grated back into place, and Kyleah squealed. The darkness was so complete she was as blind as a mole. Then she heard a sharp 'click,' and stars flashed in the lightless dungeon.

"Thanks be to Gaelathane for flint and steel, and tinder, too!" Marlis exclaimed. The stars winked and flickered again, but this time, they joined to form a single, steady flame. "Ever since Rolin and I returned from Thalmos-future," she explained, "I have kept this stump of a candle in my pocket as a reminder of the one that made our balloon rise. I always knew this candle-stub would come in handy some day." Eerie shadows mimicking faceless Prowlers wobbled on the cavern walls in the candle's wavering light.

"So they captured you, too, did they?" said a sour voice.

"Opio?" Scanlon cried. "Is that you?"

"And Gemmio, too," said another voice. "We were hoping you had escaped that rat Larkin's dragnet. Everyone else managed to flee the tower before he took it over." The candlelight fell upon two men lying roped to the top of a stone table. One man was tall and lean. The other was built like a maple-syrup barrel. Both wore green, hooded cloaks. While Marlis lit the table with her candle, Rolin untied the trussed-up captives and helped them to stand.

Opio bowed to Rolin. "Forgive us, Sire. It is our sworn duty to protect you and the queen, yet here you are rescuing us! We were returning at dusk from hunting game with Sigarth and Skoglund when Larkin and fifteen black-cloaked rogues fell upon us. The royal huntsmen got away, but Gemmio and I did not." He patted his belly fondly. "I fear my flab put me at a disadvantage when I tried to escape. Chestnut cakes have always been my downfall!"

"Never mind that," said Rolin graciously. "We are glad to find you two alive and unharmed. Your wisdom and valor are welcome, since we are trapped here without lightstaffs or other weapons."

"What about the tunnel access?" Elwyn asked. He pointed at a door set in the cavern wall. "That way leads out to the seashore."

Rolin sighed. "The old door was broken, so I had it replaced. The new one is four inches of solid oak, and it's locked. I'm sure by now Larkin has found the key hanging in the throne room."

"I never dreamed that fellow and his followers would turn on us," said Scanlon bitterly. "We should have seen it coming. Larkin has never liked anything or anyone Thalmosian. He's been a thorn in our cloaks since the day Rolin came to Lucambra. Now we have been locked up in the very chamber that Queen Winona, Rolin's grandmother, once delved beneath our Tower of the Tree!"

"How ironic," Bembor muttered with a disgusted look.

Pointing at Kyleah, Gemmio said, "Speaking of Thalmosians, where did you find this crippled girl? Judging from her outfit, she must hail from the hill country. Why did you bring her here?"

"I'm afraid we had no choice," Rolin replied. Introducing Kyleah, he recounted how she had fallen in with the company.

"Ordinarily, we would welcome such a one," said Gemmio. "Under the circumstances, though, I wish we could disguise her before Larkin gets a good look at her. She'll give him yet another pretext to accuse us of harboring spies, traitors and turncloaks."

"In Larkin's eyes, we are already condemned; we're all guilty of treason," said Bembor glumly, straightening his mangled beard.

Treason. Kyleah was reminded of the word she had found carved into the sword-maple. "Does 'intrison' mean 'treason'?"

Medwyn demanded, "Who told you about intrisonment?"

"Nobody told me about it," Kyleah mumbled. "That word was part of a riddle that I found cut into the bark of an old maple tree growing in the sugar bush above Mapleton. What does it mean?"

Medwyn swayed over Kyleah like an aspen waving in the wind. "What else was written upon that tree? By your life, hold nothing back from me, hill-girl! Our fate hangs upon your answer."

Kyleah pictured the callused letters that had been hacked into the maple's trunk. "The riddle went something like this: *This sword was driven for a reason/To capture king of leafy treason/Remove the sword, and you will see/Why he's intrisoned in this tree!*"

Groaning in anguish, Medwyn collapsed in a heap. "It is much worse than I feared," she wailed, pulling at her long hair. "Of all the trees you could have happened upon, you found Malroth's!"

"Who is Malroth?" Bembor asked her.

Medwyn hoarsely replied, "His tale is best told in the merry woods of spring when the sun is shining in its waxing strength, not in this lightless prison beneath the earth. Nonetheless, if you would hear the oldest legends of the memerren, I will speak of dark and desperate days beyond mortal memory. I will tell you how the tree-folk first had their revenge upon the race of men."

Coughing from the terrible stench, Medwyn began, "In those bygone times when two-legs walked Gaelathane the Leaf Lord's new worlds, trees were more numerous than they are nowadays and could move about, though not as quickly as your kind can."

"Move!" Bembor said. "How is that possible? Tree roots are firmly fixed in the soil. Trees are predictable: They remain where they are planted. I should know, for I have planted a fair number of them in my lifetime. Not one of those trees has ever moved."

"I agree," said Rolin. "I have yet to see a tree walk. Dear old Lightleaf has stood in the same spot ever since I first met him."

"Still, it is true," Medwyn said. "By stretching and tightening their roots, trees could 'wade' or *wealty* over the earth for great distances. How do you suppose vast forests have come to stand upon hills and mountains, valleys and plains? Beginning with the first one of every created kind—the first beech, the first fir, the first birch—the tree-folk established themselves in those places.

"Dropping their seeds and nuts wherever they went," Medwyn continued, "the trees spread their kinds throughout the land. It is no accident ashes and cottonwoods occupy wet places, or that pines are found on sandy soil. In autumn, whole forests would descend from the mountains into warm, protected valleys for the winter. Then all trees ceased wandering until spring. Now they must rely upon the wind, birds and beasts to spread their seeds."

"Why can't the trees move about anymore?" Kyleah asked.

"That comes later in my tale," Medwyn said. "All was well in the woods until men began fashioning axes and turning them upon the leafy tribe. No tree was safe then. Many a brave nymph and dryad perished in those distressing days, as they still do."

"What does any of this have to do with us?" asked Opio.

"Patience! I am coming to that," said Medwyn. "As men cleared forests to make way for their villages and farms, certain of our high dryads, or *hamadryads*, secretly plotted revenge. Malroth was their leader. A creature of supreme strength and beauty, he was the first and foremost of all the tree-spirits the Leaf Lord created.

"Malroth and his fellow conspirators swore allegiance to the sorcerer Felgor. In return for their fealty, Felgor forged them a fell blade, which he named *Felgroth* after himself and Malroth. With this black blade, the ruthless hamadryads smote their enemies hand and foot, for no shield or weapon could withstand its bitter edge. Yet, Felgroth proved to be far more perilous in the forest than on the field of battle, for it enabled the rebels to multiply.

"For many a bloody year, the hamadryads prevailed over men's armies. At night, the moonslipping sprites would fall upon sleepy towns and hamlets, capturing or killing any mortals they found. In retaliation, men torched the woodlands, burning the good with the bad. Finally, Malroth was seized and his forces defeated.

"In shedding innocent blood, the rebels were doubly cursed of Gaelathane. They grew disfigured, returning to the wood from which they were made. Still, they kept their two-legged form, walking upright as men do, though no man was ever so hideously misshapen. They became known as *woodwalkers* for their stiff gait. In the dryadin tongue, they are called *trollogs*, or 'man-slayers.'"

So the "Prowlers" are really tree-sprites! Kyleah thought.

"And the second curse?" asked Gemmio expectantly.

Medwyn replied, "As punishment for the trollogs' rebellion, the Leaf Lord stripped all trees everywhere of their power to move. Since that day, trees have remained rooted in one spot, unable to wealty from place to place or to flee from their enemies."

Kyleah's heart sank. She would have loved to watch the trees gliding through the earth like stately ships sailing the Green Sea. Indeed, had she known the black blade's bloody history, she would have trekked over the Tartellans to cast the sword into the sea.

"It is no wonder men so fear the forest!" Timothy remarked.

"Didn't I see a black sword in the square?" Marlis asked.

"Yes," said Medwyn. "Alas, that accursed blade has fallen into Malroth's hands again. It was he who tried to kidnap Kyleah."

"I alone am to blame," said Kyleah softly. Thirteen pairs of eyes glowed at her in the candlelight as she described Larkin's failed attempts to pull out the black sword, her own success at retrieving Felgroth and her unfortunate choice of hiding places.

"How could she remove that sword when Larkin could not?" Mycena marveled. "She's but a slip of a girl, as I was at her age."

"And why was Larkin pulling out those spikes?" Emmer said.

"Once, I found him snooping around the royal library," said Gwynneth. "I even caught him rummaging through my room."

"Then it was he who stole Winona's diary and my *Chronicles of Lucambra*," Bembor said. "I wonder what he was looking for."

Medwyn replied, "As Rolin has pointed out, Larkin and his flunkies could not seize Lucambra's throne alone. Instead, Larkin has been looking for a way to raise his own ready-made army."

Iron rang on stone, raising goose bumps on Kyleah's arms.

"An army? What sort of army?" Rolin asked Medwyn.

"Evidently, Larkin's 'snooping' must have led him to the trees where Malroth and much of his army were intrisoned. By pulling out the iron spikes rusting in those trees, Larkin released a trollog-legion like the one that originally ravaged the worlds of men."

Intrisoned. There was that odd word again! "You never told us what 'intrisoned' actually means," Kyleah reminded her.

Medwyn explained, "It means 'to imprison in a tree'—often with a nail or spike, since Wood Folk cannot endure the touch of iron. The trollogs themselves invented this cruel practice, first intrisoning any memer who refused to join their rebellion, and later their mortal captives as well. In the end, Malroth suffered the selfsame fate. In his arrogance and wrath, he dared to raise the black blade Felgroth against the King of the Trees, and Gaelathane intrisoned him with his own weapon in the maple you found."

By pulling out that black sword, I freed Malroth! thought Kyleah in despair. "What happened to the other trollogs?" she asked.

"After Malroth's defeat," said Medwyn, "a few worldwalkers won the trust of men, showing them how to intrison the lesser hamadryads with a hammer and nails. Some of those wretched creatures eluded capture and continue to wreak mayhem and havoc, but most of them have been shut up for hundreds of years inside the ancient trees of various worlds, chiefly your own."

"How did people know which trees to spike?" asked Elwyn.

"Often they did not," Medwyn sadly replied. "Then Wynnagar hatched a brilliant plan. Those nymphs and dryads faithful to the Leaf Lord were told to remain in their trees for a time. At dawn, mortal women then took balls of colored yarn into the woods, tying a length of yarn around each tree. The next day, their menfolk would drive an iron spike into any tree whose yarn had been snapped, for a trollog had broken that string leaving his tree.

> The trogs were tricked, the trogs were trapped
> In trollog trees; while sunlight lapped
> Upon the leaves, men's hammers rapped
> The tap of doom as tree-souls napped.

Timothy asked, "Why couldn't the trollogs that were still loose release their intrisoned friends? After all, if Larkin could pull those spikes, surely the renegade hamadryads could do the same."

"No, they could not!" said Medwyn. "Iron will burn even the most thick-skinned of trollogs. However, the black sword's touch wounds them worse still. Though Felgroth was forged neither of metal nor of stone, it still scorches our enemies' woody skin."

"Is that why Malroth was wearing gloves?" Kyleah asked her.

"Yes, it is," Medwyn said. "In battle, Malroth always wore leather gloves to protect himself against Felgroth's deadly sting."

"Hush!" said Mycena. "Don't you hear the tide rolling in?"

Everyone fell silent as a rhythmic sighing echoed through the dungeon. Kyleah thought it sounded more like a bear's heavy breathing—or boiling syrup bubbling in a sugarhouse cauldron.

"That cannot be the sea!" said Scanlon. "How could we hear the El-marin's breakers when the tunnel door is shut fast?"

"Gemmio and I also have often heard that sound," Opio said.

"And other noises, too, as of chains clanking," added Gemmio. "We feared our minds were playing tricks on us in the dark."

"Not unless our minds are being tricked, too!" said Rolin.

By now, the candle had burned down too far for Marlis to hold it any longer. She placed it on the table, and everyone gathered around, letting out a collective groan when the stub's feeble flame finally surrendered to the darkness. Squeezing her eyes shut, Kyleah hoarded the candle's dying light behind her eyelids.

Above the stairs, stone ground on echoing stone. *Clank.* Iron jangled in answer, ominously clinking and rattling. The dungeon's reek grew worse, as if the darkness itself were rotting away.

"What a dreadful smell!" Marlis gasped. "We should have aired out this room when we had the chance. It has been shut up for so long that the air has become stagnant and foul."

"I do not think it is the air," said Emmer in a low voice. "I smell sulfur. Mt. Golgunthor must be erupting again, releasing fumes underneath us. Do you not feel the vapors' warmth?"

Elwyn said, "If only our griffins would rescue us! They have deserted us in our hour of need. What has become of them?"

"Knowing Larkin, he has cooped them up in a cage or cave somewhere," said Scanlon gloomily. "Thus far, he hasn't slipped up. He is always one step ahead of us, as Felgor was at first."

"Lord Larkin has made one mistake," rumbled Malroth's harsh voice from the head of the stairs. "He has let you two-legs live!"

CHAPTER 11

INTRISONED

"Do you take me for a fool?" Larkin roared. Clattering down the stairs with a torch, he swung Gannon's sword against the wall, and it shattered. "How dare you foist off this cheap tin laundry stick on me! If you don't tell me what you have done with Elgathel's sword, your whole family will suffer for it!"

Rolin blandly replied, "Of course I knew you would catch on sooner or later. With these wooden-limbed friends of yours, I'd say you already have plenty of laundry sticks at your disposal."

Roaring with rage, Malroth bounded down the stairs, taking the steps five at a time. He grabbed Rolin by the throat and shook him like a rat in a mastiff's jaws. The others beat on the trollog's back, but they might as well have been hammering a tree trunk.

"Careful there, Malroth," said Larkin, leisurely making his way across the floor. "*After* he has told me where to find Elgathel's sword, you may tear him to pieces and eat him, if you wish."

"I wish!" hissed Malroth. He opened his huge hand, and Rolin dropped to the ground. Marlis ran to his side and helped him up.

"Are you all right?" she anxiously asked him.

"I will be, once my head stops ringing," he ruefully replied. "I should not have provoked Malroth so rashly, as big as he is."

Larkin thrust his flaming torch in Rolin's face. "Now tell me where you hid that sword, or Malroth here will fold you in half!"

"Do whatever you wish to me or to my family, but you won't find the sword that way," Rolin grunted. "I entrusted it to one of my faithful servants, who took it into another torsil world. Which one, I do not know. That sword lies beyond our reach now."

"Don't be so sure!" snapped Larkin. "I have eyes in every torsil world. Wherever that sword has been hidden, I will find it!"

Bembor said, "If I were you, I wouldn't lose any leaves over Elgathel's sword. I'd be watching my back. These trollogs will turn on you when you least expect it. Surely you don't believe they will serve you as their king! By nature, hamadryads are traitors; they are bent on wiping out the entire two-legged race to a man."

Larkin sullenly replied, "They need me more than I need them. Besides, the parchments prophesy I shall be king of the trollogs."

"What parchments?" Rolin asked suspiciously.

Larkin threw back his head and cackled. "Now there's a piece of irony! When it came time to muster my army, I found all the clues I needed in a stack of parchments lying right under your nose in Gannon's cellar! They had been gathering dust for years, but you never bothered to read them. I beat you to their secrets!"

Meghan sniffed, "I suppose like a true villain you're going to flaunt those secrets in our faces, whether we like it or not."

"Of course!" replied Larkin fiendishly. "And you won't like what I have to tell you, either. Most of the parchments contained recipes, but on one I discovered the first two staves of a riddle written in Winona's hand. The remaining verses were too faded to make out. I still learned all I needed to know from these staves:

> Steal not the nails o'er dripping pails,
> Where wicked wight awaits;
> The first to free intrisoned trees
> Shall open Gundul's gates.
>
> For buried sword of Gundul's lord
> Shall fit the slotted stone;
> A fateful twist of weaponed fist
> Shall seat him on his throne.

"What does that mean?" Marlis asked, looking bewildered.

Larkin sneered at her. "So Lucambra's clever queen has met her match at last, eh? Where you are going, you will have the lifetime of a tree to puzzle over that riddle. I'll give you a hint: As the 'first to free intrisoned trees,' I have become the trollogs' master."

In a flash, Kyleah understood. From the riddle, Larkin had correctly guessed the "dripping pails" referred to sap-buckets. On the other hand, he could not have known at first which "nails" to "steal"—the iron spikes that were keeping trollogs intrisoned in their trees, or the spiles supporting Branagan's sap-buckets.

As Larkin's torch dangled loosely in his grip, Kyleah saw her chance to stir up some excitement. Awkwardly swinging her crutch, she knocked the fiery stick from Larkin's lax grasp. Before the Lucambrian could pick it up, she seized the torch and hurled it at Malroth. The burning end struck his cloak, which burst into flames. Howling, the trollog beat at the tongues of fire with his hands, but the torch's hot pitch stuck to everything it touched. In mere seconds, the cloak had gone up in a cloud of smoke.

"That was a mistake," said Larkin.

Malroth stood before them in stark fury, a nightmare woven out of wood. Though the flames had scorched the trollog's massive frame, he was unharmed. His twisted features seared themselves into Kyleah's horrified eyes. In the Beechtown market square, what she had taken for a malicious mask of wood was Malroth's face, if such a grotesque mass of gnarled knots could be called a face. As Malroth clenched and unclenched his long, lumpy fingers, Kyleah recalled the sticks she had found lying on Gannon's cabin floor. Those were no ordinary twigs, but trollog fingers severed when Gannon's guests had slammed the door on trollog hands.

"Gaelathane, have mercy upon us," whispered Marlis.

Bellowing, Malroth came for Kyleah. Terror turned her knees to jelly. She collapsed and crawled under the stone table, knowing she could not escape. She hoped the end would come swiftly.

"Not yet!" cried Larkin, and Malroth's warty, splayed feet stopped inches from Kyleah's nose. "We can burlip this girl with Felgroth. As young as she is, she'll make us some fine burlies."

Malroth's feet stomped off, only to return. Then the flaming torch dropped next to Kyleah's head, singeing her hair. "I fear not even the hottest flames, two-legs!" growled the trollog. "Though fire may scorch me, my burns will quickly heal, for my skin is tougher than any tree-bark, and much thicker than your skin."

With a sharp kick, Malroth sent the torch skidding under the table and into Kyleah's body. She screamed and grabbed the stick by its cool end. Sputtering dangerously close to her face, the flames illuminated wispy words inscribed underneath the table:

Steal not the nails o'er dripping pails,
Where wicked wight awaits;
The first to free intrisoned trees
Shall open Gundul's gates.

For buried sword of Gundul's lord
Shall fit the slotted stone;
A fateful twist of weaponed fist
Shall seat him on his throne.

Though hidden horde obey his sword,
No mortal can prevail
O'er deadly sprite that gnaws the night,
Intrisoned by a nail.

Then she shall come who cannot run;
This two-legs goes on three;
She'll hold the blade not mortal-made,
Who touches heart of tree.

Though wooden band will fear to stand
Before the royal tree,
The living staff who lacks a half
Will root the trolls who flee.

She had just finished reading the riddle when Malroth grabbed her feet and yanked her out from under the table, torch and all.

"Bembor is right," Rolin told Larkin. "Malroth and his friends will obey you only as long as it suits them. However, you will never be their king. The first stave of your riddle promises only that you will 'open Gundul's gates,' a rash act you might live long enough to regret. Once opened, those gates are difficult to close again. Felgor breached them, and it nearly destroyed Lucambra."

"Felgor was a fool!" Larkin snarled. "He commanded a great army, but his minions could not think for themselves. Once he fled, his followers fell into disarray and were easily defeated. *I* have marshalled an army of cunning hamadryads five hundred thousand strong, every one of them capable of tearing down this tower single-handedly, every one of them itching for revenge."

"Every one of them with sawdust for brains," quipped Elwyn. Malroth shot him a venomous look from his scowling mask.

"My tolerance for you simpletons is wearing thin!" Larkin spat. "I must introduce you to my pet. Maybe then you will understand the full extent of my power and the utter futility of resistance."

Following Larkin and Malroth, Kyleah and her companions crowded into a dark corner under the stairs. They jumped back as a greenish-black form lunged at them, its baleful red eyes glowing in the darkness. A scaly creature was straining at a massive iron chain whose end was bolted to the stone wall. Thick leather straps secured a heavy muzzle over the beast's tapering snout.

"Why, it's a . . . it's a marsh dragon!" Gwynneth exclaimed.

Larkin smirked. "I see you still know your serpents."

"That explains the stench we've been smelling," said Marlis.

"Look!" cried Emmer. "Here are our stolen weapons!" Sheaves of swords, spears and longbows stood stacked against the wall.

"Where did you find the marsh dragon?" Elwyn asked. "They're all supposed to be dead! Gaelathane destroyed Vineland's dragons, and the one that survived in Thalmos drank itself to death."

Looking smug, Larkin said, "I'll tell you how I found *Glunt*. I hung around those stinking Beechtown docks—and listened."

According to the river gossip, Greenies had been attacking Beechtown's barges again. Still laden with cargo, the unmanned vessels were running aground in the stagnant Rattlereed Marshes. However, Larkin knew that when Greenies robbed a barge, they always took the goods. He also knew that the only Greenies left in Thalmos had given up their vines and their former way of life.

"What are Greenies?" Kyleah interrupted, but Larkin ignored her and went on with his tale. On the pretext of visiting some ever-so-distant relatives in Thalmos, he had hitched a ride on the next barge south. Exchanging his green cloak for a bargeman's billowing red blouse, he had helped his companions pole the craft downriver, stopping at villages and hamlets to trade bolts of cloth, plows and horseshoes for venison, vegetables and fruit.

One afternoon, the barge had shuddered and picked up speed, traveling much more swiftly than the Foamwater's current. The bargemen had tried in vain to slow the craft's progress with their poles. Some of the frightened men jumped overboard and swam for the safety of shore, but not one of them ever reached dry ground. With terrified cries, they had disappeared beneath the river's swirling waters. After that, no one dared leave the barge.

When the meandering Foamwater lost its way among thickets of reeds and willows, the flat-bottomed barge stuck fast in the mud. Larkin scanned the marsh for telltale green humps before collecting his baggage and bidding his fellow bargemen farewell. He steeled himself against their raucous taunts and warnings.

"Ye'll never leave this marsh alive!" they solemnly predicted. Waving at them, he had hopped off the barge and slogged away through the treacherous muck. After whittling himself a sharp ash spear, he had hidden in the top of a tall willow—and waited.

That night, *she* who had dragged the barge downriver came for the men on it. Larkin listened to their frantic cries, knowing the hapless Thalmosians were giving their lives in order that he might become king of Lucambra. In the morning, he returned to the barge, where he found the gorged dragon asleep in the hold. First, he securely bound and muzzled "Glunt," as he afterwards called her. Then he prodded the snoring beast awake with his spear.

My, what a ruckus that dragon raised! Unable to spit fire at her tormentor or bite him, Glunt wore herself out at the point of his spear. Cajoling and threatening the beast by turns, he tamed his reptilian prize. Even so, he very nearly lost his life in the bargain. Weary but triumphant, Larkin had set off with his marsh dragon on a grueling overland journey to the nearest Lucambra-torsil.

"I have purposely kept her on short rations so she'll fit through the door," Larkin concluded. "That means she is very hungry!"

"Those poor Thalmosian bargemen!" Mycena cried. "How could you be so heartless? Why didn't you try to save them?"

"It was all for a good cause," said Larkin smoothly.

"For *your* cause, you mean," Opio shot back.

Larkin laughed. "How do the Thalmosians put it? 'You can't make an omelet without breaking some eggs.' Nasty, disgusting things, those chicken eggs. Only brutish barbarians eat them."

"You should try them raw," Meghan said, her eyes flashing.

"Glunt also prefers her *meat* raw," Larkin coolly replied.

"Just give us the chance to round up our griffins, and they will make short work of your marsh dragon," growled Gemmio.

"You won't have that chance," said Larkin. "Besides, I have sent off Ironwing, Windsong, Smallpaw and your other sorcs on a pressing errand in the king's name. They'll be gone for months."

"Then we will ring Elgathel's bell to summon King Redwing's griffin legions from the Willowah Mountains!" Elwyn said.

Larkin grinned. "Alas, that bell's clapper has gone missing."

"What are 'griffins'?" Kyleah asked. Again she was ignored.

"You still have not explained how this marsh dragon came to live in the Rattlereed Marshes!" said Rolin.

"I owe you no explanations, pretender!" Larkin snapped. A sly smile traced his lips. "Still, did you or your bumpkin father find the memento I left on your shelf in place of those parchments? I thought it only sporting to give you one small clue at least."

"Memento?" said Rolin, a frown creasing his forehead.

Gwynneth groaned. "That green flake was a piece of dragon eggshell, wasn't it? I should have known! I have such an eggshell in my bedroom. I'll bet I know how this dragon ended up in a Thalmosian marsh. Bart and his Greenies were making green mist on the Foamwater with a marsh-dragon egg when their ship sprouted and sank. That egg must have dropped out and rolled downriver with the current. When I was trapped in the Glynnion Wood of Feirian, I saw an oblong green rock tumbling along the Foamwater's bottom. I'm sure it was Bart's marsh-dragon egg."

Kyleah clutched her growling stomach. She hadn't understood a word of the Lucambrians' discussion. If only she could snap her fingers and return home, she would happily stand laundry duty until both hands blistered. She wondered if Barley missed her.

"What are you going to do with us?" Elwyn asked Larkin.

"You'll find out soon enough," the turncloak purred. "Why spoil the surprise? I am fond of surprises, aren't you? I cannot promise you'll enjoy this one. You'll likely never recover from it."

"You don't want our blood on your hands," said Marlis. "Why not just send us back to Thalmos? After all, since you have turned the torsils against us, we'll be forced to remain there in exile."

"Your wish is granted," Larkin said with a mocking bow. "This very night, you and your family will be returning to that world."

Larkin and Malroth herded their captives up the stairs and out of the Hallowfast. Runnel and his men were waiting for them. Under a star-milky sky, the Greencloaks marched Kyleah and her friends into the woods and up a torsil tree. When they climbed down again, sugar maples surrounded them. An orange moon was rising as the prisoners were driven farther into the sugar bush.

Rustling and creaking, more lanky, black-cloaked figures joined the procession, hemming in the captives on all sides. The grim-faced trollogs stiffly loped through the woods with impossibly long, stilted strides, singing out a rumbling, grumbling chant:

> The trogs are here, the trogs are there;
> We've come to drag you by the hair,
> Or lure you to our lonely lair
> And work you till your bones are bare!
>
> The trogs are big, the trogs are black;
> They creep thru cranny and thru crack
> To cram your children in a sack
> And take them for a tasty snack!
>
> The trogs will tromp, the trogs will tread
> Upon their takings till they're dead,
> And if they find you when they're fed,
> They'll make you cook for them instead!

Kyleah felt sick. She would rather die than become a trollog's slave. Before long, Larkin stopped in a clearing high in the forest.

"This will do!" he announced. The trollogs gathered around their captives, forming a black-cloaked wall of wooden bodies.

"Take the half-breed first," Larkin said, his voice dripping with disdain. He looked on with grim satisfaction as the trollogs shoved Rolin outside their circle, despite his family's attempts to protect him. Then Larkin and Malroth marched Lucambra's king away into the forest. Marlis, Gwynneth and Meghan quietly sobbed.

"Good-bye, dear husband!" Marlis shouted after him. "May Gaelathane keep you till we meet again. I will always love you!"

"And I you, my bride!" Rolin's reply faded into silence.

One after another, Larkin called out the praying captives. At last, only Medwyn and Kyleah were left. Then one of the trollogs grabbed Medwyn and dragged her struggling to a nearby maple.

"Not the iron!" she screamed. "Please don't intrison me with the iron! Help me, Scanlon! Leaf Lord, save me from this death!"

Wrapping Medwyn in his long, stiff arms, the trollog stepped back into the tree, dragging her with him, much as Kyleah had done with Barley when hiding from Malroth. Moments later, the creature reemerged, leaving Medwyn trapped inside. The other trollogs thumped their chests like drums and hooted in triumph.

Then Larkin approached Medwyn's tree carrying a bag and a hammer—but it was the wrong time of year for tapping trees. Taking a spike from the bag, Larkin drove it into the trunk with ringing blows of his hammer. Cold rage mingled with fear in the pit of Kyleah's stomach. Larkin had intrisoned Medwyn with one of the spikes he had removed months earlier from a trollog-tree!

"Worldwalkers cannot moonslip, or so I have heard," Larkin told the trollogs. "However, I am not taking any chances. We mustn't allow the queen of the Golden Wood to escape this tree."

"Now it is your turn!" said Malroth, and he jerked Kyleah off the ground by her hair, staff and all. Then he backed into another tree, taking Kyleah with him. The tree's woody insides were as cold as the Grieving Ground during the dead of winter. Malroth then slipped out the back of the tree, leaving Kyleah by herself.

Outside, the trollogs were ponderously circling beneath the trees, their arms raised over their heads as if reaching for the misty moon. Chanting fell words of death and destruction, trollog voices raucously rumbled in time with the rhythmic tramping of trollog feet. Kyleah shuddered in horror at what she heard.

Trollogs stamp and trollogs stomp,
Under rising moon we romp,
Seeking two-legs to intrison,
In our private leafy prison!

Merciless we are to men,
Whose hatchets shall not hack again!
Driven spikes for nymphs and dryads,
Iron nails intrison naiads!

No more singing, no more mirth
When trollogs triumph on the earth!
Not a two-legs left to live,
For trollogs never will forgive.

Trollogs tread the treeless hills;
Trollogs steal and trollogs kill;
Trollog sword makes burlies burge;
Trollogs are a scurvy scourge!

Then the trollogs stopped singing, and Malroth's rasping voice cut through the chorus of creaking joints. "Friends and fellow trogs!" he said. "In days of old, men did whatever they wished to us trees. Henceforth, they shall learn to fear us! Now those two-legs who served the Detested Tree are intrisoned, and their shining sticks shall trouble us no more. This night marks the beginning of a new age—the Age of the Trollogs. Let the burlies burge!"

"Let the burlies burge!" his listeners harshly echoed.

Malroth drew the sword Felgroth and stepped up to a large, black burl growing on a tree. Swinging the sword over his head, he struck the burl. Even inside her tree, Kyleah could hear the sharp 'crack.' The burl split open, and a dark, dripping head emerged, followed by flailing limbs. Wriggling out, the creature dropped to the ground. Several trollogs bent over it with grunting sounds.

Wood swallowed up Kyleah's gasp. She understood now what Medwyn had meant when she said the trollogs used the black sword to "multiply." Horrified, she watched as Malroth went from tree to tree, slicing open other burls. Before long, the forest was swarming with the black hatchlings. Then Malroth came to a burl-less maple. He struck the trunk once with his sword and moved on. Darkness gathered in the weeping gash. A new burl was sprouting where Malroth had wounded the tree.

Then he came to Kyleah's tree and struck it with the edge of the black sword. Pierced to the core, Kyleah let out a muffled scream. As the burl began swelling on the trunk, it sapped her strength like a malignant tumor. The world around her grew dark.

Mocking their captives' distress, the trollogs croaked,

Let the black blade bite and the bloody burls swell
From the trees where our two-legged trisoners dwell;
Make the captive souls breed an army of trolls,
Till the trisoners shrivel into shapeless shells!

Still singing, the trollogs melted into the woods. Their black burl-babies scampered after them. Meanwhile, Kyleah's agony was worsening. She tried to leave the tree, but the bulging burl was paralyzing her mind and body. Who was she? Where were her friends? Where did she belong? What was happening to her?

Two last, stubborn thoughts refused to surrender to the burl: *These "trollogs" are really "trolls," and they have intrisoned me!*

CHAPTER 12

THE BROKEN BED

*D*arkness. Kyleah could neither see nor feel anything. She had become a numb, formless spirit wrapped in a wooden overcoat. Emblazoned in fire, a word suddenly appeared before her face. *Gaelathane*. With ebbing strength, she whispered that name. The blackness behind her eyes lifted, and in a new light, she saw a white-cloaked figure striding through the forest.

Too short for a trollog, the bearded stranger was carrying a shapeless leather bag over his shoulder. Stopping at one of the maple trees, he took a wooden mallet and a handful of white pegs out of the bag. After fitting one of the pegs into a tap-hole in the trunk, he drove it in with a few solid whacks of the mallet.

The Plugger! When Kyleah had last seen him, he had not been wearing a cloak. But why was the hermit working so late at night in the forest? Didn't he know of the terrible danger after dark?

Laying aside his mallet, the hermit touched a burl sprouting where Malroth had "planted" it on the maple's trunk with the black sword. *Pop!* The black burl dropped off like a sated deer tick, leaving no scar or other trace behind on the bark. Then the Plugger moved on to the next infected tree, repeating his actions. Kyleah held her breath. Would the Plugger overlook her tree?

Picking up his bag and mallet, the hermit moved away from Kyleah. Seized with a terrible despair, she tried to cry out, but her mouth wouldn't open. Instead, she willed her tormented heart to pour out its last, desperate plea: *Don't leave me here—please!*

The Plugger glanced back, gazing through the tree right into Kyleah's agonized eyes. Something about the man's look calmed her anxious spirit. As he approached her leafy prison, she was sure her pounding heart must be shaking the maple from the ends of its far-flung roots all the way to the tips of its topmost twigs.

Then the Plugger stood before her, a smile wreathing his face. Raising his arm, he touched her burl. The swelling lump of gnarled wood and bark fell off, and Kyleah could breathe freely again.

"One day soon I shall remove the burl you cannot see," said the Plugger, his voice full and clear. "Though you have yet to pass through water and through fire, your healing begins this hour. To make amends for the great evil you have unleashed, you must free as many of your friends as you can! You must also lean upon your brother Barlomey, for his gift will multiply yours a hundredfold."

Before Kyleah could ask what he meant, the Plugger simply disappeared. Fearing Malroth would return with his black sword, she wasted no time in pushing herself out of the tree. All around her, spent, split-open burls littered the moonlit earth. But which of the maples held her friends? At night, the trees all looked alike—dark, brooding beings not unlike the spiky trollogs themselves.

The spike! Searching the trees around her, Kyleah found the thick iron nail Larkin had driven into Medwyn's maple. She thrust her hand inside and drew out the spike. Then she plunged her arm back into the tree and flailed about. Suddenly, another hand gripped hers with such terrible strength that her knuckles cracked. She pulled on the hand—and out popped a disheveled Medwyn.

"Thank you! I don't know how you got me out, but I shall always be indebted to you," the worldwalker gasped.

"Never mind that now," Kyleah replied. "We must find the others." Medwyn's eyes goggled as Kyleah fished around inside tree after tree. She had just found and rescued Meghan when tall, hooded shapes slunk toward them with heavy footfalls.

"The trollogs are coming back!" Medwyn whispered.

"I can't leave my family here!" Meghan protested.

Kyleah said, "We can return for them after sunrise, when the Prowlers—I mean *trollogs*—are sleeping in their own trees."

The three hurried down the mountainside. Desperate to keep up with Medwyn and Meghan, Kyleah vaulted logs and gullies with her tall staff. Thudding footsteps followed, growing louder by the second. Kyleah wept with relief as the Grieving Ground came into sight. However, even as she and her companions passed Mapleton's sugarhouse, the trollogs were catching up to them. One tried to grab Kyleah, but she knocked its gnarled hand aside with her crutch. "This way!" she cried to the two women, and they all swerved right to scurry up the hill toward Kyleah's dark cottage.

Kyleah staggered up to the door and flung it open. Once her friends had passed through, she was about to enter herself when something like a lightning bolt struck her back. Gasping with the awful pain, she staggered through the door, slammed it shut and bolted it. *Whump!* The door shuddered under a heavy blow.

"They're going to break through any second!" she exclaimed.

"Is there another way out?" Meghan asked her.

Kyleah shook her head. She and her companions were trapped, just as surely as they were when intrisoned in the trees. Then she remembered Wynnagar's words: *When they come for you, take to your bed! It is your only way of escape.* Dragging Medwyn and Meghan into the tiny bedroom, Kyleah ordered them to lie down on the passage bed. With puzzled looks, they did as she asked.

Kyleah had just thrown herself down beside them when Barley appeared at the bedroom door. Rubbing his sleepy eyes, he said, "Here you are, Sis! Where is Father? Where have you been all this time? We expected you home ages ago. I have missed you!"

Seeing the impish look in her brother's eyes, Kyleah cried, "No, Barlomey!" She was too late. Barley took a running leap and with a whoop, landed squarely on the bed next to his sister. Wood cracked and splintered. Then the groaning frame gave way, and Kyleah's magnificent passage bed folded up with a great crash.

She wailed, "Look what you've done! You broke my bed!"

Looking baffled, Barley was staring at the forest crowning Mt. Argel. Kyleah gazed up at the moon shining through Wynnagar's filmy white canopy. Then she climbed out of her ruined bed.

"Where are we?" her brother asked. "Am I dreaming again?"

"If you are, then I'm having the same dream," said Meghan.

Medwyn blinked dazedly. "How did we get up here?"

Kyleah sighed, "My bed is to blame." Yet, *she* hadn't touched the headboard and footboard at the same time—and Barley was too short to reach them with his head and toes. Unsupported, the bed's two end boards now tilted drunkenly toward each other.

That was it! When the bed buckled, the passage-tree footboard and headboard had folded inward like the walls of a collapsing tent, touching everyone's head and feet. Suddenly, Kyleah herself felt the need to collapse. She leaned heavily upon her staff. The searing pain in her back wrenched a groan from her throat.

"Look! Her back is bleeding!" Meghan exclaimed. She and Medwyn poked and prodded Kyleah, causing still more agony.

"What happened to you?" asked Medwyn.

"I don't know," Kyleah miserably replied.

"How odd!" Meghan remarked. "It looks as though someone sliced through her dress and into her flesh with a sharp knife."

"This is no knife wound," countered Medwyn. "Knives don't leave such ugly raised welts. Something has flayed her back raw!" She lowered her voice. "This wound bears all the marks of a *tollash*. She'll—" Medwyn murmured some words Kyleah couldn't hear.

Meghan gasped sharply. "Really? What can be done for it?"

"Nothing," muttered Medwyn. "We'll know soon enough."

A tollash? thought Kyleah. *I've never heard of such a thing.*

Meghan stitched up the torn shift with a needle and thread from her sewing kit. "There!" she said. "That should hold for now. We ought to be thankful for coming away from those trollogs with nothing worse than a broken bedstead, a ripped garment and a few welts. Now, when can Kyleah release the rest of our family?"

Medwyn replied, "We can't go back while the trollogs are still lurking about her home. I am hoping that old man who wandered by to knock off our burls will free the trisoners himself."

"That was the Plugger," Kyleah said, and she told Medwyn and Meghan of the hermit's peculiar habit of plugging tap-holes.

"I suppose the trogs intrisoned him, too," said Medwyn. "They are always on the prowl for more mortals to intrison and *burlip*."

"Burlip!" Meghan exclaimed. "What does that mean?"

"You were burlipped yourself," Medwyn replied. "As you saw, wherever Malroth wounded a tree with the black sword, a burl sprouted. Such a burl can swell to washtub-size, but nothing will come of it unless the growth is gashed with Felgroth. Then a young trollog will hatch out. We call the hatchlings 'brollogs,' or 'burlies.' They're every bit as dangerous as full-grown trollogs."

"That explains the writing on the sword-blade," said Kyleah.

"What did the writing say?" Medwyn asked.

"'With this blade he will make them, and with this blade he will break them!' It sounds like what you just described."

"Is that what burlipping means?" Meghan persisted.

"Yes, it does," said Medwyn. "A burl will remain barren unless someone is intrisoned inside its host-tree. The young burlie feeds on that unfortunate victim. The trollogs 'burlip' a person when they plant a burl on the tree where he is intrisoned. We can be thankful the first rebellion was put down before Malroth could release all the brollogs he had bred, or he would have prevailed."

"How awful!" said Meghan.

Kyleah frowned at Barley, who was climbing on the collapsed bed. "Leave my bed alone!" she scolded him. "Haven't you done enough damage already? Thanks to you, we're stranded on the top of this high mountain, and it's too steep to climb down."

"You should thank Gaelathane for your brother!" came a voice from the night. Still garbed in black, a youthful Wynnagar stepped out from the linden trees. "As I see it, if Barley hadn't broken your bed, you might not have made passage in time to escape."

Barley beamed and strutted like a cocky rooster.

"Hail, Wynnagar of Thalmos!" cried Medwyn.

"You two already know each other?" Kyleah asked.

"We do indeed," said Medwyn. "I am a worldwalker, too. We met on this mountain many years ago at one of our Conclaves."

The two women embraced. Then Medwyn introduced Meghan and Barley to Wynnagar, who already knew Kyleah's brother.

"What is a Conclave?" asked Meghan.

Medwyn explained, "Once a year, memerren and worldwalkers from every passage world meet on this mountain for the Conclave or *Cyngor*. As trees listen with root and leaf for woodland gossip, so we worldwalkers like to keep up with our own kind. You will find that we listen deeply, see much but speak little. That reminds me, Cousin: Why have you told this mortal about our ways?"

Wynnagar raised an eyebrow. "Who said she was mortal?"

Medwyn laughed. "Don't be silly, Cousin. Her homespun dress and vulgar manner of speech give her dead away. Mark my words, she is nothing more or less than a Thalmosian hill-girl."

"Is she?" said Wynnagar. "Have you forgotten the Oracle?"

When blessed babe be noble born
To her who mortal walks forlorn
Without the home where once she slept;
Of kith and kindred since bereft.

Then build the *blairn* a proper bed,
Of passage wood its foot and head;
This grant the Gifted Girl to keep
Until she stretches in her sleep.

"You gave this mortal girl the Leaf Lord's bed-boards?" Medwyn gasped. "Why? Have you gone soft in the heart in your old age?"

"That's what I want to know, too!" sniffed Kyleah. "I didn't ask to have this traveling bed. Anyway, my mother and I weren't noble born. She was the sugarmaster's wife, and I am their daughter."

Wynnagar smiled mysteriously and mischievously at Kyleah. "Tell the queen of the Golden Wood your mother's name."

"Larissa—though I can't see what difference it makes," said Kyleah. Honestly, these worldwalkers could be so difficult!

Medwyn underwent an astonishing transformation. First, her face turned pink. Then all the color drained from it, leaving her skin paler than the whitest dogwood blossoms. She cleared her throat. "By any chance, you don't mean *that* Larissa, do you?"

"Yes, she does," said Wynnagar. "Thanks to Larissa, the blood of the high memerren flows in Kyleah's veins. If she is not 'gifted,' how did she rescue you and Meghan from intrisonment?"

Medwyn regarded Kyleah with wondering eyes. "I thought I sensed a kindred spirit in her when we first met. Who would have ever imagined the 'Gifted Girl' was a Thalmosian hill-dweller?"

Wynnagar said, "Pray the enemy does not realize who she is, either. This one must not be revealed until the proper time."

Kyleah burst into tears. "My mother wasn't a memer!" she wailed. "She didn't live inside a tree the way you say nymphs and dryads are supposed to! She lived her whole life in Mapleton. I wish Father had never made me this bed in the first place."

"In her youth, dear blairn," said Wynnagar, "your mother did live in a tree. To foil our foes, she chose to leave her beloved forest and live in hiding as a worldwalker. Even then she was not safe."

"Excuse me," said Meghan. "What is a 'blairn,' anyway?"

"A blairn is the offspring of a memer and a mortal," Wynnagar explained. "In rare instances, the Leaf Lord blesses a blairn with unique abilities or talents, as Kyleah obviously possesses."

Barley pouted. "I don't have any special talents."

"Kyleah can also understand tree-speech," Meghan said.

Wynnagar's eyes shifted uneasily to the bed and back again. "All nymphs and dryads are born with the gift of understanding forest-speech. Most blairns are not. If a blairn is able to enter a tree and leave it again, though, that ancient blessing will fall upon him or her without the necessity of smelling amenthil blossoms."

Kyleah knew just when the Gift had come over her. She and Barley had hidden from Malroth inside the maple tree. When she had emerged the following morning, the forest had sung for joy.

"Something is wrong here," Wynnagar was saying. All at once, Kyleah's bed sprang into the air and flew to pieces. The splintered frame shattered, pillows exploded in clouds of goose-down, and even the mattress lofted skyward, returning to earth in shreds.

"It's the trollogs!" Kyleah gasped. "They're in my room! Oh, dear. That means Dolora and my stepsisters are in harm's way, too. How can I warn them? What if the trollogs intrison them?"

"It is too late to help them now," said Wynnagar. "Besides, we cannot risk giving away the secret of your passage bed. If those trollogs realize how we escaped, they could follow us here!"

"How could they follow us when my bed is broken?"

Wynnagar retorted, "They need only the headboard and footboard. Let us hope the fiends destroy those pieces as well!"

"If we threw the boards off this mountaintop, the trollogs couldn't find them!" Kyleah declared. She started to seize the headboard, but Wynnagar and Medwyn firmly held her back.

"Don't!" Wynnagar warned her. "If you so much as nudge a splinter, the trogs are sure to notice! As former dryads, they may know the Oracle's words and might recognize the bed. We are in terrible danger here. Come! We must leave this place at once."

As if to confirm Wynnagar's words, the footboard flipped end-over-end to land flat on the ground, while the headboard rose above it. A shadowy form took shape between the two boards.

"Run!" cried Wynnagar.

Medwyn, Barley and Meghan dashed away. However, Kyleah lagged behind, waiting for Wynnagar. Mapleton's oldest resident had grabbed a broken leg from the bed and was holding it at the ready. Suddenly, a trollog appeared, standing on the footboard while pressing the headboard against its hooded head. With a fierce cry, Wynnagar struck the trollog with the bed leg, knocking the beast onto its back, where she continued thrashing it.

Seeing Kyleah frozen in place, Wynnagar cried, "Flee, you fool!" Even as the headboard lifted into the air again, Kyleah limped after her companions into the moon-shadowed forest. When she glanced back again, Wynnagar was grappling with her powerful enemy, while a second trollog was pulling her hair.

"Wynnagar! Wynnagar!" Kyleah cried.

"Fly . . . to the lake!" gasped Wynnagar. Then the hulking trollogs carried their struggling captive into the dark woods.

CHAPTER 13

THE HEARKENING HALL

Hobbling on her crutch, Kyleah was hard pressed to catch up with her companions. She plodded by moonsilvered trees, rocks and bushes in a sweaty haze until the ground sloped downward. Was she approaching another cliff edge? Then she spotted the glint of moonlight on water. As she came closer, Kyleah saw a placid lake nestled among the trees below her.

"Hurry up, Kyleah!" reedy voices called to her from the dark water. Small figures were stepping across the lake's surface. Kyleah stared and blinked. Surely the moonlight was muddling her eyes. Barley, Medwyn and Meghan were waving and shouting at her from the middle of the lake! Dumbfounded, Kyleah waved back.

Weak with grief and fatigue, she tottered through the trees down to the shoreline. Suddenly, woody fingers closed around her neck. "No intrisoning for you this time, shrimpy two-legs!" a harsh voice rumbled. "We'll spit you and your friends and roast you over a nice, hot fire. We trollogs never give up the chase!"

All at once, water geysered out of the lake, dousing Kyleah and her captor, who loosened his hold on her neck. Tentacles curled around her calf and yanked on her leg. Still gripping her crutch, she fell backward, screaming as rocks scraped her lacerated skin.

As the enraged trollog bent down to seize her again, she fought him off with her staff. More water sprayed the trollog's face. Then Kyleah was dragged feet first down the shore into the frigid lake.

The tentacles pulled her down, down into the deep water, where the moon's rays drowned in the darkness. Unable to swim, Kyleah panicked and drew in a lungful of icy, unforgiving lake water. Choking and gasping for air, she found no relief. Her ears popped from the pressure while stars danced before her eyes. Then even the stars winked out, leaving a black forgetfulness.

She was lying next to a radiant, glassy tree. Cool, sweet air flowed into her burning lungs, and sweet peace filled her heart.

"What are you doing here?" asked a voice from the grave.

Kyleah looked up to see Einwen sitting beside her. "My dear Einwen!" she cried. "I have missed you terribly! Where are we?"

"Hush!" said Einwen. "The King wishes to speak with you."

A pair of sandal-shod feet came to stand beside Kyleah, and she gazed up into a face shining like the sun. Yet, she felt no fear.

"You do not yet know Me, though others have told you about Me," said a strong, deep man's voice inside her head. "As I have loved you and gave My life for you, will you love Me, serve Me and follow Me all your days? The choice is yours to make, Kyleah."

"I chose Gaelathane and His Tree before coming here," Einwen said. "If you choose them, too, then we can always be together!"

Weeping, Kyleah knelt beside the Man. "I will!" she replied.

His hand touched her head. "Welcome to My family, dear Kyleah!" He said. "You must return now, for your work is not yet completed." Instantly, the Man, His Tree and Einwen vanished.

Kyleah awoke in darkness. Was this death? Had she really just seen her twin sister Einwen, or had it all been a dream? Freezing water lapped around her chest, and violent shivering racked her body. Even as she spat up water in spasms, she felt a warm glow spread throughout her being, as if someone had just told her a secret more marvelous than any heart could possibly contain.

The tentacles returned, crawling and tapping eel-like over her head and back. Terror seized her. Had the trollog dragged his prey underwater, first to toy cruelly with her and then to devour her?

"Do not fight the water, child," murmured a woman's voice. "Let it come up as it will. I nearly lost you, but by the grace of the Water Lord, I managed to revive you again. Forgive me for so hastily bringing you down here without the air to breathe. There was no time. That woodwalker was about to strangle you."

"Thank you for saving me," Kyleah croaked. "Where am I?"

"You are beneath the Listening Lake. What is your name?"

"Kyleah." Her echoing words sounded flat and unfamiliar.

"Here is your staff. It is rather heavy for one so young."

A familiar solid shape brushed against Kyleah's arm, and she grasped the crutch Rolin had lent her. "If we are truly under the lake," she said, "how is it I can still breathe air down here?"

"Let me show you." The tentacles grasped Kyleah's arm and guided her gently along a watery passage. After she had waded a few dozen yards, Kyleah felt the tunnel gradually rising and the water becoming shallower. Following her mysterious rescuer, she limped through the spacious passage until it opened onto a vast, glowing cavern. In the cave's center, a massive crystal column rose treelike from the floor, supporting a transparent, domed ceiling.

A silvery light shone through the dome, revealing Kyleah's guide as a slender, stately woman with greenish hair. She wore a loosely-fitting, gray frock that shed the water in beads. What Kyleah had mistaken for grasping tentacles were actually nimble, webbed fingers, which appeared red and swollen, as if burned.

Kyleah openly stared. She had never met anyone with webbed hands before, much less green hair. Once, while she and Einwen were swimming in a stagnant pond near Mapleton, floating water plants had entwined themselves in their hair, lending it a sickly, leafy-green tint. However, her rescuer's dripping, tangled locks were the color of sea-swells running before a gathering storm.

"Who—who are you?" Kyleah stammered.

Following her gaze, the woman smiled. "Do my hair and hands intrigue you? My name is Aquilla. The Water Lord gave us *naiades* and *daiades* green hair to help us blend in with the waters of lakes, rivers, and seas. Our hands and toes are webbed for swimming."

"But what are—what did you call yourself?" Kyleah asked.

"We are the *Maiades*—Memerren of the Water—or Water Folk, if you please. The naiades are water-women, or *naiads*. Daiades are water-men, or *daiads*. The Water Lord made us the caretakers of the Listening Lake. Mt. Argel is mostly crystalline rock, which amplifies sounds and funnels them into this lake, making it a sort of watery drum. We have trained our ears to detect the least of sounds, from the croaking of frogs in the shallows to the staccato pattering of raindrops on the forest floor. You are now standing in the Hearkening Hall, delved under the lake bed long ago. We often come here to gather news of the wide world outside."

Kyleah realized then that the chamber was echoing with strange, distorted noises. She heard measured thumping sounds that might have been trollogs tromping toward the lake. Next, confused splashing noises resounded in the Hearkening Hall.

Aquilla pointed a webbed finger overhead. "That is the sound of your pursuers swimming across the lake. We cannot let them reach the far side, where your friends are trapped on the shore between the lake and the cliffs. Ever since the maiades discovered this world years ago, we have prepared for this very day and hour. Our enemies must not escape; nay, they shall not escape!"

Kyleah looked up and quailed. Tons of dark water hung over her head. Only the fragile-looking crystal dome stood between her and the lake's great weight. High above the dome, pallid rays of moonlight filtered through the twilight like sunlight through torn clouds. Higher still, several dark specks that might have been paddling trollogs marred the lake's mirrored surface.

Clutching her crutch, Kyleah watched as Aquilla lightly laid her hand upon the central crystal column and tapped it twice.

Thunk. A dull, heavy sound echoed through the Hearkening Hall. Then the roaring began, a waterfall thundering that grew louder every second. Kyleah plugged her ears with her fingers.

Jabbing her hand at the crystal dome, Aquilla shouted at Kyleah, "We're straining the rake!" Or so the words sounded.

Far above the dome, where moonlight met water, a silvery dimple was forming under the lake's surface. The dimple widened and deepened, gradually stretching into a shiny, twisting rope.

Down, down the rope dropped until it was fluttering like a silver flame over the supporting pillar. Lowering and retreating as if unable to make up its mind, the rope finally touched the pillar's top and fattened into a writhing cable. The roar became a shriek.

Sometimes when the last dregs of maple syrup were draining from a cauldron in the sugarhouse, air would get into the pipes, making a sucking sound. The noise that now beat upon Kyleah's ears was a million times worse. She imagined the earth itself were in the throes of drowning, choking by degrees on air and water.

Wincing from the noise, Aquilla made a circling motion with her arm and webbed hand. In a flash, Kyleah understood. The naiad had really said, "We're *draining* the *lake!*" Torrents of water were sluicing through the hollow crystal column that supported the Hearkening Hall's domed ceiling, creating a huge whirlpool. The maelstrom dwarfed all the puny vortices Kyleah had ever seen forming and collapsing in the bottom of a maple syrup cauldron.

Transfixed, she watched the whirlpool snaking from the lake's surface to its bottom, drawing down air, leaves, debris—and a spinning mass of jumbled sticks and chunks of wood that she guessed were the remains of the swimming trollogs. After an hour or so, the Listening Lake gave up its last waters with a gurgle.

"Where did all the trollogs go?" Kyleah asked Aquilla.

The naiad gestured toward the floor. "We won't be seeing *them* again. What was left of them went down the main drain, which empties out of Mt. Argel's flank a thousand feet above the plain."

Aquilla rapidly opened and closed her webbed fingers, making a popping sound. Startled, Kyleah gasped and staggered back.

"I'm sorry!" Aquilla said. "I should have warned you. We maiads *cwelap*—clap our webs—to express emotion or raise an alarm. Now let us find your friends." Leading Kyleah out of the Hearkening Hall, Aquilla took her through a rising passage that ended under the stars near the steeply sloping lake shore. As she gulped in draughts of fresh night air, Kyleah gazed down into the emptied lake's shadowy, bowl-shaped bed. Tiered seats had been cut into the bowl's sides to create an amphitheater filled with thousands upon thousands of animated, murmuring maiads.

"Where did all those maiads come from?" Kyleah asked.

"From the Listening Lake," replied Aquilla. "Our friends who excavated the Hearkening Hall also created this fine amphitheater. Ordinarily, when convening a Conclave, we drain the lake straight down. However, if our home has become clogged with debris, we sit on those seats and push the water in a circle with our webbed hands while the lake is draining. The resulting whirlpool draws in all the flotsam and handily flushes it right out of Mt. Argel."

"How do you avoid being sucked down, too?"

"Once the whirlpool forms, we join hands!" Aquilla replied.

"But how can you hold your breath for so long?"

The naiad laughed. "We don't! We can breathe underwater."

Just then, Medwyn, Meghan and Barley ran up. Waving his arms, Barley jumped up and down like a jack-in-the-box.

"Wasn't that a *huuge* whirlpool, 'Leah?" he shouted. "It drained those Prowlers down the hole like bugs in a syrup kettle!"

"I saw the whole thing," said Kyleah. "Now please calm down!" After introducing her companions and Aquilla to one other, she described how the brave naiad had delivered her from the trollog on the lake shore. She didn't mention meeting Gaelathane and Einwen beside the Tree. Instead, she asked the others, "Didn't I see you all walking across the water? How did you manage that?"

Meghan giddily laughed. "It may have appeared so from afar. We were actually stepping on the backs of floating maiads!"

Aquilla explained, "In the Hearkening Hall, we heard your footfalls approaching as those woodwalkers pursued you, and we positioned ourselves in a line across the lake. When the first woodwalkers reached the water, we dove below the surface to avoid being seen. I swam up just in time to pull you in after me."

"Where is Wynnagar?" Medwyn asked Kyleah.

Kyleah burst into tears. "She is gone! To help me get away, she stayed behind and fended off the trollogs. I haven't seen her since. I wish the trollogs had taken me instead. I'm as useless as ever."

"No, you're not!" Meghan told her. "You rescued Medwyn and me from intrisonment, remember? Wynnagar gave her life for you because she loved you. We'll just have to go on without her."

Kyleah sniffled. "I always thought she was just a harmless old busybody who liked to whittle spiles in her spare time. Now it seems she was the best friend I ever had, and I didn't know it."

"We're your friends, too," Meghan assured her.

"If Wynnagar had a plan, I have no idea what it was," said Medwyn. "What shall we do now? We can't go back to Thalmos, because more trollogs might be lurking about Kyleah's house. We can't stay here, either, or the woodwalkers will find us again."

Meghan wistfully said, "Long ago, Gaelathane gave our King Elgathel a prophecy to help deliver us from Felgor. If only we had a new prophecy now to guide us! The Oracle tells us about Kyleah, the 'Gifted Girl' and her bed, but not how we are supposed to go about driving back the trollogs and rescuing our loved ones."

Reminded of the verses she had read in Winona's room, Kyleah said, "I found more of Larkin's prophecy under the stone table!

Steal not the nails o'er dripping pails,
Where wicked wight awaits;
The first to free intrisoned trees
Shall open Gundul's gates.

For buried sword of Gundul's lord
Shall fit the slotted stone;
A fateful twist of weaponed fist
Shall seat him on his throne.

Though hidden horde obey his sword,
No mortal can prevail
O'er deadly sprite that gnaws the night,
Intrisoned by a nail.

Then she shall come who cannot run;
This two-legs goes on three;
She'll hold the blade not mortal-made,
Who touches heart of tree.

Though wooden band will fear to stand
Before the royal tree,
The living staff who lacks a half
Will root the trolls who flee.

"I don't recall hearing those last three staves," Medwyn said.

"Neither do I," Meghan remarked. "Long ago, Gaelathane must have entrusted this prophecy to Queen Winona. To ensure its preservation, she recorded the verses in two places—under the table in the Hallowfast and on a parchment in Gannon's cellar. By the time Larkin found the parchment, only the first two staves had survived. That old cellar is full of damp, pests and mold!"

Kyleah said, "I know the first and second verses of this riddle have already come true, but what does the rest of it mean?"

Barley piped up. "I can answer that! You 'cannot run' 'cuz you're a *three-legs*. Your third leg is a crutch." He smirked at her.

She glared back at him. "Three-legs," indeed! She would give her brother that third leg in the teeth if he didn't stop his teasing.

"Speaking of 'thirds,'" said Medwyn, "the third stave bears out Bembor's warnings of the trollogs' treacherous ways. But if Larkin was the 'first to free intrisoned trees,' how will he 'open Gundul's gates'? If the 'buried sword of Gundul's lord' refers to Felgroth, 'buried' in a tree, what 'slotted stone' does the sword 'fit'?"

"What is 'Gundul'?" Kyleah asked her.

"It is the underworld—a place of eternal suffering and regret. Gaelathane died to deliver us from Gundul's awful torment." She added, "You alone among us have held Felgor's sword—'the blade not mortal-made.' Yet, I always thought Felgor was a mortal."

Meghan said, "He was, until he took an ashtag sythan-ar to prolong his life. Anyway, I don't see how this riddle can help us."

"Could 'the living staff' be a lightstaff?" Kyleah asked.

"I would agree with you, except that 'who' usually refers to a person," Meghan replied. "That verse simply makes no sense."

Medwyn turned to Aquilla. "What will you do now without your lake? The dawn swiftly approaches, and you have nowhere to hide from the sun. You and your people don't wish to become worldwalkers like me, do you? The life of a mortal can be bitter."

"Indeed we do not!" Aquilla replied. "We will retreat to our sunless tunnels and caverns below the lake until it refills." She waved a webbed hand at the empty lake bed. Water was gushing into it from hidden inlets, forming a rapidly rising pool.

"May we join you?" Kyleah asked the naiad. "We can't return home because of the trollogs, and we have nowhere else to go."

"I was hoping you would be our guests, in the Water Lord's name," said Aquilla merrily. "Our King Corwyn will wish to meet you. It has been many a year since we have entertained any of the 'webless ones,' as we call all who live upon the face of the earth."

Aquilla led Kyleah and her companions to a hole in the ground beside the lake shore. Glancing into the opening, Kyleah saw no stairs or handrail. The tunnel looked altogether uninviting. "How are we supposed to climb down there?" she asked suspiciously.

"You aren't!" Aquilla replied. "This is the quickest route to the Chamber of Living Waters that lies beneath the Hearkening Hall. I will see you in half a cwelap!" The naiad hopped into the hole and disappeared into the darkness. Kyleah was still staring after her when the sun's bright eye peered above the world's distant rim, and golden light flooded Aquilla's tunnel.

CHAPTER 14

KING CORWYN

E eeeiiiiiyy!" Kyleah yelled as her heart sprang into her throat. She had just eased into Aquilla's tunnel when her feet flew out from under her, and she began hurtling down a winding, slippery chute. Clasping her staff, she barreled feet first into darkness. Her companions were screaming close behind her.

Just when she thought her wild ride would never end, Kyleah shot out of the chute, sailed into space and plopped into a frigid subterranean pool. As she sank under the numbing water, all the air in her lungs whooshed out in a painful, bubbling shriek.

Then webbed hands seized her and drew her out of the water. Panting, she lay beside the pool clutching her crutch, wishing she were a better swimmer. Her wounded back ached and burned.

Just then, three shrieking bundles whizzed out of the chute and splashed into the pool. The maiads retrieved the new arrivals as well and helped them dry off with soft, thick sea-sponges.

Aquilla's companions were also green haired. The naiads wore frocks of pastel yellows, browns and gray-blues, in contrast to the brighter greens and reds of the daiads' shorter tunics. The maiads cwelapped in wonder at the visitors' webless fingers and toes.

"How can you swim without webs?" a naiad asked Kyleah.

"I don't," she confessed. "I sink!" After nearly drowning twice in one day, she wanted nothing more to do with the water. Barley, on the other hand, was begging her to go down the chute again.

"Not on your life; once was quite enough!" she retorted.

"Is this any way to treat your guests?" Meghan was telling Aquilla. "You could have warned us we were in for a dunking!"

"Forgive me!" laughed the naiad. "I had forgotten not everyone enjoys the water as much as we do. This 'maiad-slide' is a quick way of escaping our foes or the deadly light of dawn. Countless generations of maiads have slid down that race, wearing its stone smooth. We also feed water into the chute to keep it slippery."

Kyleah and her dripping companions followed their maiadin hosts down a dark hallway. Feeling thoroughly miserable, Kyleah was relieved to find the floor of this tunnel was comfortably dry.

The passage drove on straight and level for some thirty yards, ending in a shimmering curtain. Suddenly, two burly daiadin guards armed with three-pronged stone spears popped out of opposing alcoves in the walls. The guards lowered their tridents across the curtain to block the entry, barring further progress.

"Halt!" growled one guard. "Who goes there? State your names and your business in the Chamber of Living Waters."

Aquilla touched the guard's cheek. "Don't be so stuffy, Terrill; it's only me and some friends! Now let us pass, for you wouldn't want to keep the king waiting, would you? These are his guests."

"Very well, madam," said Terrill. He and his fellow guard raised their tridents, allowing Aquilla and the other maiads to move through the curtain. Medwyn, Barley and Meghan followed.

Last of all, Kyleah limped through. To her astonishment, the curtain was not made of fabric, as she had supposed. Rather, it was a shining sheet of continuously flowing water. Passing through it, she was briefly showered with a spray of fine, cool droplets.

Beyond the water-curtain lay an immense chamber echoing with the sound of splashing water. In the cavern's center stood five tall crystal trees spouting fountains of water hundreds of feet into the air. Across the cave rippled another water-wall. The Chamber of Living Waters had been aptly named. Kyleah crossed the floor.

The glowing, glassy fountains reminded her of the Tree she had seen while visiting the King. When she touched one of the trunks, it rang like a neck-bell. The shining trees encircled a lily pond where the falling waters collected. Amongst the pink water lilies stood a throne carved from a single block of rose quartz.

The far water-wall parted around the figure of a tall, erect man garbed in flowing, golden robes. A crown woven of white water-lily blossoms graced his greenish-gray hair. Yet, his noble face wore the long years lightly. Wading into the fountain pond from the far side, he ascended the throne and sat back. Then he beckoned to Kyleah and her companions, inviting them into the water.

"I'm not going in there!" Kyleah protested. "After sliding down that chute, I won't dry out for a month and a year as it is."

"No ordinary waters flow into the King's Pool," Aquilla said, brushing a stray green hair from her smooth forehead. "These are the living waters that spring from the Tree-scions the Water Lord planted for us here. However, if you have misgivings about the pool, I will enter first and speak with the king on your behalf."

"Please do!" said Kyleah, shivering in her wet clothes.

Wading into the pond, Aquilla bowed and said, "Good King Corwyn, I pray your mercy. These webless folk have evidently found their way into our world by the passage-wood bed of which the Oracle speaks. They are Medwyn, worldwalker and Queen of the Golden Wood; Meghan daughter of Marlis; Kyleah, the girl to whom the bed belongs; and her brother Barley." Aquilla's face clouded with concern. "I know neither her origins nor his."

The king waved his hand dismissively. "The origins of our honored guests do not concern me so much as their purpose in coming here. Water is water, no matter whence it springs. We are all the Water Lord's creations. First, though, I must ask everyone to remove your rings and other articles of metal. You may give them to Aquilla, and she will return them when you leave us."

Looking puzzled, Meghan dropped her necklace and Medwyn her wedding ring into a cloth bag that Aquilla held open for them. Holding the sack at arm's length as if it were filled with poisonous snakes, the naiad gingerly hung it on a smooth crystal branch.

"I intend no offense, dear guests," said King Corwyn. "Though most memerren can tolerate the touch of all metals but iron, we maiades cannot abide the presence of any metal whatsoever."

Kyleah thought back to the day Wynnagar had confronted her with the bag of intrisoning-spikes. It was not rust Kyleah had seen on the worldwalker's palm, but fiery welts the iron had raised.

The king sniffed the air and frowned. "Are you sure you have no more articles of metal on or about your persons?" he asked.

Barley surrendered a set of jacks Branagan had once given him as a Yuletide present, and Meghan found a pair of gold earrings in her pocket. These objects also went into Aquilla's sack. Kyleah noted the naiad was careful to avoid touching any of the items.

"Now that we have dispensed with that trifling matter, let me introduce myself properly," said the king. "I am Corwyn, King of the Mt. Argel maiades, by the Water Lord's leave. Welcome, guests; what brings you to my lowly kingdom beneath the lake? We rarely have mortal visitors from the worlds of tree and sun."

As Medwyn and Meghan spoke in turn of their adventures, the king's head bowed, his eyes sank into their sockets, and his cheeks hollowed. "You say Malroth walks the earth again?" he rasped. "These are ill tidings indeed! If we do not stop him now, he will finish the rebellion he began when the world was young. Having the black sword Felgroth, he may prove difficult to defeat."

Aquilla said, "If we mustered the memerren from all the Water Lord's worlds, surely then we could overcome Malroth's hordes!"

Pop! Pop! Corwyn cwelapped his webbed hands. "I think not," he said. "Now that the brollogs are hatching, they will multiply like frogs. We must exile Malroth by felling his passage trees."

"You can't cut down those trees!" Meghan gasped. "My grand-father and great-aunt would be exiled. They live in Thalmos!"

"My relatives do, too!" Kyleah said, but nobody paid her any attention. The others had apparently forgotten she was there.

"Alas!" moaned Medwyn. "Must we choose between killing our own kind and saving the Leaf Lord's worlds from the trollogs?"

"Anyway," Meghan added, "we can't possibly find and destroy all those torsils, and Malroth needs only one to make passage."

"Mortals used trickery to intrison the trollogs before," Medwyn said. "I doubt the trogs will fall for the yarn-trick a second time."

"Nonetheless, we shall beat them!" Meghan fiercely declared.

"In the meantime," said Corwyn, "allow me to offer you and your friends a proper maiad greeting. Please step into my pool."

Barley, Medwyn and Meghan waded toward the king. Instead of shaking their hands in Thalmosian fashion, however, Corwyn sandwiched each proffered hand flat between his webbed ones.

When Kyleah's turn came, she unsteadily lowered herself into the pool on trembling legs. The water was curiously warm and soothing. Steadying herself with her staff, she approached the king. Corwyn pressed her hand between both of his own. His webs felt moist and supple, like strips of sun-warmed seaweed.

Suddenly, the king's face paled. Gasping, he released Kyleah's fingers as if she were infected with some dreadful disease.

"I smell the scent of gold upon you!" he hoarsely cried.

"I have noticed the metal taint upon her as well," said Aquilla. She held up her arms, which bore crimson streaks and blotches.

Kyleah's stomach was aching with hunger. Her head detached itself from her body and floated above it. As in a dream, she looked down upon the gold bracelet still hanging from her neck. Then the tree-fountains began to move. They spun 'round and 'round faster and faster, until crystal trees and gushing water blended in a white blur, and her body sank beneath the fragrant water lilies.

She awoke lying beside her crutch on the brink of the King's Pool. Her back was burning unbearably. Shadowy shapes were gathered around her. "No wonder she fainted!" said one of the shapes. "She hasn't eaten a blessed thing since Gannon's oatcakes yesterday morning in Thalmos. It's a marvel she made it this far."

"Don't forget she's been *tollashed* as well," said another voice. Then cool, sweet liquid poured down her throat. She coughed.

"Sit her up, or she'll choke!" someone said, and several hands pushed Kyleah upright. A soft petal nudged her lips. Tilting back her head, she swallowed more of the syrupy liquid. Medwyn, Meghan, Corwyn and Barley were standing over her, while Aquilla was offering her a lily blossom filled with a clear fluid.

"That's it; drink some more!" she urged Kyleah. "The juice of the river-cane plant slakes thirst and eases all hunger pangs."

"Get away from me!" Kyleah croaked. "The metal will sting you again. I forgot a gold bracelet is hanging around my neck."

"Not any more!" said Meghan. She held up Kyleah's bracelet by its leather cord. "I removed this before you woke up."

"My bracelet!" Kyleah gasped, reaching for it. "Give it back!"

Meghan shook her head. "You don't want to hurt our maiad friends, do you? If Barley and I hadn't dragged you out of that pool, you might have drowned. Aquilla didn't dare touch you again for fear of being burned even worse." Meghan shook Aquilla's cloth sack, and it clinked. "After I dry off your bracelet, I'm going to place it in this bag with the rest of our trinkets and jewelry."

"I've never seen that bracelet before," Barley told his sister. "Is it really gold? Where did you get it? Did you steal it from the mayor? I've heard he's got gobs of treasure under his house."

"I didn't steal it!" Kyleah snapped. "Mother gave it to me."

"She didn't give me anything," Barley pouted.

Medwyn asked to see the bracelet, and Meghan handed it to her. The worldwalker turned it over in her hands. "I haven't seen one of these in years!" she said. "In days of old, a dryad-suitor might offer such a bracelet to his beloved in token of betrothal."

"But Larissa married a mortal, did she not?" asked Meghan.

"Apparently," said Medwyn sadly. "Perhaps she loved a dryad before she surrendered to the sun. We memerren have a saying:

Nothing shall our love betray
Except the coming of the day;
With the dawn the old has gone,
When moonlit loves must pass away.

"What does that mean?" Kyleah asked.

"Once a dryad or nymph becomes a worldwalker," Medwyn explained, "he or she drifts away from those friends and loved ones still bound to their trees. Long and bitter are the ballads our bards have sung in memory of the doomed love between memer and worldwalker or mortal. Love often demands a terrible price."

"How well we maiads know those tragic tales!" said Corwyn. "Many a mortal lad or lass has drowned while chasing a water-sprite frolicking in a moonlit river or lake. For that very reason, we are careful to hide ourselves from prying eyes, even at night."

"My mother never loved anyone else but my father," Kyleah said. "Wynnagar would agree, for she knew my mother well."

Medwyn handed the bracelet back to Meghan, who wiped it dry with her sleeve. "Why, look at this!" she said. "I've found an inscription engraved around the inside. The script is too fine for me to read. What tool could engrave words so small and neat?"

"I've never noticed any writing on my bracelet before," Kyleah sniffed. Taking it from Meghan, she pressed the gold band to her eye. Silvery threads of flowery script flowed along the bracelet's curving inner surface. "I can't read the words, either," she said, disappointed. "Why didn't I see this inscription earlier, anyway?"

Medwyn observed, "The Tree's light can reveal much that has long lain in darkness. Even in the light of day, that lettering might never appear. Such inscriptions were meant to be read only by moonlight. In bygone years, we memerren often called upon our faery friends to etch messages of love upon these 'troth-braces,' as we call them. Larissa's love must have composed this poem to his betrothed before she walked into the world of mortal men."

Defeat clouded Aquilla's blue eyes. "If faery fingers penned those words, then only the sharpest of faery eyes can read them."

Suddenly, Meghan frantically patted her pockets. Pulling out an oval lump of clear glass, she announced, "I have something better than faery eyes! This lens from my father's old starglass can magnify small objects many times." Taking the bracelet back from Kyleah, Meghan put the glass to her eye and held up the golden band. When she lowered the lens, she wore a triumphant smile.

"What do the words say?" asked Kyleah breathlessly.

Meghan replied, "This troth-poem was not addressed to Larissa. I believe she herself wrote it to her first and truest love."

"To my father?" Kyleah asked with a gleam of hope.

"I'm afraid not," Meghan answered.

CHAPTER 15

LARISSA'S LOVE

Kyleah's cheeks burned, and she hung her head in shame. Then it was true. Her mother must have given her heart to a dryad before she had met Branagan. Yet, Kyleah had always felt the love between her parents was deep and enduring.

"Who was he?" Medwyn asked, leaning forward expectantly. Meghan smiled slyly. "Here is what Larissa's bracelet says:

To Gaelathane I plight my troth,
Who loved me ere I knew Him well;
While men be mean and trollogs wroth,
I shall await the tolling bell.

Kyleah went weak with relief. Her mother's first love had been no ordinary memer, but the great King Whom Kyleah had met!

"It is well Larissa gave herself first of all to the Leaf Lord," said Medwyn. "'The greatest love is that which cometh from above.'"

"From above?" Kyleah asked. What did Medwyn mean?

"Why, yes," said King Corwyn. "The blessed Water Lord lives in *Gaelessa*, a wondrous land far above any world watered by the rain He sends. In His world, we memerren need not fear the light of day, for the Tree's light brings only healing and wholeness."

126

Medwyn nodded. "We look forward to the day when naiads and daiads, nymphs and dryads no longer must hide themselves from the sun's burning eye whilst it rides high in the sky."

"But what is the 'tolling bell'?" Kyleah asked.

"Wait—let me read the rest of this riddle," said Meghan.

A perfect glass for limping lass
Lies waiting in the wood;
The perfect sword Lucambra's lord
Gave up for greater good.

The flashing thing fit for a king
Hides fast within a tree;
In darkness sealed, to be revealed
When fire shall set it free.

Not made by hand of maid or man,
This trollish bane shall be;
With bloodless bite the blade shall smite
The mocking enemy.

King Corwyn said, "By the Living Waters that flow from the Five Crystal Trees, I hear the Water Lord's voice in this riddle. Yet, the maiades have no need of swords, for the water conceals us from our enemies, and no mirror of mortal make can rival the Listening Lake when it lies still as glass beneath the watchful moon."

Aquilla waved her webbed hand at the cavern ceiling. "Sire, surely this riddle was written for nymphs and dryads, for it speaks of a 'wood' and a 'tree.' We maiads have no part in this matter. The deep waters of our lake shall shelter us, whatever may betide."

Corwyn's face darkened. "I think not. Malroth would find a way to drain our lake and enslave or destroy us all. Like it or not, we must do all we can to assist these our guests in their mission, whatever that may be, though it cost us both lake and life."

"And what is their mission?" Aquilla asked him. "In addition to the Oracle, our visitors have brought to light two prophecies hitherto unknown to us. Is it not folly to send these people back whence they came without knowing what they are supposed to do? I wish the Water Lord would make His will plainer to us!"

Meghan dropped the bracelet into Aquilla's bag. "Gaelathane rarely gives us but one prophecy to follow," she said. "Rather more often, He speaks through several of His servants, as He has done through Queen Winona and Larissa. Since each new prophecy tends to shed further light on previous ones, I believe our two riddles must tie together somehow. Both speak of swords. Larissa's prophecy mentions a 'perfect sword' that 'Lucambra's lord gave up for greater good.' As I think of it, those words can refer only to my father, who gave up Elgathel's sword rather than let it fall into the hands of Larkin and his cutthroat band of renegade trollogs."

Kyleah decided she must be the "limping lass" in the riddle's second stave. "What do maiads eat for breakfast?" she asked. Though tasty, the river-cane juice hadn't staved off her hunger for very long. "And what does the 'perfect glass' mean, anyway?"

"If by 'breakfast' you mean the morning meal," said Corwyn, "we are preparing a light repast that I hope will suit your tastes."

"'Glass' refers to a mirror, in our people's parlance," Medwyn explained. "However, the Leaf Lord may have intended a symbolic meaning or an actual piece of glass, such as Meghan's lens."

Aquilla said, "I fear we maiads cannot supply you with any mirrors, since their backs are coated with silver or other metals."

"Hand-mirrors are easily found," said Meghan impatiently. "If the second stave speaks of the sword Elgathel forged, though, why does the fourth describe a blade not made by human hand?"

"Why indeed?" said Medwyn. "Winona's prophecy also speaks of a 'blade not mortal-made.' Since that ancient *pos*, or riddle, tells of the 'buried sword of Gundul's lord,' Felgor's and Elgathel's swords may one day both cross on the battlefield of prophecy."

"One of those swords shall be a 'trollish bane,'" Meghan said. "I suppose Elgathel's sword 'shall smite/the mocking enemy' 'with bloodless bite,' since our cruel foes lack both flesh and blood."

King Corwyn put in, "Perhaps we should rather ask ourselves, 'When is a sword not a sword, and a mirror not a mirror?' If I am not wholly mistaken, therein lies the crux of this riddle."

Meghan groaned. "If Bembor were here, he could interpret this prophecy. On past adventures, he has always led us aright."

"What about breakfast?" Kyleah broke in. Her poor stomach was rumbling and grumbling most dreadfully, to Barley's delight.

"Breakfast? Of course. Let us adjourn!" said Corwyn grandly. He and Aquilla led their dripping guests out of the Chamber of Living Waters, down a long passage and into yet another cavern hewn out of the mountain's heart. This room was lit by green-glowing globes set in wall-alcoves. The cave featured more water-curtains, which sectioned the space into neat cubicles containing mattresses made of some smooth, milky material. Aquilla led each of Kyleah's companions in turn to a different water-booth.

"Hullo! What are you doing here?" a voice called as Kyleah passed one of the booths. Robin son of Rimlin was sitting on a mattress, pouring water from a tin pitcher into a glass globe.

"I should ask the same of you!" Kyleah said in astonishment.

Robin shrugged. "That 'Vinegar' woman brought me here. She said I would be safe underground. These webby people keep me busy filling their globe-lights for hours on end. Otherwise, I guess I'd be bored. At least the webbies feed me three meals a day."

"'Vinegar'?" Kyleah laughed. "Don't you mean, 'Wynnagar'?"

"Her name sounded like 'Vinegar' to me, and she looked just as sour." Robin yawned. "Did you come here to bring me home?"

"No, at least not now. What makes those globes glow?"

"It's the water I put in 'em," Robin said. "Once each day, the webbies fill a big stone basin with hot-springs water they draw from a deep well that's five levels beneath us. After a month or so, the water stops glowing, so these glass balls have to be refilled."

"But why are you the one to refill them?" she asked him.

"I can answer that," said Aquilla, entering the cubicle to join Kyleah. "It has always been a chore to carry the luminescent well-water up from the collecting basin. Since all our vessels are made of stone, glass or crystal, they shatter when dropped, and most are very heavy. The glass globes are especially delicate. When Wynnagar brought Robin here, I realized he could handle this ceremonial silver pitcher without harm to himself or the pitcher. That's when I put him to work filling our water-lights."

"Time for a refill!" said Robin, scurrying out of the cubicle.

Kyleah followed Aquilla to a booth next to Barley's. Inside, the water-curtains musically murmured as Kyleah flopped down on the cubicle's mattress and stretched out with a grateful sigh.

All at once, a girl of about Kyleah's age stepped through one of the water-curtains. She was carrying an earthen basin, which she set down on the floor. Water streamed off her lithe limbs and from the long green hair plastered onto her head. Her twinkling blue eyes and pleasant face were a startling mirror of Aquilla's own.

Kyleah reluctantly sat up. "Who are you?" she asked the girl.

"I am Hannith," she replied. "Aquilla is my mother. She sent me here to bring you some nourishment and to look after you."

Kyleah peered into the large pot. Four wooden bowls shaped like lotus blossoms floated on the surface of the water that filled the basin. One bowl held slices of a dark bread; another contained pieces of a white fish; nuts were heaped in a third; and chunks of something like golden radish roots swam in the fourth dish.

"What is in these bowls?" Kyleah warily asked Hannith.

"This is bulrush-seed bread," the naiad replied, pointing at the first dish. "The other bowls hold broiled trout, roasted lotus nuts and candied water ginger. I hope you will enjoy your meal. I have heard that mortal palates are sometimes difficult to please."

Kyleah's palate was not at all difficult to please. Still famished, she devoured the contents of all four bowls. The trout tasted moist and flaky; the bread was heavy and rich, while the crunchy lotus nuts reminded her of roasted chestnuts. The candied water ginger was as tangy and sweet as the wild ginger roots her mother used to gather in the deep woods and boil in Branagan's maple syrup.

While Kyleah ate, Hannith stood under the water-curtain. She looked as comfortable in the curtain as a fish lazing in a stream.

Kyleah stared at her. "What are you doing there? Bathing?"

Hannith laughed. "If we maiads are deprived of water for more than a few hours, we dry up and die. Water is our very life and breath, for we take it in as naturally as you mortals breathe air."

"So you cannot drown, then?" Kyleah asked her.

"Does the dryad suffocate in his tree? Neither can the maiad perish beneath the sea. Now you must eat to regain your strength."

Kyleah was scraping the last morsels of ginger root out of the bowl when a rhythmic *thump-thump-thump* came from the cubicle next to hers. She followed Hannith through the water-curtain to find Barley gleefully jumping up and down on his mattress.

"Look how high I'm going, 'Leah!" he shouted.

"No!" Hannith cried. "You mustn't—"

It was too late. When Barley came down again, the mattress burst asunder, flooding the floor. Stunned, Barley stood amidst the remains of the mattress. "What happened?" he whimpered.

Kyleah couldn't help herself. Laughter bubbled out of her in a merry torrent. When her giggling fit had passed, she told Barley, "You may not think you have any 'special talents,' but you do! You have a talent for getting into mischief, dear little brother."

Hannith stared in dismay at the ruined mattress. "I see nothing amusing about destroying one of our beds! It takes weeks to make a watertight mattress from the air-sac of a Giant Sea Pillow."

"A Giant Sea Pillow!" said Barley. "What is that?"

"It's a kind of jellyfish," Hannith replied with a scowl.

Barley gulped. "I've been jumping on a *jellyfish*?"

Kyleah suddenly felt ill. "And I've been lying on one!"

Overcome with weariness, she returned to her cubicle and lay down. Lulled by the sound of splashing water and the mattress's undulating motion, she fell into a deep sleep. When she awoke, her back felt better, as if the living waters in the King's Pool had soothed her welts. Hannith was standing in the water-curtain.

"I trust your sleep refreshed you!" said the young naiad.

Hannith then took Kyleah and Barley to rejoin Meghan and Medwyn, who had also eaten and rested. All at once, a daiad rushed into the hall from a side entrance and frantically cwelapped his finger-webs. *Pop! Pop! Pop!* In turn, other maiads cwelapped their own webs. Like ripples spreading across the Listening Lake, the echoing alarm swiftly traveled throughout that vast cavern.

"Our worst fear has come upon us!" Hannith told her guests. "Some horrible hamadryads have sneaked into our tunnels. We can't hide in the lake; it isn't full enough yet. Let us flee to the Chamber of Living Waters. The trees' light will protect us there."

"No!" said Medwyn. "If we split up, we'll force the trollogs to divide their forces. While you, Kyleah and Barley hide in the Chamber of Living Waters, Meghan and I will go elsewhere and act as decoys. May the Leaf Lord be with us all and protect us!"

As if on cue, dark figures appeared at the cavern's far end. Maiads scattered as the trollogs advanced upon Kyleah. "She who bears the black sword's brand belongs to us!" they bellowed.

"Run!" cried Hannith.

While Meghan and Medwyn dashed off to draw the trollogs away, Kyleah tried to keep up with Barley and Hannith. Through a twisting tunnel she followed them until they ducked through a bright doorway. She caught up with them by the King's Pool.

"Hooray! We're safe!" Barley crowed. His celebration was short lived. The cavern's water-curtains parted, and out stepped fifteen trollogs. They were wearing their black cloaks backward, hooding their faces and shielding their bodies from the trees' light. Blinded by their hoods, the weaving, black-gloved woodwalkers shuffled toward Kyleah, snuffling as they smelled out their prey. Others hung back to guard the chamber's two curtained entrances.

"Oh, no!" Hannith wailed, waving her webbed hands like fans. "We're surrounded! We can't possibly fight off so many trollogs."

"We could try climbing these trees to get away," said Kyleah.

"They're too slippery," Hannith said. Then she gasped, "The King's Pool! I forgot it has a drain. We can swim down that outlet into the main drain below us. It is our only chance of escape."

"Swim?" said Kyleah doubtfully. "What if we get stuck?"

"I'll go down first," said Hannith. "Then you and Barley can follow. The current should carry you through. If either of you hangs up inside the drain, I can swim back in and pull you free."

Noticing Aquilla's sack hanging from one of the tree-branches, Kyleah cried, "My bracelet! I can't leave my bracelet behind!"

"There's no time!" Hannith said. "See you at the bottom!"

Hannith dove beneath the water lilies. Barley followed. In spite of his small size, he was a strong and fearless swimmer. Kyleah was neither. As she reached for Aquilla's bag, a groping trollog backed her up to the pool's edge. Hugging her crutch, she fell in.

Diving under the water's surface, she yielded to the relentless pull of a powerful current that sucked her into the black depths of the pool's drain hole. Heart hammering and lungs screaming, she hurtled helplessly along until the drain spat her out into a swift stream. A webbed hand snatched her from the icy water.

"Up we go!" said Hannith, depositing Kyleah and her crutch on the stream's damp bank. Kyleah struggled to catch her breath.

"Wasn't that fun, Sis?" Barley teased her.

"No!" she sputtered. Her brother could be so insufferable!

"We must make haste!" Hannith said, her voice echoing over the sound of running water. "If my people drain the lake again to flush out our foes, this tunnel will be the first to flood. We had better find a side passage leading to higher ground. This way!"

However, all the side tunnels they found led to disappointing dead ends. As they tramped farther, the suffocating darkness began to lift, and Hannith said, "We are nearing the drain's outlet in Mt. Argel's flank. If we go much farther, I'll become a worldwalker!"

Then Kyleah heard splashing sounds behind her. "Hush!" said Hannith. When everyone stopped moving, the splashing noises also ceased. "Our enemies are following us!" the naiad whispered. "They must have smelled us out. Pray to the Water Lord we can find a proper passage before they catch us—or the sun does."

Kyleah prayed. The deadly daylight lay lurking just ahead when a tunnel branched off to the left. Wading across the stream, the three fled down the passageway. With her every faltering step, Kyleah's crutch tapped loudly on unyielding stone, betraying her presence. Down, down the tunnel sank into unguessable depths.

At length, a distant light glimmered ahead. As Kyleah and her companions approached, they found two sputtering torches set on either side of a riveted iron door. The words, "POSITIVELY NO ADMITTANCE!" were boldly stamped into the door's face.

"May the trollogs take me!" gasped Hannith. "We have come upon the kingdom of the *gonomia*, where all tunnels end. We must find a way around or through this door—or die trying!"

CHAPTER 16

TOEFOOT

G onomia!" Kyleah exclaimed. "Who or what is that?"
"I haven't the time to explain," said Hannith. "Those wood-walkers will catch up to us any minute now! Please help me find a way to open this metal door before it's too late."

"But it hasn't got a doorknob or latch or bolt," Kyleah argued. Except for the rows of rivets, the door was completely smooth.

Hannith beat on the barrier with her webbed fists, crying out in pain as the iron burned her sensitive hands. "In the name of Gaelathane, please let us in!" she shouted. No voice answered from within, nor did the door budge. *Tramp! Tramp!* The sound of marching trollog feet echoed down the clammy corridor.

Pulling Hannith back, Kyleah raised her staff and drove it with all her might end-first into the door. *Boom! Boom!* The iron slab thundered under the impact. She was drawing back the crutch for another blow when—*Click! Clack! Screech!*—a succession of harsh metallic noises ran through the door from top to bottom.

At last, the door groaned open an inch or two, and a long, bulbous nose poked out. "What do you want?" growled a voice through the crack. "Can't you read what's written on this door? 'Positively No Admittance!' That means you. Now go away!"

Quick as a flash, Kyleah jammed her crutch tip into the crack before the door could slam shut. "Please, sir! Open the door and let us in! If you don't, the trollogs will catch us and devour us."

"What! Trollogs? Down here? Why didn't you say so before?"

The crack widened just enough for Kyleah and company to slip through. Then it banged shut again with terrible finality.

Inside, Kyleah found a narrow room with a raised brick fire pit at its center. In the pit, a roaring fire sent sparks and smoke swirling into a conical metal hood that funneled them into a sooty chimney-hole. Around the cone's lip hung pots, pans, bellows, rolling-pins, pokers, shovels and assorted other utensils. Wooden picture-frames by the thousands lay stacked willy-nilly on the floor. Hundreds more were heaped on sagging shelves. Some of the frames were empty, but most held ornate silvered mirrors.

Surrounded by so much metal, Hannith wilted. Scuttling away from the door, she crouched whimpering against one wall.

Click. Clack. Clunk. A bald little man was perched on a ladder affixed to the back of the door. He was deftly twisting, pushing and turning an astonishing array of locks, dead bolts and catches. After reaching the bottom, he hopped down from the ladder.

"There!" he said, dusting off his calloused hands. "No trollog will get through that door, I'll wager. I've got thirteen locks, one for each of the ancient gonomial monarchs. Who are you three, and why have you come here with trollogs at your heels? Speak up, now; didn't your elders teach you it's not polite to gawk?"

Kyleah couldn't help staring. Never in all her life had she seen such an odd little person. Wearing a heavy leather apron over his grimy jerkin and trousers, he stood only three and a half feet tall. His neatly brushed gray beard hung down to his knees. The shining dome of his bald head reflected the firelight like a glass Yuletide ornament, while his nose and ears looked too large for the rest of him. The mirth of many a private jest sparkled in his deep-set eyes, as ageless and blue as glacier-fed mountain lakes.

Kyleah introduced herself, Barley and Hannith. Then she said, "Thank you for letting us in here. You have saved our lives! But who are you and what is this place? And why all the mirrors?"

    The little man drew himself up, thrust his thumbs behind his apron strings and propped one of his battered boots on a stack of framed mirrors. "Toefoot's the name. This is my workshop, and these are my mirrors. I'm known as the 'Mirror Master.' Now what do you want? People hardly ever come down here unless they want something. And how did you find me in the first place?"

Barley gaped at Toefoot's oversized boot. "Golly, you do have awfully big feet!" he said. "And you're even shorter than I am!"

"But I'm awfully strong!" Toefoot gruffly retorted. Grabbing Barley by his leather belt, the sturdy Mirror Master hoisted him off the ground with his sinewy arms before setting him down again. Barley's eyes grew as large and round as copper syrup cauldrons.

Kyleah wasn't sure whether she could trust Toefoot. "We weren't looking for you," she said. "We ended up here by accident while trying to escape the trollogs. You're not a trollog, too, are you?" Some of the burlies she had seen were about Toefoot's size.

Toefoot snorted indignantly, and a pair of thick eyebrows inched up his shiny forehead like twin furry caterpillars. "Me, a trollog? Hardly. I've knocked a few in the head with my pickax, though." He chuckled to himself as if relishing the memory. "I'm a *Gonomion*, or a 'Gnome.' Gaelathane created our kind to burrow and excavate beneath the earth. Some of the silver we mine finds its way onto my mirrors. How do I know you are telling me the truth? After all, the maiads don't let mortals into their kingdom."

All at once—*Bang!*—the door shuddered under a heavy blow. More thudding shocks followed one upon another. Kyleah backed away from the door, fearing it would give way before the relentless pounding from the opposite side. Terrified, Barley clung to her.

Toefoot's beard bristled and his face darkened. Scurrying up the ladder, he slid an iron beam across the door, barring it. Next, he climbed down and pulled over four low wooden stools. At his invitation, Kyleah and Barley seated themselves on two, while Hannith huddled forlornly on the third. The plucky gnome settled on the fourth. Then he took out a long-stemmed pipe and lit it, puffing perfect smoke rings that lazily sailed around the ceiling.

"Now let's hear your tale from the beginning!" he said.

Over the din of the booming door, Kyleah retold her many adventures. When she had finished, Toefoot stroked his beard and eyed her speculatively. "So you think you're the Gifted Girl, eh?" he remarked. "That's a mighty tall claim. You're not much to look at, but then, neither am I." He glanced ruefully down at his round belly. "Since I can't test your 'tree-burgling' abilities without a tree, I suppose I will just have to take you at your word—for now."

"Our friends Medwyn and Meghan could vouch for me, if they were here," Kyleah stoutly replied. She wondered whether the pair had successfully drawn away the trollogs without being caught.

"I wish I could tree-burgle, too," Barley wistfully told her. "Can you teach me how to hide in a tree from Gyrta and Garta?"

"I don't think so," Kyleah said. "You can't learn tree-burgling; it's just a gift you're born with. Besides, you've got to stop avoiding those two and start standing up to them. If you don't, they'll never leave you alone." If only she could take her own sage advice!

Just then, the trollogs' thumping and hammering gave way to an ominous silence. Barley crept up to the door and put his ear to it. "I don't hear anything now," he said. "They've all gone away!"

Toefoot blew another smoke ring. "I doubt it," he said. "They may stop for a bit, but don't be fooled. Trollogs never give up."

Kyleah glanced around Toefoot's workshop. "Do you live alone?" she asked him. "I mean, where are the other gnomes?"

Her host pointed his pipe stem toward the room's far end. "In the floor back there, you'll find a trapdoor that opens onto more workshops below this one. Sometimes, my friends come up or I go down to sit a spell and share a pipe. Otherwise, uninvited guests can be a nuisance—present company excepted, of course."

"Who but gnomes would bother you?" Kyleah asked.

"Other than Gaelathane, Who is always welcome in our workshops, we see maiads, mostly." Toefoot winked at Hannith. "We gnomes excavated this mountain for their kind long ago. When we were done delving the halls, tunnels, drains and caverns, I put up this door so no one would disturb us again." He sighed. "It didn't work. Unwelcome visitors still drop in from time to time. That's what I get for living so close to the surface, I suppose."

"What do your visitors want from you?" asked Barley.

Toefoot waved his pipe at the ceiling. "Someone always needs a new tunnel dug or an old one unblocked; a cavern roof repaired or a drain unclogged. Nowadays, I leave the pick-and-shovel work to the younger fellows. My friends and I are too old for that sort of thing. Our digging days are over. Most of us have turned to more profitable work—cutting and polishing gems; smelting precious metals; forging swords and maces; fortifying castles; designing siege catapults, and the like. Mirror-making is my specialty."

The mirrors in Toefoot's cluttered workshop came in all sorts of shapes and sizes. Recalling her own smashed mirrors, Kyleah wondered why the renegades hated them. Perhaps they sought one mirror in particular. Might Toefoot already have created the "perfect glass" of the bracelet prophecy? If so, which one was it?

"How many mirrors have you got here?" Kyleah asked him.

"Three thousand, seven hundred and fifty-six," said the gnome. "No, make that fifty-five. I sold a full-length mirror last week to the queen of Hammerhaven. A plump lady she was, and as vain as a trollog's wife. I spent a whole day showing her some of my most flattering curved models. Mortal women pay me very handsomely to see themselves as something other than what they really are."

Hannith's eyes widened. "You lug your mirrors to the surface just to sell them in another world? That must be very tiring."

"Hah! I have a better way," Toefoot grunted smugly. "I—"

A whistling shriek interrupted him. The sound reminded Kyleah of Larissa's teakettle singing on their ancient wood stove.

Leaping up from his stool, Toefoot dove into a pile of tools and rubbish. He emerged seconds later with a coil of oily rope. "I knew this shipwright's caulk would come in handy some day!" he chortled. "I'm surprised I still remembered where it was. Now help me seal the door," he told Kyleah. "Your brother is too short to be of much use, and your naiad friend can't tolerate iron. Hurry!"

Kyleah understood. Desperate to rid their mountain of the trol-log menace, the maiads were flooding their tunnels, forcing pent-up air whistling shrilly through the cracks around the door. If those cracks weren't plugged, Toefoot's workshop would flood.

As quickly as Toefoot laid the rope around the door, Kyleah tamped it into the cracks with her crutch. Then she climbed the ladder to finish the job. She was just clambering down when a roar sounded in the passage. The door creaked and groaned.

"As the Tree lives, it's a blessing I barred that door when I did!" Toefoot marveled. "The lower tunnels haven't flooded like this in fifty years—and those trollogs cannot swim very well!"

"Oh, look!" Hannith cried, pointing. Water was seeping under the door. Using her crutch, Kyleah crammed the rope deeper into the crack, but the water kept coming, first in a dribble, then in a steady stream. Soon, water was running underfoot everywhere.

While Kyleah and Barley sat perched on their stools trying to keep their feet above the flood, Hannith happily romped in the water like a child playing in a shallow creek. The young naiad seemed unaware of the peril the water posed to her companions.

Crash! Bang! Toefoot was digging through his tall stacks of mirrors. Then Kyleah heard a gurgling noise, and the water began to recede. Hannith padded around in the remaining puddles with her webbed feet. Then she plopped down in the thin stream still spurting under the door and glumly splashed water on herself.

"If we were all maiads here, I would open that door and let the water in!" she said to Kyleah. "I am already starting to dry up."

Maiads or not, we would all be crushed by the onslaught of so much water! Kyleah told herself. She absently scratched her arm. First her back had begun itching painfully, and now her forearm.

Toefoot clumped up, his beard and boots dripping. "The last time my workshop flooded, the water damaged some of my best mirrors, so I installed two drains," he said. "That was so long ago I plumb forgot where I put the drains! Since the tunnels won't be passable for a couple of days, I'm afraid you three will be stuck here with me. I'd be glad of some real company; my mirrors look back at me, but they don't answer a word when I speak to them!"

Kyleah stifled a groan. Three days was a long time to be cooped up inside a gnome's workshop. She scratched her arm again.

"Let's have a look at that," said Toefoot. His nose twitched as he examined the itchy red blotch spreading across Kyleah's skin.

"That's a bad 'un," he observed with a grim scowl. Rummaging through a wooden box, he brought out a jar of some foul-smelling salve that he rubbed on Kyleah's rash. The itching subsided.

"Thank you!" she told him. "That feels better. Maybe your iron door is making my skin break out like a maiad's." Still, she wondered what had bloodied her back outside her cottage door.

As the water in the passage outside decreased, the leak under the door dwindled to a trickle. Then it stopped altogether. After mopping up the stray puddles, Toefoot led his yawning guests into a side room containing two beds. "I usually reserve these beds for guests from the Upper World," he explained. "Besides, we gnomes prefer to sleep on the floor. We like the feel of solid stone against our backs. Now rest well; in the morning, I shall prepare you a first-rate breakfast, and none of that fishy maiad fare, either."

"Then what shall I eat?" Hannith protested.

Toefoot cocked his head. "Don't you worry; I'll come up with something," he said. "Now off to bed with you all!" After banking the fire, he lay down on the floor inside the bedroom doorway.

Kyleah and Hannith took the left-hand bed, while Barley took the right. Kyleah snuggled under the thick quilted comforter and laid her head on the feather pillow. Then she stretched out and touched both the headboard and footboard at the same time, just to be sure they weren't made of passage wood. She didn't want to wake up in another strange place! To her relief, she stayed put.

While Toefoot snored and Barley moaned in his sleep, Hannith thrashed about in her waterless dreams. Unable to sleep herself, Kyleah turned over so she could look through the doorway into Toefoot's workshop. A single mirror stood propped up against the fire pit's bricks. By some trick of the flickering firelight, Malroth's hideous face leered back at Kyleah from the glass.

CHAPTER 17

TORSIL MIRRORS

Kyleah awoke to the sound of singing and metal clanging and banging. She tried to bury her head in her pillow, but Toefoot's happy, rasping voice still cut right through.

Polish the glass and silver it right!
Glue down the frame and clamp it up tight!
Lay in the mirror and nail it in snug!
Hang it up high or hold it up to your mug!

That's how the master makes all his mirrors,
Big ones and little, for persnickety peerers;
Wide ones and narrow, for nice mortal tastes;
Cunningly curved to mend wide mortal waists!

Leaving Hannith and Barley still asleep, Kyleah rolled out of bed and quietly crept out the door. She felt groggy and ravenously hungry, as if she hadn't eaten in days. In the workshop, she found Toefoot standing at the fire pit, frying eggs and bacon in a big cast-iron skillet. Kyleah's mouth watered and her stomach growled.

"Good morning!" said Toefoot. "I hope you slept well."

Kyleah yawned. "Not especially. I didn't realize gnomes snored. How do you know it's morning, when you can't see the sun?"

"I have my ways. And if you had a nose like mine, you'd snore, too!" Toefoot indignantly replied. "Would you rather eat your eggs and bacon now, or wait for Barley and Hannith to come out?"

"Eat now," said Kyleah, slavering. She reached for the skillet. It was too hot to touch. *Food.* She could think of nothing else.

"You must be starving!" Toefoot observed. "Hold on; let's have you a proper plate. You don't want burnt fingers." He lifted a tin plate from a hook on the fire pit's hood and handed it to Kyleah. Gripping the plate, she watched intently as Toefoot doled out two eggs and a rasher of bacon. No sooner had the food touched her plate than she shoved it all into her mouth and swallowed.

"Greedier than a gnomling, you are!" Toefoot exclaimed.

"More, please!" said Kyleah from the pit of her stomach.

"Very well," Toefoot sighed, and he dumped the remaining eggs and bacon onto Kyleah's plate. Neglecting to thank her host, she devoured those portions as well. Still famished, she licked the plate and demolished a loaf of bread lying on the edge of the fire pit. She was licking bread crumbs off the bricks when she glanced up to see her brother standing in the bedroom doorway. He looked small, alone and frightened, and his eyes were as big as skillets.

"Jumpin' jellyfish!" he gulped. "I've never seen you eat so much—or so fast! You must have been awfully hungry, 'Leah."

"Very impressive, I'll grant you," Toefoot grudgingly agreed. "She just put away ten eggs and fifteen rashers of bacon. As the Tree lives, that lame leg of hers must be completely hollow."

Kyleah felt her face redden. She looked down at her fingers. They were sticky with egg yolk and coated with bread crumbs. What had she just done? Where were her table manners? She still felt hungry, but her body's need was no longer as urgent.

"I—I'm sorry," she told Toefoot, scratching her arm. "I haven't left anything for you—or Hannith or Barley, either. I didn't mean to eat all the breakfast. Something just came over me, I guess."

"That's quite all right," Toefoot gruffly replied. "I've got lots more eggs and bacon and bread. I went out early this morning to fetch provisions. I knew you had gone long without eating."

"How'd you find eggs and bacon down here?" Kyleah asked.

"Water," croaked Hannith. The naiad stood swaying in the bedroom doorway beside Barley. Her face was pale and drawn, while her lips, webs, toes and fingers were cracked and split.

Toefoot clapped a hand to his head. "By my father's beard, I have forgotten proper gnomish hospitality! I'll find some water."

Disappearing into the rear of the workshop, he returned with a wooden flagon nearly as tall as he. Hannith drained the pitcher in one long draught and smacked her lips. Then she shook the last water drops onto her head. "Do you have any more?" she asked.

"Why don't I ever get any normal guests?" muttered Toefoot. Taking the flagon, he tromped along the rows of stacked mirrors. Kyleah, Barley and Hannith hurried to catch up with him.

"I still don't understand where you find your food—and your firewood!" Kyleah said, her curiosity getting the best of her.

"And where did that water come from?" Hannith asked.

"Come along, now, and I will show you," said Toefoot. The gnome took his visitors to the rear wall of the cluttered workshop. Propped against the bare wall's stark gray stone stood a handsome mirror-casing of a rich burgundy-brown color. The glassless oval frame measured just over three feet high and two feet wide.

"Where is the mirror that goes inside?" asked Barley.

"This is not an ordinary mirror," Toefoot explained. "Touch the frame at the top and bottom, and you will see what I mean."

Barley's arms were barely long enough to reach both ends of the frame at the same time. As soon as he touched the wood, a lifelike landscape appeared inside the wooden casing, as if painted there by an invisible brush. Verdant fir and pine forests climbed over the backs of foothills marching toward snowy mountains. Sleepy villages nestled along the silken strings of shining rivers that connected the emerald beads of deep-green lakes.

"An enchanted mirror! This is white magic!" Barley gasped.

Toefoot rounded on him with a fierce look. "There is no magic in this mirror! Black or white, all enchantments are from the Pit. Felgor the sorcerer invented magic and witchcraft, and he became enslaved to Gundul. All those who practice the dark arts weave webs to snare their own souls and will come to a black end."

"Then what makes your mirror work?" Barley asked.

Toefoot told him, "This frame is carved from torsil limbs, much like the bed that brought you here—if your sister's tale is true."

Kyleah blinked. Clouds were scudding across the landscape's sky, forming a billowing white backdrop for soaring eagles. "This isn't a painting at all!" she said. "It's a window on a real place."

"Of course it's real," snorted Toefoot. "Where do you think I get my vittles and firewood? I pop through this 'torsil mirror' and climb down the tree that grows on the other side. Then I visit the nearest village. Even when I have plenty of provisions, I like to go out now and again just to feel the wind and sun on my face and breathe some fresh mountain air. My workshop is rather stuffy."

"Look at all those rivers and lakes!" said Hannith dreamily. "I wonder if any maiads live in them. I'd love to visit this land."

"My arms are getting tired," Barley said. As soon as he stepped back from the torsil mirror, the framed scene faded into stone.

"Do you have any more mirrors like this one?" asked Kyleah.

"A few," said Toefoot. "Torsil wood is hard to come by these days. Most people burn it for fuel or make furniture out of it." He chuckled dryly. "You would be surprised how many folks have disappeared after sitting in a torsil chair or digging around in a torsil cabinet. Now look over there: Those are torsil mirrors."

The gnome pointed out four more glassless frames leaning against the wall. "I don't recall where those mirrors lead," he said. "I usually engrave the name of the particular world in the wood at the bottom. Are you three in the market for such a mirror?"

Kyleah frantically scratched her blotchy arm, which did little to ease the maddening itching of her spreading rash. "Now that you mention it," she said, "we are looking for a 'perfect glass.' Do you have any perfect mirrors lying about your workshop here?"

Toefoot frowned. "All my mirrors are crafted to perfection. If you mean a perfectly flat mirror that flawlessly reflects your face, then such a thing does not exist. Why do you need this mirror?"

"I had a bracelet inscribed with a prophecy," Kyleah replied. "Part of it said, 'A perfect glass for limping lass/Lies waiting in the wood.' Have you ever seen or heard of a mirror like that?"

"I might have, my 'limping lass'!" Toefoot remarked. "Just let me noggle for a moment, and I may come up with an answer for you." Toefoot hummed one off-key, rumbling tune after another, all the while tapping his fingers in time on his round potbelly.

"What does 'noggle' mean?" Barley asked the gnome.

Toefoot ruffled the boy's hair. "'Noggle' is a gnomish word that means 'to think with your noggin.' Now, where was I? Oh, yes. *Hum-ti-dum-di-dum-a-rum-rum.* That's it, all right! Gaelathane

146

once wrote a lay for King Pagglon the Pickfisted. The words were inscribed in the Hammering Hall far below us, where ten thousand gnomes used to hammer gold and silver into cunning works the like of which the world has not seen before or since. Alas, many of my relatives lost their lives when that cavern flooded long ago. As for Pagglon's Lay, I can noggle out only the first stave:

> The perfect glass, once forged anew,
> Will root the rebel to the rock;
> When trollog sees his image true,
> He'll gasp his last and stand a stock.

"What does your riddle mean?" Hannith asked.

"As I understand it," said Toefoot, "when a woodwalker sees his image reflected in this 'perfect glass,' he will root on the spot, returning to his original tree-form. 'Stock' refers to a senseless log or stump or block of wood. We gnomes have long tried to fashion this perfect mirror, but all our creations were flawed. I fear we misread Pagglon's Lay, for it says the 'glass' was once reforged. Molten mirror-glass is rolled out in a foundry, not a forge. Only metal tools and weapons are forged, as any gnome can tell you."

No wonder the trollogs had broken all Kyleah's mirrors! They must have known the "perfect glass" would be their undoing, and they had set about destroying all the mirrors they could find.

Kyleah coughed. Smoke was spreading beneath the ceiling, swirling through the room like threatening storm clouds.

"Dratted flue must be plugged again," Toefoot grunted.

Batting at the thickening smoke, Barley said, "I'm hungry! Can we have potatoes fried in bacon grease?" Hannith loudly gagged.

Toefoot sighed. "You young 'uns are always hungry. Very well. I'll heat up the skillet. If your leg is as hollow as your sister's, I'll have to restock my larder. Now, where did I put those spuds? I hope they haven't sprouted like the ones I bought in Thalmos."

Thalmos. Kyleah ached with homesickness. Had her father recovered yet from his head-wound? Had the trollogs razed her house and carried off Dolora, Gyrta and Garta? Kyleah wouldn't wish intrisonment on anyone, not even on her stepsisters.

While the potatoes browned, Toefoot fried up more eggs and bacon. As the smoke continued to thicken, he climbed a ladder and poked a long iron rod into the chimney-hole. Only a few black clots of creosote fell out. Muttering, he returned to his skillet.

When the second breakfast was ready, Barley ate three eggs and four pieces of bacon. He shared the hash browns with his sister and Toefoot. For Hannith there were fresh minnows, which she delicately swallowed whole. After his guests had eaten their fill, Toefoot ate the rest of the bacon and eggs straight out of the skillet. When his back was turned, Kyleah licked up the grease.

After breakfast, the gnome pulled out his pipe again. He was cleaning out the stem when a queer look came over his face. Putting aside the pipe, he twirled the cleaner in the leaping firelight.

"Maybe the 'perfect glass' must be grown, not made," he said.

"What do you mean?" Kyleah asked him.

"Have you ever heard of the *firebird*?" he said.

"Is that a bird that has caught fire?" asked Barley.

"No, it is a rare bird with feathers of silver," Toefoot replied.

"Then it should be called a *silverbird*," Hannith said. "Anyway, there are no such birds. You are just teasing us, silly old gnome."

"Oh, but they do exist, and this is one of their feathers," said Toefoot. "See for yourself." He handed Hannith his pipe-cleaner. Though frayed, it resembled a feather quill dipped in silver.

"Firebird tail feathers make the best pipe-cleaners anywhere," he said. "I've had this one for nigh on two centuries. The wing feathers are prized as mirrors, because they reflect only the finest features of a woman's face while hiding her flaws. Naturally, such feathers fetch a king's ransom. I'd rather make my own mirrors."

Kyleah quipped, "Trollogs haven't got any fine features, so maybe they couldn't see themselves at all in a firebird's feather!"

Barley and Hannith laughed, but Toefoot scowled. Cleaning his pipe, he asked Kyleah, "What else did your bracelet say?"

Thinking back on Meghan and her glass lens, Kyleah recited:

The flashing thing fit for a king
Hides fast within a tree;
In darkness sealed, to be revealed
When fire shall set it free.

Not made by hand of maid or man,
This trollish bane shall be;
With bloodless bite the blade shall smite
The mocking enemy.

"Aha!" Toefoot said. "Of course. It's perfectly obvious! *Bird* feathers are 'not made by hand of maid or man.' As the 'perfect glass,' a firebird feather's 'blade' will 'smite' our enemy, bloodlessly turning him back into a tree. Also, fire sets these birds free!"

"How does fire set free a bird?" Kyleah asked him.

"Pardon me. In my haste, I seem to have tripped over my beard. I have failed to tell you about firebirds and how they live, haven't I? Like woodpeckers, owls and tree-swallows, they lay their eggs in tree holes and hollows. Then the parents abandon the eggs. In time, the tree will grow over and enclose the unhatched eggs."

"Then how do the babies get out?" Barley asked.

"Often they don't. The eggs may lie dormant for years without hatching. Only if fire consumes the tree will the hard shells crack, allowing the young ones to hatch. They emerge fully formed."

"No wonder firebirds are so rare!" Hannith exclaimed.

"Indeed," said Toefoot. "Kings often burn whole forests to the ground just to hatch a few clutches of eggs. The birds are kept in cages not only for their feathers, but also for their melodious song. Bitter wars have been waged over a single caged firebird."

"How cruel to keep a bird in a cage!" said Kyleah. At home, she had felt like a caged bird herself, unable to escape the ever watchful eyes and long arms of her stepmother and stepsisters.

"Are you saying that we could defeat Malroth and his army with just one feather?" Hannith asked the Mirror Master.

"Hardly," Toefoot replied. "We would need a whole bundle of feathers to defeat Malroth's army. Also, I want a new pipe-cleaner to replace this one. It is growing a bit worn and thin. A gnome must have a pipe, and his pipe must be properly cleaned. All we have to do is capture some firebirds and pull out a few feathers."

"We?" Kyleah said, her hopes suddenly reviving. "Does that mean you will help us find these firebirds? Will you, please?"

With a wink, Toefoot slid off his stool. "I am growing stale from being cooped up underground," he said. "A little excitement might breathe some new life into these old bones. For years, I have surrounded myself with mirrors; everywhere I turn, I see Toefoot. I need a new view. Besides, the trollogs won't rest until they have destroyed all the mirrors they can find. That means mine, too."

"When can we leave? When can we leave?" Barley shouted.

"Hold on, now," said Toefoot. "We mustn't set off for the mines with dull pickaxes. I haven't seen a firebird in—let me noggle—one hundred and fifty-six years. I left King Wortlewig's service shortly after he burned down his firebird forest again. If any firebirds still live there, capturing them might prove hazardous to our health."

"Why is that?" Kyleah asked. Burning down a forest to catch any firebirds that hatched didn't sound too dangerous to her.

Dropping his pipe into his pocket, Toefoot said, "Because King Wortlewig beheaded anyone caught stealing his firebirds."

CHAPTER 18

PENODDION

O h, dear," said Kyleah, clutching her throat. She wasn't sure this firebird quest was worth risking her neck. "Why couldn't we use your pipe-cleaner instead?" she asked.

Toefoot laughed. "Why, we could never clean off all the soot. That feather is too tattered and tarnished to make a decent mirror. To take on the trollogs, you must have fresh, shiny feathers."

"Speaking of soot, it's becoming terribly smoky in this room," Hannith said. "Anyway, how do you know the Water Lord wants us to search for these firebirds? Your own prophecy tells us the 'perfect glass' was 'forged anew.' How can a feather be forged?"

Toefoot pursed his lips. "Maybe that means the birds must pass through the 'forge' of a forest fire before hatching. By my beard, I can't think of any other interpretation that makes sense."

"Then where is King Wortlewig's forest?" Hannith asked.

"It lies in a world known as 'Penoddion,'" Toefoot replied.

"And how do we get there?" asked Kyleah.

Toefoot drummed his fingers on his apron and coughed in the smoke. "There's the rub," he said. "I don't know."

"But you told us you once lived in that land!" Hannith said. "Why can't we go there the same way you did in the first place?"

"That was a long time ago," Toefoot said. "In those days, I traveled to and from Penoddion by climbing passage trees, since I had not yet discovered how to make torsil mirrors. Seeing we are trapped down here, climbing trees is out of the question, and I doubt we would find a Penoddion-torsil on Mt. Argel, anyway."

Kyleah groaned. "You're saying we can't go to Penoddion?"

"No, no, not at all!" said Toefoot briskly. "I am hoping I had the foresight to make a mirror frame from the last Penoddion-torsil I climbed. If so, we could reach that world directly from my workshop. Of course, we would have to find the frame first."

Kyleah groaned again. How could they find a single frame among three thousand, seven hundred and fifty-five of them? Then again, maybe the odds weren't so bad. "Since the torsil mirrors lack glass," she said, "we only have to look for empty frames."

Toefoot's face brightened. "You are right! Except for a few of my favorites I keep hanging on the wall, most of my torsil mirrors are in that back corner there. I hope we can find the right one."

Toefoot led Barley and the girls into the corner, where they found a towering stack of mirror frames. A few held mirrors, but most were blank. The gnome eyed the daunting heap with dismay. "I haven't gone through these frames in years," he confessed. "I used to keep the torsil mirrors in alphabetical order, with the 'A' worlds on top and the 'Z' worlds on the bottom. I'm afraid they're all mixed up. Penoddion could be anywhere. Let's get to work."

Waving her webbed hands, Hannith protested, "I can't touch those things! They're all put together with metal nails and wire."

"Very well," said Toefoot. "You can still help us look for names on the frames." Pulling over a ladder, he climbed to the top of the stack and began handing mirrors down to Barley and Kyleah, who grasped them only by their sides to avoid making passage.

Hannith inspected each of the frames before Barley and Kyleah piled them elsewhere. Toefoot was nearing the bottom of the stack when Kyleah held out the next torsil mirror. Hannith squinted at it. "Pen-odd-i-on," she read. "Penoddion. Yes! This is the one!" She pointed out some obscure lettering on the bottom piece.

"So I did carve the name on the frame!" Toefoot said.

Humming tunelessly to himself, the gnome rummaged through more of his wares until he had found three brass hand-mirrors. Two he gave to Kyleah and Barley, keeping the third for himself.

Kyleah gazed at her reflection. She looked well, except for her matted, greasy hair—and the Rash. It had spread up her back, over her right shoulder and down her right arm. She smeared more of Toefoot's salve on her skin, and the irritating itch eased.

"You'll want to take that jar with you," Toefoot told her.

Kyleah was appraising herself in the mirror again when she noticed a fine black rain falling into the fire pit behind her. Then something snaked out of the flue-hole in the cavern roof. It was a sooty hand attached to a long, thick arm. A wooden arm.

Dropping the mirror into a pocket in her shift, Kyleah sidled over to Toefoot and pointed up at the flue-hole. The gnome's face tensed. "They found the one passage that the water couldn't reach!" he grunted. "Quickly, now—we haven't a moment to lose!"

Leaning the Penoddion-mirror against the wall, Toefoot held the frame at the top and bottom, steadying it. At his touch, a moonlit forest appeared. "In you go!" he barked. Kyleah grabbed her crutch and the salve jar just before Toefoot booted her through the frame. Falling freely, she landed in the top of a passage tree.

She had just hooked her crutch around a stout limb and was swinging herself onto it when Hannith and Barley tumbled into the tree above her. Foliage broke the naiad's fall, but Barley bounced from one branch to the next, hollering with each bounce. Kyleah grabbed him as he flew past and seated him beside her. Last of all, Toefoot emerged in the treetop, looking fierce and bedraggled.

"Dratted trollogs!" the gnome grumped, brushing twigs from his beard. "I should have roasted them out when I had the chance. Now they'll smash all my mirrors. Well, what's done is done. If those rebels want the Gifted Girl badly enough to crawl all the way down a sooty chimney-flue, they're welcome to my mirrors."

"Can't they follow us through your torsil frame?" Kyleah asked, anxiously peering up through the passage tree's silvery leaves. At any second, she expected to see knobbly trollog feet and legs plunging pell-mell toward her through the tree's canopy.

Smiling grimly, Toefoot hoisted a curved length of carved wood beveled at both ends. "Even if they could figure out which was the right frame, it wouldn't work," he said. "I tore off this top piece as I came through. Without this stick, those trollogs can't make passage through the same Penoddion-mirror we used."

"Thank the Water Lord we arrived after sunset," said Hannith. "Otherwise, I would be a worldwalker now! Before dawn, I must find some water to hide in. I'm sorry to be such a nuisance."

"You're not a nuisance," Kyleah assured her. "My lame leg is more apt to hold us up than you are. Now let's climb down."

Once on the ground, the four surveyed their surroundings. The slumbering forest breathed out a sweet scent, refreshing after the stale, smoky air of Toefoot's workshop. Leaf-shadows shifted in a rustling night breeze. A shrill bird-cry shattered the stillness.

"Was that a firebird?" Kyleah whispered to Toefoot.

"I believe so," he replied. "They like to lay their eggs in woods like these. We must first find food and shelter. Then we can search for the birds. They don't fly about until after the sun has risen."

"Then I will never see one," said Hannith gloomily.

Creeping through the forest, the four companions broke out of the trees onto a well traveled path. Toefoot studied the ground.

"Horses have passed by this way recently!" he observed.

Hannith clapped her hands over her ears. "How the sound of clashing metal hurts my ears! It's coming from that direction."

She pointed left, where fireflies darted in the distance. As the lights approached, Kyleah realized they were swinging lanterns held aloft by three dark-cloaked figures mounted on horses. The animals' hooves pounded out a dreadful, thundering rhythm.

"Woodwalkers!" cried Hannith. "Flee! Flee for your lives!"

Before Kyleah and her companions could escape, however, the horsemen were upon them, hemming them in. The riders bore bright swords and long spears, and they wore heavy chain-mail hauberks. Their faces were masked in the thick night shadows.

It struck Kyleah that no trollog would take up weapons of steel, much less wear metal armor. She glanced at Hannith, who stood with hands clasped behind her back to hide her webs.

"Hold thy places, peasants, lest we run thee through!" roared the closest rider. Dismounting, he thrust his smoking lantern into the travelers' faces and triumphantly declared, "Forsooth, we have caught us our poachers red-handed! These four must be the miscreants who have been killing the king's firebirds. See how this shrinking brat's face flames with the guilt of her bloody deeds!"

Kyleah knew better. Poor Hannith's face was flushing beet-red from all the metal in the horseman's lantern, not out of guilt.

"Never have I laid eyes on a more motley lot," continued the rider. "Three guttersnipes and a—" Toefoot's bald head and seamed face brought him up short. "By the feathered crown, Kirkin," he exclaimed, "what manner of mongrel man is this? Do I see a boy too swiftly and cruelly aged, or a graybeard not yet fully grown?"

From his horse, Kirkin said, "Let the knave speak for himself." Poking Toefoot with his spear, he asked, "Pray, what are you?"

Toefoot bowed. "A gnome, if you please, good sir. My tender companions and I have lost our way in this wholesome wood."

"Beware this one's honeyed tongue, Reinhardt!" Kirkin warned the first man-at-arms. "For a scurvy trespasser and a poacher in the royal preserve, he is a well spoken villain. Methinks that when the noose is cinched about his neck, he will sing a different tune!"

"Nay, no poacher am I!" Toefoot protested. "In sooth, we four friends have journeyed from a distant country to entreat the favor of your good King Wortlewig. We have heard that no finer mirrors may be found in any other land than in this blessed kingdom."

"What is thy name, slyboots?" Reinhardt demanded.

"I am called the Mirror Master," Toefoot modestly replied. With an elegant flourish, he produced his hand-mirror and gave it to Reinhardt, who held it up to his face with an amazed grunt.

"By the Tree, here is cunning craftsmanship!" he marveled. "Yet, would not such a glass also serve to lure our prized birds?"

Toefoot said, "I have heard firebirds will flock to a mirror, mistaking it for another firebird. I would not stoop to such a trick."

"This trinket will please the missus!" said Reinhardt.

While his back was turned, Kyleah whispered to Toefoot, "You *were* planning to catch firebirds with our mirrors, weren't you!"

The gnome grinned up at her. "Yes, I was," he whispered back. "But I couldn't very well admit to it, or my life would be forfeit!"

"We have parleyed long enough with this rabble," Kirkin told Reinhardt. "Let us take them with us and return to the castle."

Reinhardt seated Toefoot on his horse, while Kirkin mounted Barley and Kyleah on his. Kyleah's lame leg complained as she gripped her crutch with one hand and Kirkin with the other. The third rider, whose name was Dunstan, roughly swung Hannith onto his horse. The naiad soon started kicking and squirming.

"Giddyup!" shouted Reinhardt, and the horses set off at a brisk trot. Sitting behind Dunstan, Hannith moaned and wriggled.

Dunstan growled, "What is the matter with you? Hold still!"

Then Kyleah realized Dunstan's chain mail was burning the helpless naiad. She kept crying and groaning as the clinking metal links scorched her delicate skin. Filled with dismay, Kyleah wished she had never listened to Toefoot's advice in the first place.

Beyond the forest, a moonlit fortress loomed, its spires, towers and turrets shrouded in night mists. Surrounded by a moat, the castle dwarfed the horses and their riders. When Reinhardt raised a horn to his lips and blew a long blast, a drawbridge rattled down to span the moat like a gigantic dragon's jaw. The horses had clop-clopped halfway across the bridge when Hannith slipped off her mount's back, ran to the side and hurled herself off the bridge. Kyleah held her breath. Seconds later, she heard a muted splash, and she smiled. Hannith had finally found her watery haven.

"Halt!" Dunstan shouted. He and Kirkin dismounted and ran to the edge of the drawbridge. After stiffly climbing off Kirkin's horse, Kyleah joined them. Only a few telltale ripples marked the spot where Hannith had plunged into the moat's black waters.

Kirkin asked Kyleah, "Why did thy friend take her own life?"

Kyleah shrugged. "You might say she was thirsty!"

Continuing onward, the procession stopped before the iron portcullis. Kirkin whistled piercingly, and with a clanking of chains, the grating lifted. Under his prodding, Kyleah hobbled beneath the portcullis, and the castle's dark maw swallowed her.

CHAPTER 19

THE FEATHER KING

While Dunstan stabled the horses in a smelly courtyard, Reinhardt and Kirkin escorted their prisoners down a well lit marbled hallway decked with flashing feathers. Kyleah decided her captors looked less sinister by torchlight. The taller of the two men-at-arms, Reinhardt was sandy haired with stern features and piercing gray eyes. Brown-eyed Kirkin wore a perpetual hangdog look under a thatch of shaggy black hair. Both men were garbed in dark blue cloaks emblazoned on the front and the back with the faded likeness of a striking silver feather.

Other passages opened on the right and left, but the men-at-arms silently marched down the hallway until it ended in a tall feather-shaped door that was overlaid with glistening silver leaf. Two blue-liveried guards armed with spears flanked the entry.

Kirkin and Reinhardt exchanged words with the guards, who then opened the door. Passing through, Kyleah entered a grand mirrored hall blazing with reflected torchlight. A shining fabric woven of countless silver feathers covered the walls and ceiling.

By the door stood an ornate, gilded cage. Inside the cage, a long-tailed bird sat on a perch, its feathers a tarnished silver. On a second look, Kyleah saw that the bird was stuffed and mounted.

Against the opposite wall on a feathered dais sat a throne also overlaid with the metallic-looking quills. On the throne slouched a withered figure, his face lined and gray. A robe woven of the same reflective feathers was draped over his stooped shoulders.

Bowing, Reinhardt addressed the king. "Forgive this unseemly intrusion at such a late hour, Sire. Kirkin, Dunstan and I have found four trespassers in the firebird preserve. We have brought three of them here. The fourth, a girl, cast herself into the moat, driven to some thirsting madness by the dread of her doom."

"Name yourselves, vagabonds," said the stone-faced king.

Bowing, Toefoot was about to introduce himself when Kyleah limped past him, moved by some inner prompting that she could not understand herself. "O King, we come in the name of Gaelathane to help you," she announced. "My name is Kyleah, and this is my brother, Barley. Toefoot the Gnome is our guide."

A harsh, bitter laugh escaped the king's lips. "How could a crippled girl, a lad and a dried-up old goblin assist the Feather King? I should say rather you three have been slaughtering the firebirds whose feathers adorn this hallowed royal chamber."

"I'm a gnome, not a goblin," Toefoot muttered. "Feather King," he said more loudly, "surely nothing is hidden from your sight. We have indeed come to your kingdom seeking the fabled firebird, but not in order to destroy those resplendent winged creatures. We require but a few paltry feathers to vanquish an enemy who fears neither blade nor arrow—but only a perfect mirror."

Reinhardt plucked the pipe-cleaner from Toefoot's pocket and held it up. "Your Highness, this fellow already possesses such a feather. He also showed me a mirror with which I am sure he and his companions intended to lure our firebirds to their deaths."

Toefoot tried to snatch the frayed feather from Reinhardt's grasp, but the man held it just out of the gnome's reach. "Give it back!" Toefoot cried. "That feather rightfully belongs to me. It was a personal gift from King Wortlewig the Third of Penoddion!"

Suddenly alert, the Feather King sat up and leaned forward on his feathered throne. "I am Wortlewig the Sixth!" he declared. "You knew my great-grandfather? He passed on many years ago."

"Knew him?!" said Toefoot. "I stood at his right hand as Chief Counselor. I left his service only to make mirrors of my own."

The Feather King's features sagged with shock. "You are that Toefoot who served my great-grandfather? You are that Toefoot who taught us how to ensnare the firebird and to weave its silver feathers into such works of splendor as we see here today?"

Toefoot bowed again. "The very same. As I served your great-grandfather, so shall I serve his heir, King Wortlewig the Sixth."

The king stood, wrath written in his face. "Knave! Is this how you repay our ancestor's kindness, by killing the firebirds in our royal preserve? Death is the penalty for merely possessing a single firebird feather! I should have you hanged here and now."

"You will not find the blood of your birds upon our hands, O King," Toefoot replied. "Rather, I believe we are sent of Gaelathane to aid you in hunting down the scoundrels who have committed this cowardly offense against your realm and your people."

Wortlewig the Sixth sagged back into his throne. "I fear we are beyond all help—even Gaelathane's," he said. "This spring, our servants came across some firebirds slain in the forest. Every bird had been stripped of its feathers. We sent forth three companies of yeomen to catch these vile poachers, but the patrols disappeared. Beginning a fortnight ago, scores of our subjects have also been vanishing during the night, to the great detriment of our realm."

Kyleah and Barley exchanged worried glances. The king's grim account of disappearing townsfolk sounded all too familiar.

When Wortlewig lapsed into a morose silence, Kirkin took up the tale. "Two nights ago, four horsemen cloaked in black came knocking on our gates, demanding to see the king. Very tall they were, and they shrank back from the torches we bore. We escorted them to these chambers, but they refused to enter. They delivered their message to our liege from the doorway, with hooded faces.

"'If you wish to see your missing people ever again,' they said, 'bring two hundred bushels of firebird feathers to the castle gates seven days hence, one hour after sunset. Otherwise, we will not leave you a single soul alive. We will also demolish this citadel stone by stone and burn your firebird forest to the ground.'"

"If it were a matter of a few feathers," the king said, "we would gladly give them in exchange for our subjects' lives. Yet, I fear we would not find ten bushels' worth of those mirrored treasures in all the kingdom, though we should plunder this room's bounty."

"What will you do, then, Your Highness?" Kyleah asked him.

"We must torch the forest to hatch more firebirds," he said.

"No!" cried Kyleah, waving her crutch. "You mustn't, I mean, please reconsider, Your Majesty. Don't you understand? If you burn your forest, you will be playing into the trollogs' hands!"

"Trollogs?" asked the king. "Pray tell, what are they?"

Kyleah explained, "Those are the black-cloaks that have been snatching your people. We know of these creatures firsthand." Then she told the king what she knew of Malroth and his rebels.

All the color left Wortlewig's face. "What do these renegade tree-sprites want with us, our subjects and our firebird feathers?"

"Above even fire itself," Toefoot broke in, "these trollogs fear mirrors, particularly perfect mirrors. No mirror-master has ever created a glass as flawless as a firebird feather, as you well know. By killing your birds and removing their feathers, the trollogs are eliminating this threat to their existence. Even if you gave them all the feathers in your entire kingdom, the black-cloaks would not release your subjects. On the contrary, they will still set fire to your forest and kill all the birds that hatch out. Worse still, in burning the trees, they will also destroy your intrisoned people."

"Then what are we to do?" asked Reinhardt.

"I think I can help you," Kyleah said, and she outlined her plan. When she had finished, Toefoot tugged on his beard.

"It might work," he said. "Still, you would have acres of forest to cover in only five days, and none of us could assist you."

"Gaelathane will show me what to do," Kyleah declared, though she was already beginning to regret her rash proposal.

"I pray that He does," said the king. "Our lives and fortunes depend upon your thwarting these trollogs' wicked ambitions."

"I will stake my life upon the success of this venture," Toefoot added. "Should Kyleah's daring strategies go awry, you may keep me here in your castle as your vassal till the end of my days."

"Loath am I to maltreat one of my forebear's faithful servants," said King Wortlewig. "Besides, if the lame lass's plans come to naught, we are undone and shall all perish defending the realm."

"Then may Gaelathane grant us good success!" Toefoot said.

"For the present, kindly accept our meager hospitality," said King Wortlewig. He clapped his hands. "Prepare a banquet!"

Kirkin and Reinhardt disappeared through the feather-door, returning with more of the king's servants, all cloaked in the same feathered blue livery. Before you could say "firebird," tables had been laid out and piled with platters of meats, fish, cheeses; breads and pastries; jams and jellies; fruits and nuts; potatoes and leeks.

Meanwhile, Kyleah had fallen into a frenzied scratching fit. In a matter of hours, the rash had spread to both her arms and legs. Though she attempted to hide her condition, the Feather King stared at her with alarm and dismay. "Does the poor girl suffer from the mange or the scab?" he asked Toefoot much too loudly.

The gnome shook his head. "It is merely a pesky rash, Your Highness. She has neglected to apply the salve I supplied her."

Excusing herself, Kyleah escaped into the hallway, where she rubbed Toefoot's salve into her itching skin. This time, the smelly lotion failed to relieve her discomfort, for the skin on her back and arms was thickening and puckering into hideous brown ridges, creating a vein-like network that restricted her arm movements. She tried to cover herself, but her sleeves were too short.

Hiding herself in a doorway, she watched courtiers and nobles pour into the feather chamber. Tortured by the banquet smells, she finally entered, too. By now, the feast was in full swing. Guests were filing along the tables, scooping steaming food onto their wooden trenchers. Unable to wait her turn, Kyleah shoved her way to the front of a line. Ignoring the protests of the other guests, she tore a leg off a fat roast goose and devoured it, bones and all. Next, she shoveled a meat pie down her gullet. The murmur of polite conversation in the hall died into a shocked silence.

"You are making a spectacle of yourself, my dear," Toefoot whispered to her. "Gobbling your food in public like this reflects badly upon us all. Please do try to restrain yourself for once!"

The gnome briskly rapped the butt of his knife on a tabletop, and the banqueters looked up at him. "No doubt you all have been marveling at my young friend's prodigious appetite," he boomed. "Please pardon this breach of courtly etiquette. The Gifted Girl is merely preparing herself to do battle with our mutual enemies."

A babble of approving chatter echoed through the mirrored hall. Mortified, Kyleah wondered why she could not stop eating.

After the feast, Reinhardt and Kirkin took their visitors to three adjoining rooms on the castle's ground floor. Each room was furnished with a straw-filled mattress. Apologizing for the plain lodgings, the men-at-arms bade their guests a good night and left. Toefoot stretched out on his room's bare floor and began snoring.

What with her itchy rash, the scratchy mattress and the dread of her spreading skin disease, the Gifted Girl found no sleep that night. When a gray morning light struggled through her room's window, she sat up and hugged herself against the damp chill.

"Gaelathane," she whispered. "Please help me today."

After rubbing the last of Toefoot's lotion on her bumpy skin, she rousted out Barley. Her brother stared at her arms in disgust.

"Your skin looks worse," he said. "What's wrong with it?"

"I don't know," she replied. "It's just a rash, I suppose."

"That's no ordinary rash," said Toefoot, who was lounging in Barley's doorway. A tear quivered in the corner of his eye as he turned to one side. Pulling out his pipe, he chewed on the stem.

"If it isn't just a rash, what is it?" Kyleah asked him.

"You've been 'troll-lashed,'" he said, facing her. "Old trollogs can peel off strips of their thick hide to make ropes and whips and the like. Wherever a troll-lash draws mortal blood, an itching rash forms and spreads over the skin. In time . . ." Toefoot stopped.

"In time?" Kyleah prompted him.

"In time, you will become a trollog yourself. There is no cure for it. I am sorry, my dear limping lass. I am so very, very sorry.

Beware the lash that brings the rash
Of scaly flesh and skin;
Though slow to spread, you'll feel the dread
When wooden gait begins!

CHAPTER 20

THE FORGOTTEN BLAIRN

Toefoot's words knocked the wind out of Kyleah, leaving her doubled over and gasping for breath. When Medwyn and Meghan had examined her flayed back on Mt. Argel, Medwyn had evidently said "troll-lash," not "tollash." Weeping, Kyleah collapsed on her lumpy mattress. Now she recognized the ridged pattern on her arms. Her skin was turning to tree-bark!

"I don't want . . . to become . . . a . . . trollog!" she wailed.

Backing away from his sister, Barley tearfully asked Toefoot, "Will she eat me? Can I catch the trog-sickness from her?"

"No, she is perfectly safe—for now." Toefoot took Kyleah's hands in his gnarled ones. "You still have some time," he told her. "The change may take months. Meanwhile, you must try to eat as little as possible. Food fuels the growth of the trollog within."

"How long have you known?" Kyleah dully asked him.

"Since that breakfast in my workshop," Toefoot softly replied. "No mortal girl your age possesses such a voracious appetite. You have not been feeding yourself, but the trollog-that-is-to-be."

When Medwyn had laid eyes upon Kyleah's torn back, the worldwalker must have known even then what lay in store for her. Hope drained from Kyleah like sap from a leaky tapping-pail.

"What's done is done," she announced, echoing Toefoot's words in the torsil tree. Wiping her eyes, she continued, "Since my time is short, I had better get to work. At least while I'm in the woods, there won't be any food readily at hand to tempt me."

Unfortunately, Kirkin and Reinhardt appeared just then with bags of apples, bread and cheese. Having a trollog's acute sense of smell, Kyleah could not bear the tantalizing odors and had to leave the room. Otherwise, she would have devoured everything.

After the others had eaten, Kyleah followed them out to the courtyard stables, where the saddled horses waited. Her eyes burned in the bright morning sun. No wonder the trollogs so hated the light! Reinhardt seated her on his horse, while Kirkin mounted Barley and Toefoot on his steed. Then off they rode.

As the horses drummed across the drawbridge, Kyleah glanced over the side at the stagnant, oily water. If Hannith was still living in the moat, there was no sign of her. But then, being a naiad, she would be hiding from the sunlight in the darkest, deepest water.

When the company had ridden for about a half-hour, the fire-bird forest came into view. Though the woods looked cheerier in the light of day, a hard lump of dread grew in Kyleah's heart. Then she recalled her plea to Gaelathane for help earlier that morning. He would not forsake her, "troggirl" though she was.

"Here we are!" said Reinhardt, helping her off his horse. "May Gaelathane grant you good success. Kirkin and I shall await your return here, for we shall not venture into this wood again."

Kyleah explained there was nothing to fear from the trollogs until darkness fell, but the two men-at-arms refused to ride any farther. They would linger outside the forest only until sunset.

As Kyleah passed beneath the trees, their leafy branches seemed to reach toward her like grasping trollog fingers. She flexed her own fingers, and the stiff joints creaked. Already cold wood was replacing her warm flesh. If only she had stayed one more step ahead of the trollogs, she could have escaped their lash's sting!

She sighed and stretched her thickening arms. Miles of trees marched before her. How could she explore the entire preserve in less than a week? Her companions would be of little or no help.

Toefoot and Barley looked expectantly at her. Squaring her itching shoulders, she limped to a nearby tree and thrust her arm into it. Flailing about, she encountered nothing solid. She wished the trollogs had marked the trees that held trisoners inside.

Barley stared at her with a perplexed expression as he followed her every movement. "Why are you doing that?" he asked.

Kyleah withdrew her arm. "Weren't you listening last night?" she snapped at him. "I thought I explained everything then."

"No, no," said Barley. "I mean, why did you pick *that* tree? There's nothing inside it except wood. You're wasting your time."

"I know that now, you ninny!" Kyleah shouted. Her stomach was knotting with hunger. What a cruel fate awaited her! If she gave in to her urges, she would be hastening her "trollification." If she denied herself, she would starve. Still, death was preferable to turning into another Malroth, a night-stalking creature of wood.

As she moved on to the next tree, Barley was hopping on one foot and then the other, making grunting noises. Finally, Kyleah turned to him in exasperation. "What is it now?" she demanded.

"That tree is empty, too!" he said in a single breath.

Kyleah groaned. Why couldn't her brother have stayed in his own bed that night instead of jumping on hers and breaking it? Then he wouldn't be nagging her. *If the trollogs had found Barley in his bed, he might be dead now*, Gaelathane's voice reminded her.

"How do you know the tree is empty?" Toefoot asked him.

Barley waved his hand at the trunk. "It's easy! I can see there's nobody inside. But someone is in that other tree right next to it."

"Well, I can't see anybody in there!" Kyleah retorted. She hated arguing with her brother, especially when he was right. She fished around in the first tree, finding nothing. Then she moved to the tree Barley had pointed out. When she stuck her hand inside, she felt a warm human arm. Pulling on it, she drew out a befuddled old woman garbed in a plain woolen dress and linen blouse.

"Where am I? Who are you?" the woman asked her.

Ignoring the trisoner, Kyleah asked Barley, "How did you know someone was intrisoned in that tree? Did you hear her? Do the trollogs leave a special sign on the bark? *How did you know?*"

"I already told you how," Barley retorted. "I looked inside, and I could see that lady trapped there. I thought you saw her, too."

For the first time, Kyleah clearly saw her brother. *He is also a blairn*, she reminded herself. What was it the Plugger had said about Barley? *His gift will multiply yours.* "How long have you been able to . . . see inside trees?" she asked him huskily.

He shrugged. "Just a few months. Can't everybody do that?"

Thick tears oozed out from beneath Kyleah's itchy eyelids. "No, Barley," she said. "You alone possess that special gift. Tell me, can you see anything or anyone else in these trees around us?"

While Toefoot led the old woman back to Reinhardt and Kirkin, Barley pointed out trees that held arrowheads; trees with people in them; and trees containing oval, white objects that turned out to be firebird eggs. In every case, his predictions were accurate.

Kyleah knelt before her brother and enfolded him in her arms. Sobbing, she said, "I am so sorry, my little maple-bear! Will you forgive me? All this time, I treated you as nothing more than a nuisance. Now I know Gaelathane sent you along to help me. I cannot search this wide forest without you. Will you guide me?"

When Barley happily nodded, Kyleah raised her crutch and shouted, "Then look out, you trollogs, for we are about to plunder this whole forest, and there is nothing you can do to stop us!"

After that, Kyleah made rapid progress. As quickly as she could free a trisoner or filch a firebird egg from a tree, her brother would point out another tree to burgle. By the day's end, they had sent a long line of former trisoners happily trudging toward freedom. Kyleah's burgling had also filled two food bags with firebird eggs, which Toefoot and Barley grudgingly lugged out of the woods.

"By my mirrors, this sack is heavy!" Toefoot groaned.

"What are we going to do with all the eggs?" Barley asked.

Toefoot replied, "I am praying we will find a way to hatch them out. Then we'll have plenty of firebird feathers to go around."

Just as Kyleah, Barley and Toefoot emerged from the forest, Kirkin and Reinhardt rushed up to congratulate them. Kirkin was so excited that he grabbed Toefoot and cleanly lifted him off the ground. The gnome sputtered and spluttered indignantly.

"Put me down! Put me down!" he howled. Laughing, Kirkin set the furious gnome back on the ground and brushed him off.

"Well done, dear friends!" said Reinhardt. "Thanks to you and Gaelathane, our missing countrymen are safely returning home."

Kirkin said, "Reinhardt and I have taken a goodly number of the people back to the castle on horseback. By the feathered crown, look at all the eggs you have collected! If each one hatches, the kingdom shall never again lack for firebirds or their feathers."

Toefoot muttered, "If you don't want to wear those firebird eggs on your head, you had better not try to pick me up again!"

That night, no one else went missing, for King Wortlewig made certain his subjects hung a mirror on every cottage door and in every window. For the next four days, Kyleah, Barley and Toefoot returned to the forest to release more trisoners and gather more firebird eggs. By noon of the last day, Barley could find no other trees for Kyleah to burgle, and she felt so famished she was tempted to devour some of the firebird eggs raw. For five days, she had eaten nothing but eight apples and a few slabs of cheese.

The three companions returned to the castle with Kirkin and Reinhardt amidst great fanfare. The drawbridge was lined with former trisoners waving banners and cheering their rescuers. However, the celebration was cut short to make the preparations Kyleah had requested. All that afternoon, the castle was an anthill of activity. After supper, King Wortlewig joined his honored guests on the battlements overlooking the main gate and drawbridge.

"All stands in readiness!" he told Kyleah, rubbing his hands together in gleeful anticipation. Having gorged herself at supper, Kyleah was scratching again. From her vantage point, she could see servants still scurrying about below, putting finishing touches on their handiwork before retreating behind the castle walls.

The lengthening evening shadows had just reached the firebird preserve when the sun sank behind forested peaks. Then Kyleah noticed a deeper darkness gathering where the castle road entered the wood. The darkness flowed along the road and rumbled over the drawbridge, stopping before the raised portcullis. Malroth's voice rang out, and Kyleah covered her ears with knotty hands.

"Where is our feather tribute?" Malroth demanded.

"Here are your feathers!" bellowed King Wortlewig from the battlements. So saying, he hurled a spear over the parapet into the blackness beyond. The lance arced gracefully through the air until it thudded into the drawbridge scant yards from Malroth's horse.

On that signal, the portcullis was lowered, and the castle lit up like a Yuletide tree. Mirrors mounted on the portcullis threw back the light of a thousand torches, candles and lamps flaring in windows, along the parapets and around the moat. Thirty-five trollogs stood stunned in stark relief. Blinded and confused, they retreated across the drawbridge to regroup. Then their leader raised his black sword, piercing Kyleah's heart with madness.

"You have one final chance to redeem yourself, O King!" Malroth rasped. "Bring the girl known as Kyleah out to us, and we will leave your dominions, never to darken your gates again. She is already one of us, and she belongs with her own kind."

"Do not trust him, Sire!" Toefoot warned the king. "Even if you give them the girl, those fiends will not rest till they have rid Gaelathane's worlds of every last man and woman, boy and girl."

"Kyleah stays with us!" Wortlewig roared down at his foe.

"So be it!" snarled Malroth. "You have decided your own fate! Now we shall burn down your forest and reduce your castle to rubble! We will still have your firebirds, pretty feathers and all—and your intrisoned subjects shall perish in smoke and flames!"

The woodwalker and his cohorts reined their horses around and were riding away when the moat's waters suddenly rose up, gathering in a mighty wave that towered over the trollogs' heads. The wave crested and toppled forward, thundering toward the fleeing woodwalkers with frightful speed. It overtook and crushed them like so many matchsticks before sweeping them toward the firebird forest in a tumbling, helpless heap.

CHAPTER 21

TROLLOGS AT BAY

W hat brought forth that great wave?" King Wortlewig gasped. "Was it a geyser or a waterspout? How could all that water rise up so swiftly from a shallow moat?"

Smiling at him, Kyleah quipped, "You have friends in low places! Anyway, I doubt we'll be seeing those old trollogs again."

"I wouldn't be so sure about that," Toefoot cautioned her. "Nothing can kill or destroy a trollog except a searing-hot fire."

The king said, "All the same, we sent the scoundrels packing, did we not? If they should have the temerity to return, we will drench them with burning oil and pitch from these parapets!"

Cheers erupted from the castle, which was still ablaze with light. The portcullis was raised, and a throng of King Wortlewig's subjects poured onto the drawbridge to gawk at the nearly empty moat. Owing to the rising lay of the land around the fortress, the floodwaters were already draining back into the circular ditch.

Kyleah waited until the murmuring spectators had drifted back into the castle, leaving the drawbridge vacant. Then she crept out and peered over the side into the moat's muddy waters.

"Hannith!" she hissed. "Are you still down there?"

"I am right here."

Kyleah jumped as a webbed hand touched her shoulder. Hannith was standing behind her, dripping wet and grinning.

"Hannith!" Kyleah cried, embracing the naiad. "I am so glad to see you again! I had feared you were dead. Thank you for your help. But did you create that tremendous wave all by yourself?"

Hannith laughed. "Alone, I scarcely could have raised a ripple. However, when we maiads work in concert, calling upon the small skills the Water Lord has given us, we can accomplish much." She cwelapped her finger-webs, and some fifteen heads bobbed above the moat's rising waters. Webbed hands gaily waved at Kyleah.

"I found some friends in this moat," Hannith explained. "We have been watching and listening—and planning. The wave was lovely, was it not? Now that the trollogs are no more, we can—but I see you are feeling unwell. What is wrong with your face?"

Kyleah touched her cheek. It felt itchy and rough. Despite her meager rations, the trollog skin had not healed or sloughed off. The awful infection was still spreading. Raising Toefoot's pocket mirror to her face, she shrieked. Hopeless eyes set in mottled, grainy flesh stared back at her. When the metal handle began burning her trollish fingers, she flung the mirror over the moat.

"What is the matter?" Hannith asked her in alarm.

"Go back to your water. You cannot help me now. When the time comes to leave, I will tap my staff on the bridge to call you."

Trudging into the castle, Kyleah did not look back, not even when a familiar splash echoed up from the filling moat. She had helped defeat the trollogs, yet she was becoming one herself.

The sun still slept behind the mountains when Kyleah sat down to an early breakfast of eggs, sausage, toast and jam. Although she was hungry enough to consume everything on her trencher and more besides, she could only pick at her food. All around her, the sounds of revelry filled the castle's passages and halls, but Kyleah ate alone. People were already avoiding her, though she was not yet wholly trollog. Surely when her trollification was complete, all her former friends and loved ones would shun her. Men would drive her from their homes and villages into dark, waste places where she would weep alone in trollish misery among the rocks.

Stiffly, she left the table to stagger back to her room, where she slept all morning and into the afternoon. When she awoke, Toefoot was standing over her. He avoided her questioning gaze.

He sees what I have become, she thought. *He sees me and loathes me. I don't blame him a bit. I have seen me, and I loathe me, too!*

"I saw you talking with Hannith on the drawbridge last night," he said. "By Pagglon's pickax, that water-wave of hers taught those trollogs a lesson they won't soon forget! Tell her if she wishes to rejoin us, we will leave at dusk, for her sake. If she doesn't want to be seen, she can follow us at a distance. Now that our enemies have suffered this setback, we should be safe after nightfall."

But for how long? Kyleah wondered as the gnome hastily took his leave. She sat up and tried to stretch her rigid limbs. Now she knew why the trollogs were also called "woodwalkers." She felt just like an awkward, inflexible wooden doll. Too weary to move further, she flopped down on the straw mattress and fell back asleep. When next she awoke, Barley was pulling on her arm.

"Get up, sleepyhead!" he told her. "It's nearly sunset, and we're leaving; everybody is waiting for you. Hurry up! This way!"

Barley dragged Kyleah out the doorway and through the castle gates beneath the raised portcullis. On the drawbridge outside, King Wortlewig was talking with Toefoot. Next to them, Kirkin, Reinhardt, Dunstan and three other men-at-arms each sat astride a horse. Three of the animals bore two burlap bags apiece filled with firebird eggs. Dunstan helped Barley climb up beside him.

"I see no reason for haste," Wortlewig was saying. "If these trollogs are creatures of the night, why risk departing after dusk? Tarry with us a few days longer. We have only begun to express our gratitude to you and your companions for all you have done."

Toefoot bowed. "You have been most gracious to us, Your Highness. As I have said, our errand is urgent. To find the 'perfect glass,' we must quickly hatch these eggs. Also, the Gifted Girl is gravely ill. If we do not soon seek a cure for her, she may die."

"As you wish," sighed the stooped king. "Then may Gaelathane bless your journeys, and may you return to us in better days, when we may bestow upon you such rewards as you rightly deserve."

Grimacing, Toefoot let Reinhardt pick him up and seat him on his horse. Kyleah had just enough presence of mind to stamp her staff twice on the drawbridge before Kirkin gently hoisted her—crutch and all—onto his mount. Clinging to him from behind, she realized Toefoot hadn't told her where they were going.

Amidst much cheering and well-wishing, the procession set off. Kirkin's horse brought up the rear. Straining her eyes in the failing light, Kyleah gazed back at the castle. Its massive outlines were already growing hazy in the evening mists. Just then, a slight figure appeared at the moat's edge and moved into the tall grass.

The men-at-arms rode their mounts at a brisk trot along the road, which was still puddled from Hannith's moat-wave. Not far from the castle, Kyleah saw several drowned horses lying bloated beside the track. She also noticed a number of muddy black cloaks scattered amongst broken legs, arms and other trollog parts.

Stopping at the forest's edge, the men-at-arms lit pitch torches. Then they urged their horses into the woods. No one spoke as leafy darkness enclosed the company. Hearing a rustling in the underbrush, Kyleah stared about but saw nothing. Kirkin flicked his reins, and his mount's pace quickened. All at once, a horrible hand grabbed Kyleah, and she came face to face with a one-armed trollog bounding along behind Kirkin's panicked horse.

"You are coming with me, troggling!" he grated.

"No!" Kyleah yelled. "Help me, Gaelathane!" She brought her crutch down on the creature's head, to no effect. Fear and rage flashed through her veins. Grasping the arm that held her, she wrenched it violently. With a splintering noise, the limb came away in her hand. Bellowing with pain, the trollog staggered back. Kyleah dropped the severed arm only to find more of the woodwalkers loping along beside her horse. Kirkin tried to fend them off with his sword, but they easily brushed it aside. Then a trollog seized Kirkin and attempted to drag him off his mount.

"No, you don't! Get away from my friend!" Kyleah screamed, and she tore off this trollog's arm as easily as she had the first. When the attacker's other arm shot out, she broke it off as well. Roaring in confusion, the woodwalker fell back into the bushes.

Now scores of trollogs—many of them maimed—fell upon the horses, pulling down their riders and creating havoc. Spears and swords flashed in the torchlight. Men shouted and horses reared.

When the trollogs beset Barley and Dunstan, Kyleah seized her crutch, leapt down from her mount and tore the legs off the nearest attacker. Another trollog tried to grab her, but she climbed onto its back out of its reach and twisted off its wooden head, which she hurled at a third trollog. In a frenzy, she waded into the fray, thrusting her crutch to trip here, rending and ripping there. Before long, any woodwalkers still able to walk had retreated to nurse the terrible wounds Kyleah had inflicted upon them.

With wondering glances at her, the shaken men-at-arms opened their egg sacks. Miraculously, none of the precious cargo had been damaged. As Kyleah climbed back on Kirkin's horse, he marveled, "How have you come to possess the strength of fifty?"

"Ride! Ride!" Toefoot roared, and the horses galloped through the dark woods, rattling Kyleah's teeth as she jolted along. At last, the pace slowed, and the horses turned off the track to pick their way among groves of trollishly twisted oaks. Toefoot called a halt, and the men-at-arms piled the egg-bags in a neat heap. Then they furiously spurred their mounts back the way they had come.

Kyleah slung four egg-sacks over her shoulder, leaving the other two bags for Barley and Toefoot. Into a moonsilvered sea of bracken ferns they plunged. Toefoot's torch bobbed above the bracken like a beacon-fire burning atop wave-worn cliffs. At length, the three reached the gnarled base of the Penoddion-torsil.

"What are we doing here?" Kyleah asked the gnome.

"We're going home—I think," he grunted.

"I don't understand. I thought your frame was broken."

"It is," Toefoot replied. "I left the top member around this tree somewhere. If I put that piece on my head, the torsil mirror may let me back into my workshop. Now, where did that stick go?"

Kyleah blinked in the torch's searing light. Shading her eyes, she sniffed her way around the torsil's trunk until she smelled the sharp scent of varnished wood. Following her trollog's nose, she found the beveled frame-piece lying underneath an azalea bush.

"Here it is!" she called to Toefoot, holding up the stick.

"Very good!" he said. "Now I must find a way to keep it from falling off the top of my head. If only gnomes had more hair!"

"Let me try this," said Kyleah. Grabbing Toefoot's beard with both hands, she divided the hair in half. Then she pulled the two halves up past his droopy ears and tied the ends together over his head. Finally, she shoved the frame-piece into the hairy topknot.

Kyleah and Barley burst out laughing at the sight of the gnome's new hairpiece. Toefoot grunted and turned red in the face.

"Very clever," he growled, patting the board. "Don't ever tell a soul about this, or I'll be the laughingstock of all my relatives!"

"Why are you complaining?" Kyleah retorted. "You wanted some hair on the top of your head, and now you finally have it!"

Just then, a shadow crept into the torchlight. Kyleah jumped back, but it was only Hannith. The two girls warmly embraced.

"I'm sorry to be late," the naiad whispered. "I had to sneak past some trollogs that were watching the road. How can I help?"

Toefoot told her, "We must get these egg-bags into this tree!"

Kyleah easily climbed into the torsil, dragging her crutch after her. Being the tallest, Hannith handed the sacks of eggs up to her, and she lodged them in the tree's crotches and forks. With her newfound strength, Kyleah then hauled her companions into the passage tree. Toefoot had to stand tiptoe on Barley's shoulders in order for Kyleah to reach his brawny hands. He felt feather-light.

"If my passage-plan fails," he said, "we must spend the night in this tree. After sunrise, we'll find another torsil out of Penoddion. Hannith may become a worldwalker, but it can't be helped."

Leaving the torch with Kyleah, Toefoot disappeared into the tree's top. A night wind sprang up, ruffling Kyleah's hair. Weary beyond words, she idly wondered whether all her hair would fall out when she fully became a trollog, or whether the hair would turn to wood. She was asking Gaelathane to help Toefoot safely make passage into his workshop when she noticed glaring eyes glittering below her in the torchlight. The trollogs had found her.

"Don't you wicked things ever give up?" she shouted, and she flung a dead branch at them. The trollogs did not flinch. On the contrary, one of them picked up the branch and began eating it.

"Come down to us!" they croaked back. "You belong to us. You are becoming as we are—tough, indestructible and immortal! Neither you nor those floodwaters can keep us down for long."

To her absolute horror, Kyleah saw the trollogs were sprouting new legs, hands and arms from the stumps of the old. "Go away and leave me alone, you ugly old trolls!" she screamed at them.

The trollogs crowded around the torsil. "Climb down, and we will let your companions go free!" they told her. "We want you and you alone. Do not be afraid of us. We will not harm you."

"What do you want with me?" she cried despairingly.

Suddenly, a tin plate came bouncing and banging down through the torsil's branches, landing smack at the trollogs' feet.

The creatures laughed hideously. "Trinkets cannot hurt us!

Trogs we are, and thick our skin!
Tough we are, than all our kin!
Sword may strike but glances off;
We cannot cringe; we only scoff!

"I'll bet Toefoot dropped that plate to signal us that he made passage!" Kyleah told her companions. "Now it's your turn. Take those sacks with you. Hurry! This torch won't last much longer."

While Kyleah held off the trollogs with the torch, Barley and Hannith manhandled the egg-bags to the torsil's top. Kyleah heard rustling noises above her as the two climbed down again with the sacks. Then the passage tree fell utterly still. Kyleah was alone.

Suddenly, the torch flickered and went out. Leering at Kyleah, the nearest woodwalker leapt onto the tree and climbed froglike up its trunk toward her, his eyes gleaming. Waiting until the last second, she thrust her smoking torch into the trollog's face. Then she scrambled into the torsil's top and slid partway down again. She was fending off more trollogs with her crutch when she felt the torsil mirror invisibly squeezing her shaking shoulders.

"You cannot escape us!" the trollogs taunted her. Then they all faded away like nightmares before a glorious summer's dawn.

CHAPTER 22

TOEFOOT'S HATCHERY

Kyleah and her crutch tumbled out of the torsil mirror. She had hardly picked herself up when Toefoot pried off the frame's top piece, which he had tacked on again.

"There!" he said, dusting off his hands. "Those woodwalkers won't be coming in here again, at least not this way." Using a brush he had pulled out of his pocket, the gnome rhythmically stroked his disheveled beard until every hair fell neatly into place.

"I can't bear an unkempt beard," he explained. "Of course, I can't see myself any longer, anyway. All my mirrors are gone." Toefoot waved his arm at his workshop, and Kyleah gasped.

Twisted frames and shattered glass lay strewn everywhere. Nothing shiny had been spared, including Toefoot's pots and pans, which were crumpled into shapeless lumps. The door hung open, most its locks and bolts bent or broken. Cold ashes filled the fire pit, leaving the drafty workshop as chilly and damp as stone.

Toefoot remarked, "Those old trollogs did a thorough job of mirror-wrecking. Either they were seeking to smash the 'perfect glass,' or they hate looking at themselves—with good reason."

Kyleah was relieved none of Toefoot's mirrors had survived in one piece. She dreaded seeing the trollog she was becoming.

She was terribly hungry. However, the trollogs had eaten or spoiled all of Toefoot's food. After piecing together one of his torsil mirrors, he went off in search of provisions. Meanwhile, Kyleah helped Barley collect the broken mirror-glass, which Toefoot would melt down again. Hannith swept up the remaining shards, though she could not touch the silvered glass. Then Kyleah picked up the mangled mirror frames to burn in the fire pit.

Those dratted trollogs! Kyleah thought as she worked. She gripped one of the broken frames so hard that the wood crumbled to dust in her hand. Responding to a ravenous urge, she tossed the fistful of powder into her mouth and gulped it down.

Barley stared at her fearfully. "What did you just swallow?"

"Nothing," Kyleah replied, licking the sawdust off her lips.

"You won't eat me when you're a trog, will you?" he asked.

Kyleah wrapped him in her arms. "How could I eat my own brother?" she said, her voice husky and wooden. She wondered whether Barley would still love his ungainly woodwalker sister.

Presently, Toefoot returned with his purchases. Building a fire with the mirror frames, he fried up a hearty breakfast of fresh trout and red potatoes in a black cast-iron skillet the trollogs had left intact. Hannith ate her fish raw, much to Barley's disgust.

Kyleah chewed slowly, savoring her food. The sawdust she had consumed had taken the edge off her appetite. Still, she put away six trout and a veritable mountain of potatoes. Afterwards, she felt famished again. "Could you please make us a firebird-egg omelet?" she begged Toefoot. "Surely we could spare a few eggs."

"Certainly not!" Toefoot indignantly retorted. "Those eggs are strictly for hatching. We need all the wing feathers we can get."

"How are you going to hatch the eggs?" Barley asked him.

"You'll see!" Toefoot replied. After closing and barring the door, he stirred the fire's glowing coals with a poker. Opening one of the bags, he then removed a firebird egg and carefully laid it on the embers. Finally, he stepped back and folded his hairy arms.

"So you *are* making an omelet!" Kyleah said. Already she could taste the egg's delicious contents, and she scratched herself.

"I hope not," Toefoot chuckled. "Now we'll watch and wait!"

Tensely watching the egg, Kyleah recalled the morning she had placed a hen's egg on the coals underneath a simmering syrup cauldron. The egg had burst, spattering its contents everywhere.

Though fierce heat waves rose around it, the firebird egg did not blacken, crack or explode. An hour passed, and still the egg had not changed at all. Toefoot's forehead crinkled with worry.

"During a forest fire," he reflected, "the eggs heat up slowly inside their trees before the fire reaches them. When I put this egg directly on live coals, the shock might have killed the hatchling."

He had just finished speaking when the firebird egg rocked and made a sharp clicking sound. Then a long beak poked through the shell and began pecking at the hole's edges, enlarging it. Finally, a feathered head popped out, followed by the rest of the body. Swiftly, the hatchling spread its wings and darted out of the fire.

"Look out!" cried Hannith as the bird swooped past her, its new feathers flashing in the firelight like sharp, polished sabers.

Barley tried to snatch the bird as it circled Toefoot's workshop, but it easily evaded him. "How do you catch 'em?" he asked.

"I'll show you," Toefoot replied. "Give me my mirror, please."

Barley handed over the pocket mirror Toefoot had lent him for their journey to Penoddion, and the gnome propped it up on a work table. Before long, the firebird had alit on the table and was pecking at the mirror. Grabbing the fledgling, Toefoot plucked out a tail and wing feather before giving the bird to Barley.

Next, the gnome laid the Penoddion-frame's missing top piece back in place. Touching the bottom board at the same time, he nodded at Barley, who released the firebird into the mirror.

"Our very first firebird has returned home to roost," the gnome announced. Bowing, he handed the wing feather to Kyleah. "The silly bird was attracted to its own reflection in my mirror. That trick works every time." Pulling out his pipe, he twirled the tail feather into the stem to clean it out. Afterwards, he clamped his teeth around the mouthpiece and sighed. "At last, a clean pipe!"

"Just don't light it while we're here!" Hannith scolded him. "Maiads don't care for smoke, and I've already breathed my share from your fire. All that soot is unhealthy for maiad or mortal."

Making a wry face, Toefoot put away his beloved pipe.

Kyleah pointed at the Penoddion-frame. "Shouldn't you take off the top piece? What if some trollogs try to come through?"

"They won't now," Toefoot said. "The sun has already risen in Penoddion, and the trollogs must hide themselves from its face. If the dawn catches them—or if they look into the 'perfect glass'—they will turn into trees, sprouting leaves, shoots and roots."

Kyleah glanced at herself in the wing feather and saw a face more trollish than human. Revolted and frightened, she turned away. Then she started hopping up and down on both feet.

Toefoot stared at her. "What are you doing?" he asked her.

"If I'm almost a trollog," she said, "I might root, too!"

The gnome laughed. "You have nothing to fear for now." He sobered. "Hereafter, you should avoid looking into mirrors."

"'Leah!" Barley exclaimed. "You can jump again!"

Kyleah looked down. Her brother was right! Though she still walked with a limp, her leg was no longer as lame. Becoming a trollog had somehow strengthened her crooked bones. Gaelathane had allowed her troll-lashing for a special purpose after all. As Kyleah-the-girl, she never could have covered the entire firebird forest on foot, much less repulse the band of pursuing trollogs.

Now she and Hannith helped Barley and Toefoot lay out more eggs on the coals, until the fire pit resembled a gigantic nest. When the eggs all hatched, the workshop was a-flutter with squawking, screeching birds. Instead of trying to catch them all, Kyleah tied Barley's mirror to the top of the torsil frame, luring the fledglings back into Penoddion. Hannith funneled the birds into the frame with her webbed hands, while Kyleah plucked a wing feather from each bird as it passed through. In this way, the two girls could clear the workshop while Toefoot and Barley filled the fire pit with more eggs and hatched out another batch of lively firebirds.

Several hours later, the last flock of hatchlings flew through the frame into Penoddion. Kyleah and Hannith carefully stuffed the feathers they had collected into two of the burlap bags. One bag Toefoot kept as a gift for King Wortlewig. The other he set by the door, which he unbarred and ceremoniously opened.

"You three had better be moving along," he told his guests.

"You're not coming with us?" Kyleah exclaimed in dismay.

Toefoot shook his head. "I wouldn't be much help. Besides, I must get back to making more mirrors. Don't tarry anywhere long, or the trollogs will sniff you out. I'll keep the fire hot, in case a few of them come slithering down my chimney again. Above all else, follow the prophecies Gaelathane has given you!"

Weeping, Kyleah and Hannith hugged the blushing gnome. After shaking Barley's hand, he said, "Off you go! Please stop by any time you're in the neighborhood. You'll always be welcome in my workshop. Next time, I hope it won't be in such a shambles."

Before she knew it, Kyleah was standing outside the door with Barley and Hannith, grasping Rolin's staff and the bag of feathers. The tunnel was inky black, since the floodwaters had doused the sputtering torches flanking Toefoot's door. Hannith was giggling.

"Gnomes don't like long good-byes!" she said. "That suits me. I am drying up. It's time for me to rejoin my people. Let us go!"

Fortunately for Hannith, the tunnel was still damp from the recent flooding. Splashing through unseen puddles, she quickly revived. After the three companions had been tramping through passages for what seemed hours, Kyleah smelled fresh air and heard quavery, echoing music, like flutes being played in a cave.

"We must be approaching the main hall," said Hannith. "It sounds as if there is a celebration in progress. I cannot imagine why, after all the commotion those woodwalkers caused. Here is another drain outlet. Maybe it will take us where we want to go."

The three scrabbled up through the narrow passage and poked their heads out. They had emerged at one side of the main cavern, which was ablaze with light. Clad in long, flowing robes, myriads of maiads crowded the hall. At the front stood a row of twenty gigantic, long-stemmed crystal goblets between four and five feet tall, with translucent bowls of various widths. The goblets were arranged from shortest to tallest. All contained water. At each delicate piece stood a maiad, webbed hands either poised over the gleaming rim or running lightly along it, calling forth ringing tones that harmonized in a haunting, melancholy melody.

Bare-headed, King Corwyn came forward. In his hands, he cradled a tapering velvet bag and a wooden-handled silver pitcher. Kyleah recognized the pitcher as the one Robin had used to fill the glass globes with luminescent water. "In the beginning," Corwyn said, "Gaelathane created the liquid-that-gives-life to cover the earth. Before He formed the dry land, He made us maiades from the water. 'Rejoice in lake and stream, river and sea,' He told us. 'You must look after all the other creatures of My watery world.'"

Raising the pitcher, Corwyn continued, "This pitcher calls to mind our frailty, for its metal galls us. The Waters of Life that fill it symbolize the spirit the Water Lord pours into every living soul. Now He has taken from us Hannith, Kyleah and Barlomey, and we rightly grieve over our loss. May they now rejoice in the River of the Water of Life that forever flows from beneath the One Tree."

King Corwyn poured the pitcher's contents into the tallest of the crystal goblets. Next, he opened the velvet bag and removed a sledgehammer with a wooden handle and an iron head. "As their lives were poured out," he said, "so let this water be poured out. As their lives were shattered, so shall be this singing goblet."

"No!" Hannith screamed. "Don't—!"

She spoke too late. Corwyn swung the sledgehammer, and the goblet exploded in a shower of glittering shards and sparkling water drops. Scowling furiously, Hannith pulled herself out of the drain hole and marched up to King Corwyn. "Why have you held a Goblet Ceremony for the living?" she demanded, cwelapping. "My friends and I are not dead, but alive. We have returned!"

The hall fell silent. Corwyn stared at her. "Can rivers that have flowed into the sea and mixed with the salt return fresh to their source? Can the rain return to the clouds whence it has fallen, or can this shattered goblet be restored? Yet here you have come back to us alive and whole. May the Water Lord be praised!"

The cavern echoed with cwelapping as the assembled maiads welcomed back a daughter from the dead. Hannith's mother rushed up to greet her, smothering her with kisses and embraces. Wistfully watching the reunion, Kyleah wondered whether her and Barley's homecoming could ever be as joyful as Hannith's.

Dolora would no doubt scold them. "Ragamuffins! Where have you been all this time? There are clothes to launder and dishes to wash; weeds to pull in the garden and water to tote from the well; and the horses are wanting their feed. Now get to it, unless you want to go to bed hungry tonight without your supper!"

Barley broke into Kyleah's musings. "Can we get out now?"

Tossing the feather-bag out onto the floor, Kyleah and her brother emerged from the drain. Together, they approached the maiads who were surrounding Hannith. Shrieks and gasps went up as the water people caught sight of the girl-turned-trollog. Kyleah had forgotten how drastically her appearance had altered, and she self-consciously covered her face with her hands and hair.

"A she-trollog has sneaked in among us!" some cried.

"No, it's a gonomion!" others shouted.

"It is just Kyleah!" Hannith called out. "She has changed on the outside, that's all. Come and see the bag of firebird feathers we have collected. Surely one of them must be the 'perfect glass'!"

Kyleah opened the sack, and the maiads gathered around to marvel at the polished wing feathers. Aquilla held one up to her face, admiring her reflection. "These firebird feathers will serve nicely in place of silvered mirrors, which we maiads cannot use," she said. "If you girls don't mind sharing a few with us, that is."

Hannith and Kyleah didn't. While they passed out feathers, the maiads set up tables for a feast. Hannith was closing up the sack when two women rushed in and threw themselves on Kyleah.

"You're all still alive!" Medwyn and Meghan cried as one. They also embraced Barley, who winced and grunted in boyish disgust.

"We were sure the trollogs had taken you!" said Medwyn.

"If it weren't for Hannith and Toefoot, they would have," Kyleah said, and she recounted the terribly close calls and other harrowing adventures she had shared with Barley and Hannith.

Spreading his finger-webs apologetically, King Corwyn told Kyleah and Barley, "To flush out our foes, I was forced to order the floodgates opened, though it meant you two might perish in water. I am delighted to hear our friend Toefoot took you all in."

"You know Toefoot?" asked Kyleah in amazement.

"Of course!" the king replied. "He keeps to himself, but he's a staunch ally in a pinch—if you can persuade him to open his door. I haven't seen the gnome in years. He and his friends delved our tunnels and halls for us, since we maiads cannot make or wield metal tools. Nobody can swing a pickax like a gonomion, though that race is clannish to a fault. Stoneworms can do the job quicker, but once they have burrowed into a mountain or hill, it is nearly impossible to coax them out again. Given the choice, we would rather have gonomia living under us than giant worms."

Stoneworms? If it weren't for King Corwyn's bland expression, Kyleah would suspect he was telling a tall tale. Stone-burrowing creatures, indeed! She stretched her stiffening arms and legs.

The king eyed her pityingly. "I regret to see our common foe has infected you with the 'woodwalking disease,' for which we have found no cure as yet. Until we do, you are welcome to stay here with us. While you were gone, I commanded our people to seek out the 'perfect glass' or 'flashing thing' in all the burned-over forests within our realm, according to your bracelet riddle."

"What did your servants find?" Kyleah asked the king.

Corwyn's head sagged in defeat. "So far, only some nails and ax heads. I shall call off the search, since these firebirds and their feathers seem to fit the prophecies better than any mirror or iron weapon. Besides, objects of glass and metal could not possibly pass through a forest fire without warping into imperfect shapes."

"But how can feathers defeat the trollogs?" Medwyn asked.

"I don't know," Meghan said. "Kyleah's bracelet prophecy does state that, 'With bloodless bite the blade shall smite/The mocking enemy.' In the parlance of warfare, a 'blade' usually refers to the business end of a sword. A feather's blade makes more sense here, for its 'bite' draws no blood. If these feathers aren't the 'trollish bane,' then Toefoot was climbing the wrong torsil, so to speak."

"Feathers must be the missing clue!" said Medwyn. "From Winona's table-prophecy, we assumed the 'blade not mortal-made' was Felgor's sword, once held by our two-legs who 'goes on three.' Instead, the Leaf Lord must have meant a feather blade, which is grown naturally and is 'not made by hand of maid or man.'"

"Then what am I supposed to do with a bagful of the things?" Kyleah asked. "I can't very well march up to Malroth and say, 'Here, Mr. Malroth, take a look at yourself in some of my feathers!' Can't we just dump them on the trollogs from a tree or a cliff?"

King Corwyn laughed. "Do not concern yourself with the fate of your feathers. Rather, I would advise you to return to your own world and release your companions' tree-bound relatives."

Numbly, Kyleah nodded. She dreaded to think what she might find on the other side of her broken bed, but Corwyn was right. Marlis, Rolin and the other members of the royal family were still intrisoned in Thalmos—and Kyleah alone could deliver them.

"All right," she said. Her voice was growing rumbly and deep. She was tempted to gaze at herself in one of the firebird feathers. Turning into a tree would be better than living as a trollog.

After their four guests had enjoyed a lavish meal, King Corwyn, Hannith and Aquilla ushered them through a stone door into a vertical shaft with a wobbly wooden floor. Kyleah dragged her bag and crutch along, hoping to return the staff to its owner soon.

"Please visit us again!" said Aquilla. "After dusk, simply slap the lake three times with your hand, and we will come to you. Now you must hurry! The sun is setting in the world above, and trollogs may be lurking about. May the Water Lord go with you."

"And with you!" Kyleah replied. "But how are we to reach the surface without stairs? We cannot climb these sheer walls."

"You will ride all the way to the surface!" Hannith announced, stepping inside to join the four. "We are standing on a wooden platform that floats on a water reservoir. When we are ready, my father will release more water into this shaft, elevating us to the level of the Listening Lake. After we have left, he will drain the shaft until the platform has sunk back to its present level."

"Your father?" Kyleah said, confused. "Who is he?"

Hannith laughed. "Why, King Corwyn, of course! I assumed my mother had already told you. I am their only child and heir."

Meghan, Kyleah and Medwyn exchanged baffled looks. "If your mother is the queen," asked Medwyn, "why doesn't she wear a crown and royal robes and sit on a throne beside the king?"

Outside the door, King Corwyn chuckled. "Maiadin kings and queens do not rule together. This year, I am reigning as king, while my wife Aquilla waits upon me. Next year, I will doff my crown to serve her while she reigns as queen. In this way, we are reminded that ruling well requires the humility of a true servant's heart."

Kyleah waved at the king and queen until Corwyn closed the door. As the latch clicked fast, Meghan said, "You forgot this," and she handed Kyleah's bracelet to her. Unfortunately, the band would no longer fit over her swelling trollog's wrist. Instead, she hung the bracelet from its leather thong back around her neck.

Dull mechanical noises came from outside the chamber. Then Kyleah heard gurgling sounds beneath the platform, and it began to rise with a boat-like, rocking motion. She leaned on her crutch to steady herself, while her companions clung to each other.

As it rose, the round wooden floor scraped alarmingly along the shaft's walls. Minutes later, the platform's bumpy ascent stopped.

"Here we are!" Hannith cheerily called out. Moonlight dimly filtered down from the shaft's mouth about twenty feet above.

"You said we could ride this overgrown raft to the surface!" Kyleah grumbled. "Now we'll have to climb the rest of the way."

"I also told you the platform would raise us to the same level as the Listening Lake, which lies just below this hill," Hannith corrected her. "Water always seeks its own level, you know."

Leaping up, the naiad nimbly caught the lowest rung of a stone ladder carved into the shaft's wall. Medwyn and Meghan climbed up to join her. After tossing her feather-bag up to Meghan, Kyleah followed. However, Barley wasn't tall enough to reach the rungs.

"Help me, 'Leah! I'm falling!" he cried, jumping up and down. Sure enough, the platform was dropping back. As Kyleah watched Barley disappear into the darkness, guilt-pangs seized her. Much as though her brother annoyed her at times, she still loved him.

Crouching on the last rung, she lowered her staff until Barley could grab it. The descending platform left him dangling by his arms in mid-air. With a cracking of her thickening wooden joints, Kyleah hauled her brother straight up onto the stone ladder.

"Thank you!" he said, rubbing his wrists and arms.

"Whew!" she gasped. "I thought I was going to lose you."

Meghan and Medwyn regarded her curiously. "For a lame girl, that was quite an impressive feat of strength!" Medwyn said.

Recalling her yearning to be more "strong and sure-footed" to stand up to her stepsisters, Kyleah felt a stab of remorse. Once more, her trollish powers had rescued her—and Barley. Yet, she would give anything to go back to her old weak and gimpy self.

Climbing the ladder, Kyleah and her companions emerged from the shaft amidst a boulder-strewn, mountaintop wood. Downslope, the Listening Lake lapped quietly against its shores. A slivered moon walked a silver path across the lake's waters.

"Where are we going?" Medwyn asked Hannith.

"We are looking for Kyleah's bed. It is the fastest way for you to return to her world so she can free your intrisoned people."

"And if we find any trollogs, we'll trounce 'em!" said Barley.

Kyleah wasn't so sure of that. When it came to trouncing trollogs, brute strength would not avail. Armed might alone had failed to put down the first uprising of an enemy that could regrow missing arms and legs. Kyleah hoped her bagful of feathers would prevail where swords, spears and battleaxes had fallen short.

Meghan peered through the forest. "Finding that bed won't be easy in the dark. When we were fleeing from the trollogs that came out of the bed, there wasn't time to keep track of landmarks."

"You won't be going back to your bed," said a gruff voice.

One of the "boulders" was sprouting a head, legs and arms. What Kyleah had taken for mere rocks were hundreds of trollogs curled up in their black cloaks on the ground. Tromping and stomping, the stilt-legged woodwalkers surrounded her and her terrified companions. Soundlessly, ominously, the dark horde parted to make way for another hulking, black-cloaked figure.

"Welcome, troggling!" said the trollog. It was Malroth.

CHAPTER 23

THE FEATHERS FAIL

Kyleah shrank back, but Malroth easily trapped her in his engulfing cloak. She felt at once terrified and repulsed, yet also oddly comforted by his trollish presence.

"Did you really think you could escape me?" he growled.

Kyleah whipped a shiny feather out of her bag and thrust it in Malroth's face. "Behold the perfect glass!" she cried in triumph.

"Aarrgg!" croaked the trollog king. Clutching his craggy throat, he reeled like a drunken raftsman. Suddenly, he appeared to recover. Snatching the offending feather out of Kyleah's hand, the trollog tipped back his head and swallowed the quill whole.

"A tad dry, but not bad," he remarked. Taking a feather from Kyleah's sack, Malroth stared at his reflection and grunted, "There's a face only another trollog could love. By the black sword, this isn't the 'perfect glass,' either." As he tested more of the quills, a great weight crushed Kyleah's chest. Pagglon's Lay had promised a "perfect glass" would "root the rebel to the rock." Yet so far, Malroth's feet had sprouted no roots and his arms no leaves.

Malroth laughed hideously. "I've found no perfect glasses here, lads!" he gleefully announced to his followers. "This girl has brought me a tasty dowry. What say we have us a feather-feast?"

Malroth tossed the feather bag into the air, releasing its fluffy contents. Bright feathers flew everywhere. To Kyleah's dismay, the trollogs made a gruesome game of catching the floating mirrors and stuffing them into their mouths. Any feathers that managed to miss being eaten ended up falling beneath broad trollish feet and were crushed into the damp ground, making a muddy mess.

Still chuckling unpleasantly, Malroth asked Kyleah, "What made you think a firebird feather could be the 'perfect glass'?"

"You wanted all King Wortlewig's feathers, that's why!"

Again Malroth howled with trollish mirth. "How little you know of us, troggling! Firebird feathers are a trollog delicacy. We relish their taste. As for the 'perfect glass,' you and your misguided friends have been wasting your time. Even if that mythical mirror still exists, we trogs will find it and smash it to smithereens!"

Kyleah wept bitterly. Despite all her clever, daring stratagems, Malroth had still won. Now he was free to pursue his dreams of conquest. "What are you going to do with me?" she asked him.

The question took Malroth aback. "Do with you?" he repeated. "That depends mainly upon you. We will intrison your miserable companions, of course, but we do not eat our own kind. You are a trollog now, and a trollog you shall always be. After the whip has flicked you, there is no going back, as our Lash Chant teaches:

Once trollish lash has tickled your skin,
It won't be long till the itching begins!
Then joints will crack and flesh will fail
As bumps erupt and skin will scale!

For wood will win though flesh is fair;
Stiffening limbs and hardening hair;
Your lotions and salves cannot stem the change
Till human is hidden and trollog remains!

"I am tired of being a trollog!" Kyleah declared.

"Better trollog than human!" Malroth scoffed. "Once, you were weak and crippled. Now your legs are whole. Even if you lost one, you could regrow another. You do not realize your own strength. Why, you could easily uproot one of these trees if you wished."

"Then what do you want from me?" Kyleah demanded. "Why have you been chasing me all this time, if not to devour me?"

Malroth's wooden mask leered at her. "I would make you queen of all the trollogs, second in authority only to me."

"Queen?" The very word fouled Kyleah's mouth. "Why?"

"My present queen no longer pleases me. She has failed to find my sworn enemy, who alone possesses the power to defeat me."

Hesitantly, Kyleah asked, "What enemy might that be?"

"She is called 'the Gifted Girl,'" Malroth replied. "We know only that she is of noble birth. The riddles that speak of her have been hidden from us. Never fear! I have chosen you as my new queen, a trolless who can walk the world freely by day or by night. From you shall spring a new race, one able to fight under the light of moon or sun, moonslipping or sunslipping at will."

"No!" Kyleah wailed. "I don't want to be a trollog-queen!"

Malroth appeared not to hear her. "Just think of it!" he boomed. "Trollogs by the millions will overrun the puny race of men. No longer shall we live in terror of their axes and saws. No longer shall they burn us to heat their houses built of our wood. We shall be kings of the earth, and men shall be our slaves. As for you," he went on, gesturing at Kyleah, "you shall be '*Kylogg*'—'the Troll's Trophy'—and all shall fear you and obey your every command."

"Long live Queen Kylogg!" the other trollogs shouted as one, stamping their flat feet. "May her offspring ever increase!

> A queen we now need, for all who were freed
> From our iron-spiked prisons seek someone to lead!
> With thickening hide, she's a beautiful bride,
> And the king of the trollogs will not be denied!

"Please don't listen to them, 'Leah!" Barley pleaded with her. "I need you; Father needs you. He won't care what you look like."

"Do not deceive yourself!" Malroth rumbled. "You cannot go back to your former life. Once you are wholly trollog, men with burning brands will hunt you and hound you to the death. Your family and friends will be the first to raise their hands against you. Like it or not, you belong with trollogs. You belong with *me*."

Seen through Kyleah's trollish eyes, her fellow travelers looked contemptible—pathetically feeble and stupid next to the cunning, mighty hamadryads. Then she heard a man singing in the forest.

Are you free, truly free from the burden of the tree?
From the burl, from the knurl—are you free to be a girl?
Would you live, truly live, not to take but simply give?
Can you die to the lie and your every dream deny?

Those lilting words cleared the cobwebs from Kyleah's mind. "Queen Kylogg," indeed! How could she betray her family, her friends and Gaelathane by siding with their enemy? How could she live with herself if she accepted Malroth's enticing proposal?

Still singing, the Plugger strode out of the trees, and the trollogs scattered from him. He wore a hooded white cloak and carried a staff over his shoulder. Eyes blazing, he approached Malroth.

"How did you find me, my ancient enemy?" Malroth growled at the intruder. "Must you forever dog my footsteps? Begone! Your pitiful presence is neither welcome nor needed here. Go find some tree-holes to plug before I decide to plug a tree with you!"

"Your disobedience has left much larger holes in my creation," the Plugger shot back. "It is time to repair the damage. You were made to serve mortals, not to destroy them. If you and your rebel followers return to the trees whence you came, you may perhaps forestall your fate. Otherwise, be warned! My prophecies are about to be fulfilled upon your head, and you shall in no wise escape."

Malroth waved his long, limblike arm at the tattered firebird feathers littering the moonlit ground. "If you are referring to your perfect mirrors, old man, we have eaten them! Your prophecies have utterly failed, and I have proclaimed a new vision: The Age of Men is ending, and the Age of Trees has begun. This time, we shall have our revenge upon those who have mistreated our kind. This time, you will not hinder us as you did at the beginning."

"Then you shall have to slay me," said the Plugger simply.

"With pleasure," Malroth said. He drew the black sword with gloved hands. "I should have killed you when I had the chance."

"No!" Kyleah cried, and she threw herself on Malroth's arm.

He shook her off. "No!" she repeated. "Leave him alone. He has done nothing wrong. He's just a poor old man who never hurt anyone." Kyleah hardly knew the Plugger, but she loved him. Had he not rescued her from intrisonment and from the burl's curse?

Looking at her, the Plugger spoke into her heart. *Do not trust the trollog! All his promises are lies straight from the pit of Gundul. As his queen, you would spend all the rest of your days locked up in a tree infected with his black growths. When he had used you up in making his "burlies," he would cast you aside like a dry branch.*

Malroth snorted. "Never hurt anyone?" he said. "This *man* intrisoned me with my own sword for an age and a year." He shoved Felgroth back under his cloak. "The sword is too swift an end for him. Let us first give him a taste of troll skin." Malroth ripped off the Plugger's cloak and jerkin. Two other trollogs grabbed the old man's arms and pinned him against a tree. A third handed Malroth a bundle of long, flat thongs knotted together at one end.

A troll-lash! Kyleah thought. Her back tingled painfully at the memory of the cruel whip's sting. The thongs wriggled and danced in Malroth's fist as if possessing a life of their own. He twitched his arm, and the wicked trollskin strips sang through the air to rake the Plugger's back. Again and again the lash fell upon him, yet he uttered no word or cry of anguish, though his skin hung in tatters from his bloodied back. Then his legs gave way, and he collapsed. Picking up the Plugger's ruined body, Malroth backed into the bloodstained tree, dragging his limp victim inside as a trisoner.

The trollogs thumped their hollow chests and guffawed. "The Plugger saved others; now let him save himself!" they hooted. "Let him come out of the tree and turn us all to stone, if he can!"

As their harsh laughter echoed through the woods, Kyleah noticed Hannith was absent. Then she heard a splash. The naiad must have escaped into the waters of her beloved Listening Lake.

"Let the water-imp go," said Malroth tersely. "When we cut off the head, the whole body will perish. Now we shall see to the head."

He held in his gloved hands three stout iron spikes and a mallet. With the mallet, he drove the spikes into the Plugger's tree—two higher up on the trunk and one near the bottom.

"Two for the hands and one for the feet," he declared. "That should keep him out of my way for good!" Drawing his sword again, Malroth sharpened it on a gritty granite rock. *Whick! Whick! Whick!* went the long black blade. Meanwhile, the other trollogs were thumping their woody chests in time with a dreadful ditty.

> Death! Deal him death! Give him not another breath!
> Let him suffer as a duffer in his tree!
> Strike! Let us strike! Drive the sharpened iron spike;
> Let it enter to the center of his tree!
>
> Hack! Let us hack, till the trunk begins to crack;
> We will chortle as the mortal bares his blood!
> Die! Let him die! Drive the iron through his eye!
> In the killing we'll be spilling all his blood!

After sharpening his sword, Malroth gave Kyleah his gloves. "As my queen," he said, "you must be the first to strike the tree."

Cringing, Kyleah dropped her crutch and took the oversized gloves. She put them on and grasped the sword's proffered hilt. Instead of the usual pangs of pain, she felt a surge of power. Then she understood. Felgor had forged Felgroth for Malroth and his minions. Since Kyleah had become a trollog, too, the sword was responding to her as it did to Malroth. She swung the blade, and it whistled through the air. A slashing downward stroke clove a stump cleanly in two. Malroth nodded and grunted approvingly.

Kyleah quivered with excitement. With this sword, she could lead armies to victory, making mincemeat of her foes. She would also make her tormenters pay, beginning with Dolora, Gyrta and Garta. *Gimpy. Lame-leg. Cripple.* Bitter rage possessed her as she relived the shame of those mocking names. If only the witless people of Mapleton could see her now! She would take immense pleasure in hacking the soft, spineless mortals to bloody ribbons.

She raised the black sword to hew the Plugger's tree. Once the deed was done, she would become Queen Kylogg the Great.

"For the love of Gaelathane, don't do it!" Meghan cried.

Kyleah dropped the sword as horror, fear and shame filled her fractured heart. What was she doing? What had she become?

You must forgive your enemies, came the Plugger's voice again.

"Pick up the sword!" Malroth ordered her.

"I—I cannot!" Kyleah protested.

"PICK IT UP!" roared the trollog king.

Kyleah sank sobbing to earth. Killing was beyond her now.

Malroth spat. "Too much of the mortal still lives in you."

Stripping the gloves off Kyleah's hands, he took up the sword and pointed it at her. Now the pain began. As Malroth twisted the blade, Kyleah's insides were ripped apart. Blood poured from her mouth and nose. Desperately, she tried to crawl away from her torturer, but the other trollogs hemmed her in. Helpless to defend herself or stop the pain, she could only thrash about in torment.

"'I am Queen Kylogg!' Say it!" Malroth bellowed at her.

Kyleah could not speak. She was choking on her own blood.

"Say it!" Felgroth twisted again, and white-hot knives stabbed her. Somehow, she knew if she broke down and repeated Malroth's four words, the last shreds of the girl Kyleah would die, allowing the trollog within to consume her. Malroth's queen would become a bloodthirsty trolless bent on destroying the human race.

Raising her head, she told the trollog king, "Never."

The agony crested within her like Hannith's giant moat-wave. Then the wave crashed down into a numbing darkness.

CHAPTER 24

THE FIRE SETS FREE

Thack! Kyleah opened her pain-bleared eyes. Lifting her head, she saw Malroth striking the Plugger's tree another resounding blow with the black sword. *Crack!* After a few more blows, the trunk splintered and toppled with a great crash.

Feebly clutching her crutch, Kyleah let her head fall back. She was finished. Either Malroth would soon turn on her and hack her to pieces, or his sword would rip her apart from the inside out.

The troll king dragged Kyleah over to an oak. She shut her eyes as her body lurched. Ice shot through her aching limbs.

This is death, she thought. *Maybe I have descended to that place the Lucambrians call "Gundul."* When she cracked open her eyes, however, she saw she had been intrisoned inside the oak. Outside, Malroth was also intrisoning Meghan, Medwyn and Barley. Kyleah gasped. Dark blood was oozing from the Plugger's fallen tree.

Kyleah's eyes welled with trollish tears as the life ebbed from her broken body. Trapped inside this tree, she would die unloved and unmourned. No one would ever find her. Even if she survived the night, Malroth would plant a burl on her oak, and the burlie would snuff out her last sparks of life. Alive or dead, Kyleah was utterly powerless to help the others in their intrisoning trees.

Malroth returned to Kyleah's tree and pounded an iron spike into the trunk, piercing her heart with terrible pain. "After a few years' intrisonment, you will change your mind!" he snarled at her through the wood. "I must leave now to claim my throne in Lucambra—the first of many worlds I shall conquer, including Gundul itself. Glunt will keep you company until my return, when I will burlip you and your friends." Turning aside, he thumped his chest, and a leafy mound on the forest floor sprang to life. First, a shaggy green neck snaked out, followed by clawed feet. It was Larkin's fringe-headed marsh dragon. Malroth spoke into Glunt's ear, and the beast shambled over to flop down before Kyleah's oak. Smoke poured from its nostrils as it began to snore loudly.

Malroth and his friends moved off into the forest, leaving Kyleah alone in her oak. The night's heartbeat fluttered, faltered and stopped. Only the dragon's rumbling snores broke the uneasy stillness. Kyleah groaned with the pain of her wounds and the greater anguish of her failure. How could she have let everyone down so badly? Why had the Plugger so willingly thrown away his life? Who would plug the tapholes in Mapleton's trees now? The trollogs would soon overrun Kyleah's village anyway, leaving no one to tap maples or to boil down the sap into sweet syrup.

She tried to shift her body, but the iron spike stuck her no matter where she moved. She wondered how Barley and Medwyn and Meghan were faring in their own trees. As the moon rose, the tree-shadows slowly shortened, as if the forest were shrinking. Kyleah wished she could shrink away from the intrisoning spike.

She must have fainted or fallen asleep, because when she next looked out, the shadows had retreated before some shining winged creatures standing beside the Plugger's mutilated tree. Resembling men and women with bright robes, fair faces and flowing hair, they bent in unison to lift the prostrate trunk, placing it upright on the stump. Without even flapping their wings, they vanished.

Her agony and despair forgotten, Kyleah gazed out upon an unmarred tree that appeared wholly restored. Light burst from the trunk, and the Plugger stepped out, now recognizable as the Man Kyleah had met after her near-drowning in Listening Lake.

Stepping around the sleeping dragon, the Man swiftly strode up to Kyleah's tree. "Do you know who I am?" He asked her.

"You're the Plugger, but how did you survive being chopped down in that tree? The whipping alone should have killed you."

"I am Gaelathane," He said, and He showed her the terrible wounds Malroth's sword had inflicted. "I died once through the Tree of trees to deliver My creation from darkness and death. Now I live forevermore. Wherever evil and rebellion linger in any world, I must relive that sacrifice until My love has conquered all."

Gaelathane! So this was the One of Whom Kyleah's friends had spoken. "Who were the winged people that righted Your tree?" she asked. "Their garments shone nearly as brightly as Yours."

The King smiled. "Those were My servants. In most worlds, they are known as 'angels.' I have assigned an angel to look after you. He has been very busy lately keeping you out of trouble."

"Then can You or my angel please get me out of this tree?"

"Do you truly wish to be free?" Gaelathane countered.

"Yes! Yes! Of course!" Kyleah cried. Inside the tree, her voice sounded thick and muffled. "Please—Malroth will return soon!"

"If I freed you from this tree, you would still be intrisoned."

"What are You saying?" Kyleah wept. She was drowning in pain and dread. Did she hear Malroth's footsteps approaching?

"Ever since your accident," said Gaelathane gently, "you have lived in a prison of your own making. Hatred and bitterness are its bars. Only you possess the key that opens your cell. I cannot release you from bondage until you have released your enemies."

"I don't have any key!" Kyleah wailed. Bathed in a fear-sweat, she stole a glance down at Glunt. The dragon was still sleeping.

"Forgiveness is the key," Gaelathane told her. "Just as I have forgiven you, so you must learn to forgive others." Reaching into the oak, He touched Kyleah. One after another, she began reliving the painful events of her past. Her stepmother's and stepsisters' cruel taunts and sidelong looks of contempt; the stabs and jabs of thoughtless townspeople; the "accidental" kicks that sent her crutch flying—all of those ugly scenes played out vividly before her eyes, leaving her weeping in shame and humiliation.

"Will you forgive those who hurt you?" Gaelathane asked.

"Yes, but I don't know how," Kyleah hesitantly replied.

"Then let us go back again," said Gaelathane, smiling.

As each scene replayed, He prompted Kyleah to forgive her tormentors in the very act. When the ordeal was done, a sense of freedom flooded Kyleah's being, leaving her weak with relief.

"Now will you let me out?" she asked Gaelathane. "This spike is hurting me, and if I stay here much longer, Malroth will come along with his friends and burlip me with a nasty fat burl."

Gaelathane shook His shaggy head. "As I once promised you, I must first remove 'the burl you cannot see.'" Before Kyleah could object, His hand plunged through the tree and into her chest. She felt a tickling sensation. Then a sharp pain left her gasping.

Outside the oak, Gaelathane held up a black, dripping lump, knobbly and misshapen like a burl. "Felgor forged Felgroth from an ashtag burl," He said. "When the wicked blade wounded you, it infected your heart with one of those black burls as well. If I had not torn out this growth, it would have completely consumed you from the inside out, filling you with Gundul's utter darkness."

Gaelathane blew on the bloody burl in His hand. It burst into flames, burning down to a pile of smoking ashes. He blew again, and the ashes whirled away in a black cloud beneath the moon.

"Now I must plug the hole where the cursed canker grew," He said, puffing into His cupped hands. A warm light blossomed between them. When He opened His hands again, a glowing ball floated out and sailed toward Kyleah's tree. Passing through bark and wood, it entered her heart, filling her with peace and joy.

"Peace I leave with you; My peace I give to you!" said the King. "You are now healed, spirit, soul and body. I will never leave you or forsake you, even in your darkest hour of peril and despair."

"But I am still an intrisoned trollog!" Kyleah said. "And what about the 'perfect glass' that was supposed to defeat Malroth?"

Gaelathane sighed. "You are free now. As for My prophecies, you and your friends never bothered to ask *Me* what they meant. Had you asked, I would have told you. As it was, you relied upon your own powers of reasoning and misinterpreted My words."

"Then what do Your prophecies mean?" Kyleah asked. But Gaelathane had disappeared into the moonlit, woodsy landscape.

"Thanks for nothing!" Kyleah muttered. "I'm still stuck in this dratted tree!" Then it dawned on her: The spike no longer was burning her. She thrust it out of the oak and stepped outside. Gaelathane had been right after all. "I *am* free!" she crowed.

"Not for long, you aren't!" a deep voice growled.

Head weaving, Glunt was glaring at her with fiery eyes. The iron spike she had just pushed out was lying at the dragon's feet.

"I was dreaming of some tasty marsh rabbits when you hit me with this!" the beast rumbled, nudging the spike with her clawed foot. "Now I am going to roast and devour you!" Flames leapt from the dragon's fringed jaws, singeing Kyleah's face and arms.

Kyleah—your crutch! The weighty staff King Rolin had lent her was lying beside the oak. She must have dropped it there when Malroth had intrisoned her. Having no proper weapon at hand, she snatched up the staff and held it upright before her face.

The dragon opened her jaws again, and blazing fires burst forth, enveloping Kyleah in terrific heat. Shutting her eyes, she turned her head aside and prayed the end would come swiftly.

Oddly, she felt no pain. Choking on the dragon's breath, she screwed open one eye. Her warty troll skin was sloughing away, hanging off her body in tattered strips and lumpy sheets. All that remained of her bracelet was a golden puddle lying at her feet.

As Glunt paused to suck in a new torrent of fresh air, Kyleah opened both eyes and gasped. Her wooden crutch had burned away, leaving bright metal in its place. She was gripping a sword!

Recalling the powerful feel of Felgroth in her hands, she leapt upon Glunt, catching the dragon off guard. With two mighty blows, she severed the beast's head. It fell smoking to the ground. The rest of the creature's body collapsed in a quivering heap.

Kyleah fell back against Glunt's carcass, coughing at the awful stench of her own burned skin. She could hardly believe what had happened. All this time, she had been carrying a staff with a sword hidden inside! No wonder the thing had felt so heavy. She wiped the bloody blade on some leaves and examined it more closely.

Gleaming letters were engraved upon it. *King of kings and Lord of lords*, the words said. She had found Elgathel's sword! Rolin must have given her the sword-staff to keep it from Larkin. No one would ever suspect a cripple's crutch of concealing a weapon.

Gaelathane had told her she would "pass through water and through fire," and so she had. If He had given in to her pleas and freed her from the oak, the flying spike would not have awakened Glunt, and Elgathel's sword would not have been revealed.

The dragon's fires had exposed something else. As Kyleah picked at the scraps of gnarled troll hide dangling from her body, she discovered fresh pink skin lying underneath. She tore more troll skin off her face, her arms and her legs. Then she sidled up to a boulder and scraped the burnt skin off her shoulders and back.

After rubbing the dirt off one side of a trollog-trampled firebird feather, she looked at her reflection. A grimier version of her old self stared grimly back. She had become Kyleah-the-girl again!

Laughing and crying, she danced around the dragon. Then she started to shiver. Glunt had burned all the clothing off her body, and the night air was nipping at her new bare skin. Casting about for something to wear, she spotted the Plugger's white cloak lying nearby. She shrugged it on and wrapped it around herself.

Next, she released her brother from his tree. Barley bounded out of the trunk and stared at her. "You look normal!" he gasped. "What happened to you? Say, is that a dragon lying over there?"

"I haven't time to explain now," Kyleah told him. "Malroth could return any minute!" Dragging Barley after her, she freed Medwyn and Meghan from their trees. Her friends properly thanked her, but they wondered at her changed appearance. Pointing at the dead dragon, Kyleah described how Glunt's fires had both restored her and revealed the sword. She held up the weapon. Its sharp blade flashed menacingly in the moonlight.

"That is Elgathel's sword, all right," said Meghan. "I would recognize it anywhere. I wondered why Father had gone to the trouble of shaping that stick when he already had plenty of other staffs. He must have suspected Larkin's intentions and wanted to conceal the sword. It has been sitting under our very noses!"

"I should have recognized the Plugger was the Leaf Lord," said Medwyn. "He wears a different guise in each of His worlds. Look! Kyleah is walking without a limp; her leg looks much better!"

Kyleah's scarred and twisted leg was perfectly smooth and straight. "The 'limping lass' is gone for good!" Kyleah quipped.

Medwyn clapped a hand to her head. "Of course! It all makes perfect sense now. Elgathel's sword must be the 'perfect glass'!

> A perfect glass for limping lass
> Lies waiting in the wood;
> The perfect sword Lucambra's lord
> Gave up for greater good.
>
> The flashing thing fit for a king
> Hides fast within a tree;
> In darkness sealed, to be revealed
> When fire shall set it free.
>
> Not made by hand of maid or man,
> This trollish bane shall be;
> With bloodless bite the blade shall smite
> The mocking enemy.

"You are right!" Meghan agreed. "And 'the wood' refers not to a forest, but to Kyleah's wooden staff! 'Lucambra's lord'—my father—'gave up' his 'perfect sword' for the 'greater good' of all Gaelathane's created worlds! The next four verses fall into place now, too. Elgathel's sword—'the flashing thing'—wasn't hidden inside a real tree, but inside a staff made from a tree! The sword was 'revealed' only when the marsh dragon's fires 'set it free' by burning away the wood that surrounded it! Yet, if Elgathel himself forged this sword, then it was indeed made by the hand of man."

"But it was not reforged by a man's hand!" said another voice.

Kyleah turned to find Toefoot stepping out from behind a tree. Over his shoulder, he was carrying a pickax and a bulging bag.

"What are you doing here, you dear old gnome?" she cried, rushing to embrace him. Embarrassed, Toefoot deftly ducked out of the way. Unable to stop herself, Kyleah collided with a rock, scraping her fresh skin. For once, she missed her old troll hide.

Toefoot told her, "I'm glad to see you looking like your old self again! I gather the dragon burned away your trollog's skin—at the cost of his own head. Well done! The only good dragon is a dead dragon, I always say. Anyway, I thought you could use some more of these firebird feathers, so I came looking for you up here. I hope you won't mind my bringing along a few staunch friends."

Four more gnomes joined him. Like Toefoot, they were bald and bearded and toted one or two sharp-pointed pickaxes apiece. All wore leather trousers and jerkins. Toefoot introduced his stocky companions as Hardhand, Smoothpate, Bigtoe and Forger.

"Hardhand is a miner," Toefoot said. "Smoothpate smelts ore; Bigtoe is a tunneler and Forger makes pickaxes and other tools."

In turn, Kyleah introduced herself, Barley, Meghan and Medwyn. Toefoot's four friends bowed and chorused, "May your pickaxes never grow blunt and your tunnels never collapse!"

"Thank you!" Kyleah said. Privately, she wondered what help the gnomes could possibly offer. Then she told Toefoot what had taken place since she and her companions had left his workshop.

"I'm sorry I dragged you to Penoddion just to collect a bag of trollog treats," said Toefoot humbly. "I noggled awry. Gaelathane was correct; we never did ask Him what those riddles meant."

"That's all right," Kyleah graciously replied. "I trust Gaelathane will still use those feathers, though I don't know exactly how."

Meghan asked Toefoot, "What did you mean when you said Elgathel's sword 'was not reforged by a man's hand'?"

"According to Pagglon's Lay, 'the perfect glass' was 'once forged anew.' If I recall my history, your relative rediscovered Elgathel's sword, and the griffins of the Willowah Mountains repaired it."

Meghan nodded. "My great-grandfather found the sword on Elgathel's coffin in the Hallowfast, and the broken tip turned up in an old wooden box. Later, the griffins rejoined the two pieces."

Medwyn was eyeing the gnomes' pickaxes dubiously. "Those picks look awfully sharp. You don't use them on trees, do you?"

"Never!" Toefoot cheerfully replied. "Just on stone and coal."

"We had better be leaving," said Kyleah. "I don't want to be here when Malroth returns to find I've beheaded his pet dragon!"

Setting off for Mt. Argel's summit, the company came to the moonlit grove of linden trees where Kyleah's bed had stood. All at once, Barley gave a yelp and pointed at one of the gray trunks.

"There's someone inside that tree!" he cried.

"There is?" Kyleah said. By moonlight, she could make out the telltale head of an iron spike jutting from the linden's trunk just below a grotesque black burl. She struck the burl with Elgathel's sword. *Crack!* The lump of deformed wood split and dropped off. Then Kyleah drew out the spike and tossed it aside. Finally, she jammed her arm into the linden and waved her hand to and fro.

Grasping cloth, she pulled out the trisoner in a jumble of arms and legs. "Wynnagar!" she exclaimed. "You are alive after all!"

The freed worldwalker seemed dazed but little the worse for her long intrisonment. With her sharp eyes, Wynnagar quickly took in Kyleah's smooth stride, baby-pink skin and shining sword. She also noticed Toefoot and the other gnomes gathered around.

"Here's a tale that begs the telling!" she murmured.

"But we haven't time to tell it!" Kyleah said. "We must return to the sugar bush and free the others before Malroth catches up to us. We should find my bed over there, or what is left of it."

Peering through the trees, Kyleah could just make out the pile of shattered boards that had once been her passage bed. With a shout, she started toward it, but Toefoot suddenly held her back.

"Don't take another step," he warned her, and he sniffed the air. "These fine noses of ours aren't just for looks. Gnomes are blessed with a very keen sense of smell—and I smell a trap!"

"A trap?" Meghan asked. "What kind of a trap?"

In answer, Toefoot motioned the little band toward Kyleah's bed. For yards around it, the ground was unnaturally smooth, as if a gray blanket had covered all the branches, rocks and ferns.

Toefoot picked up a fallen limb and pitched it out a few feet. As soon as it landed, the ground rippled and rolled, flinging the branch end-over-end through the air. There came an awful *crunch*, and with a blubbering *poof*, a shower of splinters shot up.

"That old helihag didn't care for my gift!" Toefoot chuckled.

"What's a *helihag*?" Barley asked, wide-eyed.

"It's a flat, fleshy creature that inhabits deep lakes and caves far from the light of day," Bigtoe said. "We also call them 'hurla-hogs,' because they can toss a full-grown wild boar fifty yards or more—and eat it, too. We gnomes often came across whole caverns filled with helihags while we were excavating Mt. Argel."

Kyleah shivered. "What is this one doing up here, anyhow?"

Toefoot said, "Our woodwalkers are as clever as they are ugly. They laid out this hurlahog to guard the way to your bed. Being long-legged, the trollogs can still easily hop across the 'hag, but if we were to walk out there, we'd be tossed right into its mouth."

"How are we supposed to cross safely, then?" Meghan asked.

"You'll see," Toefoot replied. The gnomes spread out all along the helihag's smooth margin. At Toefoot's signal, each gnome drove his pickax through the helihag's hide and into the earth.

Kyleah jumped back as the helihag billowed and flapped like a ship's sail in a gale, all the while making horrible gurgling sounds. Still, the pickaxed sections remained firmly fixed to the ground.

"Let's go!" Toefoot ordered. "I don't know how long those picks will hold. We must reach the bed before they loosen."

Staggering across the heaving helihag's squishy, stinking skin, Kyleah and Barley held hands to keep from falling. They were half-way to the bed when a reddish hole loomed in the helihag's hide. Row upon row of sharp, curved teeth lined the fetid pit, which Kyleah gathered was the mouth. She hastened onward.

At last, they reached the broken bed. Pieces of the frame lay scattered on a patch of ground bordered by the flopping helihag. Fortunately, the headboard and footboard were still intact.

Kyleah showed the gnomes how to position the two wooden panels overhead and underfoot. One by one, the bald little men disappeared. Wynnagar, Medwyn and Meghan made passage next. Meghan had just vanished when the helihag popped one of the pickaxes out of the ground and flung it away like a broken toy.

Kyleah and Barley were standing on the footboard when the helihag worked the other pickaxes loose and vigorously shook them off. Seizing the headboard, Kyleah brought it down on her and Barley just as the helihag's thrashing bulk brushed their legs.

CHAPTER 25

THE FIELD OF FEAR

D a iawn! Well done!" Rolin said, patting Barley's head. The two stood with Kyleah beneath the scaffolding that housed Elgathel's silver bell at the top of the Hallowfast. Kyleah's brother had just finished hanging the missing clapper over its wire hook. The Greencloaks all clapped and cheered.

Rolin told Barley, "When I was a boy, I rehung the clapper on this bell while standing on Bembor's shoulders, just as you did on mine. On that day, an ashtag and a pack of batwolves were trying to tear us to pieces. Fortunately, the griffins rescued us first."

Bembor said, "Though the sorcs are no longer bound to obey the summons of this bell, may they come to our aid once again."

"We shall do our part," said Scanlon. "The rest is up to Gaelathane." Pulling on a chain, he set the bell swinging. Faster and faster the bell rocked, until it began pealing. Echoing from the sorcathel, the ringing resounded across Lucambra's green hills.

The last of their company to escape the helihag, Barley and Kyleah had stood stunned in her wrecked room. Her belongings lay smashed all over the floor. The rampaging trollogs had made a shambles of the house, sparing only the kitchen. The deserted cottage reeked of stale air, rotten food, death and disaster.

Eerily frosted in ice-white moonlight, Mapleton itself appeared abandoned. No cheery lights burned behind curtained windows; no cooking-smoke rose from crooked chimneys; no haunting harp music or laughter drifted through welcoming cottage doors.

Driven by fear of Malroth's return, Kyleah led her companions up into the groves of thick-leafed maple trees muttering in their dream-heavy sleep. With Barley's help, she found and freed all her intrisoned friends. Many tears fell in the forest that night when the royal family was reunited. Afterwards, Kyleah introduced Barley, Wynnagar and the bearded gnomes to the grateful Greencloaks. Toefoot and his friends especially intrigued old Bembor, who had always assumed the gonomia were purely mythical beings.

Rolin had never suspected Larkin's treachery. Rather, acting upon Gaelathane's promptings, he had carved a hollow staff of ash and concealed Elgathel's sword inside. Kneeling before the king, Kyleah returned the blade to its rightful owner. However, Rolin insisted that she still wear the weapon for safekeeping. "I sense its destiny and yours shall be entwined for a time," he told her.

Also obeying the King's nudgings, Kyleah dragged her friends through a driving rainstorm to Malroth's tree. After Larkin had disabled Elgathel's bell, Malroth concealed the bell's clapper high inside his tree, where only a trollog could reach it. He had not reckoned on the Gifted Girl and her brother. Once Barley spotted the clapper, Kyleah climbed onto Emmer's shoulders and neatly retrieved the precious piece of silver from the tree's heart.

Armed with the clapper, the Greencloaks had only to reunite it with the bell in order to alert their griffin allies. Without a willing torsil, however, there was no hope of returning to Lucambra.

Then Timothy blew his griffin-whistle, which would summon any sorc within earshot. To Barley and Kyleah's delight, Windsong, Ironwing and Smallpaw appeared, along with a motley assortment of other lion-eagles that had also been torsil-exiled in Thalmos.

After the griffins had shared the latest news with their two-legged friends, they carried their riders into the rain-drenched morning sky. Wishing to look into the mysterious disappearance of Mapleton's townsfolk, Wynnagar alone remained behind.

Flying with her whooping brother on a golden-winged griffin named Quickfeather, Kyleah thrilled to the sight of the Tartellans' forests passing beneath her. Barley was so excited he almost fell off the beast's back. Unaccustomed to heights, Toefoot and the other gnomes clamored to be let off at the next hill. In the end, they nearly had their wish. One of the closest hills on the Foamwater's far side boasted a solitary Lucambra-torsil Larkin had overlooked. After making passage through the tree's top, the griffins flew all their riders to the Hallowfast. They found the tower occupied, its door sealed and windows blocked up from the inside to shut out the mid-morning sun. Fortunately, the sorcathel was unguarded.

Thump. While Elgathel's bell pealed, the sorcathel's trapdoor raised, and a human hand emerged. Windsong's head jabbed downward, and Kyleah heard a muffled shriek. The bleeding hand promptly disappeared, and the trapdoor slammed shut. Though Kyleah knew the trollogs could not show themselves during the day, Larkin and his turncloak henchmen had no reason to fear the sunlight. She was glad the griffins were guarding the trapdoor!

The Greencloaks and gnomes took turns ringing Elgathel's bell throughout that day. Yet, no griffins darkened the sky.

The clouds in the west were blushing crimson when Elwyn gave a shout and pointed southeast. "Look there!" he cried. "I see something flying through the mountains. The sorcs have come!"

Kyleah could barely see a dark speck floating in the air above the coastal mountains. Was it a single sorc, or a whole battalion?

"The griffins have come! The griffins have come!" cheered the Greencloaks. While the gnomes gamboled and the young folk skipped, Elwyn grabbed Kyleah's hand and took her on a dizzying spin around the sorcathel. Before the accident, Kyleah had loved to dance, especially during Mapleton's Sugaring Festival, when the villagers celebrated the end of the sugaring season with lively fiddle music and stacks of pancakes dripping with maple syrup.

Suddenly, a lone griffin fluttered over the tower's battlements and collapsed, gasping for breath. The Greencloaks rushed to its side. All the sorcs who were not guarding the trapdoor nuzzled the newcomer and chittered to him in their own peculiar tongue.

"Why, it's Keeneye!" Rolin exclaimed. "If you hadn't given Timothy that silver whistle after we visited the Golden Wood, we would still be in Thalmos trying to find our way back home."

"I'm glad you could put it to good use!" Keeneye wheezed.

"Welcome, Keeneye!" said Bembor gravely. "May your fur and feathers never fall out! Why is it that you have come alone?"

"Last night, the tree-trolls caught us completely unawares," Keeneye began in a quavering voice. "Those hardy creatures scaled our sheer cliff faces by worming their long fingers and toes into the rock the way tree roots work their way into cracks. The climbers proved nearly impossible to dislodge. Once they got into our access tunnels, they plugged the passageways with rock. King Redwing and I barely escaped through a back entrance before the beasts blocked that, too. Redwing flew south to enlist the help of our relatives in those regions, while I flew north to answer the bell's call. I am afraid one worn-out griffin cannot offer you much assistance, but as we sorcs say, 'My wings are yours!'"

Rolin bowed. "We do not accept your allegiance lightly, brave Keeneye. Help from any quarter comes as a blessing. Yet, you bring us dismal news. Larkin's men have already seized this tower, and we had hoped your kin in the Willowahs would arrive in greater numbers to relieve us, for we are sorely beset by the turncloaks."

"We must fear Malroth as well!" Kyleah broke in. "He has come here to claim the throne of Lucambra, either by force or by treachery. This is only the first world he intends to conquer. If we do not stop him, he will enslave us all." After describing the riddle she had found beneath the stone table, Kyleah recited the second stave: "'For buried sword of Gundul's lord/Shall fit the slotted stone/A fateful twist of weaponed fist/Shall seat him on his throne.' Elgathel's sword alone can defeat such a weapon."

Opio said, "Though a mighty arm should wield it, how could the sword of Elgathel vanquish Malroth's black hordes? Besides, you have told us these tree-trolls would resprout any limbs we chopped off. Such a bloodless enemy can be beaten only by fire."

Bembor cleared his throat. "I disagree," he said stoutly. "The key to our victory lies in following Gaelathane's prophecies.

"Obviously, the black sword Felgroth was 'buried' for long years in Malroth's tree. When Felgor first discovered Gundul, he forged terrible weapons in its eternal fires. Supposedly, one of those dark devices was to serve as the key to Gundul's gates. Most of Felgor's infernal creations later perished in Mt. Golgunthor's downfall, but Felgroth escaped destruction when the sorcerer gave it to Malroth. If only I could learn more about that sword!"

Kyleah said, "When I was intrisoned on Mt. Argel, Gaelathane told me the black sword had been formed from an ashtag burl. What kind of a tree is an ashtag, anyhow? Do they grow here?"

Her companions' faces paled with alarm. "Any blade made of ashtag wood must be deadly indeed!" said Gemmio. "I did not think any trace of those trees remained in Gaelathane's worlds."

Bembor explained, "Ashtags are black, poisonous trees whose ancestors Felgor discovered in Gundul and bred with the torsils of the upper worlds. After he sowed his ashtag seeds beneath the sun, the trees acted as Gundul-torsils. Gaelathane's blood destroyed all the ashtags in Lucambra and in most other worlds as well."

"If anything could unlock Gundul's gates, it would be that sword," said Rolin. "We must pray Winona's 'slotted stone' lies buried beneath Mt. Golgunthor's ruin. If that stone has survived, then we may have much more than trollogs to contend with."

Emmer slowly nodded. "Reopening Gundul could unleash a second plague of yegs, gorks and other unclean creatures worse than the first scourge that Felgor brought upon Lucambra."

Suddenly, Kyleah heard a low rumbling sound below, like the rolling drumbeat of thunder signaling an approaching storm. Elwyn and Timothy rushed to the parapet and peered down.

"They're coming out!" Timothy cried.

Everyone hurried over to join the two young men. In dusk's failing light, a black tide could be seen vomiting from the door of the Hallowfast and sweeping around the tower. Other dark streams were pouring out of the forests, merging with the main current to form a swelling river that meandered southward. Kyleah gasped. Like hungry ants climbing a table leg, hundreds of grim trollogs were silently swarming up the Hallowfast, blackening the tower.

"We must leave at once!" Rolin yelled. "Riders, to your mounts! Sorcs, shadow those trollogs. We must hinder them from making further mischief! Take the turncloak Larkin alive if you can."

As Kyleah and Barley hopped on Quickfeather, the trapdoor flew up, and more woodwalkers piled out. One of them seized Quickfeather's back leg, dragging him down. With his other hind leg, the griffin slashed off the trollog's wooden fist. Even as the sorc rose into the air, trollogs were pouring over the battlements.

Soaring into the purpling night sky, Quickfeather joined his fellow griffins. Together, they followed the woodwalker army as it marched across streams and rivers, over hills and through dells. Malroth's dark legions ignored the griffins hovering above them, even when a recovered Keeneye began dropping small boulders on the relentless trollog army, crushing some of the creatures. Leaving their wounded behind, the trollogs tramped onward.

"I would much rather fight these tree-trolls than follow them," Quickfeather confessed. "I am looking forward to tearing some of the creatures apart before I myself am gloriously slain in battle. Unfortunately, I hear woodwalkers taste like rotten sawdust."

"Er, if it's all the same to you," Kyleah told him, "Barley and I would prefer you let us get off on the ground before you do any trollog-tearing or dying. Believe me, there is nothing glorious or honorable in death-by-trollog. Besides, heights make me dizzy."

"Nonetheless, you do seem to enjoy flying, which is more than I can say for your rude companions with the stubby legs," said Quickfeather. "I overheard their leader calling Ironwing a 'flying fur-ball.' Those rash words nearly cost him his head. Speaking of 'heads,' those bald short-legs should try eating some starberries. Doing so might encourage the fur on their scalps to regrow."

Kyleah could not help laughing. "I think that is how gnomes are supposed to look, and anyway, I actually like them that way!"

Now turning west, the trollogs marched up a gorge in the mountains Kyleah had just learned were called the "Brynnmors." The ravine at length opened onto a desolate, boulder-strewn plain hemmed in by snowy peaks. No green thing grew on that wind-blasted waste where moon-shadows lurked beneath the rocks.

Kyleah shivered in the cold, thin air. "What is this place?"

"We sorcs call it the *Agorashon*—'Field of Fear.' Felgor planted the first ashtags down there," Quickfeather replied. "Below us lies the Dreadrock, where Felgor mustered his gorkin army. Though his black trees are no more, griffins avoid flying over this spot."

Trollogs were flooding the Agorashon, filling it with their black-cloaked figures like a beach packed with mussel shells.

"How I wish the sun would rise upon them all!" Kyleah said.

"Hunh! Hunh! Hunh!" The trollogs had turned their wooden faces upward and were grunting in unison. The guttural chant grew louder, until the very air throbbed. Kyleah's ears ached.

Screeching, the griffins veered away from the Field of Fear. They landed together in the forest a mile below the Agorashon.

"The woodwalkers were making those dreadful noises to drive us away!" Quickfeather told Kyleah and Barley. "The fiends! They must have known we sorcs have sensitive ears. I am afraid you two must go on without me. I cannot risk damaging my hearing, for I depend upon it to catch conies and to navigate the twisting tunnels where we griffins live in the Willowah Mountains."

All the other sorcs said the same thing. They would remain in the woods while the gnomes and Greencloaks went ahead to scout out the enemy's defenses. Reluctantly, the riders dismounted.

"We have but one decent sword among us!" Gemmio pointed out. "What is that against a half-million of Malroth's tough-limbed warriors? I say we fly back to the Hallowfast and securely fortify it against these creatures. Come the dawn, they will find the tower shut fast against them, and they will become harmless trees again. Let us not throw away our lives and the kingdom for naught!"

"You are mistaken," Toefoot retorted, folding his thick arms. "The woodwalkers could demolish your fine tower stone by stone if they so desired. You don't know their malice and strength."

Medwyn added, "You must remember these creatures of wood cannot be conquered by mortal might or force of numbers—and they can multiply like rats and mice in a granary. Only Gaelathane can crush them as we obey the prophecies He has given us."

"Well said!" Bembor put in.

214

"Besides," said Rolin, "we must not allow Larkin to 'open Gundul's gates.' I suspect that is why the trollogs have come here."

King Rolin was still speaking when a howling mob of black-cloaked woodwalkers fell upon the company. Screams and shouts split the windless night as gnomes, Greencloaks and griffins tried to repel their attackers. Kyleah hacked off trollog legs and trollog arms with Elgathel's sword. Suddenly, a glittering cloud flew up, scattering moonlight among the woodwalkers. The wily Toefoot had tossed fistfuls of firebird feathers into the air, where they floated like a fleet of silver ships sailing beneath a pale moon.

Their ambush forgotten, the trollogs madly chased after the fluttering feathers to devour them. Before Kyleah could blink, she was alone. Then a stray trollog trotted up to her, still chewing on a firebird feather. He sniffed at her before continuing on his way.

Kyleah let out her breath. Why had the trollog passed her by? Even in the moonlight, she was plainly a mortal girl, not a troll.

Or was she? Kyleah reeked of burnt trollog skin and dragon's breath. At night, trollogs relied more on their sense of smell than of sight. This trog had evidently mistaken her for a small burlie.

She broke into a clammy sweat. To the trollogs, she would be as invisible as a mortal child in a crowd of grown-ups. She took a step toward the Agorashon. "Don't be a fool!" she told herself. She took another step. The sound of chanting shook the earth.

"Where are you going?" asked a small, squeaky voice. Barley was gazing up at her, his moist brown eyes glassy with fear.

"I am about to leave you . . . for a little while," she said.

"Can I come with you? The others flew away without me."

"No, dear brother. Where I am going, you cannot come. I must walk this path alone." She whistled, and Quickfeather dropped through the trees. "Please take my brother away and keep him safe," she told the griffin. When the sorc had flown off with Barley, Kyleah hiked up through the ravine until its walls fell away.

"Gundul! Gundul! Gundul!" the trollogs were roaring. The ground trembled under the stamping of their mighty feet. Then they began thumping their chests, making a hollow booming noise like the sound of ocean breakers pounding a rocky shore.

The woodwalkers were facing a kite-shaped rock formation that jutted skyward from the Agorashon's plain. Tilted like the proud prow of a sinking ship, the moonlit rock cast an ominous shadow over the chanting trollogs. Two menacing figures swathed in hooded black cloaks stood upon the rock's pointed pinnacle.

That must be the Dreadrock, Kyleah thought, easing herself into the dense forest of thick trollog legs. Engrossed in their foot-stamping and chest-pounding, the creatures paid her no mind.

A burlie about her size came scurrying by. Kyleah tore off its black cloak and kicked the gibbering imp away. Then she draped the cloak over her white robe to blend in better with her foes.

Ducking and dodging, she made her way to the front of the throng. The Dreadrock stood out starkly, a bare, silvery slab of crystallized moonlight fallen from the heavens. Still the trollogs ignored her. Clambering onto the rock, Kyleah scuttled up its steep incline, approaching the two black-cloaks standing at the top end. One threw back his hood, revealing Malroth's hideous features. With pounding heart, Kyleah climbed up to meet him.

"Burlies do not belong on this rock!" he growled. "Get back below before I tear off your limbs and eat them for supper!"

Kyleah cast off the burlie's cloak and pulled back her own hood, revealing her russet hair. "I am the Gifted Girl!" she cried.

Malroth's mask froze in woody dismay. "You!?" he gasped. "But you are not of noble birth! And how did you become a mortal girl again? No matter. I have just the cure for fleshlings like you." Malroth flicked a single-thonged lash at Kyleah. She ducked aside, and the whip harmlessly whistled past her ear. Malroth drew back his arm to apply the lash again, but his companion stopped him. It was Larkin. The turncloak held Felgroth in his right hand.

"Deal with the girl later," said the Lucambrian. "It is time!"

Malroth snatched the black sword out of Larkin's grasp and pointed it at Kyleah. "You are right!" snarled the troll-king. "It is time to teach this mortal whelp a lesson she will never forget—or survive." He twisted the sword, but Kyleah felt no pain. Looking down, she was amazed to see that her palm no longer bore its old black scar. Emboldened, she drew her own bright sword.

"What?!" Malroth roared. "You dare raise your hand against *me*? I shall strike you down on this rock!" Up went Felgroth.

Down came the deadly black sword like a scythe. Kyleah barely parried the blow before it could cleave her skull. The two swords rang, clashing in sparks and fire. Then Malroth knocked Kyleah's sword out of her grasp. It spun across the rock slab and skittered over the edge, falling point-first among the massed trollogs.

"No!" Kyleah screamed. Had she come so far, only to see her last hopes dashed? She would perish at the point of Felgroth, now poised at her heart for a killing thrust. She tried to back away, but her feet slipped on the dew-slick stone, and she awkwardly fell.

Larkin plucked the black sword out of Malroth's grip. "We must act now, or it will be too late!" the turncloak said. "If the moon begins its descent, the keyhole will close until next month! That's one more month you and your friends must skulk in caves and cellars during the day. You cannot properly wage war when the enemy has the sun on his side. Your revenge can wait awhile."

Malroth's eyes slitted. "Very well—but hurry! This girl has caused me more misery than a burrowing wood-beetle. My sword has not tasted blood in many a thirsty year—and neither have I."

A scudding cloud briefly drew a white curtain across the moon. When the curtain drew back again, Larkin was clutching Felgroth, its tip pointed downward. Then he lowered the blade.

Propping herself up on one elbow, Kyleah noticed a dark slit in the rock at Larkin's feet. *The slotted stone.* Somehow, Larkin had found the keyhole in Gundul's gates—and Felgroth was the key.

With a scraping sound, the sword slid into the slot nearly to the hilt. Larkin sighed. "At last!" he murmured. "After years of scouring Lucambra, I have found the gateway to Gundul! Felgor did not labor in vain, for I shall take up where he left off."

CHAPTER 26

GUNDUL UNLEASHED

alroth raised his arms and turned to face the great trollog throng. The chanting lapsed into an expectant silence. "My people!" he bellowed. "This night marks a new era in the history of trees, when we shall once again gain supremacy over the race of men! No more shall we fear the Yellow Eye in the sky, for Gundul's smokes shall blot out the sun's blinding face and hide us from its harsh light! We shall be free to walk the earth both by day and by night, my brothers. We shall be free at last!"

"We shall be free! We shall be free!" the hooded tree-trolls echoed back, stomping their feet and drumming their chests.

Basking in the worship of his followers, Malroth nodded at Larkin. Then he twirled his crooked wooden finger in the air.

Larkin grasped the black hilt's cross-guard—and turned it. *A fateful twist of weaponed fist/Shall seat him on his throne.*

Grinding and groaning, the Dreadrock tipped upward at a steeper angle. With a cry of terror, Larkin lost his footing. He flung out a hand and grabbed Felgroth's pommel, arresting his fall. Malroth clung to the rock with his rootlike feet, scornfully laughing at Kyleah as she vainly scrabbled at the slick stone with bleeding fingers, all the while sliding down the rising Dreadrock.

Abruptly, the upward movement ceased, and the slab began dropping instead, leveling out as it sank toward the earth. When the Dreadrock had drawn nearly even with the ground around it, Larkin was able to stand upright again. He proudly beat his thin chest in imitation of the trollogs' rhythmic thump-thumping.

Crabbing over to the side of the rock, Kyleah found Elgathel's sword sticking out of the earth. She was about to grab it when she spotted Malroth standing behind her, flicking his trollskin lash.

Malroth snapped his wrist, and the whip hissed toward her. She rolled out of its path just in time. Again the lash sought her, but she rolled the opposite direction to escape it. Then Malroth's misshapen mouth gaped, and the whip hung limply in his hand.

With the screech of stone scraping on stone, the ground around the Dreadrock was pulling away from it, creating a chasm on all sides. Stinking black smoke and inhuman screeches poured out of the crack. While Malroth stood riveted in the spectacle's grip, Kyleah stretched over the fissure to retrieve Elgathel's sword. However, the retreating earth had carried the blade out of reach.

Malroth angrily shook himself and strode up to Larkin, who was still pompously pounding his chest. Snarling, Malroth seized the turncloak and hurled him bodily into the widening chasm. Kyleah shuddered at the Lucambrian's echoing, pitiful screams.

"Fool!" Malroth roared into the gaping gorge. "Never come between a trollog and his prey! Did you really think I would let a mortal weakling rule over my army? Now who is the king of kings? I, Malroth, am lord of all! Trollogs, bow the knee to me!"

The woodwalkers obediently bowed, but they were running out of space. The plain was receding under the peaks surrounding it, leaving the Dreadrock a lonely pillar standing amidst Gundul's smoking gulf. As the ground retreated beneath their feet, terrified trollogs by the hundreds were tumbling into the Gundul-chasm. At the same time, hideous flying shapes with leathery wings were boiling out of the smoke like so many black cinders.

"Now for you!" Malroth snarled at Kyleah. He cracked his whip threateningly at her, and she instinctively scooted away.

"What about your army?" she shot back, stalling for time.

Malroth snorted. "If my entire army falls into the Pit, I could raise up another like it tomorrow! In fact, you shall be my first foot-soldier. Mortal flesh never forgets the lash; the second time around, you shall 'trollify' more quickly. Then I shall send you forth to do battle with the failing race of men. Prepare yourself for the Stinging Scourge!" Malroth sent the whip slithering through the air straight for Kyleah. This time, she flattened herself against the rock, and the lash whined scant inches above her head.

Malroth drew the cruel whip back, but it went taut. When he yanked on the lash, Elgathel's sword came hurtling point-first toward his chest. Evidently, the tip of the whip had wrapped itself around the hilt of the half-buried sword and pulled it free.

The trollog chief deftly snatched the sword out of the air. "All things considered," he told Kyleah, "I think it more fitting that you should die by your own blade than turn trollog. You shall be the first of your kind to perish in the second War of the Trees." Malroth held the sword erect before his face like a battle-hardened knight preparing to engage his unarmed rival in mortal combat.

Suddenly, the sword dropped from his fingers, and he let out a strangled cry. His wild eyes started from their sockets. Breaking into a slimy sweat, he staggered backward, gibbering with fear.

Kyleah shrank back as well. She wished Malroth would stop toying with her and simply slay her. Death, it seemed, was her only way off the Dreadrock. She couldn't wait to return to that place her friends called "Gaelessa," where Gaelathane lived.

However, Malroth was not tricking her this time. Thick white roots were bursting from his lower body, anchoring him to the Dreadrock. As Pagglon's Lay had predicted, "The perfect glass, once forged anew/Will root the rebel to the rock/When trollog sees his image true/He'll gasp his last and stand a stock."

Kyleah screamed as Malroth squirmed. Leaves and shoots sprouted from his head and limbs, transforming him from trollog into tree. Stiffly bending, he fixed Kyleah with a murderous glare. His wooden jaws yawned wide, ready to devour her. At the last second, leafy branches billowed from his maw, and he gagged. He was still glowering at Kyleah when foliage shrouded his eyes.

Scarcely able to believe this turn of events, Kyleah grabbed her fallen sword and headed for Felgroth. All the while, Malroth's army was bellowing at her. The nearest trollogs were also making frantic twisting motions with their hands. They were trying to tell her to close the Gundul-gap by turning the black sword back!

She hesitated. Why should she shut Gundul's gates now? Why not wait until all the trollogs had toppled into the bottomless pit? Then she realized that while those gates remained open, untold numbers of horrible creatures were escaping Gundul. Pouncing on Felgroth, Kyleah tried to twist the hilt counter-clockwise.

The black sword refused to budge. Kyleah's heart sank. What was she to do now? Neither man nor trollog could reach or help her on this island of rock in a turbulent sea of sulfurous smoke.

"You are turning it the wrong way," said a familiar voice.

The Plugger was standing beside her! Kyleah hopped up and hugged the becloaked old man, feeling Gaelathane's veiled power and love surge through her weary body. "How did you find me?"

"Did I not tell you I would never leave you or forsake you? Now let us set about undoing the damage these rebels have caused."

Kyleah and the Plugger grasped Felgroth's hilt and turned the sword clockwise. Something clicked deep inside the rock. With a mighty rumble, the Gundul-rift gradually began to narrow.

"Quickly, now; we must remove the sword before the gates close!" said the Plugger. Pulling up on Felgroth, he and Kyleah drew it out of the slot. The black blade appeared unmarred.

"What shall we do with the sword now?" Kyleah asked.

"Why, send it back whence it came!" the Plugger replied. "Since you were the first to free Felgroth from its woody prison, you alone have the responsibility and privilege of returning that sword to the unquenchable fires where Felgor first forged it."

Rearing back, Kyleah flung Felgroth into the shrinking chasm. Lit from beneath by Gundul's fires, the spinning sword hung in space, a red-and-black blur against the billowing smoke clouds. For a sickening instant, Kyleah thought the sword was spitefully sailing back to stab her the way Elgathel's had flown at Malroth. But Felgroth was dwindling, falling swiftly into the closing crack.

Kyleah was still tracking the weapon's tumbling descent when the rift around the Dreadrock snapped shut with a deafening *boom*. Roaring vengefully, the thousands of surviving trollogs rushed upon the massive stone where their leafy leader stood rooted.

"Fit your sword into the keyhole!" the Plugger urged Kyleah.

Puzzled by the command, she drove Elgathel's sword into the slot, as Larkin had done with Felgroth. Like twin lightning bolts, two bright rays shot from the hilt. One ran straight down into the Dreadrock, while the other blazed skyward. Together, they formed a shining pillar that rapidly grew into a glorious Tree of light.

"What is happening?" Kyleah cried. She was clinging to the Plugger when a ray of light flashed from the Tree, striking him. Or did the light-beam begin at the Plugger and end at the Tree? Either way, he was instantly transformed into the shining Man she knew as Gaelathane. She fell before Him and worshipped Him.

Gaelathane raised her to her feet. "Your work is not yet done," He reminded her. The King gestured at the trollogs jostling around the Dreadrock. Hoods drawn and heads down, they surged ever closer, as if pushing through waves of the Tree's powerful radiance. *Though wooden band will fear to stand/Before the royal tree . . .*

"I cannot fight without Elgathel's sword!" Kyleah protested.

"The sword is Mine, not Elgathel's," Gaelathane corrected her. "I lent it to him to destroy the dragon. I inlaid the hilt with wood taken from the Tree that grew upon Luralin. My presence will cause even the smallest splinter of that Tree to sprout and grow."

That was why the bracelet had said the "trollish bane" was "not made by hand of maid or man." Gaelathane's hand had forged it!

The King said, "My Sword is a 'perfect glass' because it not only reflects the face, but also the soul's true condition. Though the griffins later reforged it, this blade still reveals the thoughts and intentions of the heart. Now go forth and 'burgle,' Gifted Girl!"

Kyleah went to the Tree and thrust her arm into the swelling trunk. It grew around her body, completely enclosing her in an airy, light embrace quite unlike the cold clamminess of the maples she had explored. Inside the Tree, she could easily breathe and felt at peace and at ease, though the trollogs still surrounded her.

Through the trunk, the woodwalkers appeared frozen in place, as though they were encased in blocks of ice. Evidently, time was standing still for Kyleah while she was inside the Tree of trees.

Looking about, she saw a reflection of herself standing a few feet away. When the image laughed, Kyleah realized it was her twin, Einwen. With joyful shouts, the two fiercely embraced. For Kyleah, it seemed a tearful eternity passed in but a moment.

"I must leave now," said Einwen. "I will await you where death is dead, and the Tree outshines the moon and stars." With that, she ascended through the Tree's trunk, disappearing into an ocean of light. "Farewell, my sister!" her voice faintly called down.

Kyleah continued staring up into the Tree until it faded away. "Farewell, my beloved Einwen!" she cried. "One day, we shall meet again in Gaelathane's glad country at the foot of the Tree."

Bending over, she drew Elgathel's sword out of the Dreadrock, and the trollogs began advancing again. They were only seconds from overrunning the rock, which was still brightly lit, as though the Tree had not left. The light seemed to be coming from Kyleah herself. Her hands, her arms and even her robe were shining!

Gaelathane told her, "Those whom the King's Tree has touched are changed forever. Walk in its light, and you shall never stumble in the darkness. Commit your way to Me, and you shall never fail. Delight yourself in Me, and you shall find your heart's desire. Now go forth to defeat your foes in this My shining strength!"

"But how?" Kyleah asked the King.

"Those black cloaks they wear are woven of Gundul's thick darkness," said Gaelathane. "The Tree's light cannot touch them while they are thus clothed with evil. Yet, as the 'living staff,' you are short enough that your enemies must look down on you."

"What do You mean by that?" Kyleah demanded.

However, Gaelathane had vanished. In the next moment, the trollogs fell upon Kyleah. In the darkness, she felt their hard, woody fingers poking and pinching her. As she looked up in pleading desperation, her shining face illuminated their grotesque ones. Caught off guard, the trollogs howled in terror until sprays of burgeoning green foliage choked off their hoarse screams.

Kyleah's heart raced. All around her, trollogs were thrashing in a leafy dance of doom, their legs and feet rooting fast to the Dreadrock. Very shortly, all that remained of her tormenters were contorted trees smothered in greenery. As she pressed through the new foliage, Kyleah encountered more furious woodwalkers.

Though many of them fled at her approach, they all met the same fate as their companions. Passing among them, she left swaths of fresh forest behind. Battered and bruised, Kyleah was at the point of collapse when the sun rose behind the Brynnmors, rooting the remaining trollogs on the Field of Fear.

The living staff who lacks a half/Will root the trolls who flee.

"There she is! Down there!" With a rush of wings, Barley and the others flew out of the sky on their griffins, landing near the Dreadrock. Seeing Kyleah, they fell back, eyes filled with doubt.

"What is the matter with you?" they asked, pointing at her.

This was not at all the welcome Kyleah had expected! Feeling rather wounded, she shot back, "Whatever do you mean?"

"Why, your face is shining like the sun's!" Rolin observed.

Her face. Kyleah had forgotten the Tree had changed her. She retold her part in Gaelathane's victory over Larkin and his trollog army. While describing Malroth's leafy transformation, she held up the "perfect glass" before her eyes, mimicking the troll king's final gesture. In the sword's shiny blade, she saw the whole of her heart laid out—the good and the bad together. *To think Gaelathane could love a heart like mine!* she marveled, and she wept. Then she passed the sword amongst her wondering companions.

Looking into it, Toefoot wiped his eyes. "Small wonder Malroth was rooted to the rock! To see the mirrored wickedness of one's own heart would turn anyone back to the stuff from which he was made—or drive him closer to Gaelathane. I'm surprised I haven't become a pile of dirt myself. I must mend my gnomish ways."

Rolin groaned. "I've had that sword for years, yet not once did I look at my reflection in its blade. If only I had known earlier!"

"We all assumed Felgor's sword was 'the blade not mortal-made,'" said Meghan. "It just never occurred to us Elgathel's sword might also fit that description, because Gaelathane fashioned it."

"The last stave finally makes sense, too," Medwyn chimed in. "Those trollogs cloaked themselves against the Staff Tree's light, but they had failed to guard against our Kyleah, the *living* staff. One look at her, and they were all turned back into trees."

Medwyn didn't mention the last part of that verse, ". . . who lacks a half." Surely half of Kyleah had died with her twin, but now she felt whole again, knowing that Einwen was in Gaelessa.

Bembor's eyes gleamed. "Are we not all 'living staffs,' sent into Gaelathane's worlds as lights to drive back the darkness?"

"That we are!" Rolin agreed. "We have become so used to fighting with sword, blowpipe and lightstaff that we've forgotten our greatest weapon is the light of Gaelathane's life within us."

"We'll need plenty of that light, too!" Emmer said. "Did we not see those yegs and other flying vermin escaping Gundul?"

Gemmio said, "We can be thankful Gaelathane and Kyleah closed Gundul's gates when they did, or we would be much worse off. As it is, I fear we shall be hard pressed to cleanse Lucambra."

Opio rubbed his palms together. "Just give me a lightstaff, and I'll make short work of any batwolf that dares darken our skies!"

"At least Gundul is closed forever," Marlis said with a sigh.

"I wouldn't be so sure of that," said Bembor. "The underworld often breaks out where and when we least expect it. We must not let down our guard; remember how Elgathel lost the kingdom."

"If it weren't for Kyleah, we would have lost it again last night!" Rolin said. "Without the Gifted Girl's help, we would all still be intrisoned in Thalmos, if not enslaved by the woodwalkers, and Malroth would now be the lord of Lucambra and of Gundul."

Kyleah blushed. "I only did what Gaelathane told me to."

"Let us not forget Toefoot!" said Scanlon. "His firebird feathers distracted the trollogs long enough for us to flee on the sorcs."

The Mirror Master's chest swelled with pride. "By Pagglon's pickax," he chortled, "those feathers weren't wasted after all!"

"I have observed the King of the Trees puts everything in our lives to good use—even feathers!" said Bembor dryly. "I only wish Larkin had heeded my warnings in Winona's secret chamber. Now he has gone to his own place, and a terrible place it is, too."

"May Gaelathane have mercy on that wretch, who met such a wretched end," Medwyn murmured. "'Though hidden horde obey his sword/No mortal can prevail/O'er deadly sprite that gnaws the night/Intrisoned by a nail.' If Larkin had realized what treachery brooded in Malroth's black heart, he might still be alive today."

Then the whole company knelt and thanked Gaelathane for His deliverance. Even a dazed Barley appeared to understand that his sister could not have survived her ordeal without the King's help. The boy had just added his voice to the others' prayers when a rumbling sound shook the earth. Kyleah glanced up to see the Dreadrock rising above the trollog-trees like a finger of doom.

"Gundul is opening again!" Mycena cried.

However, no smoke rose above the Agorashon. The mountain shadows lay like long trollog fingers across the Dreadrock, which had returned to its original tipped position. A rending roar rocked the earth again as water gushed from beneath one of the peaks, streaming among the trollog-trees and pooling in dark hollows.

Kyleah and her friends wasted no time in taking to their sorcs. Meanwhile, the Agorashon was disappearing beneath a shining sheet of water. Watching from the air, the griffins and their riders circled over the secluded valley until the tips of the tallest trollog-trees were submerged. Then the sleek sorcs veered westward.

Seated with Barley on Quickfeather, Kyleah took a final glimpse back at the Field of Fear. Only the Dreadrock still stood above the rising lake. Poised in a menacing pouncing pose, the rooted Malroth-tree stubbornly clung to the slanting slab. Kyleah sensed the trollog's glaring gaze following her even as Quickfeather joined his fellow sorcs in gliding back toward the distant Hallowfast.

CHAPTER 27

A JEALOUS QUEEN

After slipping back into their tower through the sorcathel trapdoor, the Greencloaks retrieved their stolen weapons. Then they surprised Larkin's sleeping men and locked them up in Winona's dungeon. Early the next morning, Meghan helped Kyleah and Barley find a Thalmos-torsil and make passage. The three came out in the sugar bush near Malroth's maple. Eager to find her father, Kyleah climbed down the tree and trotted off.

"Wait for us!" Barley and Meghan cried, chasing after her.

But Kyleah was already out of earshot, bounding like a spooked deer down the mountainside, reveling in her newfound freedom. For the first time in years, she could run without pain. She was free of her crutch and free of the bitterness that had plagued her.

As she passed the Grieving Ground, she heard a peculiar huff-huffing sound, reminding her of a grunting bear. Motioning for Barley and Meghan to remain behind, she crept through the white-starred daisies carpeting the aisles between the paddles. Summer or winter, the Grieving Ground wore white, the color of the lost.

Crawling on her hands and knees, Kyleah came upon two new grieving paddles, each wearing a brass bell and a few faded asters. "KYLEAH," said one smooth blade. "BARLEY," said the other.

Jumping up, Kyleah read the inscriptions again. She staggered back in horror. Never had she expected to find her own paddle standing in the Grieving Ground! Her head snapped up. The grunting was very close now. It sounded like weeping. Leaving the two grim paddles, Kyleah sought out the source of the noise.

Two rows away, a lone figure sat hunched on a rock, shoulders shaking. As Kyleah approached, a twig snapped underfoot, and the figure turned toward her. It was a man, his hair so disheveled and cheeks so sunken that at first Kyleah hardly recognized him.

"Father?" she gasped. "Is it really you? Father!"

Branagan's face went whiter than the daisies beneath his boots. "'Leah?" he rasped. His eyes measured her in disbelief. "You're still alive? Where is your crutch? Why, your leg is all straight again! What has happened to you?" He rose to his feet unsteadily and crushed her in a fierce, trollog-like embrace. Repeating her name, he wept and shuddered in the throes of pent-up grief poured out.

"I have another surprise for you, Father!" said Kyleah gaily. She pulled away from his grasp—and piercingly whistled.

Barley and Meghan came running through the daisies. Seeing them, Branagan bawled, "Barley? My boy Barley! You have come back from the dead to me!" Laughing and crying, he buried his son in a bear's hug. After coaxing Kyleah back into his arms, he added, "How you two have grown! Where have you been all this time? I never expected to see you again, at least not in this life."

Kyleah understood his shock. No one whose paddle graced the Grieving Ground had ever returned to the land of the living.

Standing half in sun, half in paddle-shadow, Kyleah recounted the adventures that had driven her and her brother so far from their home. As her tale wound down, Branagan's face clouded, his legs wobbled and he collapsed onto the rock, holding his head in callused hands. Kyleah was afraid he might have fainted.

"Are you all right, Father?" Barley asked him worriedly.

"This can't be happening!" he murmured. "That knock on the head must have addled my wits—or maybe I'm dreaming. I haven't eaten in days, and my noggin ain't working so well." He rubbed his eyes and looked up. "Nope; you're all still here."

"You're not dreaming, Father," said Kyleah. "We're home; we're really home, and now you can pull up our paddles!"

After introducing herself to Branagan, Meghan produced a piece of bread from her pocket and gave it to the sugarmaster. He chewed on it gratefully. "That's better!" he said. "Now if we could only find the rest of our family. You don't happen to know what became of your stepmother and stepsisters, do you?" His earnest eyes flitted between Kyleah and Barley. Seeing their shrugs, his face fell, and he gingerly rubbed the sore spot on his head.

"This lump kept me down longer than I had expected," he ruefully confessed. "I slept for two days at Gannon's. After that, I was still so dizzy, he wouldn't let me leave the cabin. For a week, he fattened me up on oatcakes and honey. When at last he sent me off, I drove my wagon straightaway back to Mapleton. I found the whole village deserted. It still is. I haven't seen another living soul since. I've been wandering the woods, half out of my mind with worry, grief and fear. The Prowlers almost caught me putting up your paddles here in the Grieving Ground late one evening!"

Barley hadn't heard a word his father had said. He was staring into the forest with a curious look on his round face. "I see people inside these trees!" he announced. "Lots and lots of people!"

To Branagan's astonishment, Kyleah marched up to a maple, reached inside and pulled out Doughty, the village blacksmith. The next tree yielded Farmer Forthright. Moving down the mountainside, Kyleah and her brother released townspeople from trees left and right. A few unfamiliar faces stood out in the crowd—poor souls that had been intrisoned years or even generations earlier.

Then Barley pointed out an unusually graceful-looking maple. In went Kyleah's hand, and out came a slender, dark-haired waif of about twelve. Kyleah's heart skipped two beats. "Anna?"

The other girl stared back, blinking in the bright morning sunlight. "Kyleah?" she gasped. Screaming and sobbing for joy, the two friends hugged each other and danced around the tree.

By the time the swelling throng had reached Mapleton, most of the missing villagers had been recovered. However, Dolora, Gyrta and Garta were among those who were still unaccounted for.

Anna and Kyleah were panting and laughing as they tripped down to the sugarhouse, which stood forlorn and quiet after the busyness of the maple sugaring season. No clouds of steam poured from the roof vents; no rollicking singing echoed through the door; no delicious syrup-smells wafted from within. Then as Kyleah passed the door, she heard strange thumping sounds.

"What was that?" Anna said, her eyes wide with alarm.

Holding hands, the girls cautiously entered the sugarhouse, where they found one of the copper syrup cauldrons still wearing its massive lid. Someone was evidently trapped inside that kettle, banging on its metal sides, shouting and raising an awful racket.

With Branagan's help, Kyleah and Anna unclamped the heavy lid. Out popped Gyrta and Garta, still wearing their nightclothes.

Gyrta snapped, "Don't just stand there. Get us out of here!"

Kyleah couldn't contain herself. Though she knew it was rude to mock the misfortunes of others, seeing her gaunt stepsisters dripping grimy water on the sugarhouse floor sent her into gales of laughter. Even Branagan grinned at the two glowering young women. Kyleah quickly sobered at Gyrta's next offhand remark.

"My back hurts, and I'm starving," she whined.

Wringing out her nightgown, Garta chimed in, "I'm hungry enough to devour Sally whole, head to tail! My leg is burning, too. What on earth did that horrid old Prowler do to us, anyway?"

The night Barley had broken Kyleah's torsil bed, trollogs had swarmed into the sleeping village and carried off every man and woman, boy and girl. From the tidbits Gyrta and Garta let drop, Kyleah gathered the sisters had made such a terrible fuss that their captors dumped them in the cauldron and clamped the heavy lid over them. Fortunately, the lid had air-holes in it. Unfortunately, someone had left a pile of dirty laundry soaking inside the kettle. Neither girl could say for sure what had become of their mother.

While Gyrta and Garta stomped off to change their clothes and find something to eat, Kyleah returned to burgling the trees surrounding the village. When she and Barley could find no more trisoners, Kyleah felt a tear slide down her cheek, then another.

"Did you check inside *all* the trees?" she asked her brother.

Piqued at the question, her brother snorted, "All of them."

Kyleah sighed. She reminded herself that the trollogs didn't intrison all their captives. Some lost souls would never return.

Once she had reunited Anna with her parents, Kyleah took Barley and Meghan up to her cottage. Branagan joined them. A baffled look came over his face. "That's odd," he said, scratching his stubbly chin. "I left my wagon standing right out in front. Nobody was here to steal it. And where is Sally?" A quick search turned up no sign of Sally either in the paddock or in the stable.

Beyond the cottage's smashed-in door, the four found the place deserted. Meghan observed, "Garta and Gyrta came up here not too long ago to change into dry clothes. Where did they go?"

Branagan looked sick. He dashed into the kitchen, snatched up a brown jar—one of the few items the trollogs had spared—and shook it. "Oh, no. It's empty!" he groaned. "Now I know where those rascally girls went! They took my wagon and all the coins in my money jar, and they've gone off to Beechtown. What will I do? The Prowlers cleaned out our cupboards, and I can't buy supplies with nary a gilder to my name. Without a wagon, I can't drive to town, anyway! Pails and spiles! What those two clotheshorses need is a good licking with a stout stirring paddle, and I have just the one, too." Branagan stalked outside to find a proper paddle.

Kyleah held her tongue. She did not envy Garta and Gyrta their fling, knowing the stiff punishment that awaited them at Branagan's hands when they came sneaking back into the village.

"Maybe Dolora took the wagon," Meghan suggested.

"No, she didn't," someone said. Wynnagar sailed into the kitchen, followed by the Greencloaks and a very pale Branagan.

"Wynnagar!" Kyleah exclaimed. "Rolin and Marlis! Bembor! Emmer! Timothy and Gwynneth! Elwyn! Scanlon and Medwyn and Mycena! Opio and Gemmio! What are you all doing here?"

"I arrived earlier from another village," Wynnagar explained.

Rolin grinned at Kyleah. "After we cleaned up the mess the trollogs left behind in the Hallowfast, we made passage to Thalmos to hunt down any surviving trollogs. Our mounts are still outside. I fear the griffins gave your poor father a rather nasty jolt."

"Not at all! Not at all!" said the sugarmaster gamely, though Kyleah could see he was genuinely shaken to his boots.

"Have you got any vittles around here?" Opio asked. When Branagan shook his head, the Greencloak groaned, "After my long intrisonment, I feel hungry enough to eat your front door!"

"Don't speak of such a thing!" Kyleah scolded him. Then she recounted how she had greedily devoured the dry, gritty sawdust in Toefoot's workshop to quell her ravenous trollog's appetite.

Branagan apologized for the state of his larder. "My wife would offer you some Mapleton hospitality, if she were here now."

"You should be thankful she is not!" Wynnagar declared. Just as papery bark peels off a birch's trunk, the years fell away from the withered old worldwalker. Branagan and the Greencloaks gasped as Wynnagar was transformed into a comely young woman.

"Do not suppose all peril has ended with our foes' defeat," she said. "Though the Leaf Lord has crushed Malroth beneath His heel, the serpent can still strike in its death throes." Pointing at Kyleah, Wynnagar added, "If your stepmother had realized who and what you are, the trollogs would have taken you long ago."

Icy dread crawled up Kyleah's spine. "What do you mean?"

"Your whole family has been in grave danger ever since that creature came to live with you. Why do you suppose Dolora was not found among the other trisoners? And why were her own daughters left behind instead of being intrisoned in the woods?"

"The trollogs didn't want Garta and Gyrta 'cuz they're mean," Barley declared, much to Kyleah's amusement. She wrinkled her nose as smoke drifted through the broken kitchen window.

Wynnagar told Barley, "Not at all. The trollogs have intrisoned worse sorts than your stepsisters." Lowering her voice, she said, "Dolora is no more mortal than I am. You will not find a single iron pan, pot or spoon in this kitchen. She cooked only with utensils of wood, stone and copper. You know I am speaking the truth."

Kyleah's knees went weak. Surely her frugal stepmother was simply trying to pinch a gilder or two! Thinking back, though, she could not recall ever seeing Dolora holding any iron object.

"If Dolora is not a mortal, then what is she?" asked Medwyn.

"She was Malroth's consort—the queen of the woodwalkers!"

Kyleah's body began to shake like a maple leaf in the wind. "But Dolora didn't look anything like a trollog!" she pointed out.

Wynnagar snorted. "What trollog would want a wife as ugly as he? This one who calls herself 'Dolora' is a worldwalker of the vilest character. After Malroth's intrisonment, she began traveling from village to village, leaving a trail of misery and death behind her." Wynnagar shot Branagan a pitying look. "Under various guises, she has taken scores of mates, murdering or intrisoning them when they had served her purposes. Her sole ambition has been to find and destroy the Gifted Girl. That is why so many more lasses than lads have disappeared in Mapleton. For years, Dolora has been the free trollogs' eyes and ears. She directed the trogs to snatch any maiden she suspected might be the One."

Kyleah couldn't stop shaking. "Yet, here I was living all this time under her very nose! Why didn't she ever find me out?"

"She assumed the Gifted Girl was born of mortal nobility. After doing away with the female heirs in the Thalmosian royal family, she turned her attention to specially gifted girls of more common lineage. In her mind, however, no cripple could possibly be the Gifted Girl. Dolora disdained the weak. For that reason alone, she would have intrisoned or killed you eventually. As it was, when you first escaped intrisonment, Dolora must have caught on to you and has been searching high and low for you ever since."

"Why didn't you warn me about this before?" Branagan said.

Wynnagar shrugged. "I am truly sorry. I have long known someone in these hills was secretly in league with the trollogs, but Dolora cleverly covered her tracks. After returning to Mapleton, I snooped through her comfortable kitchen here. The absence of any iron utensils whatsoever aroused my worst fears. In order to confirm those suspicions, I have been asking around the other local villages for news of Dolora's doings. What I have learned has given me nightmares. When her daughters turned up today in the sugarhouse cauldron without their mother, that clinched it. Dolora must have convinced her woodwalker friends to leave Gyrta and Garta behind instead of killing or intrisoning them."

Branagan said, "I'd like to throttle that shrew, or whatever you call her! To think I put up with her, not knowing what she was."

A thick gray cloud billowed through the window, filling the room with smoke. Fire crackled outside. Out of the smoke loomed a black-cloaked figure brandishing a torch and a wooden club.

"Dolora!" Kyleah gasped, backing away from the apparition.

"I took you in as one of my own, you ungrateful brat!" the menacing figure hissed at her. "You have repaid my kindness by turning against me. Long and bitter years I have waited for my king to break the bonds of his intrisonment. Now I am Malroth's queen again, and I will brook no upstart rival—especially not the Gifted Girl! Yes, I know who you are, you useless, lying blairn!"

"I didn't—I mean, I haven't—" Kyleah squeaked. Feeling like the browbeaten stepdaughter again, she cowered behind her green-cloaked friends. Then she fled wailing into her bedroom.

Chasing her with upraised club, Dolora snarled, "I should have bludgeoned you to death with your crutch, you pathetic cripple! You look just as your mother did before I intrisoned her."

"Intrisoned her?" Kyleah echoed through numb lips.

Dolora laughed hideously. "Of course! After I had discarded my last husband, I needed another. Branagan was perfect, but Larissa stood in my way. I bided my time until my hamadryad friends and I could catch her outside after dusk. The rest was easy."

"Where is she?" Kyleah shouted. "Where is my mother?"

Dolora howled with glee. "Her tree was cut down years ago! Now you will join her in death, Gimpy Girl!" Still cackling, Dolora swung the club at Kyleah's head. The weapon froze mid-swing as a ray of brightest light pierced the pall of dense smoke.

"From wood you came, and to wood you shall return!" Rolin roared, his beaming lightstaff aimed at the cloaked worldwalker.

"No!" Dolora gurgled as green foliage spewed from her mouth and ears. Outside, the crackling of flames grew to a terrifying thunder. Fire was devouring Kyleah's beloved cottage home.

"Save the bed boards!" cried Wynnagar. Scanlon grabbed the headboard, but Dolora was standing on the footboard and either wouldn't or couldn't move off the polished piece of torsil wood.

As everyone stampeded for the front door, Wynnagar spoke into the riot of leaves covering Dolora's ear. "All your trisoners are freed, and Malroth shall trouble us no more. You have failed!"

"You haven't . . . found . . . all!" came Dolora's muffled reply.

Kyleah could not take her eyes off her stepmother, who was fast becoming a bushy tree. Leaves and branches were freely sprouting from her head and torso. Roots wriggled snakelike from her legs and feet. The upraised torch rained down flaming pitch and cinders on her wooden arm, setting it afire. Dolora's mouth gaped and her jaws worked as she rasped at Kyleah, "I . . . never . . . loved . . . you!" Then foliage grew over her face, cutting her off.

Still Kyleah couldn't tear herself away from the blazing bush that had once been her stepmother. Finally, Barley and Branagan dragged her out of the burning house, and just in time. Flames were licking through the windows and doorway. Dolora had left nothing to chance. She had set fire to the house, intending to burn it down around the Gifted Girl's head after clubbing her to death.

Driven by a hot, dry summer's wind, the flames rapidly spread, consuming the cottage's thick wooden walls like ravening wild beasts. Twitching their tails and growling, the griffins nervously paced, keeping their distance from the burning building.

Wynnagar screamed, "Quickly, now! Before the fire jumps to the stable, throw the bed's headboard onto the roof! Hurry!"

With puzzled looks, Rolin and Scanlon heaved the heavy torsil-wood slab onto the smoldering roof just as the straw thatch exploded in flames. Instantly, the cottage disappeared, leaving only the floor and stone foundation intact. A few stray ashes and glowing embers drifted down from the stunned sky. Some set the griffins' fur on fire, sending the frenzied beasts yowling in circles until the Greencloaks managed to swat out the pesky sparks.

"What happened to my house?" Kyleah asked weakly.

Wynnagar explained, "When the headboard landed above the footboard, everything between them made passage, from Dolora standing on the footboard all the way to the thatched roof!"

Bembor gaped at the space where the cottage had sat. "I've never seen anything so large—or fiery—make passage!" he said.

Meghan said, "This means our helihag just came in for a very hot surprise! I'll bet those flatcake creatures don't care for fire."

"I thought the Tree's light caused only trollogs to sprout," Marlis told Wynnagar. "Why did Dolora also turn into a tree?"

Wynnagar replied, "She may have been a worldwalker, but she was a trollog at heart, and the Tree's light purges all such evil!"

Kyleah began to weep. To think Dolora had been responsible for burning down her house, not to mention her mother's death! She could not take it all in, nor could she shake off the gruesome image of her leafy stepmother, torch and club still in hand, her flaming arm raised in a gesture of hatred and defiance.

"How could Dolora intrison my mother?" she sobbed. Barley clung to her as together, they poured out their long-buried grief.

Wynnagar patted Kyleah's arm and dried her tears. "Don't fret yourself!" she said. "Gaelathane will help us find Larissa."

Her head spinning, Kyleah said, "Didn't you hear what that horrible trollog's wife just told me? My mother is dead!"

"Oh, my dear, no!" the worldwalker replied, embracing her. "Never trust the word of a trollog or his wife! Undoubtedly Dolora helped intrison your mother, but I suspect the truth ends there. Dolora wanted to gloat over your misfortunes without letting on that Larissa might still be alive. If you knew the truth, you might run off and rescue your mother. Dolora couldn't take that risk."

"How can you be so sure Dolora was lying?" Kyleah asked.

"Look at it this way," Wynnagar replied. "What kind of trees do the trollogs seem to prefer for intrisoning their victims?"

Kyleah furrowed her brow in thought. The freedom to move those muscles felt wonderful after wearing a stiff, wooden trollog's mask. "Why, maple trees, I suppose. Why do you ask?"

"Exactly. Maple trees have nice thick trunks ideal for intrisoning people. Now, who in this village would cut down a maple tree?"

"No one, of course!" Kyleah said. Cutting down a live maple was frowned upon in Mapleton, where most everybody earned his living directly or indirectly from tapping the broad-leafed trees.

"Well, then," said Wynnagar. "Instead of standing here staring at one another, I suggest we set about finding Larissa."

CHAPTER 28

THE TOLLING BELL

"But where do we start?" Kyleah asked Wynnagar. "There must be thousands upon thousands of maple trees in the sugar bush. How will we know which is the right tree?"

Wynnagar suggested, "Let us revisit Gaelathane's words. Tell me, now: Which verses of prophecy have yet to be fulfilled?"

"All have been fulfilled," said Medwyn. "Gundul's gates were opened—and closed—with the 'buried sword of Gundul's lord.'"

"And we have found the 'perfect glass' for the 'limping lass'—who no longer limps!" Meghan added with a wink at Kyleah.

"I have never heard that riddle before," Wynnagar remarked.

Kyleah said, "My mother gave me a bracelet engraved with a prophecy that has also come true. It goes like this: 'A perfect glass for limping lass . . .'" She recited the rest of the riddle by heart.

"Are you sure you didn't forget any verses?" asked Wynnagar.

"Of course I'm sure!" Kyleah replied.

"Do you still have the bracelet?" Bembor asked her.

Kyleah shook her head. "Glunt melted it right off my neck."

"You forgot a stave," said Barley, climbing onto Quickfeather.

There he goes again, trying to embarrass me! Kyleah thought. She indignantly declared, "Mother's riddle had but three staves."

"What about the first one?" asked Barley, and he recited,

To Gaelathane I plight my troth,
Who loved me ere I knew Him well;
While men be mean and trollogs wroth,
I shall await the tolling bell.

"'The tolling bell'!" said Rolin. "What does that mean?"

Kyleah blushed and stared at her feet. "I don't know."

Wynnagar pursed her lips. "If the Gifted Girl cannot tell us, then we must assume that verse still awaits its fulfillment."

Kyleah thought back on the King's reproof during her second intrisonment. *Had you asked, I would have told you.* "I think," she said, "that we ought to ask Gaelathane what this verse means."

Heads lowered, eyes closed and voices murmured. After a few minutes of prayer, King Rolin concluded with, "The Tree lives!"

"Well?" Scanlon said, glancing around the circle of faces.

Eager to share what she had learned from her Master, Kyleah spoke first. "I have heard Gaelathane's voice," she announced, and she squirmed under her friends' curious stares. "When I first heard that bell-verse, I thought it meant my mother was waiting to hear the ringing of neck-bells at the end of the day, when all Mapleton's children are gathered in. Just now, I came to realize she might be awaiting the tolling of another sort of bell—one that would release her from intrisonment. Neck-bells are too tiny to toll, anyway; they just jingle—and no trisoner could hear such a jingling inside a tree. Now if I were intrisoned near Mapleton, what other bells could I hear? Beechtown's chapel-steeple houses the biggest bell in the valley, but its ringing hardly ever carries up here in the mountains, even when conditions are perfect."

"She is right about that," said Wynnagar.

Stroking his beard, Bembor nodded. "I see your point. If this prophetic verse refers to an actual bell, which bell would it be?"

"How could any bell release someone from a tree?" Scanlon argued. Nobody could come up with a satisfactory answer.

Mycena suggested, "What if the bell's tolling doesn't free Larissa but merely *signals* the time of her deliverance is near?"

"What a capital idea!" Bembor boomed.

"Then where would this 'tolling bell' hang?" Timothy asked. "The chapel bell in Beechtown is the only one I know of around here, but if it can't be heard in Mapleton, it doesn't count."

Recalling the forest sounds she had heard lying in her bed, Kyleah said, "Could the bell ring in another world altogether?"

"If so, Larissa must be intrisoned in a torsil!" said Marlis.

Gemmio threw up his hands and declared, "Every torsil world must boast at least one bell! That means young Barley here would have to look into every tree-of-passage in these mountains!"

"Perhaps not," said Bembor. "In most worlds, large bells have become scarce. Dragons single them out for destruction, because townsfolk typically ring such bells to sound an alarm. Given a choice, most dragons naturally prefer to show up unannounced."

"True enough," said Emmer. "Gorgorunth spared Beechtown's bell tower only because it was the sorcerer's command post."

Rolin said, "In matters of prophecy, I have found that the most obvious interpretation is usually the correct one, which brings me to Elgathel's bell. Since it hangs in the top of a high tower—the Hallowfast—its 'tolling' can easily be heard for miles around."

"Until yesterday, it hadn't been rung in years," Marlis added.

Everyone gazed into the forests waving above Mapleton. "If Rolin is right," said Opio, "how do we go about finding a Lucambra-torsil in the vast Tartellans, let alone the right one?"

The Greencloaks were stumped until Timothy exclaimed, "Breakouts!" so abruptly that he startled a flock of pigeons.

"What are those?" Kyleah asked him.

Timothy explained, "Where torsils grow in groves such as in Medwyn's Golden Wood, sometimes odors, voices and other sounds from another world can break through onto our side."

Bembor said, "You're saying we might be able to hear the bell tolling in this world if we stand close enough to a torsil grove?"

"Yes!" said Timothy. "Come on, Elwyn. Let's go back to the Hallowfast and ring Elgathel's bell for all it's worth!" The two friends hopped on a griffin. Just as they soared into the afternoon sky, Kyleah was sure Elwyn turned around and waved at her.

Taking their cue, Kyleah and her companions formed a single wide line and filtered into the forest above Mapleton. Moving as quietly as mice, they listened for a bell's ringing above the rustling moan of fir-boughs in the wind and the twittering of birds.

The day was waning into evening, but no bell had sounded in the woods. Kyleah was losing hope. Tramping over duff-covered ground untrodden by human foot in centuries, she wondered how anyone could possibly find a solitary torsil grove in that trackless wilderness. Moreover, she felt uneasy about spending the night in the forest. Although the trollogs had been roundly defeated, a few holdout woodwalkers might still be lurking about. She wished she hadn't returned Elgathel's sword to Rolin. *Gaelathane, please help us to find my mother before nightfall!* she fervently prayed.

Since the searchers were climbing the Tartellans' eastern slopes, however, darkness fell swiftly upon the forest. Fortunately, the rising moon shed some light on the woodland floor—and upon furtive figures Kyleah glimpsed here and there through the trees. It was too dark to get a good look at their forms or faces. Kyleah was stumbling over tree-roots when word came down the line that Rolin was calling a halt to the search for the night. Everyone was to gather in a central place and find a comfortable spot to sleep.

"Please come with me," a high, clear voice commanded. Gwynneth's ghostly figure beckoned to Kyleah. Supposing the Lucambrian princess was taking her to meet the others, Kyleah followed. Gwynneth led her higher into the trees, over a ridge and down a thickly wooded slope. At the bottom, silver star-dust floated upon the mirroring waters of a mountain lake. Gwynneth stopped on the shore and waited for Kyleah to catch up.

Yawning, Kyleah said, "What a lovely place to spend the night! I never knew this lake was here. But why are we alone beside it?"

"We are alone, yet not alone," said her guide, turning about.

Kyleah gasped. She had been following a stranger! Though resembling Gwynneth in height and build, this woman wore a long golden gown that shimmered in the moonlight. Kyleah was reminded of Aquilla and Hannith. "Who are you? Why did you bring me here?" she asked. To her surprise, the stranger bowed.

"Enid is my name. On behalf of my people, Gifted Girl, let me welcome you to the Lapping Lake. Thanks to you and the Water Lord, we are finally free to leave our lake without fear of *them*."

She must be a naiad! Kyleah decided, noting Enid's webbed hands and long, greenish hair. "How did you know who I am?"

Enid replied, "Water flows under and over and through all worlds, bringing with it tidings both good and ill. The news of your approach has created quite a stir beneath our lake. Come the twilight, we sent forth water-scouts to learn of your intentions."

Kyleah hadn't imagined those mysterious, moonlit faces after all! "And what did you find out about us?" she asked the naiad.

"If I understand correctly," said Enid, "you seek a ringing tree, though to what purpose, I cannot guess. Perhaps I can help you. Hark! Do you not now hear the object of your search?"

Kyleah listened, hearing only the lake living up to its name as its waters gently lapped against pebbly banks. Then she heard a distant ringing or clanging. Following that sound, she and Enid came upon a grove of torsils standing with their roots in the lake. The ringing seemed to come from everywhere inside the grove.

Enid said, "Why these passage trees chime, we do not know, but it is usually on occasions of rumored war or celebration." The naiad glanced at Kyleah with frank curiosity in her deep eyes.

To Kyleah's disappointment, none of the trees was large enough for intrisoning a grown-up. She would have to search elsewhere. If only Barley were there to guide her with his special sight!

Then she noticed a mossy maple standing among the passage trees. Stepping up to it, she plunged her arm inside the thick trunk and groped around. Icy fingers entwined about her hand. Kyleah pulled—and out of the tree popped a disheveled young woman.

It was her mother. Larissa looked as lovely and youthful as she had the night she had disappeared. Kyleah couldn't breathe. She had lost one mother and regained another on the selfsame day! Jumbled images of Larissa cascaded through her mind in a collage of bittersweet memories—eating "maple snow" on crisp spring mornings; quilting bees; trips to the Beechtown market; dressing up for the annual Sugaring Festival; cooking meals together.

"Mother?" she whispered, scarcely believing her eyes.

Larissa stared at her doubtfully. "Who are you, young one?"

"I am Kyleah, your daughter! Don't you recognize me?" Kyleah cried. Then she remembered more than five years had passed since Larissa had last seen her. "I have grown up, Mother," she added.

Larissa's face crumpled as tears sprang from her eyes. "Kyleah! My precious daughter Kyleah!" Weeping, the two fell into each other's arms, fiercely embracing like twin entwined tree-trunks.

Then Larissa broke away, her eyes clouding. "But where are your father and brother and your sister Einwen?" she asked.

Kyleah said, "Father and Barley are nearby, but Einwen is . . . no more." Then she told her mother of the accident that had left her a cripple and had so untimely claimed Einwen's young life.

Larissa sank onto a log and held her head in her hands. When she looked up again, she dazedly asked, "Then who is this girl?"

Bowing, Enid introduced herself. "Now I understand why you are called 'the Gifted Girl,'" she told Kyleah. "You have brought us a great gift indeed!" Bowing again, she hurried off to the shore.

Larissa asked Kyleah, "How did you know where I was?"

"Your 'troth-brace' led me to you, with Enid's help!" Kyleah replied, and she described the desperate quest for the bell-torsil.

"I have always loved bells," said Larissa wistfully. "I did not realize the Leaf Lord was prompting me to write a prophetic verse about one in particular. This bell sounded far away. It wakened me from a dark place of endless nightmares. How long have you been able to—whatever it is you just did to get me out of that tree?"

Kyleah said softly, "I guess I've always been able to tree-burgle, but I realized it only recently. You never told me I was a blairn."

Larissa lowered her eyes. "No, I didn't. I wanted you to grow up like the other girls. We have much to talk about, you and I."

"Kyleah! So you escaped after all!" cried a hearty voice.

A couple of dripping figures emerged from the lake. They ran up to hug Kyleah. Enid had summoned Hannith and Aquilla!

"I'm sorry for leaving you on Mt. Argel," Hannith told Kyleah. "I wasn't deserting you; I was going for help. By the time I came back with a detachment of our daiad-guards, you were gone!"

Aquilla picked up the tale. "After learning the woodwalkers were all assembling in the 'Agorashon,' we decided to convene a hasty Conclave of our own. The Water Lord then appeared and instructed us to divert an underground river in order to drown the Field of Fear. Those woodwalkers shall not trouble us again!"

Kyleah laughed with relief. "I doubt they will, either!" she said. "How did you make passage from your world into mine?"

Hannith smiled slyly. "Hidden waters often flow beneath a torsil tree and into another world. We know of many such trees!"

Nodding, Kyleah recalled the tales she had heard of streams and rivers that vanished underground, never to reemerge. Then she remembered to introduce the two naiads to her mother. The webbed pair cwelapped sharply and solemnly bowed to Larissa.

"It is truly an honor to meet you!" they said politely.

Then out of the forest trooped Enid, Wynnagar, Barley, Branagan and the Greencloaks. Several grumpy griffins dragged behind. Yawning, the sorcs padded down to the shore, where they keeled over and fell asleep. Branagan stared goggle-eyed. "Larissa? Is it really you?" he exclaimed. "After all this time, I thought you were dead! Where have you been? Pails and spiles! You don't look a day older than when I last saw you." He took a few hesitant steps toward her and stopped, as if unconvinced Larissa was alive.

"Trisoners do not age inside their trees," Wynnagar reassured him, reminding Kyleah of the boy she had freed. Robin had been cooped up in his tree for so long that all his relatives had died.

Weeping, Branagan rushed to enfold Larissa in his arms, and Barley joined him. After Wynnagar and Kyleah had run through the events of the past months, Larissa stepped back to gaze at her daughter and son. "How you both have grown!" she said. "I never dreamed you two possessed such special abilities. I am looking forward to picking up where we left off in our lives together."

Wynnagar hugged her. "I fear too many seasons have passed for that, old friend! Branagan has been widowed twice now—once when you were intrisoned and again when Dolora died. You'll have to help him bring up her two daughters as it is. Your former life is gone, but you can still build a new one on the ashes of the old."

Branagan grimaced ruefully. "But this time, I want the truth!"

With an apologetic smile, Larissa told her husband, "Right or wrong, I hid my origins from you in order to protect our family. As it was, if Dolora or the trollogs had guessed my true identity, they would have spiked my tree and done away with our children."

"I still don't know who you are," Branagan sniffed.

"Soon you shall," she promised him with a playful wink. Then she led the searchers in a prayer of thanksgiving to Gaelathane.

Afterwards, Kyleah's father asked her, "Who are your webby friends with the green hair? Were they swimming in the lake?"

"No, as Water People, they live in the water!" Kyleah told him, introducing the webbed women. Since most of the Greencloaks were unacquainted with maiads, Wynnagar, Kyleah, Meghan and Medwyn were peppered with questions about that peculiar race.

When the Lucambrians had satisfied their curiosity, Wynnagar grandly announced, "Now you are all invited to the coronation!"

"Coronation? What coronation?" the Greencloaks chorused.

"Yes, what coronation?" asked Kyleah. "Whose coronation?"

Cwelapping, Aquilla and Hannith exchanged incredulous glances. "Do you mean to say you don't know?" they asked her.

"Know what?" Kyleah retorted.

Aquilla said, "Your mother Larissa was—is—queen of the Wood Folk. We assumed you already knew that, Gifted Girl. Long years we have waited to reunite Queen Larissa with her crown."

Kyleah blinked. Her mother was a queen? "Do you mean queen of the Mapleton Wood Folk or of the Mt. Argel Wood Folk?"

The naiads laughed merrily. "No, silly!" said Hannith. "We mean that your mother is High Queen of all the Wood Folk who live in any of the Water Lord's myriad worlds."

CHAPTER 29

THE CONCLAVE

annith's words still echoed in Kyleah's ears as she, Larissa and Barley stood on the rocky, puddled bottom of the drained Listening Lake. *High Queen of all the Wood Folk,* the naiad princess had said. It still didn't seem possible. Larissa of the laughing eyes and ready smile—a queen? Unlike Kyleah's stepmother and stepsisters, Larissa had never been haughty or demanding, as one might expect a genuine queen to behave.

The night of Larissa's release, Wynnagar had taken everyone to a torsil that led to Mt. Argel, where King Corwyn and his royal retinue grandly welcomed them. Beneath the lake, Kyleah bathed her grimy self under a water-curtain. Then she collapsed onto a water-mattress and slept more soundly than she had in months.

During the following week, Mt. Argel hummed with activity as maiad-messengers were dispatched by hidden ways to invite their woodland cousins to the coronation. Feeling left out, Kyleah spent many moonlit hours strolling beside the Listening Lake with Hannith, who told her much about Larissa. Before walking into the waking world, the High Queen had entrusted her maiadin friends on Mt. Argel with two symbols of her royal office: a purple robe, which she now wore, and an ornate wooden chest.

The light of the rising moon softened the amphitheater's stark stone benches with silver as nymphs and dryads from countless other torsil worlds arrived and took their seats. Around the arena's base, a daiad-herald stood in each of the four arched inlets that served to refill the lake. Raising pink conch shells to their lips, the daiads blew an echoing flourish. Gaelathane emerged from one of the low openings, followed by Medwyn, who bore Larissa's box. Kyleah began shivering with a queasy, uneasy anticipation.

Gaelathane raised His scarred hands, and the great assembly reverently fell silent. Then He began speaking in the melodious tongue of the memerren. Kyleah was staggered to realize that she could understand much of what He was saying. As a blairn, she must have inherited a knack for the language from her mother.

"Dear friends," the King began, "I am pleased to address you on this momentous and joyous occasion. Thanks to the Gifted Girl and her steadfast companions, your ancient foe is no more."

The nymphs and dryads clapped, while the naiads and daiads cwelapped. Gaelathane motioned again for silence. "Until her captivity, Queen Larissa faithfully served Me and you her subjects. Now she shall do so again, with the help of her many friends."

Turning to Larissa, the King asked, "Will you, Queen Larissa, love, serve and obey Me in your new life as you did in your old?"

"Yes, and gladly, too!" Larissa answered in a trembling voice.

"Will you also in faith serve My people of tree and forest?"

With tears in her eyes, Larissa said, "Yes, I will!"

Gaelathane motioned to Medwyn, who brought Him the chest. Opening it, He removed an elegant golden crown from a plush bed of scarlet velvet. "According to your confession," He announced, "I restore this crown to you, Queen Larissa, Ruler and Monarch of all My sprightly moon-children who dwell in the midst of trees, wherever they may grow. Kneel now, blessed Queen Larissa."

Larissa knelt, and Gaelathane placed the crown upon her head. "Arise, Queen Larissa!" He said, and He raised her to her feet.

Next, Gaelathane laid a shining lightstaff in Larissa's palm. "Behold your queen, My people!" He cried. "Long live Queen Larissa. May her leaves never wither and her roots never thirst!"

"Long live Queen Larissa! May her leaves never wither!" echoed the spectators. Cheering and applauding, they all stood.

Larissa smiled radiantly down at her bashful daughter. "Now it is your turn, Princess Kyleah," she said, and she knelt before her. "I would not be wearing this crown today, were it not for you," she said in a low voice. "Nor, I think, shall I continue to wear it without the help of my Gifted Girl. Will you promise to love and serve me as your queen, even as I serve Gaelathane as Lord?"

With a lump in her throat, Kyleah replied, "Of course I will!"

Larissa kissed her. Then she slid something onto Kyleah's arm. It was a golden bracelet just like the one Glunt had melted! Boldly inscribed around the inside were the words, *For Princess Kyleah. With all my love, Mother.* Next, Larissa took a shining circlet from the box. "Gaelathane Himself fashioned this crystal crown for you from a Tree-shoot," she said, placing it upon Kyleah's brow.

"Hail, Princess Kyleah! May her leaves never wither and her roots never thirst!" the spectators cheered. Kyleah winced at this foreign-sounding royal title. Wilting under the audience's gaze, she yearned to hide inside the lake's drain hole, which gaped about eight feet away. Meanwhile, her brother had received his own Tree-circlet and was being acclaimed as, "Prince Barlomey."

Suddenly, the sounds of celebration died away. Dark shapes were emerging from the drain. *Trollogs!* Some of the woodwalkers must have survived being flushed out of Mt. Argel and were now returning to claim their prize. Kyleah staggered back. Then she noticed moonlight gleaming on bald heads, and her heart stopped hammering. It was only Toefoot and a few of his companions.

"Greetings, Gifted Girl!" said Toefoot. "We have brought you a special present." He and Hardhand lifted a framed mirror out of the hole and propped it up so that Kyleah could see herself. No trace of the trollog remained in her reflection, though she hardly looked the part of a princess. For the first time, she could face herself without regret or shame, despite her scarred cheek.

"Thank You, dear Gaelathane! Truly, the Tree lives!" she cried. After laying her circlet at the King's feet, she joined the naiads and daiads, nymphs and dryads in singing their moonsong of praise.

When in mystical moonlight we freely may sing,
Let all memerren murmur sweet psalms to the King,
Who was pierced for our pardon while intrisoned in clay,
That the blood-cancelled curse should no longer hold sway.

Now the sword of the Pit has returned to its place,
And the walkers-of-wood drown in leafy disgrace;
While Larissa the Queen lifts her lightstaff to reign,
For the Girl of the Gift has now banished our bane.

Let the rivers rejoice, while the valleys give voice!
For the King took the sting of the sword by His choice;
Let the trisoners leap, for the trollogs lie deep;
Underneath a lone lake they forever shall sleep!

Hours later, Kyleah sat with her friends and family beside the
refilling lake, whose swirling waters reflected the silent, unfolding
splendor of a crimson dawn. Reminded of the Plugger's blood and
Gaelathane's other sacrifices to deliver her from death, she sang,

A blairn I was born, but I tapped trees for sap;
In winter's deep woodlands I wore a wool cap;
Then burgling maples became my new trade
Till I found I'd released all the trollogs to raid!

Through caverns and castles I lately have passed;
In drowning discovered the love that will last;
Imprisoned, intrisoned, the guest of a gnome;
With the help of the King, I have found my way home.

A crown I now wear in the place of the cap;
Living water I drink in the place of the sap;
And when burgling trees, I no longer need hide
From a trollog who wishes to make me his bride!

"What will you do now as princess?" Elwyn asked her.
Grinning impishly at him, Kyleah said, "First, I want to go home
and eat all the maple-sugar bears in Mapleton!" Everyone laughed
at that, but Barley laughed the loudest and longest of all.

Epilogue

Kyleah and Barley helped their father build a new cottage on the foundations of the old. In later years, Barley and his family lived there. Branagan built another cabin on Mt. Argel, where he likes to retreat with Larissa. Malroth still stands on the Dreadrock in Trollog Lake, mumbling to himself, "I killed the Plugger! I intrisoned him myself and cut down his tree."

Gyrta and Garta enjoyed a truly sensational spending spree in Beechtown with the money they stole from Branagan. After buying extravagant wardrobes for themselves, they ate—and scratched—their way through the town. Then their gilders ran out, and their good looks as well. The days they had spent starving in the syrup cauldron had only delayed the inevitable. By the time Branagan went searching for them, the two girls had disappeared.

One luminous October day, Lightleaf's wish finally came true. Branagan and Larissa renewed their wedding vows under the torsil, who dampened the wedding guests with copious tree-tears.

On many a moonlit evening, you will find Larissa, Kyleah, Barley and Wynnagar in Mapleton's forests discussing nymphs and naiads, dryads and daiads, trees and ferns, moon and stars. They also love listening to the memerren singing Gaelathane's praises.

Branagan never again bored another hole in a maple tree. Even after becoming a queen in her own right, Kyleah sets her father's taps early each spring in the awakening trees. When the nectar is flowing, she also helps Gannon rob wild bees' nests. While Gannon smokes the bees into a stupor, Kyleah sneaks up behind the tree and neatly burgles the honeycomb from the nest. Everyone is pleased with this arrangement—except the bees themselves.

Just before the snows came, Branagan and his family led the entire village on a "paddle party," as Barley put it. The rejoicing townspeople traipsed up to the Grieving Ground, where they collected the corroding bells and plucked up the paddles of the trisoners who had returned to Mapleton. Afterwards, the wooden markers were burned in a magnificent bonfire. As the guest of honor, Kyleah flung her paddle on the pile last and lit the fire.

Branagan gave all the discarded neck-bells to Toefoot, who melted them down in his foundry to cast one big bell. The Great Bell now hangs in a new belfry on the sugarhouse roof and is rung once each year to open the "Paddle Festival." At the end of the week's celebration, the villagers plant a tree in the Grieving Ground, now known as "Gaelathane's Ground," in honor of the One Whose death made the Return of the Trisoners possible.

At King Rolin's invitation, Toefoot and company briefly took up residence in Winona's room beneath the Hallowfast. After overseeing some much-needed repairs to the tower's foundation, the gnomes fashioned more glass mirrors to replace those the trollogs had smashed while occupying the Hallowfast. Strange, otherworldly scenes are said to appear in some of those frames.

Kyleah herself owns three such torsil mirrors, which often prove handy when she wishes to avoid unwelcome visitors. One leads to Penoddion; the second to Lucambra; and the third to Mt. Argel, where she and Barley attend Conclaves with Larissa. Barley sees into the heart of any matter as well as he does into trees.

In exchange for the gnomes' work, the Lucambrians supplied them with plenty of starberries. After a month, the bald little men sprouted such luxuriant heads of hair that they became as vain as peacocks, spending hours preening in front of Toefoot's mirrors.

Thanks to Toefoot and the Feather King, Kyleah never lacks for firebirds. She has released many around Mapleton and on Mt. Argel, where the maiads built her mother a palace of crystal. In time, Kyleah herself came to occupy that palace. A blairn as wise as she is gentle, she heals the hearts of men and of trees, just as Gaelathane once removed the black burl from her ailing heart.

Kyleah loves visiting her Lucambrian friends. Since she still possesses the appetite of ten men—and the trollish strength to match—Scanlon and Opio have dubbed her, "the Hollow Lass." In quiet hours, she will gaze upon her restored heart's reflection in Elgathel's sword, with which King Rolin also tests his own heart.

Hannith later became queen of the Mt. Argel maiads and often meets with Kyleah at the Listening Lake. Having outlived all his friends and family, Robin son of Rimlin chose to remain beneath the lake. He enjoys devising waterwheels, water-catapults and many other clever water-inventions to help his adopted family.

Trollogs (or trolls, as they are better known nowadays) have become rare since the collapse of their second rebellion. However, a pair of woodwalkers still roams the Tartellans wearing tattered finery. Alas, Dolora could not spare her own kin from the lash.

I, Barley, am Mapleton's sugarmaster now, but I never tire of looking into trees—especially the Tree. Its Light still shines in 'Leah's eyes, even if the glory in her face has dimmed. She and I have spent many long nights in the Tartellan Mountains releasing intrisoned dryads and nymphs. We also visit other worlds, seeking out the trollogs' remaining trisoners. Hundreds of the maples in our sugar bush still bear "arrested burls," as we call them. If you should come upon such a burl growing on a tree, do not touch it or cut into it! I can promise you won't like what comes out.

Fortunately, the Plugger has knocked off most of those burls. If you have occasion to pass through a maple grove after sugaring season has wound down, follow the sound of hammering, and you may find the Plugger plying his mallet and pegs. Just have a seat beside him, and he will gladly listen to all your troubles.

GLOSSARY AND PRONUNCIATION GUIDE

Agorashon. "Field of Fear."

Anna daughter of Dyllis. Kyleah's best friend, next to Einwen.

Aquilla. A naiad; mother of Hannith.

Barlomey son of Branagan. Kyleah's brother. ("Barley.")

Bigtoe, Forger, Hardhand, Smoothpate. Toefoot's friends.

black sword. Sword forged by Felgor. (See also *Felgroth*.)

blairn. Refers to one who is partly human and partly memer.

Branagan son of Carrigan. Barley and Kyleah's father.

brollog. Trollog hatched from a burl. (See also *burlie/troggling*.)

burge. To grow or increase in size; refers to brollogs.

burlie. Young trollog hatched from a burl. (See also *brollog*.)

burlip. To plant a burl on a tree where someone is intrisoned.

Chamber of Living Waters. Chamber beneath Hearkening Hall.

Corwyn. King of the maiades on Mt. Argel.

cwelap (pr. kwell´-app). When a maiad "snaps" his/her webs.

Cyngor (pr. Kin´-gore). Conclave held on Mt. Argel.

daiad (pr. dye´-add). A male water-sprite inhabiting rivers, lakes, ponds or springs. Plural: daiades or daiads. Adj. *daiadin*.

daiades (pr. dye´-uh-deez). Plural of *daiad*.

Dolora. Barley and Kyleah's stepmother.

Dreadrock. Rock in the Field of Fear; gateway to Gundul.
dryad (pr. dry´-add). A male wood-sprite. Plural: dryades or dry-ads. Adj. *dryadin*.
dryades (pr. dry´-uh-deez). Plural of *dryad*.
Einwen daughter of Larissa (pr. Ine´-wen). Kyleah's twin.
Enid. A naiad of the Tartellan Mountains.
Feather King. See *King Wortlewig*.
Felgroth. The black sword forged by Felgor.
firebird. Bird with shiny feathers of silver.
firebird forest. Home to firebirds in Penoddion.
Gaelathane. The King of the Trees.
Gaelessa. Gaelathane's home; realm of light and love.
Garta daughter of Dolora. Barley and Kyleah's stepsister.
glass. Another name for a mirror.
Glunt. Larkin's marsh-dragon; discovered in Thalmos.
gnome. Stocky creature living beneath the earth. Adj. *gnomish*.
gonomion. See *gnome*. Plural: gonomia. Adj. *gonomial*.
Gundul. The underworld; a place of darkness and despair.
Gyrta daughter of Dolora. Barley and Kyleah's stepsister.
Hamadryad. High dryad.
Hannith. A naiad-girl; Aquilla's daughter.
Hearkening Hall. Chamber beneath Listening Lake.
helihag (pr. heel´-uh-hag). Large, flat carnivorous creature resembling a fleshy rug. Also known as a "hurlahog."
King's Pool. Pool where King Corwyn's throne sits.
King Wortlewig. King of Penoddion. Also *Feather King*.
Kirkin, Reinhardt, Dunstan. King Wortlewig's men-at-arms.
Kyleah (pr. Kye-lee´-uh). Main character; the Gifted Girl.
Larissa. Barley and Kyleah's birth-mother.
Larkin son of Gaflin. Lucambrian turncloak.
Lay. Short ballad or narrative intended to be sung.
Listening Lake. Lake where maiads live on Mt. Argel.
maiad (pr. my´-add). A male or female water-sprite. Plural: maiades or maiads. Adj. *maiadin*.
maiades (pr. my´-uh-deez). Plural of *maiad*. (The Water Folk.)
Malroth. Hamadryadin leader of tree-rebellion.

Mapleton. Kyleah's home village in the Tartellan Mountains.
memer. Nature-sprite loyal to Gaelathane. Plural: memerren.
Mirror Master. See *Toefoot.*
moonslip. To enter/leave a tree by moonlight. (See also *sunslip.*)
Mt. Argel. Last secure outpost of the memerren.
naiad (pr. nye´-add). A female water-sprite inhabiting rivers, lakes, ponds or springs. Plural: naiades or naiads. Adj. *naiadin.*
naiades (pr. nye´-uh-deez). Plural of *naiad.*
nymph. A female wood-sprite. Plural: nymphs.
Oracle. Prophecy Gaelathane once gave the memerren.
Pagglon the Pickfisted. Renowned gnomish king.
Penoddion (pr. Pen-odd´-ee-on). World where firebirds live.
Plugger. Old hermit who plugs tap holes in maple trees.
Prowlers. What the residents of Mapleton call trollogs.
Quickfeather. Kyleah and Barley's griffin mount.
Rattlereed Marshes. Swampy area at Foamwater's lower end.
Robin son of Rimlin. Intrisoned boy rescued by Kyleah.
Runnel son of Runion. Larkin's captain of the guard.
spile. A *tap* (spout) used to collect sap from a maple tree.
sugar bush. Grove of sugar maples tapped for sap.
sunslip. To enter or leave a tree by day. (See also *moonslip.*)
tap. Spout used for collecting maple sap. (See also *spile.*)
Tapwell son of Tharweld. Mapleton's founder.
Terrill. Daiadin guard.
Toefoot. A gonomion, or gnome. Also the *Mirror Master.*
tree-burgle. To remove objects or people from inside trees.
trog. Short for "trollog."
troggling. Young trollog. (See also *brollog, burlie.*)
trollog. Rebellious hamadryad.
turncloak. Lucambrian term for a traitor.
Water Folk. Water-memerren; water-sprites. (See also *maiades.*)
Wood Folk. Memerren of the forest; wood-sprites. (See also *nymph, dryad.*)
woodwalker. A trollog. (So named for its stiff gait.)
worldwalker. A memer (sprite) that has become mortal.
Wynnagar (pr. Winn´-uh-gar). Old worldwalker of Mapleton.

You may order additional copies of

KYLEAH'S MIRRORS

from our secure server website:

www.greencloaks.com

or by sending $14.95 plus $3.95
shipping and handling* to:

KOT BOOKS
3237 Sunset Drive
Hubbard, OR
97032-9635

Other titles in the *King of the Trees* series:

Book I: *The King of the Trees* ($11.99)
Book II: *Torsils in Time* ($14.95)
Book III: *The Golden Wood* ($14.95)
Book IV: *The Greenstones* ($14.95)
Book V: *The Downs* ($14.95)

Please make checks and money orders payable to KOT BOOKS.
*(Add $1.00 shipping and handling for each additional copy.)